For l
with... &
... [handwritten inscription]

AIR-BORN

LAURA POWER

Winter Goose
PUBLISHING
where words take flight
wintergoosepublishing.com

Winter Goose Publishing
2701 Del Paso Road, 130-92
Sacramento, CA 95835

www.wintergoosepublishing.com
Contact Information: info@wintergoosepublishing.com

Air-Born

COPYRIGHT © 2013 by Laura Power

ISBN: 978-0-9894792-4-0

First Edition, September 2013

Cover Art by Winter Goose Publishing
Typestting by Odyssey Books

Published in the United States of America

This book is dedicated to Debbie: in friendship, honour, memory, and love
I told you it would be, and you believed me

Dangerous Mistakes

Echoes fled into a long-undisturbed darkness as the figure charged through the tunnel, stumbling to a halt as the passage loomed into an inky cavern. With a crackle the light of his torch sparked and flared, casting ambiguous leaping shadows as it licked the ancient rock.

The figure sprang to the wall, running his clawed hands over it, urgently searching. Torchlight flickered across his lithe, dark-skinned form; droplets of swamp-water clinging to the contours of his body, black hair falling to his shoulders in tangled waves, frayed trousers soaked through, the water pooling at his bare feet. His ragged breath fractured the silence of the cave as he continued to search, desperate to be proved wrong, willing himself to find anything save for that which he now feared inevitable.

He stopped with a sharp intake of breath, hand frozen, as he felt something, and saw in the wavering half-light the four deep grooves gouged into the rock. Wordlessly he traced the gashes with his claws, numb with the realisation that this would change everything. The injustice of it all overpowering him, he slumped forward, head bowed against the solid presence of the stone as if he could borrow its strength, eyes closed in silent anguish as a hundred images raced unbidden through his mind.

I'll stop it, Racxen vowed weakly, paralysed with fear for his tribe— *and why would it stop there? The wider Realm.* Grimly, he shoved the possibility aside, stamping down his terror. Yet in the privacy of the cave, his resolve shuddered as he realised miserably how ill prepared he felt. *If only the tribe had still had a leader; if only the elders had . . .*

Against the waves of helplessness crashing into him, he pushed himself into standing. *You're all they've got left,* he admonished. Far louder and braver than he felt, he threw back his head and bellowed his defiance to the pitiless night and the shadows closing in, his voice crashing through the still air as he ran on.

As the footsteps scuffed into silence and the cry echoed through tunnels lain forgotten for almost two decades, something stirred: a ghost of a snarl, a ripple in the blackness—stirred and was gone.

"I still don't understand how you managed to lose it!" A sword swiped irritably through the undergrowth to reveal a regal-looking figure trudging through the dank forest. "Goblin's teeth, Amber—the ceremony's in three days."

"Enough about Goblins!" Frustrated eyes flashed beneath wayward pixie-short hair as, struggling to keep up with the Prince as he stomped ahead moodily, the Fairy called Amber gestured defensively, breathless after traipsing around behind him for the whole day and thoroughly fed up with him having a go at her the whole time. "And I'm sorry, Jasper," she insisted, trying to keep her voice level, "but the Dartwing just flew off with it—"

He fixed his green eyes on her severely.

"I mean: I'm sorry, Your Highness," she corrected hastily. Couldn't she do anything right?

Jasper ignored her salutation. "It was in your charge." He aimed a swipe at the clutch of creepers tumbling across the path, years over-grown. "We—*I*," he corrected pointedly, "thought you could handle the responsibility."

"I get it!" Amber's pride flared and she stopped angrily. "I told you it was my mistake, and I told you I'll fix it. You didn't have to come out here after me."

"Yes, I did," the Prince rejoined, tiredly adjusting his cloak. "*Some* of us actually have responsibilities, including to the most irritating of our subjects. And," he added hastily before Amber could get in a retort, "*all* of us have heard the stories. You didn't half choose your time for this."

Amber grimaced. "I know," she admitted quietly. "That's why I didn't want you out here after me. Let's just split up. We'll—*I'll*—find it quicker and we won't be at each other's throats for the next four hours."

Jasper examined a caught thread on his sleeve. "You're giving the orders around here now, are you?"

Her eyes rolling skyward, Amber trudged on in silence, leaving the Prince glaring after her.

"Well, it's not the worst idea you've had all day," he conceded, striding to catch up. "I shall aim north towards the Endless Forest," he advised with a vague swipe of his blade, "and you can head for the Southern Sands. Meet with me back in the castle grounds before nightfall." He sheathed the sword with an unnecessary flourish and regarded her sternly. "I mean it, Amber; *don't* go too far. Travelling so close to our borders at a time like this is foolhardy to the extreme, and it is imperative you are back before nightfall."

Amber nodded resignedly. "Fly free, Jasper."

He graced her with a curt half-smile. "Fly free. And stay safe," he admonished, his expression softening.

He strode deeper into the forest, leaving her standing alone beneath the eaves of the ancient trees, their leaves dappling the subtle warmth of the early morning sun upon the ground now that the dawn mist had cleared. Turning right, as the Prince had advised, she reached the edge of the wood. Staring out across the open grassland, Amber smiled experimentally. *I'll show him. I'll find it.*

Squinting up to the pale dawn and wincing as she shoved off the dew-soaked cloak, Amber shivered miserably as the wind tugged through her damp clothes. Hobbling on cramp-frozen feet she grimaced, stretched her back, carefully shook a protesting spider out of her sleep-tangled hair and tried to decide where in the Realm she should head now, guiltily recounting the Prince's warning. That had all been last night.

More Questions

Racxen's vision shuddered and he stumbled, adding another layer of mud to the remnants of swamp already plastering his dark skin. His claws gouged the earth as he heaved himself up, glazed eyes burning with the will to continue. After nearly two straight days of searching he'd lost the loose, tireless gait of his kind, his steps growing uncoordinated in his struggle to keep to the protection of the concealing trees as he slunk through the thick undergrowth, an erratic shadow against the gloaming of the forest, the pre-dawn quiet shattered by his progress.

Just reach the lake. He couldn't stop yet—not after what he'd found. Not with so many questions still unanswered.

Gradually the trees thinned, relinquishing their shelter as tangled forest yielded to bright, rolling meadows beneath streaming sunlight. Racxen allowed himself an exhausted smile as he saw, nestled like a glistening jewelled mirror flanked by emerald green, the Great Lake stretching before him.

Grimacing as tired muscles began to seize in complaint, Racxen let his breathing slow as he padded to the bank, wading into the chill and letting the peaceful quiet wash over his fraught mind as he drank.

Striding from the lake's numbing embrace, he sank into the shade of the solitary waterside tree and stretched out his sore limbs as he cast a wary gaze over his surroundings, mapping the rest of his route in his mind.

As he scanned the banks, something caught his eye, glittering amongst the grass nearby. Nudging mud and leaves aside, he poked it with a claw. Some sort of jewel, on a pendant. Entranced, he picked it up. Colours swirled mysteriously within the teardrop gem as he held it up to the light. He stared at it. Who would have come so far to lose such a treasure? He was at the very edge of Arraheng territory; the nearest other civilisation was probably the Fairy Kingdom, in the far meadows. And it was said that the Fairies never ventured beyond their own borders for fear of Arraheng and other 'monsters'. Racxen laughed to himself. He knew what was said of the Arraheng, and of the Fairies. Having good reason not to believe the former, he had long ago taken it upon himself not to believe the latter.

The crack of vegetation behind him sent Racxen flinching to the ground, all tiredness dissipated. Glancing back, through the shadows of the forest he could see a figure approaching the clearing. Fear lanced through Racxen and he stole behind the tree. *Goblin!*

Chancing another look, his heart scudded sickeningly. Normally, when travelling alone, Goblins adopted a path as erratic as their natures to both aid their own ambush attempts and discourage the efforts of trackers. But this one forced his way through the forest with a disinhibition that was frightening.

As Racxen reached to climb the tree and hide, the jewel flashed in the light. His lip curled at the thought of the Goblin, a filthy scavenging Pedlar who cursed his wares and sold them on to unsuspecting travellers, getting his hands on it. Flicking the pendant into the lake, Racxen darted towards the tree, his clawed hands seeking grasp expertly over the smooth trunk as he climbed it as good as silently. In a moment he was crouched, hidden and watchful, in the canopy. He should be safe. Goblins avoided clean water with the same rabid intensity decent folk avoided their foul elixirs.

Peering down through the branches, Racxen tensed as the Goblin slunk closer to the tree. He saw with satisfaction that the Pedlar skirted the edge of the lake, missing the gem. But something had to be seriously wrong for him to be this near. Goblin skin is dry and cannot well tolerate water; leading these vicious traders to haunt the barren plains of the desert almost exclusively, able to last for weeks on nothing but their own cursed potions to take advantage of unwary travellers worn down by the harsh terrain and long hours alone. Thus the one place in True Realm you could reasonably expect to be safe from Goblins was at a waterside—until, seemingly, now.

Time stretched uncomfortably. Trailing for days was one thing; getting trapped up an accursed tree for hours was another. *Patience.* He let the word wander through his mind. *Keystone of a tracker.*

Letting his thoughts sink away into the branches until his entire focus rested on the Goblin, Racxen leaned as far as he dared from the branch to watch, questions overlaying yet more questions. Goblins were bullies and sneaks who delighted in stealth and the ease of attack afforded by it, yet sticks and stones cracked and rolled beneath this one's feet unheeded—and was there more unease in the dart of those quick-shifting eyes than usual? Was he afraid of ambush by his own kind—it often happened—or was he being hunted? A chill crept around Racxen's chest as the memory of the caves refused to leave him. Such a being as to strike fear into a Goblin—what had he strayed across? Shivering, he gazed fixedly after him, trying to make sense of it.

Not that there was much sense to be made. There was no horde bickering around him, yet here was not the desert, where a lone Goblin could hope to pounce on weakened travellers.

Shifting as quietly as he could along the bough to keep his quarry in sight, willing that he would be sufficiently hidden as the Goblin neared his vantage-point, Racxen froze while beneath the tree the Pedlar's blue-grey skin flaked as he brushed against the lower branches, flinching and spitting savagely at the dewy caress of the leaves.

The malevolence in his rheumy yellow eyes shocked the tracker. *He's wishing death to the mere earth. So why does he linger?*

Racxen breathed more freely as the Goblin moved on. Then he saw something that made him lurch from his precarious position in shock, and left him fumbling for a handhold: the Goblin lumbered to the water's edge, and with a stream of potent curses, began to noisily drink. Racxen stared in horror. *A Goblin, drinking from a clean pool? Such an act for that kin would be physically painful—what had instilled in him fear to drive him so far as to make it necessary?*

Stunned, he stared as the Goblin, having slaked his thirst quickly, lumbered almost blindly on his way as he re-entered the forest. One thing was certain: with everything that had happened recently it wouldn't be coincidence that had brought him across his path. And if the Goblins were scared, it would have to be of something worse than any previous threat the Realm had faced.

His eyes fixed on the retreating form, as soon as the Goblin reached the forest border Racxen sought a lower branch, striving to still the trembling in his limbs as he resolved to follow him. As the Goblin, oblivious to all but his own ill-concealed anger, blundered still further, Racxen dropped quietly from the tree to all fours and darted towards the forest, sinking into the undergrowth to merge with the lengthening shadows as gathering clouds darkened the skies. Slipping between the trees as the drizzling rain crescendoed into a relentless drumming, he was infinitely cautious, staying as far back as he could without losing his quarry in the eerily fading light. If he were to be caught, it would take the kind of currency he could ill afford to lose to appease the Goblin.

Fateful Meetings

It would have to rain, wouldn't it? Amber reflected miserably, hugging her cloak around her chest as the downpour hissed its fury.

Trudging through the forest, she bent her head low against the rain, every muscle in her body still protesting over her attempt at sleeping huddled on the ground with only her Renë cloak to keep her warm. Not that it could have felt any less like the mild season of rebirth, seeing as how said cloak, having served as last night's bedding, was now soaked in mud, scattered with insects and smelled pervasively of the most pungent form of leaf mould ever to grace the Realm.

By the time she reached the edge of the wood the rain had all but petered out and, yawning and shivering, Amber couldn't help smiling gratefully as the first pale shards of washed-out light began to peep through the forest canopy with the hope of a warmer day. Or, at least, a new one: eight more hours of daylight in which to find the Queen's Fairy Gem. A familiar lurch of despair twisted her stomach at the prospect of how much trouble she'd be in once she found her way back.

She was shaken from her reverie by a tiny fleck of colour fluttering unsteadily through the pale sky: the Prince's Dartwing messenger. With her heart slamming in dread, her hand shook as she reached out her fingers for the exhausted creature to alight upon.

The Dartwing's spindly feet tickled her palm as it cleaned its antenna of rain droplets whilst Amber unfurled the scrap of parchment clutched between its mandibles. Her heart sank as she peered at the message scrawled in a familiar, overly ornate hand:

Amber ~

I have been injured ~ not severely; I don't want you to worry. I am per-fectly safe to await assistance here with the provisions for the night although I should have given them to you really because you've never been out this far. If you are not back, and you probably aren't because you never listen to me ~ I want you to find the Queen's Gem. If you are home, ignore that and give word to my father to send help for me.

Wherever you are, I hope you are safe. I should not have left you. Nor should I have spoken angrily to you. Forgive me.

Fly free.

~ Jasper

Amber stared at the scroll. He'd come out here after her because in his own way he did actually care, and now because of her he was injured.

She twisted her sash round her hands distractedly. He'd rebuke her for it, but if she abandoned her search for the Gem hopefully she could find the Prince and get him back home.

Right. Retrace your steps. Hesitantly, she considered her options. Every way winding through the forest looked the same, and she couldn't remember having ventured along any of them.

Amber sighed, and, raising her hood to give some semblance of protection as the rain began sputtering through the trees again, picked a trail and started the long trek back.

Amber skidded across unknown grasslands in the fast-fading light, trying to find shelter from the pelting rain that was tearing at her wings. With only a couple of hours until dusk and no idea where she was heading, she knew she had to find the Prince fast.

Worry and fear leapt in her mind, her racing heartbeat throbbing through her temples in time with her fleeing feet on the sodden ground until finally she slipped exhausted to a halt on the mud-gripped grass, a lake she'd never seen before stretching vast and choppy grey before her, beneath the storm-torn sky.

Completely lost, her mind goaded her, and for a moment she almost heard the tittering laughter of the others echo in her head in response. Okay, it wasn't all the others, just Beryl and Opal and Jade and her stupid boyfriend Sardonyx, but some days they felt like everyone in the entire Realm.

Distracted by a flicker of movement further out, Amber squinted uncertainly through the rain. Another figure was approaching the lake—a child? Misgivings coiled serpent-like in her stomach. She wasn't sure it was safe for a youngster to be out in this weather so close to such a wild expanse of water; but then for all she knew there could be a settlement nearby. Relief fluttered triumphantly—maybe, if she followed, she'd be led back to civilisation. She wouldn't get too close though; she didn't want to startle the child, and as she didn't know where she was she had no way of knowing which peoples they were from or whether they'd even seen a Fairy before. After all, how many times in class had Professor Cobalt explained that since the Sea Battle, when magic had started to fade from the Realm, its remaining inhabitants who hadn't yet passed into legend were becoming ever more distant from each other?

Amber picked up her pace, trying to keep the child—a boy—in view as he neared the lake. Intent on watching the figure, she stumbled on a root, sprawling over her feet with an off-guard yelp. Scrambling up from the sodden ground she stared out across the flatlands again, hope sinking in her stomach as she cursed herself in bewilderment. How could she have lost him?

Stumbling to the edge of the lake, she knelt at the bank to quench her thirst, and despairingly glanced to her reflection in the water. It was . . . different. A few days ago, she had had nothing to worry about apart from the nervous anticipation—well, okay, fear—of the imminent Presentation. Now she had lost an irreplaceable royal heirloom, disregarded a direct order from the Prince, and got herself completely lost in the process. At this rate, she'd be lucky if her invitation to the Ceremony still stood.

Okay, so before she'd got herself into this situation she'd have probably complained that getting through that would be scarier than finding herself alone beyond her borders at a time when such rumours as now were murmured fearfully with downcast eyes across the breadth of the Kingdom and probably beyond, but at this moment she'd have given anything to be back with Ruby and her well-meaning jibes, listening to her moan about how many dresses she had to choose from for the Ceremony, in the warmth, surrounded by friends and with food on the fire.

Noticing a familiar fern-like plant amongst the rushes drew her from her reverie, and Amber plucked a few pod-like leaves and chewed one thoughtfully, relishing the liquid that burst between her teeth. She slipped the rest of the waterleaves into a pocket. She'd probably just end up forgetting about them and sitting on them later, but at least she'd be able to tell Jasper she hadn't arrived completely unprepared.

As she turned back to the lake's glassy surface she saw something shimmer through the depths. Her heart leapt—the Queen's Fairy Gem! She peered into the swirling murk. The Dartwing must have got tired and dropped it. Opal and Beryl were probably laughing about it still, she thought angrily. To train it to do that just to get her into trouble—how petty could they get?

The cold pressed its teeth against her arm as she reached into the inky blackness to retrieve the amulet.

Wiping off the smears of mud, and gritting her teeth to stop them chattering, Amber inspected the jewel earnestly. The Queen's Gem was rumoured to hold magical powers, and it shone mutedly, glistening with water-droplets. Amber wondered, then nestled it carefully between her hands, shutting her eyes as if to wish. That was what the Queen did, she recalled. Wasn't it? It was hard to remember now, alone and far away. Doubt itched at her heart, and she opened her eyes sadly. Maybe it was just a stone, after all.

Amber watched the sunlight race along the Gem's facets as she slanted it to and fro. As a Fairy, once you came of age and took your first flight, you were presented with such a Gem. It indicated, should you stray from home, that you were under the protection of the King and Queen of Fairymead; that aid or ill treatment would be returned. And it symbolised, well, whatever you wanted—or rather *intended*—it to. During the Ceremony, before the Queen bestowed the Fairy Blessing upon you, the King would ask you this intention, and you would tell him. And for some reason, so far it had always worked out.

Amber sighed deeply as she contemplated it. Someday soon she'd be given her own Gem—even though she was the only Fairy left who hadn't yet learned to fly. Away from the snide comments of Beryl and the others who knew no better and scoffed at hopes and ambitions, she smiled confidently. It would be amazing, whenever it happened. It would be worth waiting for.

Absentmindedly swirling the Gem across the surface as she allowed herself to dream, Amber peered incredulously through the scudding ripples to glimpse a previously hidden Karp parading slowly back and forth, almost as muddy-brown and dull as the water surrounding him, his prominent eyes sparkling in the gloom. Amber shuddered—the Karp were large fish and most Fairies did not encourage dealings with them. But the Queen had always treated them with consideration, and it was even rumoured that they talked to her.

Amber tentatively cleared her throat. "Hello-o!" Her voice bounced back forlornly to her across the vast expanse of water, reminding her with a jolt how alone she was. She wasn't quite sure why she'd said it so loudly. It wasn't like the fish had proper ears or anything. But she'd heard snatches of stories of these parts, whispered by the bards driven out from Arkh Loban for reasons she hadn't understood when she was so young that her wings had been mere gossamer glinting on her back and such wordsmiths had taken refuge in the Kingdom.

She didn't understand the reason for their exile fully even now, but she remembered as if it had not been two seasons ago their tales, spoken hushed around fires in the starlight in voices she could have listened to, enthralled, for hours. Stories of such spirit weren't to the Authorities' prescription; and it was in the safe haven of Fairymead, granted asylum when they were hunted by Goblins and driven out by the Authorities, where the bards had told them last; which was why, some said, magic lingered here in strands you could find if you really, really searched. And the creatures in the Great Lake had always been worthy of ballads, even before the Sea Battle. This must be the Great Lake, mustn't it? Where did that mean she was—right at the edge of the Kingdom? Oh, perfect . . .

She flinched as the brown depths parted disconcertingly quietly and a smooth-scaled gleaming head appeared beside her like a great leviathan. Bulbous eyes glittered intelligently, peering above a cavernous, toothless mouth trailing long barbels.

Amber's eyes bulged wider as she stared into the lidless pair watching her. *Keep calm,* she told herself. *It's only a fish. It won't hurt you.*

"Keep calm," the fish advised in a rich, sonorous voice, which sounded slightly amused. "I'm only a fish. I won't hurt you." It added indulgently, almost as an afterthought: "If it helps, I have a name. Finsbury. You can call me that, if you want."

The incredulous stream of exclamations springing to her mind quelled by his educated tones and lugubrious voice, and her determination to at least attempt to match him for politeness, Amber none-the-less found herself desperately wanting to know how old this huge great individual was, how it was he seemed quite so aged and sprightly all at once, and where in the Realm he had got a name like Finsbury from. She found herself almost instinctively liking her dignified, if unlikely, conversation-partner. He seemed to exude calmness in ripples.

"Thanks, Mister Finsbury," she tried. "Is there any way to cross the lake?" She surveyed the bleak, ominously vast expanse of water. There didn't seem to be a bridge or anything, she realised with trepidation.

"There isn't a bridge or anything, I'm afraid," the Karp rejoined. "It got submerged during the floods and swept away when the Vetch Queen tried to claim dominion over the waterways. It hasn't been rebuilt since the Sea Battle."

Amber chewed at her lip in frustration. So it had been for nothing—she had trekked countless miles through treacherous terrain and now all hope of her crossing the river and getting help to the Prince had been lost. And all she had for company was a fish. *Oh shut up,* she admonished herself sharply. *It's not his fault you're lost. Or scared, for that matter.*

"All is not lost," warbled the Karp thoughtfully. "There is one way to cross. Hop on my back."

At his well-meaning words Amber felt as if a wave of pure fear had rolled right from the lake into her, and she pressed her hands into the damp grass to hide their trembling from Finsbury as she stalled guiltily. He was trying to help, and yet she was terrified: he'd be horrendously slimy, let alone the fact she'd be brought closer to the probably hundreds of murderous denizens of the deep lurking below that darkly shimmering opaque surface. Oh, why wasn't she braver? What in five seasons was she going to do now—swim across?

"Or you could swim across," the Karp mused, not unkindly. "But this way is safer. There are Anangma in these waters."

Amber flinched. "Speak plainly, sir, please—I've had enough of whispered rumours these past months." Something loomed out of the depths of her memory and hung at the edge of her consciousness, but she couldn't place it. It sank below again and was lost.

"Best they remain whispers," warned the Karp. "They are not yet fully active. We still have the last rays of daylight left. Cross while you can."

Internally recoiling, Amber forced herself to shuffle closer. But the Karp did not rush her. He gave, Amber realised, a curious and not slightly unnerving impression of reading her mind. Maybe that was for the best, she deduced. At least she wouldn't have to swallow her pride and admit she was scared. The Karp would suggest something else.

The Karp seemed to have lost his telepathic abilities, however, and continued to float beside the Fairy, fanning with his fins to keep as close to the bank as possible. Cursing her weakness, Amber tried, but she just couldn't make herself do it.

Suddenly she heard a splash from further along the bank and a high-pitched scream of terror. The child! Without thinking she was racing towards the churning water and the floundering youngster. Tearing off her cloak, she jumped, just as out of the corner of her eye her vision registered a dark, indistinct form flicker beneath the surface and move closer.

The water hit her in a stinging wall, icy fingers groping as the depths pulled and tugged around her. Gulping air mechanically as the temperature clawed at her lungs, she struck out for the child.

Grabbing him round the chest, she rolled onto her back so he could breathe. "I've got you," she gasped, spitting filthy water amongst the surging waves churned into life by their struggles as in her grasp, the child twisted round, squirming frantically.

"You're okay!" she insisted breathlessly, clinging to him, struggling to stay afloat with his added weight and kicking her legs furiously as she tried to turn with him towards the bank. But the child was looking over her shoulder, eyes wide in terror, open mouth contorted in fear, staring at the dark form knifing through the murky grey towards them.

With the surreal clarity of mortal fear it filled her vision: the lean, blackened sinuous mass, the undershot gaping jaws, the savage-glinting yellowing eye; the way the sun flashed harsh on the scales; the speed of its path and the impossibility of escape—everything was realer, faster, more important than anything ever before, until instinct over-rode all frozen thought and she flailed out for the bank, hauling the child with her. She wasn't in the water, her mind told her protectively from somewhere high above the situation. It was someone else.

But the numbing coldness slapping round her, stinging into her eyes and sapping her string-weak limbs, tore even that pitiful hope from her as her breath turned to fire in lungs threatening to burst and her exhausted joints began to seize in their ice-gripped sockets. She narrowed her mind to the bank—everything was over there: the child's life and hers. They just had to reach it.

Fear strangled as she felt something whip round her legs like a nest of snakes, writhing and clinging and dragging her sideways until, utterly trapped in the throes of the cross-current, Amber could only flounder in vain as she felt herself slip closer and closer to the fish; the bank retreating with every gulped breath she managed to snatch through the surface.

Throwing everything she had against the water, she couldn't even slow their path, feeling her strength drain with every second, knowing almost detachedly that they would be swept right into the predator's mouth. *If I let go, will the water take me before the fish?*

Immobile in the midst of the current that had taken the Fairy, the monster was hanging back now, knowing its prey was weakening, content to wait for an easier kill.

Stop! Her survival instinct fired rebellion. If nothing else, there was the child: wasn't there a rule about kids not dying like this? There was now. But all the time the current sucked and pulled mercilessly, weighting her limbs and crushing her chest. Not even the fear could give her speed or strength now; she had nothing left to give. She knew they were going to die, and all the intention in the world wasn't going to change the inevitable. *Will the child forgive me?*

Hope thinned almost to expiration—and then, as her soul refused to accept its loss, it in desperation grew itself another form. She wasn't going to let the fish wait until she was too weak to stop it taking the child! While she was struggling, he could escape. The monster would focus on the bigger meal, and the child would be swept past and be carried back to the bank. Hopefully.

With no time to think through such a tenuous plan and no other option left, Amber gasped hoarsely to the child: "We're not going to make it to the other side; we've got to get you back instead. The current'll help us; it'll drag us past the fish—then kick out for the bank as hard as you can, keep your head up and don't stop, no matter what you hear behind you."

The child nodded wordlessly, tightening his arms round Amber. "Thanks for trying to save me," he gulped, dragging his gaze from the fish to glance at her. In that second Amber saw that, just for now, she was his whole Realm, and she knew she couldn't let him die.

"Live!" Letting go of the child, she turned and struck with the current; let it power her towards the fish. She didn't have long left, but if she were due to meet with death this day, she would meet it head-on.

But now she was facing the monster, she had a different view of the lake, and her heart leapt as she saw, disguised amongst the reeds and rushes on the right, far-off but unmistakable: the swirling ripple of conflicting waters before it swept into a fast-flowing stream that banked onto a sandy shore. If she could just join that current.

New hope fired strength through her limbs once more as she surged towards the fish, the scudding waves of the current cresting with her speed. In a silvered flash of scale and fangs the monster lunged towards her, and summoning everything she had in reserve Amber flung herself sideways across the current, thrashing through the erratic grasp of the eddying waters.

Chokingly, the waters closed around her and turned her Realm to roiling foam as she powered blindly through the water, distractedly registering the weight tightening across her shoulders—the boy hadn't let go. Dread seized, but there was no time for thought; the fish could be anywhere.

Not daring to rest her burning limbs, she strove on, on, on; the new current building in power, lending them speed as at last the lake's pull yielded to the draw of the stream as it grew stronger, carrying them downriver.

As they swept round a bend Amber gagged against mouthfuls of silt, sediment stirring around them in swathes with every kick—it had to be shallower here. Trying to stand, Amber's foot oozed through she didn't want to think about what. Seizing their moment, she pulled the child to his feet and struck out hastily towards dry land with him, ploughing up the silence as they churned the stream to mud.

With half an ear, Amber thought she heard a sort of quiet swish through the water behind them. She turned.

A slack, wet fin protruded from the surface above a glassy, dead-eyed stare gleaming through the liquid murk.

"Run!" The scream tore from her mouth as if by someone else and grabbing the child by the scruff of his clothes she barraged through the sinking sands, shoving him clumsily onto the bank, scrabbling manically at the muddy sides and hauling herself out of the water after him.

Amidst an eruption of foam and silver scale the monster exploded through the surface, plummeting in an arcing crash that sent battering waves sluicing over the bank and threatening to sweep the companions back to a swift and savage death.

Spluttering hoarsely as the waves crashed over her, Amber felt herself pushed to her knees by the force, one arm wrapping protectively around the child, tucking him against her chest as she sprawled under the onslaught, the other hand burying into clumps of grass as the sodden earth slipped beneath them and she could do nothing but cling on.

As the fear subsided with the wave she lay gasping fitfully, all strength spent; just thankful for the icy slaps of wind billowing through her soaked clothing, for the shaking numbness that seized her body, for the gritty taste of mud that clung in her mouth and for the salt-teared water that stung in her eyes as she finally managed to push herself up onto her knees. She was alive, and just for now she didn't need to think any further than that to be grateful.

Beside her the child stood wordless and immobile, staring blankly past her as crouched eye-level to him she tried and failed to reach into that hollow gaze.

Not knowing what else to do to bring him back from his terror, she wrapped him in a hug. He felt like cold bones in her embrace, as if his life had drained away into the water.

"It's over now," she promised, her voice hoarse from the river and shaking from their ordeal even as she strove to steady it. *We're alive. We're okay.* Drawing a deep breath, she tried without success to stop herself from trembling quite so violently. "Let's get you home."

The child nodded, before being consumed in a coughing fit that wracked his whole body. He returned Amber's helpless looks of concern with a weak grin. "So who are you?" he asked, watching her through large dark eyes as he wiped his hand on the ground to dry it and extended it. "How come you saved me?"

Troubled that the second question could spring from anyone's lips, let alone a child's, she turned her attention to the first instead. "I'm Amber," she answered readily, grinning at his formality as she extended her hand in return.

Stone-cold pinpricks pressed at her wrist in his grasp, and her eyes flew to his hands before she could stop them. His palm was stretched with skin as warm as hers, but after the first couple of joints each finger tapered into a—the word that skittered fretfully in her head was "claw". You couldn't call them nails; they looked like talons, only—

Mentally, she gave herself a good kick for staring. He'd been in danger and she'd helped him and she'd do it again in a wing-beat if the need arose—although preferably it wouldn't be before she'd got him back home and they'd both grabbed a set of dry clothes and a mouthful to eat. Plastered with mud, gazing curiously up at her through widening eyes beneath an unruly mop of curly black hair, wearing shorts and sleeves that had long since turned the colour of the river bank, he could hardly have looked less fearsome if he'd tried, claws or none.

"I'm Mugkafb!" the boy offered eagerly, looking her up and down in turn. "Where do you come from? No one round here has *wings!*"

His voice trailed into an impressed hush, and Amber grinned self-consciously. "I'm a meadow Fairy; I've never been round here before. But I lost this Gem so I had to go looking for it with the Prince and now he's injured so I've got to find the King and—" she broke off despairingly, unsure of how she could finish that sentence. What *was* she going to do now?

"Wow, I bet you're hungry after all that," Mugkafb surmised confidently. "I would be—especially if I'd just rescued someone. Come and have wyshep with us." He danced away in front of her, beckoning impatiently for her to follow.

Amber blinked. Was she supposed to know what he was talking about? Yet a grin escaped her; she had to admire his ability to forget so swiftly what was probably going to plague her mind for nights to come. And she had to make sure he got home safely, didn't she? The Prince would understand. Or not, but there'd probably be horses where Mugkafb lived that carried healing supplies, or if she was lucky something vaguely resembling Dartwings that could send a message on ahead, so it would be better for him too whether he realised it or not.

Her steps schlurped noisily over the oozing ground as she ran to catch up with Mugkafb over increasingly marshy terrain, her frozen feet thawing as she splashed through puddles of warm swamp-water. Steam drifting from the hot pools sprawled on either side of their path billowed into a disorientating haze, the vapours shifting once-familiar colours and sending the sun's rays sliding into the kind of brooding twilight that usually heralded the most unearthly of storms, until the air above the swamp hung heavy and wet and strangely shimmering. Patches of smoke drifted above reed clumps, and now and then flashes of wisp-light winked through the mist.

Amber began to shiver in her still-wet clothes as cold doubt snaked around her. *Yes,* her mind goaded callously. *You are certainly far beyond the borders of the Fairy Kingdom—and possibly more completely lost than anyone in the entire Realm has been before.* She glanced uneasily to her companion, wondering where exactly he was leading her.

"Ooawacawacawacaooagh!"

Amber started violently before she realised it was Mugkafb bellowing out the call, and in a flurry of near-silent movement dozens of swamp-dwellers materialised around them, striding forth from the mists or slipping fluidly from the marsh's watery embrace.

Stunned, Amber peered through the gloaming, trying to focus on their audience. Mugkafb's people.

Proud, watchful eyes returned her stare. Through the vaporous air glinted weapons the like of which she had never seen, held silent and still.

"They're moonshafts," Mugkafb explained, seeing Amber's nervous gaze flit to the scimitar-curved stone blades wrapped round their bearer's wrists with swinging cord. "Don't worry, I've got one too. Not that it should come to that."

"Should come to *what?*" Amber hissed, pulling him up short as she stalled.

Mugkafb wrapped his claws round her hand and carried on in front of her. "You saved my life! Don't be scared, they'll love you; I promise."

Still jittery with the adrenalin backwash from earlier, Amber seriously doubted that; but she was also pretty sure that it was too late now to do anything other than react to events as they unfolded.

Searching the crowds, Mugkafb called out to one young man in particular, slightly taller and possibly a year or two older than Amber, who was watching them intently but with less of a murderous glint in his eyes than the others: "Esh Amber mwaf uhg menb vike! Engo ro wevy!"

He nodded confidently as he glanced back to Amber, translating in a low voice: "I'm telling them that you saved my life and they're not allowed to attack you."

Amber swallowed dryly, unable to tear her gaze from the encircling shadowy forms half-hidden amongst the marsh. "Oh. Good," she managed faintly, realising she still had tight hold of Mugkafb's claws and releasing them, trying with difficulty to stand a little straighter and breathe a little slower.

In response the man leapt out, smiling broadly. He had the same dark skin and eyes as Mugkafb, but his black hair was longer and swept back, cascading in unruly waves to his shoulders. He held up a warning hand to the others, and Amber couldn't help noticing how scuffed the points of his claws were and that one was veined with splits.

Turning back to Amber, he sprang into the air, landing in a kneeling crouch, his left fist half-clenched, leaving his claws indenting lengthways in the moist earth. He rose, the mud clinging to the dark spears extending from his fingers. "Sen?" he asked, brow raised questioningly.

Amber watched him warily. His hand was still, waiting for her response, palm towards himself so that the points of his claws were not turned to her.

"Sen," Mugkafb answered. The man didn't move; he kept his gaze on Amber, not rushing her.

Amber felt tendrils fear clutching through the mists towards her heart as her mind raced. They knew she'd rescued the child. They wouldn't do anything wrong, would they. Would they?

She searched the man's gaze for a long moment, saw something she felt safe with in his eyes, took courage, and allowed cautiously: "Sen."

Moving slowly so as to allow transparency of motive when she couldn't speak his language, in a fluid stroke he wiped the earth onto Amber's cheek with the curved back of his claws. "Ka' shen," he murmured softly.

"Ka' shen," the echo rippled respectfully through the observing crowd.

Less scared now, Amber risked a smile to the man. "Kar shenn?" she offered hesitantly.

Smiling warmly, he bowed his head. Then with a barking call he strode back, and at once the enchantment was broken and the swamp-dwellers returned to their business.

"Now what?" Amber asked in bewilderment as she exhaled a breath she hadn't realised she'd been holding.

"Wyshep!" Mugkafb exclaimed gleefully, clapping his hands and grabbing her wrist once more.

Hastening after him, Amber fought the urge to pick off the drying mud crinkling itchily against her skin. "Why did he do that?" she hissed while they were still out of earshot.

Mugkafb shrugged. "It's our mark."

"He was *marking* me?" she retorted angrily.

Mugkafb rolled his eyes. "We're people of the earth; it sustains everything we rely on for life so it has our utmost respect—'marking' you with it is a badge of honour. Racxen's our tracker so he does stuff like that 'cause he's got to look out for the tribe and he's my brother so he's the only one of my family left to thank you for saving me. And don't think he can't understand what you're saying, by the way. We always use our own language for ceremony. Don't Fairies do that too?"

"I'm really sorry." Amber lowered her gaze, embarrassed.

"'S all right," Mugkafb shrugged comfortably. "Not everyone can be as clever as me. Come on, this is our cave right here!"

"Where?" Amber followed his gaze, and despite her light-headedness at the day's events couldn't help grinning. Carved into the rock-face, the low entrance obscured by a curtain of tangled swamp-plants, it looked just like something out of the books she was always reading. Once they stepped through, it would open up into a yawning great underground network to rival the splendours of the outside world. Things were starting to look up.

Parting the trailing weeds, Mugkafb's brother ducked quietly into the waiting darkness of the tunnel before motioning the others inside.

Amber held her breath as she crawled through the tunnel after Mugkafb. It smelled old and damp and earthy, like a fallen tree soaked through with rain and pocked with toadstools. Gritty detritus imbedded itself in her palms and shins as she shuffled forwards on hands and knees, the scuffles of her painfully slow progress amplified in the confined space. Things were *not* starting to look up.

Scrambling out at the other end into deeper darkness she heard the *plip . . . plip* of water echo expansively from somewhere far away unseen, and for a minute she felt a stab of fear, standing there unseeingly in the unknown, all senses robbed and not knowing what to expect. Yet through the pressing blackness a welcoming glow greeted her as the softest of lights winked through the darkness, the rocks glittering with phosphorescence like the sea beneath moonlight, sprinkling their enchantment until Amber found herself wondering what in the Realm she'd been scared of.

Flames coiled and quivered, bathing the cavern in warmth as Racxen stepped back from the fire, passing the flint to Amber and slipping a terracotta-coloured woven rug across her shoulders. It was rough and heavy, and when she pulled it closer around her it felt as if the heat of the earth were infusing right through into her.

Beside her, Mugkafb poked at the leaves, coaxing more flames to dance. "'Course, it's pretty dark normally; we can't really have fires down here or we'd smoke the whole place out," he divulged. "We've only got the two entrances and we don't want to advertise our presence to the, um, well, anything. But Racxen says Fairies don't have night-vision, do you? I think it's cooler to have wings, though."

Mugkafb retreated to pester his brother for food and Amber, bundled comfortably in the rug, watched intrigued as Racxen, at the edge of the light, unwrapped a bundle of sacking that he had pulled from a hole in the earth to reveal a steaming-hot loaf of dark, sweet-smelling bread. Breaking it into chunks he piled it onto clay plates with what looked like exotic kinds of roots and tubers. Mugkafb almost snatched his portion, and Amber had to admit it beat loitering bored by the kitchen stove for an hour under direction from Ruby. Now that the rug and fire had taken care of the deathly chill, she realised she was starving.

Mugkafb enthusiastically waved a half-chewed root to get Amber's attention, ignoring the disapproving looks of his brother in the process. "So," he began amiably, hastily gulping down the offending root. "You've found the gem; the Prince is next, right? Bet he won't have come this far though—Fairies don't exactly make a habit of travelling in these parts."

Amber grimaced. "I know. It wasn't until I reached the lake that I realised just how lost I was. What were you doing there?"

Mugkafb jammed another mouthful of root into his mouth, and waved the rest of it around in an attempt to clarify the point. "I was about to go swimming."

Amber stared at him. "You can *swim?*"

Mugkafb returned her look blankly. "'Course. I live in the swamps.

Why wouldn't I be able to swim? I just didn't see the Pygon," he continued, pausing for effect so his brother could appreciate the full drama of his adventure. "It was the biggest I've—"

"This," Racxen addressed him quickly, his voice sharp with guilt, "is what I've been talking with you about. When I take you tracking I put you in danger and when I don't, I leave you in worse. I care about you more than anything in the whole Realm, and it kills me that I can't get this right."

Shrugging, Mugkafb changed tack and wrapped his claws around Amber's wrist. "Stop worrying. She saved me from the Pygon. And she's a Fairy," he continued, impressed. "She could've flown away, but she didn't." He beamed hopefully up at his brother, whose keen gaze had settled on the Fairy. "Can I have some more food, Racxen?"

Amber shifted uncomfortably. "I kind of thought he couldn't swim; I didn't actually see the fish until I was about to jump. And I—well, I can't even fly."

Racxen smiled at her honesty. "You still saved my brother. And he's right; you could have run, you could have swum away, even if you couldn't use your wings. You stayed with him, when it would have been easier to have just saved yourself." He gave her an odd, direct look. "Especially as you have been warned Arraheng roam these parts, and I've heard how much Fairies fear them."

Amber shuddered at the memory of their attacker. "I wouldn't have left an Arraheng to that monster," she protested vehemently. "And I've never actually seen one, so I can't exactly talk."

"Evidently," Mugkafb grinned, his eyes dancing. "And are you sure?"

And I thought I felt stupid when I lost the Gem, Amber groaned to herself as she kneaded the lumpy bedding into a tolerable shape. Racxen and Mugkafb had both assured her amusedly that she didn't need to apologise, but she still felt hideously embarrassed, and fervently wanted the moss mattress to swallow her up and spit her out back at home.

She turned as the older Arraheng—*yes, Arraheng, get used to it,* she reminded herself firmly—materialised at the entrance of the alcove chamber that he had prepared for her use that night.

"My brother and I will keep watch," he reassured her. "Get some sleep. We will easily make up the lost ground later—our steeds can fly faster than your wings."

Amber nodded, exhausted. "Thanks, Racxen. Wake me when they're ready."

He slipped quietly from the chamber, leaving her alone to rest.

A second later, Amber sat bolt upright in the darkness. "What steeds?"

At Midnight

"Five more wing-beats . . ." Amber pleaded distantly as the warm clutches of oblivion that had finally enveloped her, despite the contents of the mattress proving determined to stick her like a pincushion full of twigs, were systematically peeled away by a young voice altogether too chirpy for this forsaken hour of darkness.

"But it's gone midnight!" Mugkafb insisted reproachfully, grabbing her pillow and trying to yank it out from beneath her head. Succeeding after a fashion, he lost his grip and fell back, connecting loudly with the bedside table and dislodging the considerable contents of a clay wash-pot all over where the pillow had been.

"*Mugkafb!*" Amber's squawk as she was doused in stunningly cold water echoed through the chamber even as the Arraheng was already scrambling hastily away. "That'll teach you for not listening to me," the boy grinned, staring down at his feet in an unsuccessful attempt to stop himself laughing. "Come on, check this out!"

Stumbling along behind him, Amber just managed to follow him through the shifting darkness without falling over as Mugkafb danced ahead excitedly through tunnel after tunnel until moonlight spilled through the exit ahead.

As she wriggled through, a deep inky expanse of sky opened above to greet her, the soft breeze murmuring through the marsh grasses to cool the humid swamp air making it sound as though even the night itself had space to breathe out here as the clear moon turned the still waterways to silver.

Mugkafb dashed off again, leaving Amber squelching through the waterlogged ground after him. As they left the encampment to traverse the uninhabited reaches of the swamp she found herself noticing the stars as she never had at home: clustered jewels shining brightly, glinting far more sharply than they'd had the chance to whilst competing with the lights of Fairymead.

The swamps seemed to stretch out forever, but as the ground grew solid beneath her feet again she caught up with Mugkafb. Ambiguous shadows shifted into solid form as she approached, revealing sheer strange rock formations sweeping through the impressionistic darkness. Moonlight spilled between the clouds to touch the scene with an otherworldly aura.

Mugkafb pointed to the top of the cliffs with a breathless grin. "I got my brother to call the Zyfang," he revealed proudly. "You know how everyone says Fairies are humans evolved from Dartwings? Well, these're kind of *our* spiritual ancestors. Like us, they're the *best* allies. They fly like the wind and are as invisible as the night itself."

High above Amber saw Racxen, crouched at the cliff edge and silhouetted by the light of the moon, his head thrown back in the process of a long, low wailing call that echoed around the boulders and rang through the night.

In response a huge leather-winged creature swooped out of the darkness towards them, keening a harsh braying cry.

Amber eyed Mugkafb accusingly. "That's a *bat*."

"What's a bat?" Mugkafb countered innocently. "He is a Zyfang. He is the most loyal of warriors and will not let you down."

Amber stared in awe, trying to squash down the anxious thoughts flittering about in her head over what the Prince was going to have to say about being taken home on a bat. She grinned to Mugkafb. "You're going to teach me how to ride one, right?"

Seated at the Zyfang's shoulders, with Racxen's arm tight around her to stop her from falling, Amber stared into the night between their steed's daggered ears, the wind whipping across her face and stealing her breath as she awaited their launch into the unknown.

Racxen shifted behind her, watching the sky. "Ready?"

Amber buried her hands in bunches of wiry fur. "Sen!"

She whooped as they lurched forwards, Racxen's excited laughter in her ears as the creature responded with a ready guttural cry and the pulsing slap and pull of heavy wings throbbed through the air as the Zyfang launched, surging powerfully into the sky until they were surrounded by inky darkness, flying through the night with the stars twinkling above and the rolling shadow of the ground unfolding into an ever-changing landscape below.

"There!" Amber called back finally in relief, glimpsing the Prince's white shirt caught by the moonlight amongst the darker shadows at the edge of the wood, and Racxen reached round to help her guide the Zyfang in.

Relieved to slide to solid ground after the swiftest of flights and breathing her thanks to the Zyfang, Amber ran to the Prince as the Arraheng dismounted. "Jasper, you're going to be fine! Racxen and Mugkafb are—"

"Fiends!" the Prince barked, his eyes flashing murderous fear as his hand flew to his dagger.

Racxen pushed Mugkafb behind him and locked his eyes on the Prince, one hand hovering over the moonshaft still hanging casually from his belt. He didn't move.

"You want to stay out here the whole night?" Amber snapped, rounding on the Prince as she stepped between them. Jasper removed his hand grudgingly, his eyes flitting suspiciously from Amber to the strangers.

"These are my friends," she cautioned more levelly, guilt twisting in her stomach at having led them here if Jasper was going to be like this. "If it wasn't for them I wouldn't be able to get you back to the meadows, yet you dare to threaten them? And before you shout at me, you might technically be my Prince but you're not theirs."

"*Definitely* not ours," Mugkafb divulged emphatically to the air as he seated himself comfortably on a nearby rock and fixed stony eyes on the Prince.

Jasper sniffed disdainfully at the interruption. "Ignorant little worm."

"Sure," the boy retorted swiftly in his own tongue. "That's why I can speak your language perfectly and you don't know what I'm saying, isn't it?" Feeling better about the situation, he rattled off a string of Arraheng expletives and smiled at the Prince sweetly.

Glaring acidly at Amber, Jasper made a show of painstakingly turning his attention to his injured leg as he avoided the Arraheng's gaze and feigned indifference to his presence.

Keeping his eyes on the Prince a moment longer, with a word to his brother, Racxen withdrew with Mugkafb to tend to the Zyfang.

Jasper turned to Amber, spitting malevolence. "You expect help from them?" he hissed, barely caring if Racxen was out of hearing or not. "These are Arraheng, Amber! They're nothing but ignorant savages—"

"I will not state the obvious one more time!" Amber interrupted warningly, crouching down to glare at the Prince, her eyes flashing fire. "You talk about them like that again and I swear I'll tell them to leave you here."

The Prince looked deflated for a moment. "Well," he tried lamely. "There's no need to—"

"Obviously there is," Amber insisted curtly. "You seem to think it's acceptable to badmouth my friends and I don't give a Goblin's coin whether you're royalty or not I'm not going to let you."

Jasper snorted. "I only drew my blade to protect you—you're acting so thoughtlessly that someone needs to."

"Oh, whatever," Amber spat back in retort, angry with herself for not being able to think of anything less childish, but so furious that it was hard enough just to keep it verbal.

"Don't be horrible to Amber!" Mugkafb shouted suddenly, reappearing. "I'll protect her! My moonshaft's better than your sword anyway! It's made from the shards of fallen shooting stars, 'scepts you wouldn't care would you 'cause you prob'ly think it's made of bone or something horrible because you believe everything you hear, don't you!" He gasped for breath as tears squeezed into his eyes as if welling up through his throat. "And savage? You're the one who wanted to stab my brother!" he sobbed as Racxen ran back at the shouting, glaring with bitter disappointment at the Prince as he wrapped his arms around his brother to comfort him, murmuring softly in Arraheng.

"Oh, Mugkafb," Amber pleaded, kneeling down to talk eye-to-eye with him. "I'm so sorry, I should have thought. It's horrible when people shout at each other isn't it?"

Sniffing fiercely against his hand, Mugkafb studied the ground, his voice tiny and tremulous. "I just don't want you getting hurt. We've already lost so many of our tribe."

Her eyes welling up as she squeezed Mugkafb's hand tightly, Amber stood back to steady her breathing and fixed the Prince in a measured stare, forbidding herself for Mugkafb's sake to become angry again. "You owe our youngest friend a sincere apology."

Jasper seemed to shrink, completely cowed, as Mugkafb stepped forwards, his face streaked with tears and trying to look stern instead of upset.

"Good grief, I've got to stop this," the Prince muttered wretchedly, aghast. "I thought—everyone says that—how was I supposed to know otherwise; I've never . . ." he trailed off, unable to look Mugkafb in the eye. "I need to give you apologies, not excuses. I'm deeply sorry. I took rumours for truths, and hand-me-down scare-stories for history; this was unpardonable and I will not stoop to it again."

Mugkafb wiped his face with the back of his hand. "Sen," he offered, subdued, and without another word followed his brother, leaving Amber staring at the Prince and trying not to look as accursedly annoyed as she felt with him.

"It's a start," Amber acknowledged grudgingly, seeing Jasper's expression and consciously making an effort to shove the past minutes aside. "Now," she added more equably as she saw Racxen approach, "don't say anything about the bat."

Jasper's face paled at the sight of the dark-furred, fang-mouthed creature dragging itself with hooked thumb-claws into sight over the wet grass as Racxen walked calmly at its side apparently engaged in conversation.

Leaving the creature with a word a short way off, Racxen knelt beside the Prince.

"What do you think you're doing?" Jasper cried in alarm as the Arra-heng swiftly inspected his foot, and having assessed the injury shook out a cloth pouch from a pocket, its dried plant contents spilling over the rock.

"Oi! Those took me half a day to gather!" Mugkafb protested in dismay as the Prince brushed the items aside. "And I don't know why we're the ones who have to act twice as good just so's you can think we're half as important as you."

Jasper bit his tongue, cringing as if he'd just been shaken awake to realise what he'd said whilst half-asleep. "Forgive me," he mumbled awkwardly. "Although I know it's more than I deserve."

"They're healing herbs, you need allow me to apply them," Racxen admonished, dripping water from the Prince's skein onto the broken leaves. "Then we'll take you home. Amber will help you with the poultice, and our friend here will carry you."

By the time the Prince had finished complaining, they'd managed to seat him far more comfortably than the mumbled stream of curses escaping his lips suggested.

"Don't worry," Amber reassured him in a hiss. "You won't find a safer steed, and I'll make sure you don't fall."

"Like I made sure you wouldn't get lost?" Behind his usual dismissiveness she heard his embarrassment.

Biting back her retort, Amber wrapped a steadying arm around his waist as Mugkafb hopped up behind them.

Glancing back to check that everyone was safely seated, Racxen scanned the terrain laid out before him, his eyes gleaming in the moonlight. "Hold on!" he called to the others, and urged by whispered words their chiropteran steed launched once more into the sky.

After minutes of breath-robbing wind and darkness, the twinkling lights of the meadows began to fleck the sea of night as Fairymead grew closer on the billowing tapestry rolling out beneath them.

"The Ring! The castle!" Amber shouted the landmarks against the wind streaming in their faces, and the Zyfang dove at a motion from Racxen, splaying its wings to steady itself after the descent.

"They don't normally land on the ground," Racxen explained, murmuring his thanks to the creature in a tongue Amber guessed must have been its own. She slid from its back to help Racxen lift down the Prince.

Clambering unceremoniously from the Zyfang, Jasper waved their help away. "I'm not *that* injured," he muttered sullenly. The ground shuddered under him even as he spoke and he clutched at Racxen. Rolling her eyes, Amber took the other arm and the Prince begrudgingly let them guide him as they wound their ponderous way to the castle.

At the gates the Prince stopped, leaning heavily against Racxen's shoulder as he tested putting full weight on his leg. He turned to the

Arraheng, with the grace to look embarrassed. "Sir—and young master," he added quickly to Mugkafb, "it appears I have misjudged you, or rather worse, I judged you by less than yourself: an unforgivable lapse, particularly from one in power. I thank you for your assistance, and ask your forgiveness. You are nobler than I. Believe me, I will endeavour most fervently to change my ways. It should not have taken so extreme an act on your part to change my attitude."

Racxen searched his face for a moment. "Sen," he shrugged resignedly before awarding him a tired smile. "It is granted."

A noise skittered from the windows of the castle, and the old haunted look flashed across the Arraheng's face as he exchanged warning glances with Mugkafb.

Jasper nodded, chagrined. "I understand. There are many of my people who still think as I until so recently thought."

Amber kept her eyes on Racxen. "But not all."

Jasper waved a hand at the Arraheng. "Go, before you are seen. For your own sake."

At a second noise Racxen nodded sadly as, meeting Amber's eyes briefly, he gave a low call to his brother and the pair darted away, melting into the night's long shadows.

Amber let her gaze follow them for a moment before she fumbled open the ancient door and, more slowly now that she was alone with him, managed to steer the Prince into the mutedly lit corridor which served as the entrance to the recovery hall.

Hearing muffled voices, she called out softly, and the Matron hurried out from a side room, bustling about expertly while Amber told her as much as she could about what had happened, nodding and querying and preparing even as she soothed her patient with low confident words and eased him into bed.

"The medicine will have worked by morning, love," she advised with a reassuring smile as the girl loitered awkwardly by the door.

"Thanks, Sarin. He had me worried," Amber admitted, shaking her hand as the Matron withdrew to attend to other patients.

She tiptoed to the bedside. The Prince was sleeping already, a soft shaft of moonlight spilling onto his pillow; his face looked untroubled for the first time in days.

"I'm sorry," she breathed, her voice barely audible so as not to wake him. "I really didn't mean for this to happen."

Without opening his eyes, Jasper parted his lips in a slight smile. "Get some sleep," he murmured, no trace of bitterness in his voice.

Embarrassed and relieved, she slipped out quietly.

A Kind of Normality

As the Fairy lay on the verdant grass, the gentle Recö breeze warm on her skin, the air seemed to buzz with the anticipation of wondrous adventure. Yet the sky grew chill with foreboding as she remembered the wise warnings of the elders: this was how all dire endings started— she had better run home to more sensible things; then, as long as she was willing to cut out her tongue, she might be graced enough to be won in marriage by someone who would find her useful and suitably subservient. Although she might have to wait for a hundred years.

A frustrated growl punctuated this unfurling blossom of literary genius, and Amber, with no small amount of satisfaction, sent the book flying unceremoniously through the gentle Recö breeze and scudding across the verdant grass. *If I read this for just one minute longer,* she promised herself grimly, *I'm going to scream. Preferably at whoever wrote it. Or at least whoever decided it was a set text for that forsaken exam. No wonder the magic's fading from the Realm.*

She yawned leisurely. At least she never had to read it again; as soon as Ruby turned up she could have it back now that the exam period was over. What was going to happen now that school had finished, however, she was still worried about. Ruby had an apprenticeship with the seamstress Opal, Tanzan was journeying beyond the borders to become a fletcher, Beryl and Jade had no plans and no ambitions to go with them—but what was *she* going to do?

Shoving the book aside, Amber stared blankly into the distance as her mind squirmed away from the question. Ask Sarin for an apprenticeship in the recovery hall? Uncertainty twisted in her gut. If she let herself be honest, although she'd be more than proud to call it hers and felt tugged by responsibility to undertake such a role, not to mention desperately wanting to help and feel useful, the contrast between this reality and the free-spirited dreams that danced wildly through her head felt like it was pulling her apart even as she tried to grapple her thoughts into a solution to manage both scenarios.

Sighing fretfully, Amber surveyed her surroundings with a critical eye. The warm breeze buzzed with nothing more than the lullaby of drowsy insects, and the very air seemed fat and languid in its determination to not seem in the least bit adventurous at all. Fairymead was possibly, she hazarded, the least eventful place in the whole of True Realm.

Ah, well, she accepted resignedly. She couldn't really complain. She'd had enough of excitement after losing the Gem and all the trouble that had caused, not to mention the terror of the fish monster that loomed large in her mind and had invaded her thoughts in the quiet darkness when she had been about to fall asleep last night. At least the Prince was going to be all right. And she'd got the Presentation celebrations to look forward to. Well, she *should* be looking forward to it; everyone else was, apparently. But even if she hadn't been churned up from all that had happened, she knew she would still be dreading it just as much as she was now. Amber groaned inwardly at the prospect: Ruby would spend the whole night trying to steal a dance with the Prince while she'd be left standing alone, permanently gravitating around the banquet tables to try and hide the fact no one wanted to dance with her.

With a conscious effort, Amber sculpted her grimace into a smile. It would be the night before she received her Fairy Gem, she reminded herself. How bad could it be? Maybe she should focus on turning her mind back to less threatening fears—like the fact she *still* didn't have a dress to wear and was *still* the only Fairy to not be able to fly before the Presentation.

Distractedly she stared across the meadows, wondering where Racxen and Mugkafb were; whether they were okay. It was no use; she couldn't concentrate on anything else after last night's events: it was like a part of her was following them.

Her gaze wandered out to the horizon, where the green merged with the sky in a gradually darkening band behind the distant indistinct silhouettes of some far-off forest she had never been to and suddenly wanted to know the name of. Somewhere beneath the indistinct haze of distance lay the encampment of the Arraheng: people whom until yesterday she had never seen; "monsters" she'd never wished to meet under any circumstances. Friends she now cared about.

She squinted against the sunlight as the horizon's line was invaded by a slender, irritatingly voluptuous figure accompanied by out-of-tune singing floating closer. Forced back to the present, Amber hailed her warmly, "Hey, Ruby!"

"Hi, babe!" Ruby danced up, her shiny chestnut hair bouncing and her eyes sparkling mischievously. "You excited?"

Amber shoved her worries to the back of her mind. "Yeah," she admitted.

"I hear the Prince will be there," Ruby prompted dramatically with a satisfied smirk, leaving the suggestion hanging in the air for as long as she could resist before shooting a none-too-subtle sidelong glance at her friend to judge her reaction.

Amber rolled her eyes with a grin as she let Ruby help her up. "Give it a rest, Rube—I've spent enough time with him to last me a lifetime."

"Oooh, all right for some," Ruby countered dreamily, trying to achieve a suitably glazed, misty expression and instead going cross-eyed and giving herself a headache in the process. "Oh, come *on*," she insisted. "He's such a . . ."

"Creep?" Amber proffered flatly, pulling a face.

Ruby wafted a perfectly manicured hand. "I hear he once slew an *Arraheng*," she continued undeterred in a conspiratorial hiss.

"What?!" Amber spun to face her, snatching her hand free as disgust rose like bile in her throat. "Ruby, that's *evil*."

Ruby shrugged. "Well, okay it was Beryl who said it so he probably hasn't. But it's not as evil as Arraheng," she dismissed, ignoring Amber's glare. Then she lowered her voice nervously, glancing quickly around before pulling Amber closer.

"I've heard stories," she divulged darkly. "Did you know that instead of the last joint of their fingers they have claws that are like five inches long? And they *drown* their own youngsters—Jade was down by the swamp, well it wasn't Jade it was Sardonyx but he's her boyfriend so it's practically the same thing. Well there was this kid, you know, one of those; and he called out to it, but out of nowhere the water exploded and this, this *thing*, reared up and grabbed it with its claws and this poor kid was struggling and everything but it just went down in all this splashing, and he never saw it again. It never even got another breath of air." Ruby sniffed. "I know they're monsters, but to do that to a little one."

Amber's heart tattooed against her chest so thunderously it made her feel physically sick. "Well, it was Jade who told the Prince that I'd made the Dartwing fly off with the Queen's Gem," she suggested hesitantly. She stretched the silence in an attempt to force her nerves to calm. If she placed more weight on rumours from the likes of Beryl and Jade than her own experiences she was hardly standing up for her new friends.

New, her mind goaded maliciously. *Virtually unknown.* She swallowed awkwardly as she squashed down the thought. She knew how much of a drama-queen Ruby could be.

"You know how many stories have been floating around recently," Amber reminded her more steadily. "Eyes in the forest, weird noises in the sky . . ." *Giant bat-steeds and claw-handed rescuers and flesh-eating fish straight out of nightmares,* she felt tempted to add. "Maybe they've just been made up to try and scare us into staying at home obediently instead of having adventures. Maybe if you met an Arraheng you'd feel differently."

Ruby snorted with laughter. "Meet one? Feel differently? Yeah right, Amber. What Realm are you in?"

Amber kept her eyes to the horizon as they walked in silence. She felt as if someone was digging their nails into her heart.

Ruby linked arms with her, humming. "You okay?" she checked. "I know you're a bit too, you know, sensitive about these things. Hunting and stuff. No offence. I didn't mean it."

"Yeah you did," Amber muttered, quicker than she'd intended to. "You never used to be like this before you started hanging out with Beryl and that lot."

"Sorry," Ruby offered, more apologetic now.

"But not going to change."

Silence pressed as they walked, each shrunken into their inner worlds.

Ruby tugged on her hand, worry filling her eyes. Amber sighed. She couldn't change Ruby's mind for her. She knew leadenly that there was no point pushing it further. She was still Ruby, she reminded herself firmly, although her heart was skittering. Still the friend who'd been there since the beginning, still the one she'd walk through fire for despite any stupid argument they'd had. Maybe she'd just have to work on showing her the truth about the Arraheng.

"Look, I really am sorry," Ruby insisted more gently, brimming with concern. "You're my best friend, Amber, and I don't want to upset you. I won't talk to Beryl and that lot about hunting any more."

Amber looked at her, hope vying with sorrow in her eyes. "I can't ask you to do that."

Ruby squeezed her hand. "You don't need to. I only started hanging out with them because they're doing seamstressing, too, and I got freaked that we'd lose touch because you're not."

Amber hugged her suddenly, holding her tight. "You mean more to me than I tell you, Rube." She grinned. "And seriously? You're so good you could sew skins for Selkies; you're going to outclass them all. Garnet's going to have you flying off to Arkh Loban and rubbing shoulders with the elite—you'll be able to drop me for someone so much more awesome than Beryl."

Ruby giggled. They walked on, the silence spreading comfortably.

"He is a total creep, you know," Amber offered to permit a change of subject.

Ruby huffed gratefully. "All right," she conceded. "But he's a royal creep."

They both laughed. Ruby took her friend's arm again. "Come on. Let's go get ready for the party."

Amber shrugged helplessly. "It's in two days!"

Ruby grabbed her hand and grinned. "Precisely! It's about time you helped me choose my dress."

Amber stared worriedly. "You've got more than one?"

"Airborne!" Amber screamed exultantly as Ruby soared above her in yet another successful flight, racing after her as she flew towards home.

"Keep going! You're doing great!" Squinting into the sky, she watched her best friend perform a shaky turn and begin gaining altitude with effortful beats of her wings. Her outline faded as she rose and rose, her wing-beats becoming quickly more steady with the practice, her altitude controlled and her turns precise.

On the ground far below—to where Ruby hadn't looked back down once—Amber shielded her eyes as the sun made them water a little. Or maybe it was something else, too, she admitted quietly to herself. Something to do with the fact that Ruby was so good at something she still couldn't be part of. It had always been a pattern that Ruby was better at everything than her; normally she'd just be proud of her friend, and she still was, of course. Yet now Ruby seemed to be leaving her behind in more ways than one. Through school, they'd been together almost always. Now, for reasons known only to Ruby, she had taken to hanging out more and more with Beryl and Sardonyx and their friends instead.

Amber ran to catch up, bodily breaking Ruby's stumbling landing and snorting with laughter as the pair of them scrambled awkwardly to their feet, grinning breathlessly in shared triumph. "You were awesome!"

Ruby beamed in response, then grimaced as she whisked out a hairbrush secreted somewhere about her person and tugged it through her wind-tangled locks. "Why can't flying be more elegant? I look such a mess!"

Amber shoved her playfully, squinting against the sunlight across the vast green of the meadows, and accepted her cue to change the subject. "Rube, you took your first flight in Restë, back when there was still snow on the ground. When we were younger you always said you couldn't wait to enter the Ring. I mean, come on: your first counsel, that night with the King—we both dreamed about it. What changed your mind?"

Okay, so technically the Fairy Ring was just a circle of giant toadstools, but its traditional function as the place of receiving counsel with King Morgan himself—which was customarily granted from the eve of your first flight onwards—coupled with the fact that the peaceful site always seemed shrouded in serene dusk-light even during night-time, had earned it almost mythic status amongst the eager young Fairies who had yet to visit it themselves. If you had a serious problem you needed to talk to someone about, it's not like the King would ever turn you away before you could fly, but times had been peaceful and no one Amber or Ruby knew had mustered the courage to go there earlier.

Ruby twirled a tendril of hair round her finger. "Oh, I don't know," she murmured vaguely. "Beryl and that lot, they didn't go; they reckon all that stuff's just for winglets."

Amber bit back something uncharitable about the clique, managing to turn it into a sufficiently savage snort instead. She stared off to the far horizon, where the setting sun was misting into the dusky skyline. "When I take my first flight, I'm going to go there that very first night," she promised. "I can't wait." She grinned. "I'm going to be so scared— but it's going to be so awesome."

Ruby arched a perfectly plucked eyebrow. "Yeah, well it had better be. You're going to be expecting like a Gargoyle sentry and Sea Maidens singing and a Phoenix exploding through the night sky; and the first's a legend, the second all left after the Sea Battle and the third's physically impossible, so I wouldn't dwell too much. I know you, Amber. You get your hopes up too high. It's just a bunch of toadstools, at the end of the day."

Amber rolled her eyes good-naturedly. "Shut up! It'll be the best bunch of toadstools in the whole Realm ever on the eve of my first flight where I'll take my first counsel with King Morgan. It'll be perfect."

Ruby grinned. "I hope so, babe. But you've got to fly first."

Amber cringed. "I know. The thought of crashing again scares me into last Restë."

Ruby squeezed her hand. "I can tell. It's why you've been practising for twice as long as the others, and why you're going to end up doing it better than all of them." She flicked her hair back, and her eyes danced mischievously. "Maybe even better than me."

Amber laughed affectionately. "Only you could make that sound like a compliment. We're nearly at yours now—grab that dress you wanted to show me and I'll wait here."

With an excited squeak, Ruby ran off, punctuating every third bouncing step with a flurry of wings.

"I get the hint!" Amber yelled, watching her dart away between the round little Fairy homes scattering the grass, and she stretched out beneath a fruit tree to wait in the dappled warm shade.

Once enough time had elapsed for anyone else to have tried on about thirty articles, or twenty of the silly fiddly ones you could never get your wings through the back of properly without almost ripping something, Ruby reappeared, iridescent in a pink and red creation that shone with speckled jewels, waltzing up dramatically and smirking like a Goblin at a market.

"Ruby!" Amber stared with pride, speechless, grinning almost as widely as her friend. "I mean, it's stunning."

"Thanks." Ruby plopped herself down on the grass beside Amber, adjusting her jewelled hair-band and smiling brightly. "What are you going to do with *your* hair?"

Biting back an indignant retort, Amber sighed distractedly. Ruby didn't mean it. Anyway, her knotting fear that she was going to make a complete fool of herself at the Presentation was eclipsed only by the total horror of still not having been able to find a dress, coupled with the abject humiliation that she was going to be the only Fairy there who hadn't yet flown, so it wasn't like she could be *that* much more embarrassed even if she stuck a bird's nest on her head for the night. She tried to zone back into the conversation, although she wasn't sure she wanted to, as Ruby was in the middle of pointing out that the Prince (it was no use hoping he wouldn't be there) officially preferred—because Jade told Beryl who was told by Sardonyx who was a guy and so knew about these things—red hair like hers to Amber's mousy tint best identified as a sort of dirty blonde when Ruby was feeling charitable.

Amber groaned to herself. Ruby would probably spend all the night she wasn't stalking the Prince with those girls instead of her. Never mind—the Prince wouldn't be the only royalty there. She'd see the King and Queen for the first time. She'd have the Fairy Blessing bestowed upon her. She'd receive her Fairy Gem. She'd—

Ruby, having finished her soliloquy on the Prince, grabbed Amber, eyes widening in sympathy as a truly horrifying thought struck her. "You do know that you are literally the only one who's going to receive their Gem who hasn't managed to fly yet?"

Amber shot her a stony look. "Thanks, Ruby."

Ruby pushed herself off the grass, flicked a few stray leaves disdainfully off her dress and regarded her friend severely. "Now look, you've got two days. Plenty of time for another go."

She held out her hand and Amber took it, grinning as she pulled herself up. "I guess. Where's that hill you went from your first time?"

As the two friends walked off, chatting easily in the gathering twilight, their lilting voices and laughter floated across the meadows to the forest and reached inhuman ears.

A low, uneasy snarl rippled through the darkness as from the shadows a pair of glowing red, bloodshot eyes watched them leave before sinking back into the deeper patches of shade beneath boughs where no mortal still walked. The eyes seemed to stay burning in the darkness for a second as the form shifted, and then in the next heartbeat they had faded, melted back into the dusky gloom of the further forest between skeletal branches, until they were no more than a fickle, half-imagined memory of something not quite seen; a mere trick of the light within deepest shadow, witnessed by none but the new moon as anything more than a deceiving wisp of smoke and carried away on the whispered breath of Recö wind that sang still of better things.

Hunter and Hunted

Infinitely cautious as he flitted from shadow to shadow, Racxen dropped to all fours and disappeared into the vegetation, keeping as far back from the lumbering Goblin as he could without losing him. The creature's gait path was erratic, but Racxen was a tireless traveller, slipping through the trees as if he were no more than a trick of the light: the Arraheng had long ago had to learn how to avoid being seen when the need arose.

Yet it was sundown before the Goblin showed any sign of slowing. Rounding a corner, Racxen felt ice prickle along his spine as he realised he could no longer see him. Cursing himself for having allowed his concentration to stray, he noiselessly flattened himself to the ground. Every sense strained, every nerve jumping, he crept forward again.

"You've been following me for half the day now, son. Got nothing better to do?"

Racxen sprang to his feet, adrenalin flooding with memories at the unmistakable, harsh-voiced whisper as a starving-eyed, scuffed-skinned Goblin materialized as if conjured from the earth itself. Racxen's mind raced with his heart, and he felt all possible control of the situation spiralling away as if the distancing seasons since drawn across him by the waxing and waning moons had counted once again for nothing.

"No? Fair enough. But I'm beginning to get bored of you now," the Goblin warned in a casual, amused tone, his savagely darting eyes beginning to glaze fixedly. "And—as you know—that's when I start making things interesting. Let's consider the possible reasons for a young, reckless, and may I say stupid individual to make the mistake of trying to follow me. Perhaps you consider yourself a hunter, almost worthy of myself? It seems, good sir, that your quarry eludes you—I know I would, if by some laughable chance I were it." He ran a blackened tongue over dry teeth and fixed his eyes on the Arraheng wistfully. "You're doing a rather stunning impersonation of prey yourself, I might add."

Racxen flexed and relaxed his hands subtly, fervently grateful that the heaviness of his claws dulled the violence of the tremors he strove to suppress in a tenuous effort to disguise his fear from the Goblin, knowing the continuation of his quest, and even his life at this point, relied upon the next few moments not falling apart. *You need information. He's your only chance.*

"You're right, I'm hunting," he insisted awkwardly. "But my game is being driven away. You haven't eaten for some days either," he hazarded. "Mayhap yours is as well."

The Goblin eyed Racxen licentiously. "Hunger's what keeps some of us going, son. I hunt anything, me. Now I run, too. I taste what I make them feel. I expect you might call that irony."

His lips parted in a snarl, his eyes harder than flint. "Why did you say you were following me? Hah!" the Goblin barked before Racxen could answer, nodding sagely to himself. "Game—or something. Fairies? I bet it was Fairies. Stupid young buck like yourself with fire in your belly and no sense in your head. I never got my teeth in a Fairy, 'though not through lack of trying." He laughed mirthlessly. "Wretched things have wings," he explained with feeling as his eyes clouded in frustration.

"You know what's driving them away," Racxen tried again, striving to keep his voice steady while the Goblin's eyes seemed to squirm into the core of his being. *Probably the same phantasms that are being driven towards our caves,* he reminded himself in an attempt to stay focused as he struggled to keep the Pedlar's unnerving gaze. *And if they're scaring Goblins into the open we've got more to fear than we anticipated.*

The Goblin eyed him for a tense moment. "I'm going to ignore that," he continued conversationally, "because there are many things I like about you. You have a rather convenient habit of frequenting lonely places, for example. And you're just that *bit* more confident than your not inconsiderable—but by no means unconquerable—abilities should allow. I like that too. And—pay attention here, because this is my favourite—you smell of fear." He fixed a hypnotic gaze on the Arraheng. "I really do like that."

The Goblin jumped sideways without warning. "But this tracking lark, son. It ain't your strong point." He gave a sharp, gravelled laugh. "I'd have thought you'd have learnt—all these years since. I mean," he threw back his head, bellowing lustily off-key, "I'll take all your gold and silver, peddling my wares—and I'll take oh so much more than that if I catch you unawaaaaares . . . Fear," the Goblin hissed as he jumped forward again, pushing his mouth too close into the Arraheng's face and teasing the words around slowly like they were little half-dead prey too weak to escape, "is a very powerful tool. I do like powerful tools. And it is also a very. Dangerous. Thing. And do you know what else is a dangerous thing?" he murmured, his voice poisoned honey as his eyes cleared and he glanced beyond the Arraheng for a second. "Trying— and failing—to be cleverer than me."

Something changed in the Goblin's demeanour that sent Racxen's hand flying to his moonshaft, heart pounding. "I have no money," he reasoned hastily.

"Oh, that's all right, son," the Goblin reassured him brightly, striking an elegant leg and springing forward again as his voice changed. "It ain't money I'm after."

Racxen shoved him back hard with the heels of his palms, but the Goblin lunged; on him in an instant and snapping for his face, teeth flashing through the twilight as his groping hands sought the Arraheng's neck. Racxen staggered back, clawing wildly at his adversary, the fetid stench of rotten meat in the Goblin's wide festering jaws rolling over him in nauseating waves as all else dissolved into the fight.

Muted somehow as if belonging to another Realm and time, Racxen heard an explosion of noise rip jaggedly through the forest behind him: an animalistic roar he registered only as an irrelevant distraction as the immediacy of the struggle closed again.

It seemed another age when the Goblin relaxed with a quiet, barking laugh as Racxen's claws grabbed into his cloak, twisting it round his neck. "Make it quick, son. I'd hate to still be here when the monsters catch up."

"*Monsters?*" Dimly, Racxen's mind placed the roar from earlier. It sounded again—slamming through the silence, viscerally close.

"That'll be them," the Goblin responded comfortably, with not an inconsiderable amount of satisfaction. "On the way to your encampment, no doubt, judging by the straightness of their path." His voice slowed in mocking, sadistic enjoyment. "I know you had no way of knowing whether it would be today, or tomorrow, or three days yesterday. But now I'm *sure* you're asking yourself: shouldn't I be there, protecting them? Or, should I say, *trying* to protect them? Don't you wish you'd stayed closer to home; close enough to track their progress and warn your tribe—isn't that your job? Instead of following me all this way—so very far from home and all alone—to indulge your little vendetta fantasy?

"Recklessness costs lives, son. Surprised you've forgotten, since you came so close before. Well, your lesson approaches. I trust you will learn it well. Go on now. Run and hide. They won't find you. They're too fixed on your encampment. You can save yourself.

"Mark, mind: there are some things—some darknesses—that cannot be erased, not by all the sunlight of this Realm. And you will lie fevered and fitful, sunk into nights so far from now, trapped in the uneasy place between sleep and waking as the images flit and burn unbidden and unconquerable beneath the lids of your eyes, and you will think, when you at last have time to think on such things: I could have done more. I could have done *something*."

He pushed his face closer to the stunned Arraheng, his voice tripping lightly over words of horror. "Whatever will you say, when you return to find your tribe massacred? Whatever will you tell their shades that you did?"

Blindly Racxen loosened his grip, staring in abject terror towards the source of the noise. The Goblin sprang away through the trees, fleeing for his life in a straight path of fear.

Left alone beneath the ghostly shivering trees, Racxen stood frozen in anguish, panic flooding him, the Goblin's words biting in his ears.

"Trees of this forest!" he bellowed, as fear threatened to close his throat and rob him of all action. "For you are the only ones who will know—bear witness! This is my answer! I did this!"

And as the crash of undergrowth merged into the blur of black fur and slavering jaws, with every instinct screaming at him, Racxen ran. Away from home, away from safety, away from any hope of respite or rescue, he ran to change their course from his tribe, leading the monsters off beneath the trees—with them all the time gaining, gaining . . .

All for a Reason

"You can *so* do this!" Ruby yelled perilously far below as Amber prepared to launch. "Remember what we talked about!"

"Yeah, well, you've done this hundreds of times," Amber muttered to herself, teetering on the edge of the spindly precipice and trying to trick herself that it wasn't that far up anyway. Why in the Realm had she agreed to do this in virtual darkness? She looked down inadvertently, and her thoughts skittered. *Failed again.* Even in the twilight she could see for miles up here: over the meadows of the Fairy Kingdom to the sprawling swamps of Arraterr, across the Endless Forest curving its shadow along the horizon to the vast swathes of empty plains signalling Arkh Loban beyond.

She shivered as the wind caught against her wings. Having sprung open when she'd first psyched herself up for the launch, they were now fluttering ineffectually and in danger of folding completely with nerves.

"Go on!" Ruby persisted. "What've you got to lose?"

"Yeah!" Amber snapped back down. "What are a few limbs among friends?"

"Amber!"

"Fine," she admitted testily. "So I *am* scared."

"That's okay!" Ruby's voice floated back up to her.

Relieved, Amber made to get down.

"Like you told me—and look how long I've been flying for now—

'as long as you don't let it stop you,'" Ruby reminded her, a little too smugly.

Amber swallowed back the rising bile, and a retort. Ruby was right—and if she didn't learn to fly soon, she wouldn't even get to meet the King before the ceremony. Although, thinking about it, Ruby hadn't either, as she'd let Beryl and the clique's sniping get to her. Amber's legs quivered. *You'll never get the chance if you never take the risk.*

"*Aaaaaargh!*" Amber leapt, and her wings snapped rigidly open. For a second she rose, exultant, and then after the initial lift everything rushed too fast for thought and she forgot all she'd learnt about waiting for the updraft and started in a panic to beat her wings frantically, fighting in the thin air.

The next instant the ground slammed into her, knocking her off her feet and sending her sprawling; and once again the whole thing was over.

Pushing herself numbly from the grass with scuffed, smarting hands, Amber cautiously prodded her face for anything broken that would earn a rant from Ruby's mother that evening. Pain and potions from Sarin would pale in comparison to that. Her lip was swelling and throbbing—she must have bitten it landing—and her neck lanced sharply from the jarring, but despite feeling like it had squashed right inside her head her nose was thankfully intact and she could tentatively move everything.

Taking an experimental step, Amber grimaced as her leg seized with sudden pain from the bruising of landing on her hip. "You better go on ahead if you want to meet the girls for dinner," she warned Ruby resignedly. "I can't walk any faster."

Ruby gave her a sympathetic hug—gently. "You know, you didn't do badly today. I think you're nearly there, Am, I really do."

Amber grinned tired thanks as Ruby ran off across the meadows, and winced as she absentmindedly chanced another step. Casting a look towards the wooded area they'd passed on their way here, Amber considered. Maybe she could find a shortcut, winding through one of these forest passages. It wasn't completely dark yet, after all. And it wasn't like she'd be straying outside the borders of Fairymead. Probably.

Once she'd passed through the wood, the pain of walking was settling into a duller, manageable ache, and she was greeted by the welcome sight of the Eastern Hills rising up against the murky twilight. Now at least she knew in theory where she was, although she had never been this far out before. All she would have to do now would be to follow at the foot of these hills until the Fairy homes came into view again in the distance.

Relieved, she quickened her pace—and then stopped in confusion. This next hill-foot yawned into a narrow black opening fissure. She stared. It'd be tall enough to get through if she stooped. She walked closer, the darkness before her betraying nothing, the air close and still. It could have continued forever—or stopped a yard behind.

Experimentally, Amber felt for a stone on the ground, and threw it lightly in.

There came no *crack* against the wall. Seconds later, she thought she heard a muffled rattle as it settled on the floor.

At the tunnel mouth she stood, undecided yet intrigued. Surely there weren't any caves in Fairymead. But it was the wrong direction to be anywhere near Arraterr, as Mugkafb had called his home.

But you don't have a torch. And there could be anything in there. Amber hesitated. It didn't have the musty, excrement-esque smell of having been used by animals. There was no sign of broken vegetation, no stools in the clearing where she was. *Oh, so you're the tracking expert?*

Amber sighed. She thought of what she had to go back to tonight: Ruby embroidering her dress perfectly, making well meaning comments about how she really should get organised and sort hers out. Jade and Beryl tittering about one thing or another they deigned to take issue with her over. Fending off suggestions from Garnet, the cook, or Opal, the seamstress, about who she was going to do her apprenticeship with at the end of the year. She felt like the only Fairy in the Realm who hadn't decided yet. Ruby was going with Opal; it was all she talked about, save for the Prince and the upcoming party. She was still thinking about asking Sarin for an apprenticeship in the rec hall, but although she knew that out of all the jobs on offer it would be the one she'd be most proud of it wasn't, for the moment at least, what she dreamt of doing day and night.

Not like finding caves and having adventures, she reminded herself with a grin as she ducked into the entrance.

She stumbled forwards blindly, cautiously stretching out her hands as she advanced. Her fingers chancing upon the rough, dry wall of what had to then be a tunnel, Amber ventured further into the yielding dark, her vision swimming in the blackness as she wondered with trepidation what horrors could be hiding themselves within. *You could turn around right now and go back,* her inner voice taunted, unbidden. *Everything would stay the same. Everything would be so much easier . . .*

Amber sighed and took a deep breath, stiffening her resolve. "And so much more boring," she breathed to the shadows as she slipped further into the darkness.

Padding quietly along the tunnel, getting more used to feeling her way now, Amber couldn't tell how far she'd come when the wall slipped from under her hand and she felt a current of air whisper around her feet as the tunnel yawned into a cavern. Water was dripping somewhere, echoing through what felt like eternity so deep within the rock. Willing herself to stay calm, she stood enveloped in a darkness so absolute it seemed to be holding her still.

She drew breath in amazement as, rewarding her efforts, her vision began to shift, revealing gnarled stalagmites rising wetly through the surreal twilight of phosphorescence to stand like dark sentries to an underworld domain, and her eyes travelled lingeringly across the calcite cascade of milky-white folds hanging in frozen relief against the far ceiling.

Her previous misgivings a far memory, she explored further, enraptured, trailing a hand over the damp, gritty walls as imbedded in the cave walls rough gems of every colour twinkled back at her to soften the darkness. Here there lay a strange slab, almost as if nature had hewn a table from the rock. She stepped quietly past the accompanying chair and—

Chair?

She wheeled round, unease prickling her skin as she turned for the exit tunnel. This place was used, but by whom, and for what? They could be back any minute.

Even as she thought it, she was aware of footsteps other than her own disturbing the silence. Realising the tunnel was too far away to reach in time, she froze, panic-stricken, for a heartbeat, and then in despair darted towards the broadest stalagmite, her pulse slamming as she pressed herself into the welcome cloak of its shadow and held her breath.

As the footsteps—booted, solid strides—advanced closer until she feared they would stop right in front of her, Amber shrank further into the shadows until there was nothing else to do but freeze and hope.

She let out a measured breath of relief as the steps continued heavily without pause and grew quieter. Curiosity itched as she heard the scrape of the chair being pulled out across the stone floor and then the hypnotically repetitive clinking of metal instruments. Peering out, she saw a Fairy man sitting at the stone-slab desk, bent over his work, his face softly illuminated in the glow cast by the fireflies milling from a large open glass votive.

From the shadows, Amber studied the figure. In the guttering light, the grey hair that fell to his shoulders gained a warmer hue. His face was weather-beaten, and the lines etched on his face betrayed his age. But the years had not dimmed the sharp eyes, nor diminished the confidence of his gaze or the assuredness of his bearing. He would be, Amber found herself contemplating, a formidable adversary. Yet something in his manner made her feel safer now than she had in a long time.

"If you stay calm, your vision will adjust and allow you to realise that darkness is never absolute. Come out of the shadows, child." The gravelled voice addressed her calmly without the man looking up from his work.

Amber was so startled she forgot her usual retort about not being a child any more. Shamefaced, she left her hiding place, stepping awkwardly into the light. "I'm sorry," she blurted, "I wasn't spying—at least, I didn't mean to—I wouldn't have come if I'd known anyone was down here—" She broke off, partly because she needed to pause for breath but mostly due to a growing realisation of how stupid she must be sounding.

The man regarded her through stern grey eyes. "Apology accepted. Although unnecessary; I am surprised no one has found me down here before, and these items can only be taken by another with their owner's permission." He turned his attention back to his work.

Relieved and intrigued, Amber found herself watching with fascination. A collection of tools nestled amongst roughly cut precious stones of different sizes, their forms in various states of completion. She grinned in delight. "You're making the Fairy Gems? For the King?"

The man held one to the light and studied it closely. He chipped a sliver from an edge. "Indeed."

Amber stared entranced as the man held one up for inspection, the liquidescent jewel sparkling in the soft light of the table's single gnarled candle.

The jeweller smiled. "You will receive your Gem tomorrow."

She nodded proudly, gazing at the different pearling droplets of colour swirling encased in their gleaming stones. "Do you know who will receive which?"

The man's eyes twinkled in the candlelight. "Only the King knows that. What brings you so far from home so close to the Ceremony?" he asked, blowing away dust so fine it caught in the air and shimmered like stardust.

"I've just been trying to fly," Amber admitted miserably. "Trying and failing."

The jeweller chipped and tapped at a glittering drop of precious stone so clear it appeared almost liquid, using tools so fine it seemed as if magic itself must have been at work as the treasure slowly took its shape between his hands. "You do not fail if you do not succeed," he admonished her. "You only fail if you do not try. The time will come, when the time is right."

"Mayhap today hasn't been the right time for anything important," Amber mumbled dispiritedly, absentmindedly rubbing a bruise.

The jeweller polished the Gem until it sparkled so brilliantly that it flashed in the flickering light. "Mayhap it is not yet over, and holds some purpose as yet unrecognised."

Amber grinned. "Thanks for letting me see the Gems being made, sir."

He waved her out, and she pressed into the darkness once more.

After traipsing back out of the tunnel, hastening through the fast-fading light Amber thought it best to stick to a lakeside route not far from where she had first met Mugkafb and Racxen.

She had just reached the forest border beyond the lake when in a crash of snapping branches and thudding footsteps an Arraheng—*Racxen!* The realisation slammed a deathchill through her heart—burst through the undergrowth, drenched in sweat and staring unseeingly, and collapsed in front of her, frantic gasps wracking his exhausted body as he lay trembling on the ground.

Before she'd had time to register what was happening the forest exploded with the kind of noise her body registered before her brain, as the most primal roar of savagery she could ever have dreamt up slammed into her, draining her of all capacity for thought or movement.

Her limbs lead-limp and her mind bereft, somehow she was stumbling towards Racxen's fallen form, grabbing him round his chest and frantically hauling him, dead-weighted, to the near bushes where she collapsed hidden into the undergrowth with him.

But this was useless; they'd scent them out and would be on them any second. Wait. They were near the Great Lake, weren't they? She scanned desperately—the stream had to be close. If she crossed it, the monster would lose the scent. Wouldn't it? Hauling his body up once more, she gasped her intention to Racxen. She didn't know whether he could hear her or not but against the rasping of her own breath in the fractured silence the hurrying music of the stream reached her and she staggered down the slope, almost falling as she flailed into the stream with him, the rush of the water submerging their splash.

Slogging mechanically through the brook, the cold unfelt save for a kind of distracted ring of pain cutting around her thighs where churning water met freezing air, she just had to get Racxen across, and then everything would be okay; it had to be.

As she stumbled painfully up the other side of the bank and collapsed in the riverside rushes with the Arraheng's body, she heard words she couldn't understand wheeze amidst Racxen's gasps. "Engo ro hash'k, ga'nghek faa mun . . ." His eyes rolled back as he tried to focus on her. "Harnama . . ."

"Ssssh," she hushed desperately, cradling him to her as she heard something splash through the stream, freezing into silence as the crack of undergrowth neared.

In her arms, Racxen slumped as if dead. She sat there, clinging to him glazed-eyed, feeling alone in all the Realm with the gripping terror that the monster would find them amidst the tremulous reeds, each moment hearing a snort or seeing a flash of black through the leaves. Her pathetic idea hadn't worked. It would scent them out. It would find them. There was no longer any question, and there could be no escape. *Shut up!* she demanded silently. *There are still these moments. There are worse ways to die than trying to save a friend.*

Through her panic resounded a noise not of death, but of life: a great splash from the lake. Between the reed-stems Amber saw an arcing flash of bronze leap again, gleaming through the twilight—the Karp. A wash of stunned gratitude soaked through her whole being. The air shook with a harsh cry as the monster loped off, distracted.

Peering above the grass line and finding they were alone, Amber spurred her beleaguered mind back into action. She needed to get Racxen water and help.

At least she could manage the first. Leaving him hidden amongst the rushes, she raced back with water from the stream bunched in her sash—seeping out at an alarming rate. Racxen drank faster than she'd have thought possible as it streamed forth, and then threw most of it up, falling back and trembling uncontrollably. Amber grimaced, feeling sick herself now. The Matron would be horrified. She wished she'd started her apprenticeship—that had been a stupid mistake she wouldn't have made.

Amber watched the laboured rise and fall of his chest, tracing her drenched sash over the stricken Arraheng's skin in an effort to cool him. Then she panicked that she'd chill him too much so, shivering, she wrapped her cloak around him.

Clearly you don't know what to do, Amber admonished herself. *So get him to someone who will.*

"The Prince warned me about monsters," she muttered, feeling utterly helpless as she pulled Racxen to her, supporting his body as she tried to stand. "He made them sound like badly-drawn story ones. I don't think even he believed they were real. And I didn't listen to him. I never do." She grinned in relief as Racxen opened his eyes. "I might still not, though."

Racxen flinched convulsively, staring beyond her. "Venom-spitter! It was here. The tribe—"

"It's okay. It left, we're across the stream, and it didn't get past the lake so they'll be fine," she reassured him. *Venom-spitters?* The thought squeaked at her like a startled bat, and she forced herself to push it to the back of her mind and focus instead on the immediate.

Racxen struggled into sitting, his breathing easing now. "We were surrounded. Someone had to lead the danger off, away from the others." He couldn't look at her.

Amber stared. "But that would mean . . ."

Racxen shook his head. "Don't. It was just meant to be one life for many. There was nothing else to be done." His breath rattled in the silence.

His words coiled tightly around Amber's throat. "What kind of person does that?" she murmured finally, out of her depth.

"One who has finished living," came the subdued reply. "My life was in chains. It was better for all that I . . . made this choice. I had nothing else to live for."

Her eyes flashed angrily, overwrought that she'd had no idea that he'd felt like that, and more upset that it had come to this than she wanted to admit even to herself. "You could have tried to fight."

He looked at her sourly. "Do you honestly believe that there was the slightest chance even one of our tribe would have been allowed to live? You cannot fight these monsters—they deal in carnage. You have no idea."

"What about your brother?" She thought back to little Mugkafb. "You weren't going to abandon him to the mercy of these Venom-spitters?"

"I would rather have died trying to save him than see him murdered in front of me," he snapped. "What could my presence have bought him? A few more terror-filled seconds, to witness the deaths of more whom he loved?"

"You don't know." She didn't know what hurt most; that he had been put through this or the fact she knew she couldn't make it better when she'd have given anything to. "You could have tried."

"You don't know. You weren't there. How dare you judge me when you have not had to choose? Do not patronise me, Fairy. Not everyone has the luxury of flight. Some of us can't just flee."

Pride tying her voice into a tight, silent knot, Amber dropped her gaze miserably, the reality stinging her badly. Didn't he know she felt guilty that she'd be able to, when others couldn't? Didn't he know she wished—*No,* she stopped herself. *He doesn't; how could he? He can't read my mind any better than I can read his.* It was an unromantic truth, certainly, but at least it was a truth, she grudgingly acknowledged, forcing herself to calm.

"I'm sorry," she blurted. "I had no right to criticize you. I've never been in such a situation; you did what you could and you tried to save not just him but all of them. I'm so proud of what you tried to do, so in awe of it, but I just felt so bad for not having realised what you were going through that I took it out on you."

Racxen's eyes softened. "Curse you, Fairy, you're making this too difficult," he growled helplessly. "I can't hurt you, even if it is for your own good. Do you think I want to involve you in something as sweepingly catastrophic as this is turning out to be?"

"Well, I'm doing quite a good job of involving myself," Amber reasoned stubbornly. "I could even get as dramatic as to suggest I'm already far too caught up in it all to turn back now."

Racxen grunted. "I wish you would. It'd be better for all concerned."

"*All* concerned?"

"Fine—for you." His voice quietened with pain. "I'm sorry for what I said earlier. It couldn't be further from what I think of you. I just—" Racxen shook his head, and Amber got the feeling he was changing the subject before she could chance a thought for what it could have been.

"I am infinitely glad you have not been subject to the things that have darkened my path; long may it remain so. I had no right to say what I did; you stayed to help me. I know you can't fly yet, but you didn't flee either. You have shown so much more courage than me: I acted to save those I loved; you risked yourself for a complete stranger. I owe you a debt that can never be repaid."

"Not a *complete* stranger," Amber argued irrelevantly, the adrenalin still dancing in her system rendering her increasingly light-headed. "Anyway, it'll never have to be. You don't know as much about Fairies as you think you do if you assume we hold on to debts." She said it lightly but the gaze she rested upon him was warm and reassuringly serious.

A shadow darkened Racxen's eyes. "I hope you never have the misfortune to be bound by creatures that do."

"I can't presume to tell you what it is," Amber admitted, watching him anxiously. "But you know you've got a reason to live, right?"

"I couldn't see it," he muttered. "Nor trust that one day the cloud would lift and what was always there out of sight would be seen without such a struggle. It took facing death for me to realise."

Amber dampened his brow with the sash. "But you realised," she whispered. "Rest," she insisted as Racxen tried to answer, partly because she wasn't so sure it was just the adrenalin that was thumping through her body as his gaze melted into hers. "I'm sorry, I've kept you talking."

Racxen lay back, the earth beneath him as solid and comforting as the hollows of his own caves, and let his eyes close as he felt its residual warmth spread through his skin. His clawed hand sought hers. "Tell me how to thank you."

She shrugged, embarrassed. "You're the tracker. It would help if we knew where we are."

A smile played across Racxen's lips. "We are safe. It's good enough for me."

"Great," she muttered softly, huddling in the undergrowth beside him against the cool evening breeze whispering through the wood as dusk began to slide over the land, watching her companion drift into an exhausted sleep. But she smiled as she did. The jeweller had been right.

She woke with a start, and realised that Racxen was sitting up as if keeping watch. Mortified that she'd fallen asleep, she darted a furtive glance to the star-specked sky and tried to work out just how long she had been out, but Racxen caught her eye reassuringly, and she gave up. "I guess you weren't the only one who pushed yourself too far," she mumbled ruefully.

"Don't be so hard on yourself," Racxen shrugged acceptingly. "It goes with the territory. And you don't know much about Arraheng if you think their trackers sleep the night through with no thought for their companions."

Amber grinned her thanks.

"Look," Racxen promised, and Amber let herself think for a moment how comfortingly his voice lifted the inky silence of the night. "I will never fail to hold you in the highest regard; you must believe that. I said what I said only because it's best if—" He grimaced, and tried again. "It would be a mistake, if—"

"If you do hold me in such high regard," Amber challenged only half jokingly, "you can surely allow me the dubious luxury of making my own accursed mistakes."

Racxen tried to laugh, but it hurt too much.

"Racxen?"

"Sen?"

"Shut up and go to sleep."

Then he did laugh.

Challenge

"Oi. Sleeping Beauty. Wake up." The toe of a boot prodded her prone form. "Amber. Move." A hand clutched at her shoulder.

I can't keep dropping off like this, Amber half-thought blearily, trying to peel her eyelids apart. *The moment I get back I'm going to curl up on Ruby's sofa and not move for a week.*

Her mind caught up with her and she sat up with a start, squinting into the glaring sun. And the face of the Prince.

She jolted round, all trace of tiredness fleeing as she frantically scanned for Racxen. "Jasper." She managed to smile groggily up at him, rubbing trails of sleep from her mind as she scrubbed her knuckles into her eyes. She hoped the Prince wouldn't notice the flattened grass beside her.

Jasper rolled his eyes. "Who were you expecting, Prince Charming?"

I hope he got home safe . . . Amber's gaze flew beneath the surrounding trees to twisting paths leading off into a distance beyond sight.

Concern stilled Jasper's tongue as the girl ignored him, staring wild-eyed beyond him.

"Nothing to be frightened of," he tried, following her line of sight. "I'm here now." He'd thought that might provoke one of her usual responses, but no luck. He smiled awkwardly, offering his hand. "Why don't we both go back to where we're supposed to be? What in five seasons are you doing out here this early?" he added suspiciously, eyeing her mud-streaked garments.

"Thanks for coming to find me, I know you didn't have to," Amber managed, dragging her attention from the forest to the Prince as last night flooded back to her. "Listen, something's happened. We need to warn everyone. The Arraheng are in danger and Racxen says we're next. We were chased by these Venom-spitter monsters; something's driving them out of the caverns and they're rampaging across Arraterr and heading for Fairymead."

"Amber, this is important," Jasper broke in, his expression unreadable. "What did these monsters look like? How many were there?"

"They were—I mean, it was—" Amber broke off to stare blankly at him, suddenly feeling stupid. "I don't know, exactly. This Arraheng, Racxen, collapsed in front of me; there was a roar, and the branches crashed, and by that time I was dragging him away."

She waited for the Prince to exclaim in anger, and realised with dismay that instead he'd expected her answer all along.

"You see?" Jasper placated as kindly as he could. "You can't trust anything those savages say. They lure you far away for their own ends, then leave you lost and alone—and none the wiser. *Monsters* Amber, I'm surprised at you. He collapsed, yet he had no injuries. It's the oldest trick in the book. I'm surprised he didn't spin you some yarn about his little sister dying from some wound lying in the undergrowth miles away and you being the only one who could save her. And when did he leave, this Arraheng? Have you recounted the coin you were carrying?"

"Of course I have," Amber snapped back, wondering whether she'd brought any in the first place. "They're not criminals, Jasper. If you'd been there—"

"Well I wasn't," the Prince interrupted tersely, tiring of the conversation. "I don't know how you expect me to rationalise terrifying my subjects with warnings of night-stalkers and imminent doom, but I'd need solid proof before I deigned even consider such an outlandish declaration. Some of us need to be level-headed about such matters,

Amber: those of us whom it actually concerns." He stalked away, the matter closed.

Amber stared after him, his words stinging into her. "I'll get you your proof right now!" she shouted furiously at his retreating back; almost as angry with herself for caring what he thought as she was with him. "And if I don't come back, you'll know why!"

With that she stormed off, deaf to any response he might have thrown at her; striding off towards the swamps to see the monsters he didn't believe in with her own eyes.

Proof

Amber kept her eyes locked ahead, not daring to look back to the sheltering forest for fear she'd give up and return to it. The minutes stretched into eternity as she slogged through the marsh, the liquid mud clinging to her legs slowing her, weakening her. She was nearly in the centre of the swamp, her eyes still fixed on the safe haven of the will o' wisp-riddled firmer ground hovering spectre-like beyond the swamp-mists: Arraterr, the domain of the tribe.

"You're nearly there; you're nearly safe." But the whispered mantra fled in a spew of mud as unseen weeds wrapped round her legs to trip her and she flailed to the surface, spitting and gasping. Every step plunged her shin-deep into cloying, sinking mud. Her legs felt like they no longer belonged to her, as if they'd already sunk to the bottom, claimed by unseen monsters of the depths, and she was somehow being propelled. She grimaced as she dragged her thoughts back under control and set them pushing firmly towards the bank. Lifting her blurring gaze to follow them, her silt-smeared lips parted in an exhausted grin as she saw that Arraterr was getting nearer. She was going to be safe.

A distant scuffle from the forest broke into a roar of challenge behind her. Amber turned in horror to see as if in slow motion what could only be a Venom-spitter running low to the ground, with nightcat stealth and ox-built power, straight towards the swamp. Ropes of acrid spittle scorched the earth as its blood-red eyes bored into her, yellowed fangs protruding beneath writhing lips as it contemplated its kill.

Transfixed by fear and held fast by the sinking mud, waist-deep in the frozen, murky waters, she could do nothing but stare. It didn't feel real. Any minute she'd realise something; it'd be further away than she thought; it'd be scared of water. Yet those desperate thoughts surged only to flicker and die as the monster thundered through the surf. It would be on her in an instant. She couldn't run; in the swamp she could barely walk. There was no way of escaping.

Everything faded. There were no Venom-spitters, no Arraheng. Nobody. She was about to die alone, in this forsaken swamp, far away from the friends who had become her family. She thought with despair of all the things she was going to have done—all the things she had meant to do, but had put off out of fear. Now a fear far worse was staring at her, and it was too late. All those things would be left undone. She would never see her home, her friends, again. Racxen and Mugkafb wouldn't even know what had happened to her or find her remains. Never would she feel the freedom of flight, or attend the Ceremony to receive her Gem; never would she be welcomed into the Ring.

Hot tears welled up unbidden as defiance raged inside her head. She *would* go to the Ceremony, and receive her Fairy Gem, and curse it she'd fly there. She would laugh and talk with Ruby before; she would see Racxen and Mugkafb after. She would live out the rest of her life free from the suffocating fear of these accursed terrors in the dark—and so would the rest of the Realm. *You might die,* her mind jibed boldly, safe high above her somewhere. *You're allowed to make impossible promises.*

Churning water surged into pounding muscle and, head held high in rebellion, fists clenched futilely, Amber realised distractedly in a mixture of resignation and defiance that this was how it was going to end.

Sun flashed on the water as the waves around her slowed. The sky turned more vivid than she could remember. The icy touch of the water paled.

And then everything snapped into another kind of focus and there was only the snorting, bellowing Venom-spitter, ploughing through the foaming rage of water straight for her. As if in a trance, Amber heard a wild answering cry tear from her lungs—a cry of fear and anger and challenge and life.

What happened in the next instant didn't register until later—a blurring flash of frothing waves as something reared up out of the surge to drag her under—and she was flailing out, struggling instinctively, but her attacker was too strong. Gulping a last starved mouthful of air as the water closed over her head, her mind flashed back to Ruby's story of Arraheng killing their own kind in this way. She'd been right. She should never have trusted them. It was too late.

Her stinging sight swollen with murky, indistinct shapes in the dim water and her head resounding with the thrashings of the Venom-spitter as it churned the lake to foam, Amber was swept down, disorientated and powerless, at breakneck speed. The froth and chaos was left far above as the water darkened, slimy tongues of weeds clutching at her and licking out in her wake. Still she was pulled faster to further depths, the water clouding thickly with suspended sediment disturbed as they raced through rocky crevices into hidden waterways where the water was almost black. Amber had no time to think, no strength left to fight, her chest burning savagely as her need for air eclipsed all else and she felt her strength bubble and burst, skittering from her body with her breath.

Her attacker turned sharply, accelerating up towards a narrow tunnel in the rock. Amber shut her eyes instinctively as a stream of vertical rock flashed past her face.

She exploded through the surface into darkness, sucking sweet, precious air into her ravaged lungs as her pulse thundered sickeningly against her temples, delirious to be alive.

Then the last life-or-death minutes slammed back into her memory and she spun round in the water, fear cloying through the depths. Where was her attacker?

A blade-sharp grip dug into her wrist as she was dragged to the side. Terror-stricken, she stared up into her assailant's face.

"Racxen!" The relief she felt was almost as weakening as her fear had been.

He hauled her onto the rock. "Engo ro fash," he gasped. "You're safe; it can't hurt you."

Numbly, she nodded. *I shouldn't have doubted you. I never will again.* In the cold, wet darkness he held her tightly and, limp in his arms, fear gradually falling away and her shivering subsiding, her heart slowed until she was able to speak.

"You saved me," she breathed hoarsely, her voice raw with emotion and swamp water.

He found her hand, and clasped it. "Ank hashakka fyash nenta," he murmured.

She was about to ask him its meaning, but he gestured towards the deeper darkness of a tunnel eaten into the wall. "Once you're warm and fed, you can tell me what happened," he promised. "Our cave isn't far through here."

She followed as he padded to the opening, his form a barely visible silhouette against the glistening walls, and together they crawled into the darkness.

Huddled in front of a dancing fire with a thick, patterned rug wrapped around her shoulders, drinking spiced soup from an unglazed ceramic bowl as the horrors of earlier began to fade into the flames, Amber rested cocooned in the Arraheng cave. Racxen sat beside her, chewing on a handful of roots and prodding at the fire. He hadn't left the caves tonight. He hadn't said much, but the fact he could just be with and accept her like that—without questioning, without demanding to know—made her gradually realise she knew she could risk telling him, and with the warmth of the fire and his gaze on her, she falteringly voiced the gnawing shame and terror of those moments until they burned amongst the cinders and floated away with the sparks.

Amber watched flinching shadows scud across the walls. "How long have the Venom-spitters been terrorising your lands?" she asked afterwards, fearing the answer. "How are you surviving?"

"We have our water-tunnels." Racxen shrugged, overwhelmed at the fragility of their defences. "The Venom-spitters are not swimming creatures. So long as someone can sound the alarm, the tribe can bolt to safety. There have been sightings by trackers long before it was my responsibility," he admitted. "Just not to this extent, which is why I've been . . . asking around."

His gaze broke away and took solace in the fire. "They are as difficult to kill as you imagine. In theory our only chance is to find where they breed, and destroy them at the source. But I'm more concerned about what's driven them out of the caves in the first place. They will be the true monsters, and the real danger." He met the Fairy's anxious gaze. "But we've lost no one to them so far," he promised quickly. "We're managing."

A far-off cry floated into the cavern, as mournful and haunting as the keening of a lost Dragon. Racxen stood, his eyes alight. "The Zyfang are taking to the skies. If you feel ready to leave, you'll make it back to your home before nightfall."

Reaching the end of another tunnel, when Amber stepped out after Racxen she was greeted by open green country shimmering in the gathering twilight, and realised she wasn't far from the borders of the Kingdom. The Arraheng turned to her self-consciously. "Amber, I don't want you to put yourself in danger. It'd be best for you if you stay away from here; your wings would slow you down if you had to swim for safety."

Amber searched his gaze. "As long as your tribe is safe," she admonished. "I couldn't forgive myself if something happened and I'd turned my back."

Racxen nodded, watching the deepening horizon. "We've weathered it before."

Amber wasn't convinced. "I can't bear to think that those monsters might come back. If you don't want me here, at least tell me how I can help."

Racxen's expression softened. "You already have."

Amber grinned. "Yeah, well, you too." She hugged him impulsively, and realising with a glance at the dusk-heavy sky the time, broke away to run home, buoyed with the memory of death thwarted.

As she neared the Eastern Hills signalling she was nearly home, Amber slowed, stealing a glance at the hilltop silhouetted temptingly against the swift-falling dusk. *One last try?*

She considered. She still had a bruise on her thigh the size of an apple from the last failed attempt, and the time before that she had badly twisted her ankle even before she had left the ground. That was all she needed: to not even be able to walk to the Ceremony. But she *had* just evaded death. Her gaze lingered in the sinking twilight. Tonight of all nights was for living. She felt it in the trembling excitement of the winds, and in the whispered encouragement of the trees. She knew she could do it.

Clambering breathlessly up the hill, Amber rehearsed it in her mind: *Wings open—properly open—by fourth step; eighth step max. Two steps—beat—step—beat—spring—launch—*She tugged a hand fretfully through her hair. *What could be simpler?*

Reaching the peak she stalled, staring down the slope now ominously shadowed. Her feet had turned to stone, her hands suddenly sweating in the cool evening air. She breathed a few times experimentally. *Right.*

The ground flowed beneath her as she ran. Across the blur of silvering grass she began lengthening her strides—*start counting*—until her wings snapped open, the adrenalin quivering through their spines. She lost count, and stumbled with the sudden drag. *Keep going.* Step-step-step—a clumsy beat—step-step—stronger now—step—*launch!*

She flung her wings down as she sprang, paddling madly through the air as the ground buckled and she felt the familiar lurching rush as she lost coordination.

Abruptly the wind caught her, stealing her breath, and she flailed wildly like a swimmer trapped in a breaker. But she righted herself, letting the gust sweep under her wings and lend her its power, giving her time to focus on keeping her position—on not bringing her head too high or her legs too low to off-balance her—and then she was riding it; riding the wind almost like the Sea Folk of old rode the waves. She was actually doing it. Exultant, she whooped to the moon-silvered meadows below.

Abruptly, she miss-timed her wing-beats and gravity leapt on her with vision-blurring force, the ground pitching towards her as she spread her wings in a desperate effort to slow her descent. The ground slammed into her, just as she managed to remember to curl and roll.

And it was over. Amber lay gasping for a few seconds, laughing up at the stars with pure delight before pushing herself shakily off the ground with stinging hands. It was over—but it had happened.

"*Yes!*" she yelled in triumph, tears unexpectedly stinging her eyes as she stumbled to her feet, grinning so much her face hurt. She'd done it. All those months of practice when the other Fairies had laughed at her; all those times she'd wanted to give up and cry and accept that she'd never be able to do it or be as good as everyone else, they had all paid off.

"Amber!"

Eyes shining, she turned to see Prince Jasper running along the hillside road towards her. He'd set off that evening meaning to find her and tell her he believed her and had informed the King. But that could wait a minute longer, and for now his robe was flying, his regal demeanour cast off in the moment, genuine happiness lifting his normally impassive features as the trials of the morning were forgotten.

Dancing on adrenalin, she threw her arms around him. "I did it!"

Laughingly embarrassed, Jasper returned her hug. "You know there's still time before tomorrow, if you want," he urged, serious once more.

Catching his meaning she stared at him, her heart racing and still dizzy from the excitement. "Yeah." She swallowed, breathless with sudden nerves. "True." She'd always wanted to. Plus, she figured she owed it to herself, after today and tonight. "Thanks, Jasper."

He squeezed her hand. "I know it means more to you than most."

She grinned ruefully. "'Bout time, isn't it?" She ran off, no longer needing a reply.

"The right one," Jasper corrected, shouting after her. "Ceremony Eve—it's a good omen!"

She turned back gratefully. "Yeah?"

Jasper grinned. "Don't argue with royalty, Amber. Go; fly free. But—" his face shifted into its familiar sternness "—remember: twenty-four hours without practice. That's all it takes to lose the ability permanently."

"Stop fussing!" Amber shushed with a grin. Like she was ever going to put herself in that position. She set off at a run to the Fairy Ring, along the unmarked path she had known by heart ever since hearing the story for the first time as a winglet seasons and seasons ago around the fire before bedtime, her spirit soaring as she just had to know that soon it would become true.

Familiar doubts started invading Amber's mind as she approached. Just go up to it, she insisted, battling them stubbornly. *You've faced a*

Venom-spitter today, you can't possibly be nervous. You don't have to go in. Just go up to it, first. And take it from there.

Her self-talk dried up as she stopped in silent awe to behold the twelve towering, dusky-capped toadstools rising like mythic sentries through the mist-shrouded circle of sanctuary, emanating a serene otherworldly glow that graced the muted hues therein with a cloak of peace.

Amber swallowed. She'd waited her whole life for this moment, and now, typically, she was scared. Not just nervous. Gut-wrenchingly terrified. She'd got half a mind not to go in at all. Was she supposed to feel like this much of a wreck?

Try, she admonished herself sternly, gathering her courage. *He's probably not even here. After all, he can't exactly turn up every night on the off chance someone learns. Especially someone as late as you.*

As she stepped into the dusky haze, a grin of wonderment spread across her face as her nerves momentarily left her. She felt as though she were stepping into a dream.

"Hello?" she called softly. She didn't know why she was speaking so quietly; it wasn't as though she wasn't allowed to be there, and it didn't even look like there was anyone to disturb.

"Welcome," a deep voice hailed her.

Amber spun round as a Fairy man stepped out of the swirling mists. A long sword, sheathed, hung at his side, he wore a cloak of faded red, and his grey hair shone silver beneath the moonlight. Amber caught her breath. The jeweller from the cave. He was the *King?*

"I flew," she blurted proudly to cover her embarrassment, grinning like a winglet and unable to contain herself. She rubbed self-consciously at the stains on her shirt that bore witness to the attempt. "I mean, good evening, Your Majesty," she corrected, lowering her eyes and bowing quickly. *I could run away,* she thought wildly. *This is awful.*

"Congratulations," the man smiled. "You seek counsel?"

Amber swallowed. "I, um—first I need to give this back." She dug into her pocket and thrust the Queen's Gem forward awkwardly. "I'm really sorry; I went after the Dartwing as soon as I realised." She drew a steadying breath. "Sire, I—well, I met some Arraheng while I was searching for the Gem—I saved Mugkafb and then Racxen saved me—and you see there are these monsters they call Venom-spitters and they're ravaging their land and the thing is Fairymead's next . . ."

She trailed off, digging a toe into the soft grass. "I'm probably speaking out of line, but I just . . ."

King Morgan took the Gem, regarding her through shrewd, unreadable eyes. "You've apologised for a mistake. You've befriended and managed to gain the trust of a people between whom a decades-long rift has existed, and want to protect them. You freely gave information, which you feared would be ignored, that my son nearly did not to protect his ego. No, Amber, you did nothing you should not be proud of." He gestured. "Let us walk."

She grinned in the soft darkness as she walked as if entranced beside his tall silhouette. She'd imagined this for so long.

"Amber, the Fairy Ring is a place of safety and sanctuary," King Morgan began. "Fewer visit it than once did, saying they doubt its power, but mayhap in truth they doubt themselves and, for fear of disappointment, they dare not allow themselves the chance to mould their dreams into more. To enter this place one must risk believing in the chance of walking knowingly into your dreams; and once you have done that, you have proven that there is nothing to hold you back but your own fears."

He smiled gently. "A heavier burden than it might first sound. No circumstances to blame? No outside influence? Ah, but I digress. First let us attend to the physical nature of this place. Most importantly, no harm can befall you within its boundaries. Day or night, if you are troubled or distressed, you may come here and be assured of company of integrity and wise counsel. Or that of my son." His grey eyes twinkled.

"You have been awarded this honour because you have flown: you have demonstrated the tenacity and courage required to leap into the unknown and see it through. The ability to fly is one unique to our people, thanks to the hollow bone structure that Sarin has no doubt explained during your pre-apprenticeship interview. It renders your world now larger—you are no longer bound to one plane of this Realm. It is a privilege, and must be treated as such."

He stepped back, regarding her warmly. "You stand now, at the brink of fulfilling your future destiny. Welcome to the rest of your life, and to your new adventure."

Amber was speechless, burning with pride. Yet as he turned away to lead her back, she thought she saw a fleeting glimpse of pain pierce the King's expression.

"I wish everyone got to see how real it is," she thought out loud in concern.

Morgan turned back, his eyes calm again. "They do not seek what you seek," he answered truthfully. "Some are content to just dream, some have to do. Dreaming is the first stage to doing, but for some the first stage is enough."

The King stopped, staring intently beyond her and holding himself completely still. Stepping back, Amber followed his gaze in silence. A whispered breath fluttered across the grass, rippling in the moonlight as it sang softly through the quiet. Pink and orange light streaked purpling skies as the sun sank low beneath the horizon after a final blaze of proud gold had bowed to gentler darkness. And still they stood, as the meadow settled into a star-flecked night. Watching. Waiting.

Amber shivered, as the evening air grew colder. She stole a questioning glance at the King. What could he see?

A star-bright form shimmered suddenly through the darkness and Amber gasped, so astonished that she couldn't stop herself pointing like a winglet. She could see it only indistinctly at first, but as the vision drifted closer she could discern a hoofed creature, pale as moonlight, with a silky mane that caught on the slightest breeze and glistening dark eyes that held the ages of the world.

"The Bicorns," the King breathed softly as the creature stepped into the Ring, "are the last untamed creatures to walk the paths of this Realm."

Amber stared in unconcealed astonishment. "You've ridden one, haven't you?" She remembered the stories now: of a proud, jet-black equine warrior and her ethereally light peers like the one standing impossibly before them now.

"Bright Shadow, their herd leader, allowed me that honour." The King lowered his voice to a hypnotic whisper to avoid spooking the creature. "It was during the Sea Battle. After their ancestors the Unicorns were driven from Loban during the Goblin War—before it ended with the Arkhan hero Gorfang relinquishing his powers in a bargain with the Goblin King to save the Realm—they survived only in broken herds at the corners of the Realm. But come the next conflict, the Sea Battle, they massed and joined us in battle as one of the staunchest of allies."

At his voice, the Bicorn snorted in recognition, her coat shimmering in the starlight and her mane flowing like liquid silver. When she tossed her head, Amber swore she saw stardust fleck the night air.

And then the Bicorn was walking on, leaving as quietly as she had arrived; and, as if awakening from a trance, Amber realised that they had reached the perimeter of the Ring. She stared silently up to the eternal starry sky. She hated to leave, but she'd taken up enough of the Fairy King's time with idle talk.

Moonlight glimmered in the King's eyes. "Tonight is your night, as tomorrow will be your day," he advised before she could voice her apology. "And talk is never idle, nor time ever wasted, so long as you are aware with what and why you fill it." He rested a hand on Amber's shoulder. "You've an important day ahead of you. Sleep at peace."

Amber bowed her head. "I'm so glad I came here, Sire. It means more than I can say to be part of it."

"It will always be here for you," he promised. "And Amber?"

She lifted her gaze to meet his. "Yes, Sire?"

"All things take bravery," he acknowledged, standing before the inky blur at the edge of where the Ring met the rest of the Realm. "Each step shows you have it. No one can foretell what lies along your path, nor where it may lead you. But the steps you have taken carve the way for those to come. Let them give you courage for the journey ahead, for what they mean to you is something that cannot be stolen even in the darkest times."

Amber grinned proudly as he waved her on, her mind full of the evening as she traced the path illuminated by soft-glowing lanterns back to her house and turned the key quietly to slip inside.

Satisfied she had returned home safely, King Morgan leant back against a toadstool amidst the shadows and settled to sleep. It was Ceremony Eve, after all. It would not do for any counsel-seeking souls to attend the Ring only to find it deserted on the night before the most important day of the year.

Legends and Life

Amber woke to sunlight streaming onto her pillow from beneath the curtain-tail as a suspicious bustle of noise invaded through the window.

She groaned and scrubbed her knuckles against her eyes, trying to dispel the comfortable blanket of sleep from her mind and account for the nagging feeling that she ought to be nervous about something. Struggling to collect her thoughts, she squinted blearily up at her calendar. *The Presentation!* Panic slapped her awake and she jolted upright.

Groping for her alarm clock, she read with horror that it was eight thirty, stumbled out of bed, fumbled through the drawer and dragged out her dress. There was a sickening tearing sound as it snagged on the corner and ripped along the seam. Amber froze, staring at it in utter horror. *That. Cannot. Have. Just. Happened.* Her dress. The one that had taken her hours with Garnet to alter so it actually fit. The only one she had. She sat there in stunned disbelief. *Not today,* she pleaded with it silently. *Not this morning.*

Throwing a last despairing glance at the clock, she bundled up the dress, pushed herself off the floor and ran out of the room, the door swinging on its hinges as she fled the house.

"Ruby!" Amber hammered on the door, panting from the exertion of having sprinted all the way to her friend's. "I need your help!" She peered frantically through the window. "Ruby?"

The stairs pounded with feet and Ruby flung open the door, standing in the hallway and adjusting her earrings, ready to go. Amber forgot her predicament for a moment and stared in admiration. "Rube, you look fantastic."

Ruby grinned her thanks, arching a well-plucked brow as she accepted Amber's mutilated offering with an embarrassing lack of surprise. Seconds later she was smirking confidently, her fingers racing as the needle flew in and out of the fabric.

"There," she pronounced with satisfaction, holding it up to the light. "Good as new." Her eyes gleamed with challenge as she turned back to Amber. "Now we've got ten minutes left to get you ready, then we're going to have to fly."

"Oh for goodness sake—Amber hold still, or this wing's never going to fit through," Ruby muttered through clenched teeth and a mouthful of ribbons as she finally fastened the last section. She stepped back to admire her efforts and cast an appraising eye over her best friend, grinning as Amber stood self-conscious and doubtful before her.

"Look at you, gorgeous. We'll have to get you into dresses more often." She dodged a flying hairbrush and darted out of the door in a peal of laughter before Amber could put her hands to more ammunition, running through the crowds with moments to spare.

Spying Ruby through the sea of teenage Fairies seating themselves in a bustle of anticipation, Amber hurriedly picked her way through the crowd to squeeze in next to her.

Hugging her knees to her chest as dozens of young hopefuls squashed in around her, she busied herself by peering over shoulders and around heads to try and work out how best to catch a glimpse of the King and Queen when they arrived.

Fidgeting with anticipation, she drank in the scene. The morning air over the Renë meadows held the clean chill of the first season, and dewdrops jewelled the ground, transforming the grass into tiny ceremonial blades glittering crisply beneath the sun.

A fluster of excited murmuring rippled through the assembly and everyone started craning their necks and kneeling up in their seats at the sound of hoof-steps on the turf. There was a collective gasp as around the corner two magnificent grey horses trotted, harness-bells jangling, bearing the King and Queen in the rich hues of full ceremonial robes. Ruby squeaked with excitement and dug Amber violently in the ribs as they were shadowed by Prince Jasper.

The babble of voices rose for a moment as everyone started hastily shushing each other until the Royal Family dismounted and stepped to their appointed thrones: twisted branch-seats resplendent with foliage and berries entwined with filigree-worked metals.

Ruby had eyes only for the Prince, but Amber gazed between King Morgan—her gut twisting in mortification at having not realised his identity the other day—and Queen Pearl, whom she'd never before laid eyes on.

Seated with statuesque poise on the right-hand throne, the sun streaming through her auburn hair swept up into ringlets—a few stray ones of which tumbled rebelliously over her shoulders—Queen Pearl watched the congregation through sparkling green eyes at once both assured and serene.

It was rumoured that before she became Queen she had taken her apprenticeship with the Dragon-riding Nomads of the Arkhan desert plains and, watching her keen gaze sweep over the assembly, Amber decided it had to have been true. She wished the Nomads were still around. What an apprenticeship that would have been. She grinned in admiration and daydreamed of asking the Queen about it.

Catching the girl staring at her, Pearl winked surreptitiously, her regal features crinkling playfully. Amber found herself grinning like a winglet and feeling infinitely better about the whole proceedings.

She realised a hush had settled over the waiting crowds, and the Queen was rising with the opening announcement.

"Fairymead today bears witness to our most important annual ceremony," she proclaimed, her voice ringing out vibrantly. "The Presentation of Gems in honour of those who have come of age."

Later, most of those waiting eagerly would swear that the Queen's gaze rested upon them at that precise moment. "The giving and receiving of these Gems represents twofold your newfound freedom and your acceptance of the consequential responsibility: your lives are now entirely of your own making. You have completed your compulsory education; both those of you for whom apprenticeship is the next step and those of you choosing to carve for yourselves another path are standing upon the threshold of your future life. Embrace it."

To rapturous applause, the King summoned the first name, and the next dozen or so blurred into anguished anticipation until—

"Amber Amazonite!"

The Realm, the crowd, all faded, and Amber distractedly heard Ruby hiss words of encouragement and push her to her feet. Now she was walking towards the King and Queen, all eyes upon her. She knew every step of this ceremony; had replayed it so many times in her head. Now it was all real, all new—all now.

Reverently she knelt before the King, as in the hushed silence that fell over the watching crowd he placed the most treasured of amulets around her neck.

Placing both hands on her shoulders, he looked deep into her eyes. Amber's heart burned within her as she met his gaze.

"Amber Amazonite," King Morgan intoned solemnly for all to hear, "the time has come for you to receive your Fairy Gem."

Her fingers curled awestruck around it and she gazed at the subtle shades marbling as they swirled before her eyes. It was the most unforgettable thing she had ever seen, and she would carry it with her for the rest of her life, until it lit her final journey and marked her spirit's place amongst the stars. She looked into the fathomless depths contained within and beheld her future, stretched out before her through that ever-changing pattern whispering of infinite possibilities.

Irrationally, for half an instant she wished that she were younger; that she didn't have this responsibility. But it was in her hands, literally. She saw that now. She could touch it. Shape it. It was a thing to be cherished, not feared.

The King spoke quietly then, as if the crowd had dissipated to leave only the two of them beneath the watchful sun. "Amber, this Gem is no mere token. Over time, its patterns will constantly change, and they do not mould themselves. The clear colour expands with thoughts of integrity and actions of compassion; the opaque clouds with the immoral, the thoughtless, and the easy choice taken when the harder is right. You are the bearer; you are both responsible and capable."

"I understand, and will remember," Amber pledged, overflowing with pride as she gave the appropriate answer. "No ill action shall be reflected that goes uncorrected."

The Queen's serene countenance rested upon her now as she took her right hand into her own, and shivers traced Amber's spine as she spoke the Fairy Blessing:

"May courage stay within you, your hope ever lead you, darkness fall conquered behind you, and bright skies rise before you."

"I believe it and will help it be so," Amber answered earnestly, sealing the vow.

And then she was walking back again, grinning all over her face, the rest of the afternoon blurring until she found herself following Ruby through the castle grounds to where the great banqueting suites were set, hung with streamers and bunting glimmering in the near-twilight.

Slipping through the throngs to the closest tables reserved for the newest recipients of the Fairy Gems—the most honoured of guests tonight—Amber took a moment to savour the scene, breathing in the babble of eager chatter flooding around her as she leant back in an empty chair and tried to ignore the fact that Ruby was now ingratiating herself with Sardonyx's clique not quite far enough away to be out of earshot.

An elbow dug her in the ribs. "Like your trinket, Am," its owner hissed animatedly, his restless eyes dancing beneath spiky dark hair.

"Tanzan." Amber grinned in delight, her voice muffled against his bear hug. "What are you doing here?"

"Gotta come back and annoy you every now and then, haven't I?" His words fell over themselves as he claimed the seat next to her. "Way to go for this morning, by the way," he enthused. "Can't believe it's been so long. You should see Loban, girl. Got meself in with the best fletcher in the whole Realm. Couldn't wait to tell you."

Amber high-fived him in congratulations. "Didn't I tell you? The best archer in the Realm was never going to have to settle for less." She grinned proudly, confidence spreading through her in his presence. Tanzan was always on the move, but it was typical of him to magic up a surprise visit for her Presentation. She'd missed him like crazy when he left; she still did, if truth be told. He lived life as if he had to cram everything into a single day. It had earned him the wrath of Professor Cobalt, and the lifelong friendship of Amber.

"That you did, girl, an' I'll always owe you for it. By the way, you'll like this." Tanzan's dark eyes scanned the crowds cautiously as he drew something surreptitiously from his pocket. "Can't remember where I found it; I've never been so lost, but . . ." He opened his palm, revealing a metal amulet barely larger than a button, engraved with filigree markings.

Amber examined the talisman eagerly. Something powerful that she couldn't name shivered through her to behold it. It was so rusted it was hard to make out the symbols until they caught against the moon and shifted in the light. Amber stared. "Tan—is that *Gorfang's* insignia?"

Trumpets sang through the hall, sending any further thought fleeing to the rafters with the final notes. A murmur of wonder rippled through the assembly as the Queen swept down the steps to the feast hall, her ethereal dress feathering the stone floor; the King at her side majestic in state regalia and Prince Jasper—not looking too bad either, Amber had to begrudgingly acknowledge—following solemnly, thanking the minstrels with a stiff bow.

Queen Pearl's clear voice rang out across the feast hall. "Welcome!"

The guests stood to their feet amidst the hasty scraping of chairs. In her rush to greet the Queen and King, Amber banged her knee hard on the table and yelped. A hundred pairs of disdainful eyes glared at her furiously and she flushed miserably with embarrassment. Tanzan squeezed her hand in solidarity and she nudged him back gratefully.

A hushed silence descended as the King held out his hands in welcome. "Friends," he addressed the assembly, his voice booming warmly across the hall. "Tonight's feast belongs to you all; those who have been guests of honour before and remember its promise and excitement, and those of you for whom the time is yet to come."

Here his gaze roamed the room and rested on the newest recipients, and it seemed to Amber that it settled on her, although Tanzan would later swear that it was him he was looking at. "Yet most of all, it is for those who have today received their Gems. May the winds of this Realm bear you kindly, and should the rain fall, may it fall upon you softly." He bowed his head, and raised his glass. "Fly free!"

"Fly free!" The triumphant salutation was heartily returned to their King and Queen, and amongst an excited rush of voices the Fairies sat down. Food and conversation flowed freely as hundreds of lilting voices carried to a sky deepening into inky night.

The disquieting knowledge that Ruby had chosen to join Beryl, Opal, and Chrysocolla instead of her for the dinner needled at Amber's mind, and she tried to keep her attention on the food in front of her. She felt her face burn as Carnelian, as perfectly-groomed as he was insufferably arrogant, glanced disdainfully in her direction as Chrysocolla brayed with laughter at whatever he had just said at her expense and pawed on his arm in delight.

Amber jabbed her fork resolutely into a dewberry. "You finished that bow yet, Tan?" she asked, determined to not let the clique ruin the night.

"Nearly, girl," he answered readily, grinning thankfully at the tacit permission to launch into his favourite subject after battling inane pleasantries across the table. "Draws a beauty; just need to wax the string and . . ."

The grating tones of Sardonyx approaching with his consort of admirers drowned even Tanzan's energetic conversation, and throwing a meaningful glance to Amber he left the table abruptly. Amber knew about the threats Sardonyx had made towards the elderly master Fletcher whom Tan had started training with, and something tightened anxiously in her chest even before she registered the danger in his words.

"It was good sport, you know, with the *Prince's* hunting party, to which *I* was invited," Sardonyx was proclaiming nasally, while his surrounding gaggle duly arranged their immaculate features into expressions of adulation. He kicked back a chair and slumped down, idly picking a discarded scrap from the table and flicking it into someone's soup. "'Course, the best sport, as we all know," his party nodded animatedly, "is the *big* game. You know: two legs, long claws."

Desert lodged in Amber's throat and her stomach knotted, the peals of Beryl's laughter ringing in her ears. He couldn't mean . . .

"Arraheng," Sardonyx smirked in confirmation, leaning closer to his companions. "They're—"

"Us!" Amber heard herself shout, her voice echoing shrill and strange with indignation across the meadows, past caring that everyone was now staring at her in mute astonishment. "They're us without wings. We're them without claws—"

"They're swamp-dwelling savages," Sardonyx snarled, springing to his feet even before he could tell where her voice was coming from. "That means—"

"All it *means*," Amber almost shouted back, fighting to keep her temper as the clique recovered from their surprise and started jeering at her again, "is that some of us are born on one side of the lake and some on the other. That some of us can fly through the air, while some can see through the dark . . ." She broke off, tears squeezing round her throat, knowing her words weren't getting through. "You're talking about murder," she spat, and the crowd fell raggedly silent as the force of her accusation settled. "You want an audience for your disgusting boasts? Try a Royal Court of Law."

"Honestly, Amber, you don't half get wound up about nothing," Sardonyx spluttered hastily. "It was just a story, I was—"

"Hey!" Tanzan shouted from somewhere in the crowd, dropping his replenished plate to elbow hurriedly through the watchers. "You," he growled, jabbing an accusing finger at the clique leader, "shut up and simmer down before you disgrace yourself in the presence of the King and Queen because I'm seconds away from calling them over. And you," he warned Amber more quietly with a turn of his head, "something or someone's out there under the trees."

Horror flooded through Amber as she stared past Tanzan, dread rising with the sickening certainty that she knew exactly who that had to have been. Without another word she pushed free from the crowds and ran towards the forest at the edge of the meadows.

Behind Beryl, Ruby's face was a mask of shock.

"You're not worrying about that stupid winglet, are you?" the older Fairy demanded, rounding on her. "I'm not surprised she's sticking up for them monsters. She's never fitted in here; she'd be more at home in the swamps with them." She laughed in derision and tugged a curl of Ruby's hair in a veiled rebuke. When Ruby had seen her administer it to the other girls it had looked like innocent teasing between friends; an affectionate gesture that Ruby had almost envied. But now an implicit threat prickled into her scalp at Beryl's touch, and she slapped her hand away.

Beryl's shriek hung irretrievably in the heavy air between them and for an awful moment Ruby felt herself cowed into the familiar, sickening inertia woven so skilfully by Beryl's every scornful, dismissive effort. Fear clamping her tongue and rooting her limbs, Ruby wanted desperately to surge boldly from her chair and shout exactly what she thought of her in front of everyone, but she knew just as desperately that she could never do it.

Instead she managed to stand shakily, lifting her face to feign the dignity with which she imagined Prince Jasper would probably meet such a confrontation. Gripping the back of the chair to stop herself from fleeing, she glared at Beryl with the clarity of a veil lifting from her eyes.

"What you gonna do?" the older Fairy demanded contemptuously. "Run after her or summink?" She shot a warning glance at Ruby's jewelled heels. "You lose them slippers I borrowed you and you ain't joinin' us no more."

But Ruby was already gone; her face set as angrily as Amber's had been, her dress glittering in the darkness as she picked up its hem and ran into the darkness; ran for her real friend.

An uneasy quiet settled amongst the Fairies close enough to have seen what had happened. Tanzan flung a disgusted glance at the lot of them and pushed through the crowd again to escape.

"What?" Chrysocolla challenged. No one answered back quite loudly enough to be heard.

The tense silence disintegrated into a chorus of jeers and whoops from the clique as, hobbling painfully, Ruby returned, one shoe missing, her foot scuffed and raw.

"Lost summink?" Chrysocolla gloated with derision.

Hot tears stung as they swam in Ruby's eyes but she refused to speak and let them fall. She'd caught up with Amber, who'd mumbled something about a friend of hers and gone home inconsolable, leaving her to return little the wiser. Or not quite: even if she *had* known what was going on, there was no way she would have divulged her best friend's confidence—and most certainly of all not to that lot—ever again. Ruby kept her head held resolutely high as she approached to pass. Let them laugh and ridicule her. It wouldn't make her open her mouth.

It took a few seconds for her to register that they had, however, stopped. And that the crowd had shuffled back. What were they playing at now? She turned.

Prince Jasper. Her heart went *thwump* as she skipped back to let him pass, cursing that she'd been the last person to realise.

Good grief, she thought with a resigned merging of joy with despair, he was even more gorgeous up close. In the couple of seconds before he was bound to disappear, her gaze travelled the devilishly arrogant green eyes, the distinguished sweep of black hair, the majestic folds of riches cloth enrobing the honed form beneath . . . which was a perfectly appropriate observation, she told herself firmly as she felt herself blush, because after all she was going to apprentice as a seamstress so she needed to develop an eye for such things, didn't she?

Prince Jasper, in turn watching her with what was probably best interpreted as tolerant amusement, bowed. Ruby hastily shuffled sideways. Honestly, how could she have blocked whomever it was he needed to talk to?

There was a rustling of annoyance behind her from the circle. Jasper ignored them, turning instead to where Ruby had deposited herself in an effort to hide both her faux pas and herself. Something glittered in his hand.

"My lady? I believe this is yours?"

Ruby's heart slammed and stopped, and she thought she might actually die. The sweeping bow, the flourish of his cloak, had been for her benefit. She stared at him, too stunned to answer.

Prince Jasper knelt to replace her slipper, his touch lingering as the female section of the clique gawped in undisguised jealously.

"You did the right thing," he hissed, offering her his hand and helping her to her feet, which was just as well considering that the Prince proving himself to be as gallant as he was good-looking wasn't exactly helping Ruby feel any steadier. Words failing her, it was only the fact that Prince Jasper had one hand through her arm that stopped her from turning back and flinging foul gestures to the clique.

"Should've done it seasons ago," she managed regally, walking proudly off with the Prince, turning her back on them forever. And keeping the slippers.

Southern Sands

What the—?

In the dead of night Amber jolted from a shallow sleep, fear narrowing rather than focussing her mind. She lay, curling the blankets damp with sweat around trembling hands, her eyes darting across the room's ambiguous shadows.

Nothing had changed, she told herself sternly. The moon's was the only gaze peering under the curtain, the trees' the only fingers scritch-scratching at the window. *It's your imagination.* She shut her eyes firmly, trying to convince herself. *It always is.*

Scratching again—at the window. Her heart hammered so hard that her vision jumped with each beat. It wasn't Ruby. Ruby would knock. Sardonyx and those girls come back from this evening? She'd hear them bickering. Why was it so accursed quiet? Someone didn't want to disturb anyone.

Or be disturbed. She felt sick as she lay there, wishing futilely that she were back amidst the mocking bullies and crowds at the party—anywhere but here alone and in darkness with no one to heed a cry for help.

The silence lengthened mercifully, and Amber allowed herself a measured breath of relief.

Then scratching. Louder, more insistent.

Amber sat bolt upright, her heartbeat quickening so much it felt like it would burst through her ears. This was it. Enough.

Eyes wide in the swimming darkness, she eased herself from the bed. Scanning her room, her gaze fell on the glass bowl on her dresser, and she lifted it experimentally; it was heavy, solid—she had no time to choose anything else. Closing her shaking fingers around it she pressed herself back into the shadow of the wall, locking her eyes onto the window.

Again the scratching.

A ghostly whistle pierced the silence and the night exploded as the window shattered, smashed through by a golden arc that burned for a split-second in the air and faded into a blade on the floor. A silhouetted shape loomed at the window and dropped inside, followed by another.

Frantic, Amber kicked the blade away, sending it skidding under her bed and out of reach. Something dropped lightly onto her shoulder, and a hand flew up to stifle her scream. Overcome with terror, Amber bit down hard to a muffled yelp, and spun round, raising the bowl above her head to—

"Amber! Stop!" There was a clumsy thud behind her, and Mugkafb slammed the switch so hard the walls shook. Disorientated and squinting painfully, Amber realised in shock that she was standing over Racxen, all three of them freeze-framed, blinded in the artificial light.

Shakily she lowered the bowl and stepped back. Racxen jumped to his feet, his hands spread placatingly. "Engo ro fash. We didn't mean to scare you."

She snorted, glaring at him. "It's you who should have been scared. I was about to smash this over your head. Did you have to break in?"

Racxen stared at her, anguished. "You wouldn't open the door."

She returned his look stonily. "It's three o'clock in the morning."

Racxen stumbled, slumping heavily onto the bed, and Amber rushed to him, her anger dissipating into alarm. "Racxen. What in the Realm?"

Now the adrenalin had had a chance to disperse, the Arraheng was shivering violently, so she pulled her blanket round his shoulders, wondering light-headedly what Ruby would say about the mess when she came round tomorrow. Mugkafb promptly refused any fuss and wandered into the kitchen to scavenge food from the cupboards.

Sending the fire sputtering into warmth with a flint, Amber sat beside Racxen, listening helplessly as the Arraheng told her pieces of what had happened. "They're all safe," he kept repeating, eyes vacant, as if trying to reassure himself as much as her.

"We bring dire news," he managed at last, forcing composure into his breath. "Venom-spitters—" A nightbird called outside, and he flinched.

Amber stared in shock, the past shrinking into his words. "They're back?" she managed hollowly. It wouldn't be true until he answered.

Racxen nodded wordlessly.

"We've tried to tell people," Mugkafb explained miserably, returning to the room to bury himself in the mound of cushions on her bed. "But no one listens. Who'd believe 'swamp monsters'? They see us coming and run a mile."

"Amber, your people are in great danger," Racxen broke in urgently. "The Venom-spitters are massing in numbers too great to hold back. Our marsh settlements are no longer safe; the tribe are retreating to our tunnels permanently, until the danger has passed. We will be protected by the waterways."

Amber felt a tight hand squeeze hotly at her throat. "I'm glad you're going. I want both of you safe."

Racxen shook his head distractedly. "The Venom-spitters will continue their rampage. Fairymead lies directly in their path; your land will be next. We didn't just come to warn you, Amber. We came to help you."

The grip turned so tight it threatened to turn her eyes to water. "You're staying?"

"We have our refuge; behind the waters. Your people have none."

Amber stared at him, mud-plastered and still breathless. "You risked your life to come here."

Racxen dropped his gaze. "I tried earlier, but one of the revellers . . ." his eyes darkened. "I had to come back."

"Racxen, I'm so sorry," Amber blurted wretchedly, knowing her words were woefully inadequate. A thousand racing images spiralled through her mind with the news, the knowledge dragging at her throat and screaming at her incapacity to change it.

"We have to do something," she tried hesitantly, needing all her strength to keep her voice light and measured. "We have to think of something." Despair rose despite her words, or more probably because of them. *Racxen's misgivings the other day had been right,* she thought hollowly. *What do I know?*

She looked from Racxen, his eyes wild and haunted, to Mugkafb, sitting subdued, unable to comfort his brother and looking to her for guidance. She swallowed. "Firstly," she insisted, gathering her courage, "I understand that when the Arraheng make a pact, their word is stronger than stone."

"That's just a story," Mugkafb warned guiltily in a small voice.

"It's my kind of story," she replied steadily, determined now. "I know it is not something to be entered into lightly. But now is the time and we three together will not fail. We will warn of these monsters, we will fight them, and we will find a way to drive them out so that they never plague the Realm again. Are you with me?"

A slow smile burned across Racxen's face as he met her gaze. "I have a feeling this is going to be binding."

Mugkafb held his right hand out in accord and, wordlessly, facing each other the friends formed a triangle. Amber placed her right hand over Mugkafb's, and Racxen laid his over hers. Exchanging searching glances, they bowed their heads as the tracker took a deep breath:

"What we say shall now be done. Beneath the stars, beneath the sun.

The way is tough; it will be hard. We'll tread with care and keep our guard. Each is now each; we are one and the same. We'll not rest again till we victory claim. Through storms of thunder, and nights of black. Honour and friendship now bind this pact."

The Arraheng looked to Amber, and she invoked the Fairy promise to further bind their vow:

"Now these fair winds have our promises borne. The day turned to night must now yield to morn. Words are but words, but this must I say. None in this Realm can now stand in our way."

As one they opened their eyes and nodded in affirmation to each other, determined and committed.

Mugkafb fidgeted. "What do we actually do, though?"

Amber hesitated, feeling responsible and clueless. "Tell the King?" This was happening too fast; all of it, and she couldn't come up with anything else right now.

Shouting passed outside, and Racxen ducked back instinctively, but Amber ran to the window, staring out. The shouts weren't menacing.

A bugle sounded, pealing triumphantly through the night. Amber spun round to her friends, excitement rising. "I know that call." Her eyes shone. "The King's summoning us."

Fairies ran past along the track outside, laughing and calling and carrying lanterns. Amber ran to the door, turning back to urge the reluctant Arraheng. "Come on. Anyone notices you and has a problem, they'll have me to answer to. Mugkafb, don't laugh, that was supposed to be reassuring. Whatever this is, you're not missing out on it. And this is our chance to tell the King. He's not like his son. 'None in this Realm can now stand in our way,'" she reminded them firmly.

The door slammed as, chancing and trusting, all three decided.

Pelting through the darkness, Amber followed the shouts to the dirt-track seaward road, Racxen running silently beside her with long, loose strides, Mugkafb not far behind. They managed to avoid attention, although Amber had to hang back to make sure they weren't noticed by Tanzan, illuminated ahead of them by the blanching moon, his various acquisitions and talismans glinting on his cloak as he raced ahead. With Tan's overflowing enthusiasm, good-natured as it was, nothing stayed secret, or quiet, for long.

The soothing whisper of the sea grew like an ancient lullaby in her ears as the light-haze faded, yielding to an inky night beneath clear stars. Amber slowed as the waves swelled into view, the shore stretching vast in front, tumbling down to an endless ocean.

A tall figure stood alone, staring out, watching for something she could not see.

"Your Majesty?" Amber stumbled to a halt beside the King. "It's happening as Racxen warned—the Venom-spitters have over-run the swamp-plains and now we're directly in their path—"

Stop, she gulped to herself as he turned to her. *You're not making any sense. Breathe.*

Morgan's eyes settled on Racxen. "This is the gentleman to whom we shall soon owe so much?"

Amber nodded, realising her hand had sought his. "Yes," she said simply, finding the words that had sprung to her mind couldn't quite be done justice once formed on her lips.

Mugkafb eyed Amber innocently. "What was it you said about Fairies and debts?"

Jasper sniffed disdainfully, having materialized beside the King. "We are a people of honour."

"Rather than obligation," Morgan corrected his son dryly, before bowing his head courteously to the Arraheng and Amber. "Tomorrow, you will recount all you know to myself and Jasper, and plans shall be made."

Not the Prince again. Amber nodded resignedly. Then she glanced questioningly to the King. "What about tonight?"

A knowing smile lifted his stern face, his eyes shining with a far-off light. "Tonight you shall meet some of our oldest allies. Follow."

Amber's heart pounded as, with Racxen and Mugkafb close behind, she raced after the King through the darkness, down towards the Southern Sands.

Sea Maidens. Knights of the Sea. She'd heard about them, of course. Heard how, in times gone by, on the nights of the new moon the Sea Folk would come to shore to dance in the shallows amongst the flying foam of Recë tides when the surf sparkled against the moon-silvered sands on the most magical of nights. Nights when the sea breeze would soar with the sweet melodies of haunting songs—songs so pure and full of peace they would bring a lump to your throat and the fervent desire to change so that they would be proven true. Nights when you could hear, on the rush of the waves, the shrill ringing of the bells at the hooves of their white horses; nights when you would see, if you were lucky, the ribbons entwined in their manes flash amongst the green-blue rush of the soaring waves. Nights you feared, when the thick lonely darkness pressed around you, now belonged to a different time.

The gravel scrunched beneath Amber's feet amidst the lapping rush of waves as she skidded down towards the Sea, the wind rising in an ethereal chorus as it flapped through her clothes. Despite the flooding darkness a light seemed to grow on the water, larger than the reflection of the fullest moon, until in a thunder of water white chargers reared through the swell, their weed-entwined manes streaming in the wind and their froth-feathered hooves churning the sea to foam.

At their shoulders rode glisten-tailed knights, bearing ancient banners whipping out behind them, and as they neared the moon-blanched shore their jubilant cry rose in rhythm with the rolling waves a hundred strong:

"To the sea, to the sea; where the white horses reign and the darkness shall flee. Through night and through storm, over all fear and shadow; on to bright water—and hope for tomorrow."

All along the pale-lit strand, Knights and Maidens took up the call, their fair voices ringing out strongly against the shrill wind to chase away all fears.

Beside her friends Amber stood in awed silence, staring out across the ocean, caught in a tender web of magic she never wanted to be free of. "I feel like I've never seen half the Realm before," she managed, breathless with wonder.

Mugkafb grinned, unable to drag his gaze away. "Well, you haven't if you haven't seen *them* before. I have—seasons ago, when I was little."

Amber was about to ask him about it, but Racxen's eyes glistened with more than moonlight as she glanced to him. "I have met them too," he pre-empted her, his voice soft with a kind of longing sadness she couldn't place.

Amber nodded in quiet solidarity. As King Morgan approached, she turned to him. "Their ceremony isn't until Mid-Recö. Why are they coming this close in now?"

The King's eyes glittered, his gaze far-off, as if he were possessed of a great peace. "The Sea Folk would never abandon us in our hour of need. They never have before."

For a moment the only voice to be heard was that of the whispering waves, carrying the melodies of the Sea Folk to the listening shore. "They come to remind us that we are not alone, and that hope is not forsaken," he added, his voice now reassuringly brisk. "They come to gift us the courage and fortitude that we will soon have need of. And they come now, because they have knowledge that we cannot yet discern, suggesting that this night may prove the last lull before the storm breaks overhead."

A long-buried terror squirmed within Amber, and she could hardly breathe the words for fear of the answer they would provoke. "They know this is going to be worse than the Sea Battle?"

He pressed a steadying hand to her shoulder, but even the King couldn't shield her from the weight of this truth.

Amber nodded grimly, feeling as if splinters of ice were lodging in her stomach. She remembered hearing about the Sea Battle in class— the war raged against the Fairies and Sea Folk by the evil Snakelocks and her Vetch minions nearly two decades ago. The King had fought in it. And—she stared out to sea, letting the salt sting into her eyes and the wind whip back the sudden hot well of tears brimming her lids—so had her parents.

The cankerous fallout of those two splintered moments lodged deep into her memory could never fade even as they tortured her with details shifted and lost—the last words her father had given to her; the exact way her mother had looked when she'd smiled. She could remember Sarin's long hours trying to save them as she had saved countless others. So many seasons had passed since; she had barely been able to walk back then, and flying was a distant, un-placeable hope. And yet, as immediate as a heartbeat, moments unguarded still tore back to her the blank, denying confusion and the wrenching, final realisation. They had said that she wouldn't understand. She guessed they always did.

Her days became one long bad dream; forcing one foot in front of the other and continuing until nightfall could steal upon her with its numbing oblivion. Sometimes she would be soothed by dreams of her parents—things they had or had not yet said to her—or sometimes the nights would be the worst, when the announcement she couldn't shut down would play again; only this time the addition of fevered dark imaginings would wake her screaming and slicked in sweat.

Those nights, Ruby would tiptoe in from the next room, and listen, and plait her hair, and soothe her, and talk of other things; those boring and beautiful normal things, until the fear subsided and grey pre-dawn crept into the room.

And so time, incapable of the healing others promised it would bring, gifted her distance; and life in spite of everything swept her on, and together with her friends had borne her thus far.

She realized with a start that the King was still standing beside her, that the light on the water had not diminished, and that sweet singing yet floated across the waves.

Morgan caught her gaze and gestured towards a darker cove, further along the bay. "Now is not a time for sadness," he urged. "The crafts upon which we lay food and lanterns for Mid-Recö Night are moored at the Silent Sound, if you wish to speak to the Knights and Maidens?"

Amber nodded. The Sea Folk had been the first to populate the Realm, their skills of enchantment remained unsurpassed and their intervention in the last conflict had proven invaluable. Their riddles might be obtuse, but they were the only allies from whom she could hope to glean any semblance of advice about how to deal with the impending disaster. Amber shivered suddenly in the warm sea-wind, worry gnawing at her conscience. Despite having pledged heartfelt words this very hour, nothing had happened so far to reassure her that she would be of any use whatsoever in such a crisis.

"Of course, Your Majesty," she agreed, stamping down her self-doubt. Grateful for the opportunity to dissipate her growing unease into action, she turned meaningfully to Racxen and Mugkafb, and the three skittered down the shingle slopes, turning their back for now on the songs and laughter tumbling amongst the waves of the closest shore.

Rounding the cove, as one they slowed in reverence to witness the gravelled beach yield to pristine, sea-rippled sand shining pale beneath the moonlight. Here the depths lay calm, glittering like an opaque mirror, lapping quietly in the shallows beneath purpling cotton clouds, the distance-muted roar of the endless ocean now a hushing murmur as the dune grasses flanking the further shore rustled with a muted, nameless song that shivered across the sand-flats and settled once more into stillness.

"Welcome to the Silent Sound," Amber breathed.

Together they padded through the otherworldly solitude, their footsteps light upon the tide-hardened sand as the wave-patterns beneath their feet merged into scenes of wonder ever changing and barely seen. Snatches of exotic shore-plants pushed triumphant through the dry crust, and along the waterline mottle-hued shells glistened beneath the shallows' inky veil.

Amber's gaze lingered as she willed herself to take it all in; to not lose this moment amongst the uncertain times ahead that would fill them all with a dread sufficient to quash all such memories of goodness. She felt almost as though she were walking through an older version of the Ring.

"Fairies gather here every Recö," she explained in a whisper. "We bring food for the Sea Folk and leave it floating in the shallows on the rafts with paper lanterns. This year will be the first I'm deemed old enough—" *If we survive to Mid-Recö.* She bit back her fears just in time. Lonely as it felt, she could better live with that than with burdening Racxen and Mugkafb. Although she guessed it was too late for that now.

She refocused on their task, staring out over the inky expanse of water roiling slowly beneath the shawl of night, her eyes skimming the shore curving into the distance to merge with the pink-streaked swathe of horizon against an indiscriminate shifting dark. Biting back her frustration, she willed her vision to adjust.

The fickle gaze of the moon bright to his night-trained eyes, Racxen pointed to an indistinct lighter patch bobbing on the obsidian darkness.

"A raft," Amber grinned in relief. "Paddling it out should be our best hope of talking with the Sea Folk," she recounted, remembering the King's advice and fervently hoping that for one, they wouldn't be too late, and for two, she'd soon be able to stop relying on other peoples' ideas to know what to do. *C'mon,* she tried to reassure herself unsuccessfully. *Even the legendary Gorfang didn't do it completely on his own.*

"Some of the Folk will have remained," Racxen murmured confidently, his gaze remaining on the sea. "No tribe would send all of their kin to one gathering, no matter how momentous."

Amber nodded silent thanks in the darkness. For a moment, though, she almost stalled; an instinct last surfaced in her childhood hinting that here was a place where time stood still and sacred, untainted by the ravages of the rest of the Realm, and that if she were just to stay here she could somehow hold off the spiral of events threatening to break over the Realm and engulf its inhabitants in a flood of terror. Yet the endless ebb and flow of the waves drew her closer, whispering their timeless wisdom and bidding her continue with courage. They held a promise; their guardians knew of peace and its price, and the secrets of its keeping in the most perilous of times. Glancing to her friends in her own wordless vow, Amber strode into the sea's embrace.

The wet chill slapped against her chest as the depths yielded around her, but the water wasn't as cold as she'd been expecting. Moonlight glittered brokenly in her wake as she waded towards the flimsy craft, barely a shadow of reeds and bound together. It sloshed on the sparkling water as she fumbled with the weed-slipped knot slung across a jutting rock.

Grappling with the raft as it bobbed and shied, Amber finally sprawled onto it triumphantly, gripping sodden bunches of entwined reeds between white-clenched knuckles. Her gaze caught by the wave-shimmered vision of Racxen twisting and diving below, relishing the embrace of the open sea after travelling so far from his home-swamps, she realised that at least her undignified endeavour had gone unwitnessed.

"If you two are ready?" she teased, helping Mugkafb up as Racxen hauled himself out breathless and grinning beside her as she pushed the craft free, the water slapping rhythmically at its bow.

They paddled in silence through the soft veil of night, scanning the water as it darkened into a deep unfathomable ink, phosphorescence swirling mysteriously with each sweep of their hands.

Amber grabbed hold of Racxen as she glimpsed to the left a silver flash amidst the depths. Hushed in expectation, instinctively they stopped paddling and let the raft drift, wordlessly watching the water. All was silent save for the soft *lap-lap-lap* of the waves as lulled by the gentle rocking of the raft time seemed to stand still.

All three felt the next movement in the water, unmistakeably close now. Mugkafb leaned forward, his eyes straining. Racxen put out a hand, steadying his brother against the fathomless deeps. His own eyes were shining.

Another silver flash, and Amber gasped as a dark shape flickered indistinctly through the water until they could see the long brown hair and dusky purplish tail of a Sea Maiden as she undulated powerfully through the water. The sides rocked precariously as with a sweep of her tail the Maiden slowed, breaking the inky mirror-surface beside the raft with barely a ripple.

Water cascaded her salt-roughened, weed-entwined hair streaming unharnessed to her waist, framing a still face as pale as moonlight from which gazed the clearest eyes; light green and piercing, as if they could look right through into your soul. The darker remnants of a scar veined the left side of her face—the Vetch Queen's clawed savagery delivered as a penance for insubordination; the brand borne by all those brave souls who defied a tyrant and fought for peace on the side of the Fairies during the Sea Battle, marking them for death should the hounding Vetches find them. Guilt clung in Amber's throat to behold her. *Could I ever be that brave?*

The Maiden watched them silently, her bright eyes holding the wisdom of the ages.

"Darkseeker," she whispered, her voice lyrical, and Racxen started, staring at her searchingly, almost pleadingly. She smiled, her words the most soothing music that ever touched the soul. "What you did required the greatest courage; the truest love. You have been touched by no evil."

Racxen bowed his head, unable to speak. She turned to Mugkafb, silently waiting until he gathered the strength to return her gaze. "Stories do not end, Littleflame. They live on for as long as there are those who hold them in their heart and use them to do good. Heroes wear ever different guises, and travel many planes. Those who speak to you may yet be found."

Mugkafb grinned, bursting with pride.

Amber now found herself gazing into those ageless eyes in her turn. "What must I do?" The simplest and most unanswerable question disgorged itself from her mind as the enormity of their quest bore down on her.

In response, the Maiden sang, and her ethereal voice both haunting and calming drew tears to the eyes of the listeners in a melody that floated away across the mirror-flat water as soon as it was heard, and yet could not be forgotten, remaining in the mind long after as comfort in times of trouble:

"Flesh to stone, and ash to fire, as night must precede morn. Whate'er is gained, whate'er is lost, become more than you were born."

Amber stared, the words brimming tears in her eyes. The Maiden knew her every fear. There was solace in her riddle, and strength; and yet amidst that, so much loomed unknown: what would be gained; what lost? Overwhelmed by an uncertainty she felt too small for, Amber couldn't trust herself to speak.

"You ask too early, Amazonite," the Maiden advised. Her gaze slipped into the future, her keen eyes relinquishing their focus after holding Amber safe for a moment. "When the time comes, you shall find your answer."

She turned and dove, her tail shattering the surface in an explosion of moonlight-refracting spray that cascaded her rayed flukes before she slipped down through the murk to merge with the endless depths and be replaced in their vision by shivering reflections of stars against an endless dark.

The moment scattered, leaving Racxen, Mugkafb and Amber alone on the raft, listening to the wind whistling across the now empty ocean and carrying the far-off strains of singing back to them as they watched the scudding circle of ripples flatten once more.

Lost amidst savoured memories of their meeting and reverent wonderings at the Sea Maiden's messages, they paddled back. Their journey started in silence, but as they skirted the bay the melodies of the Sea Folk billowed all around them. Carrying words of inspiration, their music lifted worried spirits and infused peace into anxious minds, increasing in volume and pace until there was no room left for negative thoughts as it swirled and rose in ever greater waves.

With a shout Racxen pointed through the night-blackened swell, and following his gaze Amber glimpsed for her first time a Knight of the Sea.

How old he was she could not tell, but as his silvering tail blazed through the swirling gloam she could see several patches of scale were missing, and the years were in his ocean-green eyes as he broke through the surface, starlight glittering in his eyes and his voice a booming baritone: "For tonight, let your heart be free from troubles, and come dance amongst the waves!"

Their little craft darted across the water Dragon-fast, white foam cresting the bow as the Knight sped in front of them with the rope in his hands, his tail pulsing with silvery flashes as he guided them back towards the Southern Sands.

Drenched and gasping, as they neared the shore the friends could hear voices soaring on the wind, their words tumbling amongst the waves:

"Storms may rage and sea may foam, and the bravest hearts take fright. Yet the highest waves fastest carry you home, and dawn conquers the darkest night. So let the future bring its trials, to forge swords and temper steel. You've earned your spurs in battles that once held as much fear, and they passed, as these ones too will. You cannot avoid all darkness, so keep a lantern close stoked warm. You can neither force the clouds to pass nor wait, so sing amidst the storm!"

As the Knight slowed, Amber slid from the raft. Pushing to the surface, she flung back her hair from her face, gasping amidst the throbbing sea as the symphony billowed around her like a tangible force cast amongst the wind and foam. Arcs of light flashed from the waves as if their crests were lanced with flame, and she felt as though the drenching spray were initiating her into another Realm. Spiralling through womb-warm waters, she watched white horses burst triumphant through the surf, the ocean streaming from their flanks until she could not tell the sea from the two-score chargers leaping amongst the waves, their pale flanks glistening in the moonlight, the bells at their hooves jangling amidst the rush of the breakers and the laughter of song.

Treading water a wave's breadth away, Mugkafb whooped aloud as the horses turned his way, parting to flank him safely, their calls cresting the storm-sounds of the ocean as in the thunder of hoof-beats the young Arraheng was swept up off his feet by a rider and set before him on a snorting, foam-flecked grey, the horse's mane flying in the wind as they raced through the light-flashed sea.

One arm of the rider firm around him to stop him from falling, Mugkafb laid his hands aside the coarse mane to feel the horse's movements as if he were guiding him in the way of his people and the steed were his own, charging away through the foam-flung night.

Throwing a glance over his shoulder, the beach now far behind flowing out like silk along the shore, his attention caught on the

Knight; his strong otherworldly face, the trailing weed-entwined hair, the barnacled, dusk-streaked tail. "I remember you," Mugkafb blurted, emotion catching in his throat amidst the sea wind as the words escaped from a night still blurred in his memory.

"The darkness will lift as it did before," the Knight answered in reassurance, navigating easily through the rising swell as the horse bucked and danced at his guidance and the waves crashed and rolled around them beneath a pale bright moon. "And we will ever seek to bear you when the seas become too rough."

As he urged the gleaming horse on, the sea seemed to draw down the stars with his speed until it felt like they were racing through another Realm, and Mugkafb thought to himself that they could run until dawn and still not tire as his heart lifted to the sky through the rhythm of their steed's pounding hooves.

All too soon, Mugkafb saw the ribbon of the shore stream out as the waves relinquished their embrace, and spray flung around the horse as he pushed through to the shallows.

Spotting Amber watching the Folk close-by, listening to the melodic chants around her with a far-off, wistful look in her eyes, Mugkafb jumped down with a splash, shouting his thanks over the sea's roar. Before he could reach her to ask "engo ro fash?" in a flurry of bright water her hands were taken by a Knight and a Maiden, and with shouts and laughter the three swam together, gathering more to their group who darted into a dance around her until he could no longer be sure who was which, and Mugkafb contented himself with waiting astounded in the warm, lapping shallows until his friend returned, because after all she was a Fairy and none of them could swim half as well as he could, so someone ought to look out for her.

Moments later, garlanded with sea-flowers about her neck, the blessings of the dancers ringing in her ears and her face split grinning, she was splashing through the surf and swinging him into a hug and bidding him tell his story as they waded back to shore to sit exhausted amidst the surf and watch the revelry.

Scanning the waves, Amber saw amidst the thunder of hooves Racxen cantering bareback upon a glistening white horse amidst the swell, pounding through the surf, the sea-spray flung against his face and the wind whipping through his black hair as his charge raced towards the shore to halt snorting, his dark muzzle scattering sea-droplets that glinted rainbow-hued as he shook out his coarse mane and stood, great chest heaving, in the shallows.

Racxen slid from his back, laying a hand aside his shoulder with a whisper of thanks. The horse inclined his forelegs in a bow, his dark eyes already turning back towards the sea.

The starlit waters still dancing in his eyes, Racxen ran exultant to meet the others, and they turned back to watch as in a great thunder of hooves and crashing waves the herd ran on, until they were lost from view amidst the deeper sea and the carousers began at last to drift shore-wards.

Drenched, breathless with exhaustion, and wearing a grin that split her face as she waved her companions goodnight, the rhythms of the sea still thudding in her chest and its music buzzing in her ears, Amber couldn't help but find solace in knowing that whatever darkness was yet to follow, they had all amongst friends danced free beneath the stars this night.

Riddle of the Golden Fields

Infused with new spirit after last night's encounter, Amber ran down the hill, the wind in her hair, her strides lengthening as she breathlessly counted the steps between wing-beats. Her Realm blurred faster and faster into the rhythm until a gust of wind surged beneath her and she leapt into the waiting currents, catching an updraught in a flurry of wing-beats and surrendering to the rush, letting the airflow sweep her away.

The landscape fell away beneath her as she claimed her birthright, watching the far rich tapestry rolling dizzyingly below as she gasped and whooped, racing through her element as if it were all coming back to her from a dream she couldn't believe she'd forgotten, wheeling through the cloudless sky, the wind streaming at her face, stripping her mind of all worries until everything fell away save for the sun at her back and the air-currents writhing in ecstasy beneath her.

Her body felt new, nimbler, as if scar tissue from some forgotten wound were softening and regaining function. After so many years of waiting, flying was weaving itself into her nature, forming a part of her she couldn't now imagine being without. Diving over streams and rivers, watching the fields and valleys far below melt into an indistinct blur of golden colour, she felt freer than she ever had before—at one with the sky; becoming who she had been born to be. She felt the possibilities unfold before her, reading them like the currents. One day, she'd fly to the edge of the Realm.

For now, though, she was forced to slow in midair, not yet used to the energy flying sapped, her wing and back muscles sore from the unaccustomed exertion. She tried to fan her wings to remain stationary but, as nausea coiled in her stomach, she had to admit that the sensation of hanging suspended in the air supported by fickle, invisible forces whilst the ground quivered far below was going to take a lot more sessions to get used to.

Easing into what she fondly hoped would prove a controlled descent, Amber focused her attention on surveying the lands with a single-minded energy sufficient to block out, at least for now, the weighting ache in her wings.

Sprawling below, the Fairy Kingdom lay as if enchanted, illuminated by shafts of sunlight that bathed the land in gold. Amidst the vibrant green of the meadows, a dot of movement flickered. She squinted down at a tiny figure waving its arms frantically at her below. *Jasper?*

She angled downwards, plummeting in a rush of gravity and awkwardly splaying her wings far too late as the ground rose swiftly to punish her misjudgement. Stumbling jarringly to land, she had to resort to flailing her arms to remain upright, and any attempts at greeting the Prince in a seemly manner had to be abandoned in favour of gulping down bile and trying not to throw up.

Jasper took a serene step backwards. "You're getting better," he offered charitably, waiting for her to catch her breath. "We need to question Racxen."

Amber glared. "You make him sound like a criminal."

"Okay, fine," Jasper conceded in exasperation. "We need his help and I didn't want to admit to my father that I hadn't got my facts straight, all right?"

Amber rolled her eyes, but she grinned. "If you put it like that."

Jasper was already hastening onwards. "We have to make this quick.

We can short-cut through the Golden Fields, but for pity's sake don't tell anyone."

"Just as well *you're* not a tracker," Amber muttered in the direction of Jasper's retreating form as well after noon-tide she found herself traipsing through row upon weaving, twisting row of sun-blanched, golden-limbed plants now rustling their serpent-like protest as the Prince forced his way through somewhere unseen up ahead.

Exhausted from darting through the shoulder-high foliage in her efforts to follow him without breaking the brittle stems on either side, Amber stopped and stretched in relief, squinting against the glaring sun and stealing a moment to catch her breath while Jasper was still out of sight and couldn't berate her for hindering their progress.

"Mayhap we should stop for a while," his disembodied voice admitted, floating back to her from up ahead. "I'll make a fire in the clearing—I've never seen such dry plants—and we'll cook something to eat before moving on."

Amber was about to agree, hunger gnawing readily in her stomach, when the thought fled from her mind almost before she realised why. She felt like her feet had turned into roots as amidst the dried stalks in front of her golden eyes blinked cracklingly from a wizened ochre visage as thin and speckled as handmade paper. Impossibly fragile leaf matter curled and crinkled as fear flickered across its face in a wordless plea.

Stunned, Amber realised she hadn't given the Prince an answer. "No fires!" she shouted, her voice cutting unnaturally loudly through the quiet of the towering fields. "They'd . . . advertise our presence."

A sigh rustled through the field like a rain-heralding wind through bare trees after a season of drought, and Amber found her arm clutched in a dry, gentle hold.

"Beware the one that becomes many on the hour when day's eye shuts."

The voice was breathless and whispery, but the warning it held burned into Amber's mind. The speaker scanned her face searchingly for a moment and was lost amidst the tangle of greens and golds.

"Shafash!" A final hissed word floated in the pressing air as Amber hesitated, staring after the implausible vision.

She turned with a start at the crack of broken stalks behind her.

"If you're going to talk to yourself, Amber, at least speak sense," the Prince huffed, shouldering through the foliage to glare at her. "If you don't want us to stop to eat, why in five seasons won't you keep up? And dare I ask what you were prattling on about?"

Amber grimaced in bewilderment, steeling herself yet again for his ridicule. "Jasper, that wasn't me. There was a—a kind of person, made of leaves; they gave me a riddle when I shouted to you about the fire . . ."

Jasper snorted. "And this 'Leafling', or whatever, just happened to speak our tongue?"

"Well, we're not that far from Fairymead, and they gave me a word in their language too," Amber added defensively, realising how improbable it all sounded. "'Shafash.' Maybe it just meant 'thank you,' but it sounded more urgent than that . . ."

She trailed off, despairing of the sceptical look she was being fixed with by the Prince. "Maybe this riddle could help us. It's a warning of some sort, so it must be important. What if these Leaflings know about the monsters?"

The Prince waved his hand dismissively. "They're just babbling primitive nonsense. It's of no concern to us."

"It's all we have to help us so far," Amber growled in exasperation. "And if you think it's so primitive, why don't *you* go back and work it out and you can tell me the oh-so-obvious answer when I return from talking with Racxen?"

She shook her head warningly as he opened his mouth to protest.

"I know how you'd speak to him, and there's no way in the Realm I'm letting you. And," she added more evenly, "I promise not to get lost this time."

The Prince nodded stiffly. "I suppose this does require a scholar's touch."

"Fly free, Jasper." She waved him on quickly while she could still restrain her tongue.

Consequences

After several hours of trekking, watching the tired sun sink low in the heavy sky, Amber was relieved to see, glittering through the grey twilight, the pre-marsh clearing foreshadowing Arraterr spilling beneath obscuring mist.

From the edge of the swamps two familiar figures came sprinting in her direction and in relief she ran to hail them: "Racxen! Mugkafb! How come you're so far from the caves?"

They didn't answer; and now they were so close she could hear their ragged breath.

Anguish contorted Racxen's face as he skidded gasping to a halt in front of her, his brother running on. "Amber, we told you not to return here. The Venom-spitters—"

Across the swamp-plains, the thunder of pursuit broke beneath a rain-laden sky and she stared past the Arraheng to the slavering black-furred, burning eyed monster pounding through the almost-night towards them.

Racxen shoved her into action. "Split up!" he barked, sprinting for the trees.

Amber did as she was bidden, running for her life to escape the slowing, tangled forest. Her instincts screaming for open grassland and flight, alone with the constant lash of rain beginning to replace the heavy thuds of the monster's chase, she sensed that safety hovered within her grasp. Her wings snapped open on the surge of adrenaline and she was automatically timing her strides, measuring for the launch: *Step-step beat, step-step.*

Realisation hit her in the chest, stealing her focus and sending her skidding clumsily to a halt in the mud as the truth slammed into her harder than the ground ever had: she couldn't fly away. Not when it meant leaving Racxen and Mugkafb to face the monsters alone. They couldn't fly away, so neither could she.

But they'll be far away by now. Probably.

Oblivious to the wind and rain tearing into her, her agony of indecision lasted a mere second. A few days ago, had she been able, she would have launched herself into the air and been far and away from here by now, with no reason to stay and nothing to fear. But now that the option was gifted, it was at once unequivocally void. So much had changed. Her choice as vivid as lightning, she threw a last, desperate glance to the storm-hung sky, and raced to retrace her steps.

Amongst the boulder-strewn landscape where the swamps met the cliff-bases of the caves abandoned after the tribe's flight through the waterways, four gleaming eyes greeted Amber's approach to the largest rock-cast shadow.

"What're you still doing here?" Mugkafb whispered weakly. "Is the storm too bad for you to fly?"

"That must be it," Amber shrugged awkwardly, keeping her eyes fixed on the open ground as she ducked down beside her friends. "I'm sorry, I—" She couldn't find the words.

Racxen's eyes drew hers. "It's still out there. You should have flown," he admonished almost inaudibly, gathering his brother in his arms.

"I . . . couldn't," she muttered; quiet as a thought for fear of attracting the monsters.

"Wouldn't," Mugkafb corrected stoutly.

"Hush, you're supposed to be resting." Amber's grateful smile contorted in horror at the dark blood glistening thick and jellied on his lower leg. "What have you been doing?" she breathed, trying to keep her voice light as her mind raced through their pitiful remaining options.

"Looking after him," Mugkafb murmured, his eyes drifting as he tried to look towards his brother.

Amber found his claws in the darkness. "You've done a sound job," she promised. She felt his grip loosen, and panic flooded.

"I gave him soulroot," Racxen explained quickly. "I always carry it on treks, ever since—I mean, since it's a pain-blocker."

Amber choked on her reply as the night splintered into a guttural roar even closer than the last.

Seconds stretched into minutes measured in pounding heartbeats and terrified glances cast in silence as the three waited interminably. Against the burning heat of adrenalin skittering through her, Amber began to feel a creeping coldness, tingling along her back until it spread to her wings. Excruciatingly aware that the slightest movement risked revealing their presence to the waiting monster, she forced herself to remain still. Gradually, she felt herself grow numb to the prickling and the sensation was forgotten, engulfed in the over-riding, helpless horror of waiting; of bargaining for life one last time.

Panic-distorted minutes merged into real hours and a surreal smeared memory of deathly cold and unearthly night-noises as the monster prowled and stomped. Racxen, used to tracking for days, held still with more ease, but whilst he lay like a statue, Amber's whole body screamed out to move, tormenting her with tremblings and itchings and tinglings and crampings until in the depths of the sleepless night she felt it no longer and half imagined she was instead watching the whole thing bleary-eyed and detached from above.

As dawn at last chanced to inch across the horizon, a final growling cry shredded the remnants of the friends' nerves before echoing jarringly into a silence rendered unbearably sweet.

Glancing warningly to the others, infinitely slowly Racxen shifted until he could squint out to watch the shadows knifing across the paling ground fade back amongst the boulders. "No sign," he murmured as he ducked back down, his lips barely moving and his eyes still locked to the clearing. "Yet it feels too auspicious a coincidence to trust that they fear the coming daylight."

Amber nodded. Grimacing into the chilling dawn as her muscles seized in disused complaint, she shifted ever so slightly and automatically sought to flex her wings.

It wasn't happening. She sighed; she must be even more tired than she'd thought. But as she tried again, as deliberately and consciously as she could, still nothing happened. Panic flooding, she tried to think about it logically; isolate the muscles needed. She retracted her shoulder blades, squeezing them together as closely as she could behind her back. Between there were the muscle groups she needed. Why couldn't she feel them, use them?

She extended her back, stretching so much that it hurt. But the pain was swallowed by worry. She could feel each other part—why not her wings? She reached round with one hand, and her fingers touched something coldly alien and flimsy. Pulling her hand back instinctively, an awful though caught up and she twisted to look round.

No. Not this. In shock, she reached round once more, forcing herself not to recoil again as she caught the tip of one wing, stretching it carefully out as she would when she'd gone to sleep leaning on it at an odd angle and it had gone numb.

Except that it was useless: her wings weren't going to regain circulation, regain feeling, regain function. She knew it in the very core of her being, even as she clung to the wing she held now like a vestige of a better, now broken time. It felt like touching nothing more significant than the sloughed-off scale-patches of a snake, leaving her with the gnawing disquiet that she didn't even recognise a part of her own body as belonging to her anymore, and the growing fear that this trauma would somehow sever irrevocably the piece of her soul that had waited so long to experience flight.

Shaking now, she reached for the other wing, just in case, although she already knew how it would be: *The same. Just the same.*

Terror spiralled. She hadn't flown away. She'd exceeded the time limit. She'd gone over her twenty-four hours. *No one's lost the ability before,* she made herself recount, clinging to the fragile haven of denial. *You only learned the other week. It's just temporary. You'll get it back.*

But she couldn't fool herself; not even for the seconds it took to force the thought into her mind. She'd lost it. The most important part of her; the part that made her a Fairy—made her feel alive, gave her a future, made her different, made her the same—she'd lost it, thrown it away.

Tears spewed from her lids, her heart sputtering erratically as bile rose to burn her constricting throat. The truth bloomed like a fever, impossible to avoid or deny: her Realm was changed—shattered, stolen.

"*Amber.*" Racxen choked on the realisation. "I—"

"C'mon guys, this really hurts, and they'll be ages away by now." Mugkafb's fractious voice, as the pain seeped through the numbing soulroot to writhe renewed through his leg, wrenched Amber back as the young Arraheng stuck his head above the rock and, one hand clinging against his wound, scrambled awkwardly out of hiding. "See—"

"Mugkafb, get down!" Racxen hissed explosively in the sharpest tone Amber had ever heard him use. "We don't know—"

The pre-dawn gloaming shattered into a cacophony of jeering shouts and the rush of steel-grey, nimble-bodied delinquents.

"Goblins!" Racxen bellowed. "Keep together—don't let them separate us."

But something slammed into Amber, pain swelling as she went sprawling, and the next thing she registered was staring wild-eyed through smearing mud and pounding split-nailed feet, and distractedly noting the sky's vibrant hue, obscenely peaceful from its skewed angle as she curled protectively against whatever was thumping into her back, all hope of being able to gain purchase or defend herself stamped into the battered ground beside her in the suddenness and ferocity of the attack.

The shadow lifted and she was dragged backwards for a second and managed to stumble to her feet, turning to realise Racxen had hauled the Goblin off her, and then all else spun away as rough hands clamped, nails gouging into her neck and back as she scrabbled and scratched and shoved in her attempts to prise them away. A hand strayed too close to her mouth and her teeth clung savagely on the rough skin, head shaking to saw into its advantage as she irrationally wondered why the hold around her neck still wasn't loosening in the distorted hour-seconds. With a screeched curse, the weight slipped and she sent her elbow into the ribs crushing against her, stumbling backwards before the inevitable retribution.

Nothing. The Goblins had vanished. Amber spun round in shaking bewilderment.

Her eyes fell on Racxen; he bore numerous superficial cuts from the Goblins' attentions, but he paid them no heed as he paced like one possessed. "He's gone," he gulped brokenly, his voice as tortured as a shade's. "Mugkafb. They've taken my brother. It's happening again."

The Realm plummeted beneath her. "Taken?" she echoed, lost. "And what do you mean, 'again'? Why—"

"I'll worry about that when I find him," Racxen interrupted, his gaze fleeing to the horizon as he broke into a flat run.

"When *we* find him," Amber corrected as she charged after him once more, stitch burning into her side and lack of sleep mingling with adrenalin into a weird delirium.

Amber ran until she feared her lungs would burst and her heart explode. The jolting rush of surroundings, the rasping burn through her throat and the slamming pulse in her veins; they all blurred into perilous distractions from the need to reach Mugkafb, and she forced them down into the ground with every pounding step until there was only the boy in her mind, and the knowledge they'd find him.

As the weak light of morning blazed into merciless noon, Amber's gaze strayed to a shivering line of darkness tracing across the horizon ahead. Rubbing at her eyes for dread of having imagined it, she willed it to be a river, but it didn't flash in the sun like she'd expect. She couldn't focus on it properly without stopping, but she couldn't shake the feeling that it looked more like a void cutting into the very fabric of the Realm, and she could have sworn she saw it shift as she stared. But the only thing it could logically be was a riverbed, shadowed and drying up. And they could hardly stop for water anyway even if there were any left to be found.

Consumed by fighting back nausea and railing against her weakening legs, it wasn't until she realised Racxen was slowing that she registered the void-line thing had swollen into a jagged, darkening scar across the landscape and was spreading ominously closer.

She almost collapsed as he finally stopped, and it took several seconds for her vision to focus properly through the tumbling, almost root-like shadows of what sprawled inexplicably before them. The vague shadow they had glimpsed on the run had solidified into a wall-like thicket of tangled vegetation towering before them.

Squinting through the twisted mass of vines, the forms echoing into shadows as if repeating forever, Amber scrubbed at her eyes, her temples tight, too tired to be this confused. They'd run for hours. Was this some bizarre product of delirium? She felt as if they must have run further than even Gorfang from the legends; that this far out the usual rules of the Realm no longer held sway, leaving no way of knowing what could lie beyond.

But standing and staring wasn't going to get them any closer to

Mugkafb, was it? Groaning weakly against the stitch burning in her side she followed Racxen as he stole cautiously towards the mass, until they were standing no further than arm-length from it. Amber got the feeling her friend needed to get that close just to convince himself this was real, and not some desert trickery. She couldn't blame him. Reality had been fading with every mile they'd run. And now, grotesque knotted growths slumped as far as the eye could see, forming an impenetrable barrier.

Faint, unrecognisable noises shivered through the unearthly forest only to trail into heavy, oppressive silence as soon as Amber turned to focus on them. She realised uncomfortably that she couldn't hear another discernibly living thing amongst them. No birdsong fluted amidst the only greenery for miles. No insects disturbed the rich mulch. The air itself hung as if dead, unmoved by any Recö breeze. Yet issuing forth from within the vegetation rustled a deceptively soft hiss, rippling out from the heart, as if the forest were warning trespassers of what would befall them should they stray into this alien territory.

"They've got to be in there." Racxen was pacing again.

"But what else is?" Her voice sounded strange amidst the warping effect of the muffling leaves. Inexplicably verdant amidst the arid plains they'd fled across, knotted so densely it was impossible to see what it held or hid, there had to be something just not right at play here. The subtlety with which Mugkafb and his aggressors had vanished smacked of something primally disturbing, and if they were to have any hope of avoiding ending their search in the same fate, she couldn't let Racxen stumble blindly into the same trap. Did he even know where they were? Because she certainly didn't. How were they going to find their way back?

She dropped her voice to a whisper for fear of disturbing some unknown terror hidden within the foliage. "What are they?" The plants absorbed the words even as they left her lips, as if through a sentient desire to stifle any living thing trespassing from the outside Realm.

Staring hauntedly into the undergrowth, it was a long time before Racxen answered.

"They are Fekshwa in our language," he breathed warily at last. "'Stem Stranglers' in Universal."

They both fell silent, scouring the disturbing pseudo-forest for an opening and prowling around the unsayable.

"If he's got to be in there," Amber tried, throwing a glance back to her companion as she tramped around the edge of the thicket, "can't we hack a way through with your moonshaft or something?"

Peering through the thicket, just as she was about to give up on finding the slightest chink in the living armour, Amber glimpsed a narrow, dust-strewn gap snaking through. See, there *was* a trail. She reproached herself mentally for being so childish. There had to have been one all along, otherwise how could Mugkafb and the Goblins have avoided leaving a trace?

"Racxen!" she hissed, trying to shout down the rumours of Goblin sorcery beginning to roam unchecked through her beleaguered mind, and gestured to the gap in case it decided to close up for some forsaken reason.

The plants loomed repulsively around her as she ducked and entered, close enough to scratch her with dry fingers and goad her fraught psyche into fevered imaginings.

"There's no one behind you but me," Racxen reassured in a whisper, and together they pressed on.

The stagnant air sparked with foreboding as they pushed through the labyrinthine structure, claustrophobia pressing against them. She could barely see a yard in front of her, Amber realised fractiously. The best thing about the meadows was that you could see for miles; glimpse any threat in time to be away in flight before it got remotely dangerous. Her resolve shuddered. If you could fly. *Enough*, she admonished quickly. *You're alive and, right now, you have to make that be enough.*

She fastened her attention back onto their current path, turning and trailing into obscure shadows as yet more towering plants obstructed their way and restricted their vision. They both had, Amber realised even as she attempted to steel herself for the inevitable, no way of identifying the unseen cause of every auditory intrusion; no hope of knowing what dangers lay around each corner until the last second. Yet through this twisted web lay their only chance of finding Mugkafb, and they would strive through until the end.

Senses spinning, they crept through ever narrowing gaps, trying not to touch any of the leaves in an unspoken attempt to avoid awakening whatever it was that some primitive instinct told them lay dormant here. Even without their touch, the twisted stems of the plants knocked hollowly together with the clacking of dry bones shaken in a breeze.

Amber shuddered, blinking hard. It had to be just her vision failing to cope with the endless twisting of the path, but she could have sworn the plants were closing in on them.

"There's something sentient about this forest," Racxen warned, his voice low and eyes watchful. "There's no reason to fear yet; it hasn't hurt us. But we're veering into a circle while they'll have blundered straight through; it's getting narrower, yet there was an entire mob. This is not the way they came."

Amber's heart hammered in the silence, as Racxen kept his eyes trained ahead. She heard the rasp of his moonshaft sliding free.

"We're going to retrace our footsteps until we find another path; any other path," he murmured, shifting in front of her and wrapping the cord of the moonshaft more tightly around his hand. "Follow me."

Padding close enough to Racxen to risk crashing into him if he were to stop, Amber heard the softest rustle from somewhere behind them. She barely managed to suppress a cry of fear as, wheeling round, she glimpsed the path they'd just come down merging into the vegetation, lost forever.

Racxen grabbed Amber's wrist. "Labyrinth Creepers! The whole forest's a trap."

Shifting back-to-back, they braced themselves for the unknown, glancing fitfully through the otherworldly shadows cast by splicing sunlight through the eerily rustling growths; the Arraheng crouched low in fighting stance in readiness, the Fairy standing tall and alert, senses straining. It'd be no help, she knew in that moment, if her wings were to impossibly recover and spring quivering in readiness for flight. *I chose this,* the thought fluttered through her mind in the fraught near-silence. *I claim my choice. Bring what follows, for I would not have him stand alone.*

The moonshaft glinted as Racxen shifted it restlessly. "Do you have a weapon?"

"A weapon?" she hissed back incredulously. "Yes, *now* I've magically got one. I'm a Fairy. We don't do weapons. We've never had any need for them." She paused uncomfortably. "Until now."

"Wasn't thinking," Racxen murmured, keeping his eyes fixed warily ahead. "Just trying to delay our only option."

Amber tried to grin, although it didn't really work. "Well, if I had to choose someone to get stuck in a forsaken, malevolent-spirited forest with . . ."

It was Racxen's turn to look uncomfortable. "What if I can't protect you?"

"What if I slow you down?"

Drawing strength from each other's gaze, wordlessly they locked hands.

"Sen," Racxen nodded. "*Go!*"

As his blade carved a figure-eight flash of light, in an explosion of blade and branch they plunged into the living barrier, the Realm narrowing with crushing speed as they raced through.

The plants splayed sharply, disgorging them into a clearing, and Amber skidded in the dust as in front of her Racxen stopped with a shout, catching her arm before she could stumble.

Amber stepped back, stretching out cramping muscles threatening to seize as Racxen crept closer to the plants, trying to read an answer from their now-still forms. *Why this respite? Why now?*

Regaining her breath as she watched him, Amber flicked her foot out as she absentmindedly felt something cold and smooth brush against her bare ankle, gulping back a shriek as she stumbled, held fast. She flinched in horror as her stricken gaze flew to her leg, and even the movement of that attempt burned with tightening pain. A tendril of the plant had snaked out like a tentacle, wrapped itself quietly around her ankle, and was now fixing her in a vicelike hold. With a rubbery creak it tightened still further; she could feel her blood pulsing feebly now as it started to crush her leg.

Panic bubbling, she crouched to prise the thing off with her bare hands, her shaking fingers scrabbling at it manically until blood seeped under her nails, and then another stem touched her and she snatched her hand back as if burnt, lurching to her feet even as a further tendril slithered across to bind her legs.

Terror welled inside her, only a strangled cry escaping as more shoots reached out towards her, clutching greedily through the suffocating air.

"Racxen!" she cried in desperation, his name swallowed up in a death-rattle as the rustlings of the abhorrent plants burst into feverish agitation. Guilt splintered her heart at the thought that the same doom could be befalling him, and she'd rendered herself powerless to help.

Racxen yelled back hoarsely as Amber's cry cut through to him, spurring his struggles against the living barriers that had sprung up between them, his claws and blade splitting knot upon tangled knot. Light slipped between the final stems and, seizing his chance, Racxen clutched the moonshaft between his teeth and dove to roll through the hacked opening even as the plants closed in behind him.

As he jumped to his feet a slithering tendril flailed out for his leg and he fell heavily, kicking savagely at it until it loosened its grip and dropped back with an angry hiss.

Cursing as he tore down each fresh wall that sprang up to stop him, Racxen barraged through in time to see the thickest vine tightening around Amber's neck.

His own throat felt strangled as he ran to her limp form; her face was swollen unrecognisably, her fingers scuffed raw with blood and stained with green in a pitiful testament to her wretched attempts to scrabble free from the choking coils.

Washed through with fear as his gaze strayed to the tremor in his hands, in the next instant Racxen's face tightened and with a yell of love and terror his claws spliced through air and stem, the halved vine falling from Amber's neck with an empty thud. He was already ripping at the other binding tendrils, frantic until tooth and claw had loosened and broken the living shackles.

Hugging Amber to him as she crumpled soundless to the ground, Racxen sobbed as a great wheezing breath seemed to refill her body, and she spluttered and gasped, sounding as if she was choking all over again.

"I slowed us down," Amber wheezed, her bloodshot eyes streaming. "I endangered you—"

"You? I was too slow; I should have . . ." Racxen shook his head quickly, willing her to stay quiet and let herself rest, grinning through his tears in relief that she was here alive to make such a ridiculous apology, even as the blotching bruises already flourishing across her neck terrified him. "We can't always protect each other, no matter how much we want to. If we could, we wouldn't be mortal, whether Fairy or Arraheng."

He shrugged ruefully. "Of course, I'd prefer that you were safe and away from me; but you're even more stubborn than Mugkafb in that respect and I know better than to ask what I'd refuse in my turn."

Amber grinned weakly, feeling safer already. Then her eyes widened as she saw the broken stems through the branches beyond the closest wall. "They made it out," she rasped. "There's—"

Words fell away as she realised that Racxen's gaze hadn't stopped. No further than a mile ahead Dread Mountain rose, its mists bleeding unchecked across the land in an indelible staining scar knifing through a collective memory that had otherwise reforged itself in times of peace, protruding like a jagged bone through healing skin.

With leaden hearts, Racxen and Amber dragged themselves to their feet.

The sapping shadow of the mountain gathered weight above them. Despite themselves, both friends slowed, burdened suddenly by the overwhelming fear that now of all times there was no more use for their struggles, no longer the smallest hope for Mugkafb.

"You've seen through the darkness before," Racxen promised, forcing the words out against despair. "Let it come, for it will find you undaunted and undoubting. It can threaten what it will, but it cannot change your course."

Amber nodded fiercely, clinging to his hand as he stumbled, the colour draining from his face. "It is but a feeling," she answered equally firmly, believing the words more for him than she ever could for herself. "It is not who you are. It will pass as a storm-wave if you let it wash over you; frightening but transient, leaving you more ready for the next. And," she risked adding, a light glimmering in her eyes from which Racxen drew more hope than any words she could have thought up, "you'll never have to ride it out alone again."

His hand never left hers, a grim smile lifting to his face as together, the unflinching presence at each of their side urging them both on as private doubts surged and eased; stumbling but never stopping, linked in hand and heart, they pressed on through the mist-clung twilight.

As they reached the foot of the mountain now fallen into darkness, the immediacy of adrenalin pierced the dread fog groping for their minds as the friends stared up through the eerie shadows of the vast, craggy inclines.

"Mugkaaaaaaaaafb!" Racxen's yell ricocheted around the slopes and fell into an aching silence.

Faintly, from somewhere above came an answering sound—thin and high and scared.

They stared at each other, Racxen's eyes gleaming in disbelief, tears springing to Amber's.

After a heartbeat's pause, a thunderous roar broke in a second answer.

They froze; and in the next breath scrambled for the slopes.

As the mountain steepened, its carven moonlit paths narrowing treacherously between ancient rockfall and interlocking streambeds, Amber found herself resorting to one minute crawling, the next climbing, scuffing her elbows and skinning her knees in her haste, knowing any delay from her would endanger both Mugkafb before her and Racxen behind.

Reaching for the next handhold, she twisted painfully, but something pulled at her, holding her fast. Frightened, she lunged again, and her back burned.

Grim realisation trickled through. *My wings.*

Cursing, she reached round awkwardly, trying to pull the trapped one free, comprehending chillingly late the extent to which, now she couldn't feel them, the wings had become a hazard. Gritting her teeth, she grabbed hold, grimacing in revulsion as it crumpled lifeless in her grasp. How could something once so integral to her being have become such a danger?

"Engo ro fash." She felt Racxen's hand at her shoulder as he climbed up beside her, and amidst the scrape of stone and flood of relief she could move again.

"This place is an avalanche waiting to happen." The Arraheng eased the rock back warily, trying to quieten its progress and scuffing his claws in the process. "I wasn't expecting the stones to shift this much. At least we know the Goblins aren't close; we'd have heard them by now. They aren't used to such terrain."

"Neither am I," Amber muttered, furious with herself. She sucked in a deep breath. "Look, I know I'm always slowing you down or endangering you, but at least this time I can change it. I can't feel them anyway." A lump squeezed into her throat, but her words squashed it down. "I need you to—"

"No," Racxen swore, appalled. "Amber, it's not your fault, nothing has to be done; I'd never ask—"

Her resolve shuddered. "I know," she managed. "But this is a decision I have to make for all of us, and the responsibility lies solely with me. My wings have become a liability. We're going to have to flee with Mugkafb, squeeze ourselves into impossible hiding places; it's dark, I can't feel them. If anything happened I couldn't forgive myself."

Racxen watched her miserably. "If it truly is your free choice, I cannot deny you."

Amber nodded quickly. "To wish otherwise would be futile, and can have no bearing now."

The Arraheng grimaced wretchedly. "Sen."

She heard him draw the moonshaft, and felt his hand trace down her back to the basal nub of her wings; the sinewy clump of tendons protruding between her spine and shoulder blades.

Holding his breath, as gently as he could Racxen stretched both wings out to separate them. They crackled slightly at the movement, with the sound of leaves unfurling, and in the wan moonlight the veins glittered iridescently against the chiton-like membrane. They felt strangely velvety to the touch, and up close Racxen could see why: they were covered in tiny, downy-soft scales, instead of the smooth membrane he'd imagined. He couldn't help staring; they were fascinatingly beautiful.

"Are you certain about this?" his plea slipped out, one last time.

Not trusting herself to speak, Amber nodded. She heard Racxen's sharp intake of breath and the whistle of stone cutting through air twice in quick succession, and then a weight was severed from her back with a painless tug as the blade chinked against the rock.

So quickly, so quietly, it was over. Silently, in her mind, she said goodbye to that part of her.

"Thank you," she whispered to Racxen, feeling lost even amongst the sound of her own voice. "I know it was a horrible thing to ask."

As she sat up to face him, he turned away. She felt her soul crawl away deeper inside her. She'd mutilated herself; of course she repulsed him. What had she expected?

Racxen barely heard her, a haunting chill creeping upon him as his eyes lingered over the wings in his hands. He couldn't tear his eyes away, convulsed with an involuntary shudder. They'd looked so beautiful on Amber. Now they looked violated.

"Racxen?" Amber challenged, her voice tiny, steeling herself for his detachment. "After everything, why now won't you look at me?"

He rolled the wings up hastily, trying to keep them out of her view as he turned back to her. "Because I hurt you," he whispered brokenly. "And I can't stand it."

Taking his free hand, she bowed her head against his, knowing she should have given him the faith he deserved. "You're the one who soothes all my pain in this Realm," she corrected, exhaling shakily. She tried to smile. "Speaking of which, we've got to get to Mugkafb."

As she stepped back, she tried not to think about how off-balance she now felt. *Should have considered that beforehand,* logic goaded cruelly.

Racxen didn't move; she thought she saw tears glistening in his eyes.

"It's okay," she promised softly. "Pass them over, and let's go." There was no reply, so she reached to lift the bundle from his limp, entranced hands, and before the Arraheng could stop her she had unfurled it.

Racxen winced in the darkness. "Amber—"

A keening wail broke from the Fairy. Her wings. Her beautiful wings! They were the one thing that had made her feel maybe she could have one day been special, and now they looked hideous and dead and mutilated and she'd made him cut them off and it was all her fault. How could she have been so stupid—she couldn't be a Fairy with no wings and they'd never grow back and what would everybody think and . . .

She crumpled to the ground, her body breaking into wracking sobs. How could she have done this?

Ashen faced, Racxen knelt to hold her, and clinging to him Amber gulped back her tears and dragged a hand across her face. "We're nearly there," she managed, her voice empty as she steeled her resolve. "And I've delayed us long enough."

The last stretch of the climb sapped even Racxen's stamina, gouging into the last depths of both their reserves. Amber privately welcomed the ferocity of the challenge, letting the exertion swallow up every scrap of her being until she could almost blank out the horrifying reality she would be left to face when this was all over.

From the plateau above her, Racxen shouted, and just for now she'd not change their wretched situation for all the Realm, for there came a weak cry answering so close now and, flooded with hope, she scrambled after him, and they reached Mugkafb.

Pulling him chokingly into his arms, Racxen hugged his brother like he'd never let him go again.

Amber watched anxiously. Mugkafb's leg wound was at least closing up, and other than superficial cuts he appeared physically no further harmed. Yet the sheer terror of his ordeal, and the despair of having borne the burden of this accursed mountain alone, burned into the young eyes that locked fleetingly onto her as she broke her Gem against a boulder and powdered it into his leg wound now that Racxen had no more soulroot left.

"I ran off," the boy managed, burrowing into his brother's embrace at the memory once she'd finished applying the Gem-dust. "The Goblins took me into the mountain, but they ran off; they kept talking scared about the Venom-spitters; that the 'Samire' was coming; like there wasn't a dam or sire, just this one monstrosity, the worst of all the Venom-spitters."

Bile rose sourly in Amber's throat. "That's what the Leafling's riddle meant. All the Venom-spitters are spawned from one." She hesitated. "Could we use that to our advantage?"

Mugkafb shuddered. "Not with the monster they were describing. They were so terrified they legged it and left me behind so I didn't slow them down." He hugged his knees to his chest. "They don't know mountains like I do. But I got so scared, I hid, and I felt like—like I'd never get out, like you'd never come, and I told myself I knew it was just the mountain making me think like that, but . . ."

Racxen lifted his face gently, so he could look with fierce promise into his brother's eyes. "We'd come. Both of us. Even if they'd taken you to another Realm entirely, we'd have found a way."

His expression twisted with the clawing fear of what could have been. "Mugkafb, I should never have brought you here. I know you'd want to be with me if anything happened, but I'd rather die alone if it meant knowing you were far away and safe. You mean so much to me that sometimes I forget how young you are—don't look at me like that, brother, it's not a fault it's a privilege—I still feel so new at this, and I've failed you."

The pain from earlier now faded, Mugkafb poked at his leg, impressed. "I'm going to have a massive scar, aren't I?" he predicted proudly. "Wait till I show Sama. And anyway, it's not your fault; you're not a Goblin. Or a Venom-spitter."

Racxen grinned in humbled disbelief. Mayhap he'd never again see the Realm that way himself, but if his brother still could there remained the kind of magic worth fighting for.

"Come on then, hero, let's get you home," Amber promised, stepping forwards to help Mugkafb up.

At Racxen's sharp warning she flinched back violently, staring in horrified fascination as amidst the malevolent rattling of an insect-like, scale-armoured creature the Arraheng snaked out his hand and trapped it, pinning its barbed, whip-like tail beneath his claws as it chuntered its wrath.

Grimacing in revulsion, Racxen threw the reptile into the darkness, compulsively wiping his hands through the dust as he watched it land unharmed and scurry furiously down between the rocks to disappear from sight.

"You're going to tell me what that was, right?" Amber demanded as she feverishly checked the ground by her feet.

"Red-eyed Gantorna." Mugkafb looked like he was going to be sick. "They're the most poisonous creatures in the whole Realm. Worse even than Venom-spitters. One stab of their tail and a dart of poison kills you in I don't know how many minutes."

Any possible response fled from Amber as her mind retreated against a flood of nightmarish imaginings of the fate they'd brushed so closely past.

With a shaky flash of his old grin, Mugkafb scrambled to his feet, grabbing Amber's and Racxen's hands. "Definitely time to go."

It seemed to Amber an age before they'd half-climbed, half slid to the foot of the mountain. Looking back up at it she shivered, the insidious tendrils of doubt and despair still trying to worm their way in.

While Racxen took their bearings, she started telling Mugkafb all she could remember of one of the legends of Gorfang; anxious that exhaustion was gaining on him, for the boy looked worn and aged from his ordeal.

Yet once she'd got partway through and he'd corrected her on several choice points and started a spirited argument that it wasn't the Goblins who'd imprisoned Gorfang but the evil Lobanian Emperor, they both ended up laughing in relief at having for a second forgotten the whole sorry business, and when Racxen explained they'd need to skirt onto the Golden Fields to avoid the Fekshwa, his little brother didn't even complain.

Adding his own recounting of the tale, earning affirmations and rebukes in turn from Mugkafb, Racxen led on. Gradually, the dawn sun dared to reveal itself, splicing through the dread-mists and peeling away the shadow of the mountain from both the stricken landscape and the beleaguered minds of the travellers. The soil grew sandy, the vegetation sparse.

"Speaking of Goblins, and I know it was probably just the mountain-dread that got to me," Mugkafb mumbled, as if the embarrassment of revealing it as one would be almost as bad as hearing it proven as the other. "On the mountain, did you hear any other, um . . . monsters?"

Racxen watched him, quickly trying and failing to deduce a definite conclusion either way. A glance to Amber confirmed she felt the same; they'd both been so concerned about Mugkafb that they'd spared no thought for anything else.

"We can't dismiss experiences on the mountain," he offered carefully as his mind raced through the possibilities, neither wanting to scare his brother nor invalidate a warning that could be genuine. "But we'll reach decent cover soon in the Golden Fields, and they flank the Fekshwa— no monster would stray into such territory."

Unspokenly, the trio picked up their pace.

Nerves shredded by the desert wind-voice that didn't seem to worry the Arraheng but freaked her out no end, Amber was just beginning to trust they'd be okay when Racxen pushed in front of her, hissing for silence and gesturing towards the horizon.

Shimmering in the heat-haze, two low-to-the-ground silhouettes that could only be Venom-spitters were moving closer, only just too far away to tell if they'd caught the scent yet.

Time blurred and froze at once as in a silent rush the friends hastened for the fields. As the tallest leaves brushed mercifully over them, slipping between the stems the companions were finally obscured from view, enveloped instead in a softly rippling golden haven.

Not daring to rest, they crept along the corn-like rows, drawing strength from the distance gained as the glimmer of sand behind them faded.

"It means we can't track their movements," Racxen warned as he glanced back. "They could close in on us without warning. We need to change direction; make it harder for them and buy us time if we're scented."

Amber darted left, realising as she did so that even with their best intentions the noise of their progress, subtle as it was, combined with the muffling effect of the foliage left only a tremulous chance that they'd be able to hear the advance of the monsters.

She changed direction again, wiping sweat from her eyes. How long had they trekked for by now? The field hadn't seemed so endless when she'd gone through it with Jasper, and the heat was stifling. *Keep it together,* she told herself sharply. *You're alive enough to worry, so just—*

"Stop," hissed Racxen. "Stay calm. When I say, turn, and boldly. It needs to know it's no longer an ambush. Maybe that's enough—it's all we've got, and it hasn't attacked so far. Sen? Now."

Adrenalin surged through her, so fast she barely registered herself turning and pushing Mugkafb behind her. She stared into those damning, blood-pooling red eyes as the Venom-spitter stalked towards them through the gap they'd left.

For one impossible moment, Amber thought Racxen'd be right; that it would back off.

Then a second monster roared, charging into view, and in the blur of instinct taking over, they were running too.

Amber darted left and right, the Arraheng at her heels, zigzagging through into momentary obscurity. But they were so far into the field, their path so obvious, and the snorting, pounding pursuit of the monster rushed inescapable in her ears. Any second it would round the corner and there'd be no hope left.

And Mugkafb fell. All this time he'd managed, she didn't know how, to run, and now his body had refused, and he was on the ground.

Racxen was pulling him into his arms, no way of fighting now even as between the leaves Amber saw the matted fur streak past.

"*Shafash!*" she yelled in despair, the Leaflings' word leaping suddenly to her mind.

Instantly, a living wall of leaves sprang up, enveloping the friends behind a hedge-broad barrier, concealing them as if there'd never been a path this way.

As the Venom-spitters rounded the corner and burst into view, heaving flanks drenched in sweat, they saw just one more clump of impenetrable vegetation amongst thousands.

Inside the living wall, still shielding Mugkafb, Amber could hardly breathe she was so transfixed with terror. Distractedly, she noticed a tiny sand-spider scuttle deeper into the field, and with her heart tattooing against her chest she shut her eyes involuntarily against a situation almost too awful to experience and some small part of her crawled away beneath the twigs of straw after it so that she couldn't get hurt, not really, whilst back in the situation her body screamed and howled and wished wretchedly for it to be over.

Racxen's claws curled around her wrist, and her eyes opened as she found strength. Peering out amidst the stems, eyes staring with the horror of it all, she glimpsed dust-clung fur shifting across wiry muscle, the stench of rotting flesh hanging between the monster's jaws as it panted.

With a low growl it turned, to its companion Amber guessed although she couldn't see it. The ground shook as the first Venomspitter stomped horrifyingly close to their perilous shelter, swinging its head heavily in an attempt to scent its lost prey.

The monsters lashed the ground in frustration, billowing up clouds of dust that scratched into Amber's throat, rendering her almost irresistibly desperate to cough. She swallowed again and again, dryly. *It knows we're in here.* The knowledge knifed weakeningly into her, physically hurting. Somewhere, impossibly, a carrion bird called, the sound fading into electric silence.

Blessedly, unbelievably, the monsters spun in its direction, perhaps realising that their wanton blood-lust had forced them, thick-coated and exhausted, their red eyes made for night hunting blinded by the merciless desert sun, too far into the hostile dry lands, and that elsewhere close by lay easier meat to scavenge.

Amidst the gentlest rustling, the leaves spread to reveal a circle of Leaflings stepping back.

As one, the friends dropped to their knees in gratitude. Amber gazed upon the row of humanesque faces, trying to look each of their rescuers in the eye. Some were brittle brown, all spikes and jagged edges; some fluid gold with waving frond-like arms. She vowed she would remember their faces.

"There are no words enough in either of our languages to thank you," she tried honestly. "And yet we must attempt to express our thanks, no matter how inadequately." She floundered, out of her depth. "We will never forget you, or your kindness, no matter how far we must travel on our quest."

There was a ripple of voices, indecipherable as dry grasses murmuring in the breeze.

"This is the desert. Why are her eyes wet?"

"What did she say?"

"Listen to us." Another reprimanded his fellows with a rustle as sharp as the shake of a serpent's tale. "Do not be so rude. She may not be able to understand our words any better than we can hers. Be silent."

As the Leaflings settled into a waiting hush, one beckoned the newcomers to stand. His wizened features glowing with the hues of Recö merging into Requë, his leaf-arms folded as if into long sleeves, he exuded a most benign presence.

Many pairs of inquisitive eyes watched her as, suddenly shy, Amber bowed courteously and held out her hand.

The leader tilted his head and considered the extended fingers with interest. His papery features crinkled into a wide, peaceful smile as he took hold of her hand in a feather-light grip and patted it comfortingly.

"Ah, my child," he murmured, his voice the whisper of cornfields waving in the breeze. "I wish you could understand when I tell you it has always been foretold that one who cannot fly will walk furthest. The energy currently tied in the conviction imprisoning you will one day forge the new beliefs that will free you. When you see for yourself, it will prove so memorable a lesson, so great a reward, as could not possibly be obtained through my words here and now, no matter how much I may wish to save you the stretch of uncertainty betwixt and between."

Even with their meaning unknown, his words flowed over Amber with the reassurance of Renë's breath after the coldest Restë. She felt overcome for a moment that in the face of his serene acceptance she didn't have his faith, but instead she drew strength from the kindness of these strangers and bowed once more her gratitude, on behalf of her friends as with Racxen bearing Mugkafb they found their way out of the Golden Fields and continued their long journey home.

As the fields and valleys she knew once more greeted their steps, with a deepening realisation Amber knew she could no longer hide from the gnawing, irrevocable truth of what had happened. It was a step she could never retrace. She could never even shake the awareness that she constantly felt off-balance, like she was leaning too far back without their familiar weight. And no matter how unfair she claimed it to be, it wouldn't change anything.

The last comforting rays of sunlight had fallen away into bleak twilight long before the friends neared the border of Arraterr and Fairymead, and Amber's despair sank still lower as she saw through the gloom a familiar figure running, robe flapping, towards them.

Jasper's voice shook hollowly as he slowed to greet them, the ashen expressions of his friends sending a creeping chill into his heart. His gaze sank upon Amber; she looked damaged almost, he couldn't place it. "I assumed you stayed the night at the Arraheng encampment," he faltered, anxiously searching her face.

She shook her head, too despondent to look up. "You should have been right." Her voice faded to a shuddering whisper. "We didn't get that far. We were trapped by Venom-spitters. And I couldn't leave them. And Jasper—" Tears stung into her eyes, revisiting it finally shattering the tremulous barrier that had been threatening to collapse ever since that fateful moment, and she sob-gasped, turning broken to the Prince. "I went over my time; I'm never going to fly again."

Her words crushed into his chest, and Jasper's face froze in horror. "Come here." He couldn't find any other words as he wrapped his arms around her and finally the last remnants of her defences crashed, and she clung to him, crying into his robe.

"It's all right," he murmured against her tears. *No it isn't, you imbecile,* his conscience railed in his head. *She's a Fairy. She's never going to fly again. How in the Realm can you say that to her? You can't even say the right thing, let alone make it happen. Call yourself her Prince?*

She lifted her grief-ravaged face to him, utterly bereft. "What am I going to do?"

Desperate to give her a hope he feared was beyond his reach, he set his jaw, demanding his voice to stay strong for her as he answered. "You're going to let me escort you home," he insisted. "And then you're going to make a hot drink, and call Ruby, and talk about dresses, or sword-fighting, or whatever it is you two find to go on about all the livelong day, and then you're going to go to bed, and in the morning the sun will rise and you'll get up. And we'll take it from there."

She nodded, with the intensity of one needing to be saved from drowning.

Jasper turned to the Arraheng, anguish etched into their waiting faces. "I'll see to her," he promised. "You should go. Neither of us want you to get hurt, on this of all nights; you've been through enough dangers for five lifetimes."

Behind her, Racxen wrapped a strong arm around her until her back pushed reassuringly against his body, and the wing-stumps neither the Prince nor even Amber herself dared yet bring themselves to touch pressed into his chest, and instead of letting go he held her even tighter.

Overwhelmed by his silent gesture of solidarity, Amber choked on emotion, having to force herself not to speak for fear of breaking down even as her heart overflowed.

"I'll see you tomorrow," he promised, understanding.

"I'll thank you tomorrow," she managed, trying to smile, as sorrow-fully the two brothers left.

Not knowing what else to do as he steered her back, Jasper slipped his cloak around her shoulders. "For the cold," he insisted. "The days will become warmer, and you will have less need for it, and rightly cast it off; but allow me to offer it tonight."

Numbly, she shrugged it off, and the Prince replaced it. "Of course you can handle it," he promised, "but in unprecedented circumstances it is folly to waste all your energy in trying to act normally. Tomorrow you will have slept, and it will not be so raw, but I'm not letting this be any harder than it has to be; I am not having you further traumatized tonight."

She nodded, following him wordlessly. The tug of weight at her back comforted her. And, for the time being at least, no one would know, and she could stave off for a few precious hours those awful, insistent questions she felt she'd never be able to answer.

Night-Mare

That night she dreamed she was flying, higher than she could remember, the night flashing past below her more beautiful than before. But now she was falling and she couldn't save herself.

Amber woke in cold sweat and clinging darkness. Fumbling for her clock, its glowing numbers mocked her with the lonely hours of night still to be conquered.

She pushed herself upright, scrubbing at her tear-stretched eyes, and stared blindly into the darkness. Numbly, she let her head sink onto her clenched fists.

It was your own choice, she reminded herself grimly. *It was the right thing to do.*

The night offered no corroboration, and she battled creeping doubts.

So why can't I deal with it? Amber glared savagely at the clock. *I can't eat for it. Can't sleep properly, let alone think.*

"I'm not going to let it erode my whole life." She reined herself back and repeated it aloud, although it was a travesty of anything she could yet believe. "This is the first night. It will get easier."

She had to stop; the words made her physically sick. She pounded the pillow with shaking fists; her voice a hollow cry, too distraught to care that no one was there to hear. "I'm never . . ." The sound of her tremulous voice, alone in the darkness, frightened her. Putting her fear into a statement made it irretrievable.

Tears soaked the pillow as she clutched it to her, rocking inconsolably, and her defences broke into wracking sobs. "I'm never going to fly again."

Talk to someone. It was as if she heard the King's wise voice beside the pillow. *Even if you don't know what to say. Especially if you don't know what to say. Don't bear the burden alone.*

Smearing away hours of tears, Amber took a deep breath, setting her jaw. Feeling dead inside, she forced herself to—as she had done so many times before now when the world had been brighter and broader and better—quietly swing her legs out from the bed, and then grabbed her cloak and padded out of the room.

As the Realm outside swirled around her with grounding normality, the land settling into peaceful slumber and the soft Fairy lanterns of the path awaking with a twinkle, Amber darted outside, the door clicking shut quietly behind her. The faded colours of the night now held no peace for her, and she ran on with one thing in her mind.

"Majesty, I've got a problem," Amber blurted wretchedly as soon as she saw the King amidst the Ring-haze, unable to wait for his greeting as she stumbled to a halt on the eve-dewed grass.

He looked at her with the calm acceptance bought of years of experience. "Go on."

Amber chewed at her lip in anguish. "You're not going to believe me," she warned miserably.

King Morgan gestured towards a low toadstool.

"Um." She sat down, fidgeted with her sash for a moment, worry written all over her face, and in her distraction promptly stood again. She swallowed. "You know I did something really stupid?"

The King spread his hands. "I would have called it brave and selfless," he rebuked mildly. "As do you still, deep down, just as you did at the time."

Amber was too scared to take in his words. "I–I'm so sorry. I can't fly."

The King watched her calmly. "I know, my child; both that it is true, and that it is far from shameful." Before she could summon the strength to ask how, he added urgently: "It only means you cannot fly in the manner to which you were once accustomed, nothing more. Amber, you were whole before this. You are still now."

Amber bit her tongue. There was no point at all in asking how, without wings, he thought that would ever be possible again.

"You will," he repeated prophetically, as his grey eyes fixed on her, "fly again."

"You can't say—"

He waved away her interruption. "I am not asking you to believe it now; it is too early, too raw. You will fly differently, but you will fly."

She was silent, biting back disillusionment and anger. Out of everyone, she hadn't thought the King would lie to her. "Without wings?" she blurted flatly, unable to stop herself. "They prove who I am."

The King shook his head swiftly. "Wings don't make you a Fairy, Amber; they don't have to. You are who you are, and the only ones who will ever demand proof of that are those who do not deserve it."

Amber could feel the tears welling again, and she blinked fiercely. "I'm sorry for—"

The King touched her shoulder. "The Realm doesn't always seem fair, Amber, but that is no reason to give up hope. Good things are possible even in the blackest of times."

There was silence from the youngster.

"I am neither denying nor deriding what it will demand of you," he assured her. "You are the only one in your position, and I will not patronise you by saying I know how you feel. Nor will I give you false promises." He looked at her directly.

"So mayhap in the end there is but one question I can ask you, and I hope that it does not sound harsh, because it is not intended to be:

Are you going to focus on the hundred things you can do, or the one thing you cannot?"

"I—" she stared into his face, desperate to believe the hope he was offering her. "I'm sorry, I'm not ready to hear this," she muttered brokenly, her gaze falling. "I know what you're saying makes sense, and it should make me feel better, and I thank you. I didn't know what else to do apart from come here and tell you. I know I can't expect magic words and complete answers, but it didn't stop me wishing for them."

"There is no shame in that," the King nodded. "I will leave you with your thoughts, here in a place of space and sanctuary and safety. I trust that what you need will come to you."

Amber nodded silently. There was nothing else to say.

"This will not destroy you, Amber Amazonite. 'Life is a grindstone: you can let it wear you down, or use it to sharpen yourself up.'"

At the recital of such an ancient Fairy saying, Amber automatically half-smiled. Oh, to be back to the first time she had heard it, when there had been nothing of note to worry about.

Gathering her courage, she looked up into the fiercely reassuring countenance of the King.

"You may be willing to give up on yourself," he admonished her. "I, however, am not."

As Amber managed to curve her mouth into a semblance of a smile, Morgan retreated.

Amber hastily stared upwards to stem the tide as tears threatened to well once more, but her resolutely fixed gaze fell on the far stars that danced with such life when they didn't deserve to, and the unfairness of it all threatened to drag away any ruined defences she still dared cling to.

You always thought when you were younger that coming here would solve anything. Letting out a shuddering breath, Amber knew there was no way in the Realm she could ever bring herself to believe that again. And yet, hollow-hearted and ripped to pieces as she felt, she found herself scrambling up onto one of the dusky-hued oversized toadstools of the Ring as she had imagined doing so many times before when worry had threatened to overwhelm her.

You thought those times were bad, but you're still standing. She grappled with the words, but they slid away miserably. So she said them again—out loud. And again.

As the most confident of her shaky declarations floated away to be caught in the magical calm of the permanent mists of this place, the strangling pain in her throat was beginning to ease even if the deadness in her heart couldn't yet lift.

Perched on top of the lowest toadstool, Amber sank her head into her hands and gazed out into the veiling haze of dusky-purple night that always seemed to encircle the Ring. Legend held that the mists could permeate the thoughts of those attending and soothe the mind and spirit of the weariest travellers. On her previous visit, Amber had felt so sure that nothing would ever seem to matter here any more—the day's cares and worries had faded almost before she had even reached the place. She had drawn strength from the eternity of the site; it had been here since the beginning of the Realm, and would always remain, regardless of the trials and worries weighing upon the Kingdom or beyond. Only here, she had dreamed as a winglet, would she always be able to find the peace she yearned for when the rest of the Realm seemed shattering. How foolish such a wish now seemed—broken before it had even begun.

Nothing can help me this night. Reality tore into her. Stone-faced against the effort, she tried to draw her feverishly racing mind to contemplation, in an attempt to draw answers from questions she could barely understand in a situation too cruelly raw to begin to accept.

Tears slowly clouded her eyes at the futility of it. Where was the meaning, not just in hers, but in all this suffering? She demanded this of the night's ethereal twilight. What had Racxen, Mugkafb—any of the Arraheng—done to deserve this? And where would it end? Her own people, she knew, were now also at risk, and who knew how many more fates would become ensnared before the end, whatever that would prove to be?

Such a short time ago, seemingly now a past age, she had been blissfully ignorant of the fate overshadowing the Realm and the Arraheng had been a tribe she had barely heard of. Yet if it hadn't been for those little-known, misjudged marsh-dwellers the Kingdom would never have had any warning. Two of them had opened her eyes to the desperate plight ahead, become her stalwart friends, and now together they were fighting to stay alive and be believed, striving to find the truth and recover a semblance of peace as they became embroiled in a desperate, irreversible struggle that could unite or divide the inhabitants, rip apart the Realm and shake its foundations to the core.

"Help me!" she pleaded aloud to the sky at the injustice of it all, her voice ringing high and scared and angry for the first time within the Fairy Ring, too upset to check it.

The demand died away unanswered into the eternal twilight until despite the soft touch of its enveloping cloak she was left feeling utterly abandoned.

Her mind went back to the mocking jeers of Beryl and the others. *Maybe they were right after all,* she admitted silently. *Maybe there's got to be a point where you stop defiantly pretending and resign to it. Maybe it'll hurt less that way.*

She shook her head, although there was no one there to see. *They might be right, but they're not here. They might be stronger, braver, wiser than me, but they've given up, and I'm not going to. That's got to count for something. There's got to be something I can do.*

"I'll find it, I promise," she murmured insistently into the night. "I'm not asking anyone to do it for me; I'm asking for help, but I'll make it happen with or without."

As she nodded to seal her pledge, the movement dislodged a tear from her eye. It fell with an indiscernible *plop* onto the toadstool before melting into the silence.

Incongruously, she heard the smallest of returning sounds. Instinctively glancing up, Amber drew her breath sharply in wonder as she saw standing at the edge of the Fairy Ring and silhouetted against the moon's bright gaze the proud profile of a darkly glistening equine creature, her two gnarled horns jutting as if to spear the stars dotting the horizon. As the Bicorn shook out her mane to walk towards her, Amber swore she saw stardust cloud to fleck the sky.

Amber's heart slammed. *Bright Shadow—the King's friend. The herd leader.* She willed her madly thumping heart to slow for fear of startling the beautiful creature. She could do nothing but stare at her, entranced, the vision filling her mind and driving out for a moment recent horrors.

The Bicorn shimmered through the far shadows into the centre of the clearing, her uniquely pale mane glinting against her dark neck as she picked her way delicately over the night-dewed grass until, almost gleaming in the soft darkness, she was so close that Amber could have reached out and touched her.

Inches away, her coat steamed in the cool air. Amber could differentiate every strand of fur, realising that the rippling effect of the Bicorn's coat was due to the way each hair alternated black and silver. She could follow with her eyes the twist of those tapering, pearlescent horns, discern the deeper grooves of age, the scratches cutting into the points where horn had connected with horn—or most likely blade, for Bright Shadow, she knew, had come to the aid of the King during the Sea Battle.

Amber stood, speechless in awe and wonder. She had never even seen a Bicorn until now, and she knew better than to try and touch one. She remembered what the King had said: many had tried to domesticate them, and all had failed. They were their own; uncatchable and unconquerable, the last truly untameable beasts to roam these lands. They held the "Lost Sight", whatever that might be, and the ability to find the last remnants of magic in the Realm. They bore only those whom they themselves chose—those sound of purpose and pure of heart. Amber felt a chill flicker of uncertainty. Did that sound like it included Fairies who cut off their own wings?

Yet the Bicorn was standing patiently several paces from her and hadn't moved a step. *Oh help,* Amber thought plaintively, frozen with worry that she'd spook her into bolting if she moved. *She's going to get bored and wander away.*

But the Bicorn wasn't going anywhere. It was as if, Amber worried, she were waiting for something.

For someone, Amber realised with a jolt. For a young, insignificant Fairy who couldn't do anything now that she had no wings, and who had never until now even seen a Bicorn before?

Exactly, a new voice inside her chanced, audible now that the panicked chatter in her mind had been stunned into silence. In that magical starlit glade on that Recö night, she realised that it had always been her voice. But it had taken until now; until the splintering of her Realm, for her to know that she could summon the courage to listen to it. And tonight she chose, with nothing else left to lose, not only to listen, but also to follow it.

"Bright Shadow," she murmured, "you have appeared to me for a reason, and I wish to uphold the trust you placed in me. Would it please you to allow me this honour?"

The Bicorn turned to Amber, her deep, liquid eyes holding the knowledge of night and day, of past and present. *I hope that sounded all right,* Amber fretted. *How are you supposed to speak to a Bicorn?*

Bright Shadow watched Amber gravely, for what seemed to the Fairy an eternity she would never have rushed. Then her noble head dipped into a courteous bow. She had chosen to help the Fairy.

Shakily drawing breath, Amber reached out a hand to the Bicorn to prepare to mount. She stopped abruptly. The herd leader was very tall, really, once you stood close-up. And, of course, she didn't have a saddle or anything.

Amber grinned to herself. *Just for tonight, trust that everything will be fine.* The moment the words formed in her mind the Bicorn knelt in a regal bow, her forelegs brushing the dewy grass.

Mounting carefully, Amber exhaled a breath she realised she'd been holding as the Bicorn, with a shake of her silvery mane against the flowing ink of her coat, stood tall again.

Amber buried her hands in the mane flowing across the Bicorn's withers, and entwined her fingers gently. Although logic dictated it reasonable that the Bicorn had such wiry, coarse hair, whimsy still made it surprising that it wasn't all sort of gossamer-light, billowing silk.

Amber watched silently, not wanting to break any seeming spell, as the Bicorn turned her head towards the soft-hued shadows of the forest beyond the Ring, her soulful liquid eyes glistening as she glanced this way and that to take in its sights, one ear swivelling to catch far off night-noises from the depths. With a flick of her tail Bright Shadow decided her path, treading the moon-silvered meadow towards the trees until their branches darkened the night even further for the Bicorn and her charge.

Minutes stretched beneath the canopy with only the light crack of twigs and the soft tread of hooves amidst snuffled breath to break the silence. As the trees began to thin the Bicorn's pace quickened and Amber sat firmer, gripping the sweat-slicked sides tighter with her legs as Bright Shadow's strides lengthened, until the trees merged into a close dark blur as the Bicorn burst into a canter.

The light of the moon opened above them as the trees parted and, in the bunch and heave of muscles, Amber gulped for breath and shut her eyes instinctively as Bright Shadow leapt. Feeling herself rocked once more in the Bicorn's familiar gait, she chanced to open them again.

She gagged violently—in the cold rush of buffeting winds inky nothingness flashed past; the Bicorn racing through the night along some invisible pathway through the stars as the darkened landscape flowed sickeningly far beneath them, the flecking lights of thousands of homes speckling below like an inverted sky until even they dropped back into the distance.

Soaring through the deepest night she had ever seen, Amber felt all she had known drop away like so much old skin as Bright Shadow pounded a skyway studded with myriad glinting stars.

The Lost Sight, Amber recalled, exhilaration billowing. *This is what it means.*

The Bicorn lunged forward in a burst of speed and the passing stars blurred into eternity as the night seemed to stretch out forever in this one joyous ride. With a sensation like damp silk being brushed across her face, Amber found herself enveloped in spectral mist, and as the feeling passed she saw they had risen through the cloud.

Her teeth beginning to chatter as they continued to rise through the rapidly cooling air, and gasping now that the atmosphere was getting thinner, Amber found herself realising how limited her own flying ability had been in comparison.

At the time, that had barely crossed her mind. She had been so excited; all her attention fixed on what she could now do, sparing no thought to that which still eluded her. It had served her well once, she'd eventually bring herself to admit to the King. Could it work again?

The precariousness of her position tore her from her thoughts as she realised, without being able to tell when exactly it had happened, that she had lost sight of even the remotest impression of land below them. Amber clung more tightly to Bright Shadow's mane as the Bicorn galloped deeper into the virgin night with only the stars as witnesses.

Against the howl of chilling wind Amber discerned another note growing upon the air: a rumbling, like rushing water.

The sea? Why are we this far out? Squinting against the wind until her eyes streamed, and with shredded wisps of cloud obscuring her vision, it was impossible to tell. But that din was too close to be coming from the ocean, surely?

As the noise swelled around them, Bright Shadow slowed, her hooves scattering stardust like sparks as she began descending through the air at a walk, her feet as carefully placed, her steps as reassuringly considered, as if she had been doing nothing more unusual than bearing her rider down a gravelled hill.

They passed through the haze of cloud again, descending into the warmer climes of the lower air where visibility eased; but this time there grew not the twinkling lanterns of familiar Fairy-homes dotting the night, but instead the roiling glimmer of chasmic darkness etched with breaking crests of white.

As the last vestiges of cloud parted and the rumbling cascaded into an all-enveloping roar, Amber stared down in abject disbelief as Bright Shadow tossed her head at the deafening water-thunder.

A vast, chalice-shaped cavern hung suspended in the air, its jagged walls plunging a sheer drop to a swirling basin wherein raged a maelstrom of churning waters more violent than the sea's waves thrashing beneath. The surrounding splintered chunks of rock, barely broad enough to stand on, scattered through the air served to accentuate its inaccessibility.

Juxtaposed against this scene in serene defiance of the ferocious coils of water spewing and writhing below, translucent, fragile-looking bubbles were following a stately route. Rising up from the epicentre of the whirlpool, they spiralled upwards in a purposeful, ever-widening orbit. It was difficult to tell at this distance, but the bubbles at the top seemed the largest; big enough to encompass a Fairy maybe, if the Fairy in question wasn't quite fully grown, and their wings were tucked down really flat, or—

Amber didn't let herself finish that thought. Why *had* the Bicorn brought her here?

Ideas churned, half-glimpsed and unknowably powerful, thrashing amongst the heave and swell as the surge resounded through the chamber, reaching up to the stars and filling Amber's mind. The wind rushing past called out to her soul, howling a song both lonely and liberating, and dangerously alluring. And what's more, it promised to summon her back.

She couldn't tell for how long she had been staring down, as if enchanted, before she felt Bright Shadow of her own accord turn back along the unseen path. Bicorn and rider moving as though through a dream, the restless dark gradually yielded to the return of speckling lights, on a journey that seemed to Amber to have lasted both hours and seconds.

On the sleeping Realm below, a curtain twitched as King Morgan bore witness to the signature glimmer flickering across the soft horizon as the Bicorn returned with her charge, alighting in a shimmer of silver amidst the toadstools, the muted colours of the Ring alive with more promise this night than the brightest day of Recö.

Her legs leaden as she swung down from the Bicorn, Amber stumbled as she touched the dew-soaked, substantial ground again. She couldn't shake the sensation that she might have left her stomach in the clouds.

Resting her head against Bright Shadow's sweat-dampened neck, she touched the whiskery velvet muzzle. "Thank you, herd leader," she whispered.

In farewell, Bright Shadow tossed her head in what could have been a nod.

Amber stepped back, and her breath caught in her chest. The King was there, standing in the swirling mists of the Ring like some new-remembered legend.

"You have flown."

Amber was too tired to argue; too filled with new sights and experiences. "Yes, Your Majesty," she acquiesced, managing something halfway between a glare and a grin in her elated confusion. The rush of night air thrummed in her memory as if now tangled in her veins, and gratitude spilled across her face as she bowed deeply. The full memory of the journey rushed into her, and she stumbled over the recollection: "Before I forget and it fades—through the flight I saw something . . ." She tried to do it justice with her words, but it couldn't have worked, for as she trailed off the King was watching her with an unreadable expression; of complete bewilderment, she wouldn't be surprised, given the ridiculousness of her disclosure. She waited.

"I will tell you its tale," King Morgan offered finally, "although it is lengthy, and we cannot have you freezing in its telling." He shrugged off his cloak and offered it to her. She took it gladly; hers was worn and thin in comparison with the King's rich throw, lined as it was with downy feathers and tufts of exotic fur, gifted by the Kingdom's animal inhabitants.

Wrapping it snugly around her, Amber watched sparks chink the night air as the King crouched to coax fire from flint. The flames flared within their circle of stone, their light reflecting on his wing.

Amber's heart sputtered—she'd never seen before, not until now when he wore no cloak to cover his tunic—King Morgan bore only one wing.

He turned back to her, majestic and imposing, and she could not help but marvel at his stature, for in that moment she glimpsed the smallest semblance of what had happened in times gone by; of the hardships he had faced and come through to stand before her now.

His strong features softened in the flickering light. "To allude to your previous doubts, do you think any less of me for it?"

Amber stared at him, speechless, the ghost of a smile growing on her lips as an infinite weight shifted just slightly from her heart and she dared risk hope once more. "But—" She broke off; how could she put into words that which blossomed in her soul, the strength that infused once more? So she just stared, grinning with amazement. "You could have told me before," she managed.

The King's returning look was direct. "My response neither dictates nor negates yours."

Amber thought on it in the silence. Impossibly, the night felt a shade lighter. "May I ask?" she risked hesitantly, twisting her sash tightly in her hands. "What happened, that meant you lost your wing?"

He didn't answer for so long that Amber thought her question had offended him grievously. She was just about to stumble her apologies, when his gaze shifted beyond her to the glimmering horizon where land met sky and the Realm stretched on forever.

"Many things happened," he answered softly, his voice stirring with the spectres of memory. "Those days will be forever entwined with the history of the structure you saw. It is a long tale, as I advised, and its telling will take us to the dawn, but if you wish to hear it I will share it, and take you home at first light."

Amber nodded silently and, as she tucked her feet up for warmth and drew his cloak around her, the King began to speak, his words swirling around her, drawing her to another place far from here and yet not so: to a time when the Realm was changed and was younger than it is now . . .

The King's Tale

Wordlessly, the King pressed his Gem to his lips for a long moment, tears brimming slowly in his eyes. "It is a story of love and courage, hope and despair; of part of our history."

The faded whisper of his voice swept back the years over the crackling of the fire as he introduced his tale in the traditional Fairy manner:

"Far, far away and yet somehow not so, somewhere between tomorrow and a long time ago: the Sea Folk you first glimpsed the other night were plentiful and prosperous. They lived far out to sea in the deepest, bluest water, further than our wings could carry us, and so we hardly knew of their existence, save for tales about them from the Nomads.

"They had their society, we had ours; until the cold seasons deepened into a Resté harsher than any before. Those times tested us both gravely; it became necessary for the Fairies to seek food from the sea, and the Maidens and Knights took shelter in the protected bays around our lands.

"There were none like the Sea Folk. They cared little for their own appearance, instead delighting in the beauty of nature around them. Their hair flowed long and coarse from the salt of the sea, and their great tails rippled silver and shades of dusk, large-scaled and shimmering with power. Being of the sea, they had remained virtually untouched by other societies and their verbal language was not of words we could understand, but instead consisted of hauntingly sung notes that would carry miles out across the ocean and shiver into the ears of those lost at sea to convey advice and guide them home.

"Honed by life in a voiceless underwater world, the Maidens and Knights seemed almost able to read the minds of others, as they would also speak in a language of touch and movement whereby a glance or a gesture would be interpreted by another as easily as if ten words had been spoken. Thus, the rumour grew at first amongst the Fairies that the Sea Folk were cold and uncommunicative, whilst for their part, our oceanic cousins probably viewed our method of communicating laughably primitive, and must have wondered how we could attempt to say one thing with our mouths when they could embarrassingly easily discern that we meant something quite different.

"Regrettably, this caused both parties to at first keep themselves to themselves, coexisting in civility and courtesy but with no real relationship to speak of, although of course this was a failing on our part and the problem lay in our apathy in discovering a solution rather than in anyone's actual differences.

"Fatefully the survival of both our peoples would soon prove inextricably linked. Pearl—the Queen—has ever nurtured a particular talent for language, and you may well have guessed correctly that she was the first—and for a while I'm ashamed to admit, the only—Fairy who could talk with the Sea Folk. I took tutelage from her, and filtered our teachings down. Due to her skills and compassion we grew to trust these people, and they us, and we began to truly admire each other's society. In time we became allies, and for either side the bond was mutually strong. It must be said that they were more adept at learning our language than we theirs, but we gave our best efforts.

"However, such unions have a tendency to be met with fear and opposition at the best of times, and during those uncertain days sinister forces were stirring in the deepest oceans. You doubtless remember your history lessons about the 'Scourge of Snakelocks,' Queen of the

Vetches—the pitiless minions she conjured forth through darkest arts from the blackest pits of the ocean, summoning them to her in an attempt to claim dominion over both ocean and earth. Snakelocks's gaze, as you know, could literally petrify a man, and she imbued her foul army with this elemental power. Through their ability to merge with the rock the Vetches could shift through caves and tunnels avoiding detection, and spring forth upon unsuspecting victims to turn their prey to stone.

"You can imagine the panic stoked as their reign of terror grew ever more far-reaching, and land after land fell plague to this ghoulish sorcery. In gathering her forces for what would become known simply as the Sea Battle, Snakelocks sought to enlist the Sea Folk in her war against the guardians of the air, believing they, being of her domain, would hate us with the same intensity she did. But no—they had pledged their allegiance to us as firmly as we had ours to them."

Amber could hear in his voice the effort of striving to keep an even tone as Morgan continued: "For their courage our friends paid a shocking price. The Vetch Queen's savagery was enough to leech all hope from the stoutest heart, and she forced droves of the Sea Folk into submission. Still more, however, refused to surrender their allegiance. These brave souls, betrayed by the traitorous amongst their own kind, were captured by the Vetch Queen and branded with gashes across the face before managing to flee for their lives. This act of barbarism served as a terrible warning to other Sea Folk considering siding with the Fairies, as marked thus for death our allies could find scant respite through the length and breadth of the ocean and were hounded as mercilessly as ourselves by the Vetch minions, no matter how well we attempted to protect them, or give them guarded shelter through the inland streams."

The King broke off, staring into the distance in remembrance of what Amber, shocked into muteness, could only guess. "Snakelocks's claws inflicted a lingering toxin, causing the wound to fester and never heal. That is why they bear scars to this day. The Vetch Queen's brands, intended to shame the allied Sea Folk, instead bore witness to the kind of courage that is now dying out, and any citizen who does not count such faces amongst the most beautiful in the Realm shall find no ears receptive to their poison.

"The free folk of the sea stood by us, risking everything, fighting for our survival as well as their own. The battle was long and bloody, and the cost high. Lives were lost, hopes were dashed, families ripped apart. And yet needs must; and we fought for our lives and those of our friends."

"In the midst of the war—"A shadow passed across the King's eyes, and so dark and pained grew his expression that Amber feared for him. She didn't want to stop him if he needed to say it, though. He might not have done so for years.

"She captured my Queen," he managed, his voice a gaunt, hollow breath, "and myself." The latter he muttered almost as an afterthought, all his pain drowning into the magnitude of the former. "Until that day I had never known pure evil. I cannot tell you of a pain like it; that wrenching, searing agony when I wished for death in that unendurable chamber." His voice trailed, the memories locked and private.

A moment passed in silence before Morgan spoke again, his voice building in strength: "Into this hell came a Sea Maiden—she had no name that I learnt of to honour in songs of valour, but she earned renown eternal through her actions that will echo through the foundations of our future. She infiltrated a secret water vent in the Vetch Queen's chamber, the location of which she could only access through the fragmented memory of being dragged there under force before being branded.

"Returning to the place of her torture, she hauled herself through tunnelled miles of biting rock moistened only by the scummed filth left where the Vetches had dragged their own rotting bodies through the darkness, into the bowels of the enemy strong-hold frequented by Snakelocks's best fighters, with nowhere to hide and no means of escaping were she to be seen.

"This Sea Maiden—I swear to you, I have never seen anyone so beautiful as when she dragged herself into that chamber, scuffed skin bloodied, scales missing, tale in ribboned shreds—with a last exhausted effort, to this day I know not whence she found the strength, flung herself clear from the floor and slammed into the Vetch Queen, striking her with the full, terrible force of her mighty tail.

"Snakelocks was knocked to the ground, her body slumping motionless at the kind of angles that would, had it been anyone else, have sent you pounding on their chest and yelling for the white chargers.

"Instead, my attention flew to the Sea Maiden; she lay unmoving where she had fallen. Her soft command filled the chamber as her eyes fixed briefly upon mine.

"'Your Queen is alive—go to her!' the Maiden's eyes closed with relief in the knowledge that she had delivered her message.

"Pearl. It wasn't too late. New hope surged through my veins, calling me to action, but even that could not block out what I next had to do, if I was to have the slightest hope of reaching and freeing her."

His voice crumpled into fevered pain, his breathing laboured and shallow, and Amber couldn't help but guiltily wonder whether it would be better for him to not relive this agony through its retelling.

His words spilled fast, as if it scorched his lips to speak them: "I was not chained; that would not have sufficiently indulged Snakelocks's tastes. Instead she had pinned one of my wings to the rock with the crudest of nails. I had to rip my own wing off to free myself." Morgan's voice grew as empty as his eyes. "It was already septic from the wounds she inflicted; the tissue was dying, the structure irreversibly weakened.

It did not take much physical force, in the end, to sever what felt like my soul from my body. And yet my true soul was relying on me; and I would be reunited with her if only I could go through with this. I cannot tell you how I did so—I cannot to this day even tell myself—for it was lost amongst the terror of the next moments as agony flooded. But it was done," he surmised quietly.

"And yet not done with, for what could have been consumes me even now in sleep, and into my waking hours fractured memories of that time have lodged like splinters, and they dig and twist when I least expect." His sigh shivered through the night. "Against these shadows, the dawn ever bids me wake and thus, by the grace of fortune and with the strength of friends, I stand."

His gaze took solace amongst the flames. "Crazed and half-blinded by the pain I ran, I know not how long, until I blundered into yet another chamber, and when that disbelieving cry spilled like a beacon through the darkness I knew I had found my love.

"I fell to my knees to hold her, and my shaking fingers met with the manacles clamping her hands even as my lips found the wet salt of her cheek. I had not so much as my Gem to ease her wounds with, for it had been torn from me and dashed against the rocks by the Vetches. There was nothing in that barren hell to break the shackles with, and so I slicked her wrists with the copious blood still slipping from my wounds and arduously squeezed free her bruised hands, until at last she was released—her hands clutched mine without restraint and my Queen, my everything, was free and alive and safe. We flung ourselves into each other's arms, tears coursing down our faces, giddy with exhaustion, and the horrors and agonies dissolved into the delirium of relief as we clung to each other.

"But a grotesque scream shattered our reunion, echoing through from the chamber whence I'd fled as Snakelocks regained consciousness to scream her retribution.

"That our only salvation now lay, after the agonies we endured to find each other, in once more parting ways was a cruelty we had not time to rail against. Having but recently run through, I had a better recollection of the dungeon-complex than my wife. So I promised her that the quickest passage would be the left, when in fact I knew it to be the longest—and of course, blessings on her, Pearl demanded that I take that and she the longest—and before she could realise my deceit she had unwittingly saved herself without argument.

"Taking the other path, I was afforded the dubious satisfaction of hearing Snakelocks's thunderous pursuit devouring the distance along my route rather than my love's, and I pounded every spare scrap of strength into the ground as I fled. When the monster's roar no longer echoed behind me I should have known better than to have felt relieved—for in all probability she had merged back into the rock to spring forth in ambush at any moment—but I could not let that possibility slow my steps, for I had to find that nameless hero; that wounded woman.

"At last one of the tunnels seemed to my racing mind familiar, and my fear grew in a different form as I ran down the dark passage, slipping on the rocks, unsure of what I would find. As the cavern grew suddenly from the narrow blackness, my heart seized and I skidded in my efforts to stop. The small form of the Maiden lay immobile.

"*She's just resting. She said she would rest.* My tongue thickened against the words my heart refused to believe. She hadn't moved from where I had left her. From where I had left her, alone in the dark; so long ago it must have felt to her. My chest was seized with a dread chill, as if Snakelocks were already succeeding in turning me to stone, and I ran to the Maiden, my footsteps echoing obscenely loud and out of place through the dank chamber.

"I fell to my knees beside her, and as she lifted her head my heart bloomed, but her pool-grey eyes fixed just loosely on mine, and her voice trembled hoarse and strained, barely audible despite the near-silence: 'I die now.'

"I cradled her head, trying to block out the terrifying resignation in the shockingly weak voice that I could still in my mind hear singing out hope across storm-ridden seas as she once had. Yet it would have taken more than the words of a King to retrieve her, so I scanned the darkness quickly. 'Hold on, my lady.'

"The ice of her touch seeping through the dungeon-torn tatters of my cloak as she clutched my robe with frozen fingers, I gathered her chill form to me, willing my warmth into her against the fierce cold of the passage as I lifted her into my arms, and stumbled through the filth of that starless claustrophobic night.

"I heard not the echoes of my footsteps crawling into darkness, only the breathing of the Maiden. Mayhap enemy ears heard me; I was long past caring. All that mattered in those moments was she whose name I didn't even know.

"Slipping on glistening stones, I heard at last a familiar, soothing rush bubbling through the cloying dark, and the glitter twinkling on the lightless flow before us spoke of cleansing rest after the longest of journeys.

"The river's song billowed around us as I waded into its sedate flow, and I lowered the Maiden's body into the water, supporting her face just clear of the surface. She heeded not the drop in temperature; at the caress of the water washing over her she closed her eyes in relief as her lips parted in the ghost of a smile.

"'You have returned to the Realm of your brethren and sisters,' I tried to reassure her as I stroked her sea-tangled hair, holding her close and wishing so desperately that I could say something that would take her pain away. 'Do you hear the far sea singing to welcome you home?' And mayhap she did, for the swell rose like music as it lapped around us.

"I swallowed wretchedly, the tears refusing to stay in my eyes. 'Were you a Fairy, I would wear your Gem to keep you with me; to prove I will never forget you.'

"'It is not needed.' Her breath was barely a whisper now, yet her voice shivered with conviction. 'What we have done will echo as ripples across the ocean through all the years this Realm will see.'

"Her words were needles stitching the wound in my heart, but I would have given anything for her to have instead raged against me, if only it could have bought her a few more minutes or hours, for I could see her light dimming even as she spoke.

"'I'm sorry—I'm so sorry—' I couldn't stop myself; it grew like a mantra. 'I wish I could save you,' I whispered brokenly. 'You saved my life, and I left you—'

"The Maiden shook her head. 'There are some things one cannot be saved from by another, and I fear death less than dying alone.'

"'That is one fate that cannot befall you,' I promised. 'I cannot alter your course, but I will stay beside you until after the very end of your journey.'

"The Maiden's smile was like a stream easing over barren rocks to sing of better times. 'Then it is as well as it can be,' she murmured.

"Cradling her in my arms, I knelt with her in the cold swirling water, talking to her to stave off the waiting dark. And because she was a Sea Maiden and I didn't know what else to say, I spoke of cleansing streams running glass-clear through meadows, and of the ocean's spray pounding raw and elemental against the rocks, and of a green rocking sea stretching out beneath the sun forever.

"The echoes of my voice died away, and my fast breath alone filled my ears. The Maiden no longer moved. I fancied her eyes still flickered slightly to fix on things—but it could have been just that: a fancy. I could almost feel her slipping from me. But I have felt such things in battle and been proven wrong. That is what I clung to then, for even in such times there are glimmers that must be clutched at no matter how short-lived they prove to be.

"She looked at me, and more passed between us in that glance than I will ever be able to explain or fully understand, and there in the darkness I smiled at her, forgetting where we were, forgetting the pain, forgetting everything; and as she smiled back her eyes sparkled as they once had.

"That moment, in spite of the sickness I felt after, will shine forever in my mind, and oftentimes I find myself reliving it even now for fear I might unwittingly one day be unable to picture her face, or to remember what her scale-like skin felt against mine; for that was the last moment when her breath mingled in the air with mine, and her hands held mine of her conscious will.

"It lasted just a precious second or two, and then her eyes no longer followed mine. I promised myself that I was just missing her pulse amidst the frantic beating of mine as I pressed my searching fingers against her neck, and tried to convince myself that if only I hadn't been shaking so much I would have seen the rise and fall of her chest proving she was still gifted with breath. I argued with the impassive dark that I was a warrior by training, not a healer; that the final judgement could not be mine. And yet I knew, as I had no choice but to know, that she had breathed her last.

"And although I knew there had been no way she could possibly have lived, tears welled in my eyes at the suddenness and unfairness of it. I knew it was just the shell of her left beside me, but the shell was all I had, and I gathered her limp body close to me and ran my fingers gently through her tangled hair, stroked her cheek again once more as I had in life; not wanting to say goodbye, not wanting to lose one I had grown to love.

"A coldness deeper than that of the sea was clutching her now, carving a breach that could never be crossed and warning of the futility of my warmth. And still I stayed with her, in case I was mistaken, wishing so much that I was, deep down knowing that I couldn't be but refusing to accept and believe that she was really gone.

"Yet gradually I realized I could not stay here forever and that, however much it hurt me, for her sake I had to be strong and let her body go to its resting place, for that was my last duty to perform for her save for ensuring that henceforth she would dwell in the memories of all who loved her.

"Thus I let go of her body, though it hurt me so much, and I watched her sink beneath the surface for the last time, as the gentle current carried her away along unseen passages to the open sea—well, in my mind it did, for even though I feared that the clinging weeds of the tunnels would catch her body, I knew her spirit would flow with the clear waters far beyond the misery of this hellish place to where the ocean spray glitters on far beaches beneath bright sunlight.

"And then I was standing alone again, staring after her in the darkness with only the numbing embrace of the water to block out the pain, until at last I turned to wade wearily back through the clinging slime of the pools and across the jagged echoes of the rocks.

"My ragged cloak weighed sodden and heavy upon my shoulders, and I found myself half-wishing that it would drag me down and hold me there so I would not have to trudge, my heart gouged through and soaked to the skin, through a Realm devoid of such a soul, while the river still twisted and played in a cruel parody of life when no light should ever glimmer on water again.

"Lost in memories I staggered through the passages, imagining her beside me and knowing that she never would be again; the hollow realisation cutting so raw it physically hurt.

"As my final tears mingled to entwine forever with the water that would flow out to meet her beloved home, I heard—was it simply wishful thinking and a breath of wind through the tunnel?—her lilting voice clear once more in my mind: *Where the sea meets the sky, you will see me once more.* I held the memory close in my heart, and clinging to it, found my way out of the tunnel."

In the King's heavy sigh, Amber heard a door closing on the past.

"As you know," he continued gravely, "the battle eventually ended. This was Gorfang's last stand before he gave up his powers for his people and passed into legend, but this was not Gorfang's hour. He fought astride the mighty Dragon Akutan—yes, the blind old albino lizard upon whose back he was borne unnoticed into the besieged town of Arkh Loban. You remember that Snakelocks and her minions had the power to turn their victims to stone just by meeting their gaze? Akutan was therefore the only foe she could not vanquish, and he did what Dragons do best. With their leader destroyed, the Vetch force attempted to evade capture by melting back into the rocks. But without the fell power of Snakelocks they were weakened to the extent that the Sea Folk were able to bind them captive in their rock form. They remain held there to this day, their evil effectively banished through their imprisonment."

The King paused. "There were celebrations, of course there were, as one must ensure for those who have risked and lost so much. But inevitably, and not just for the fighters, mark, the next weeks and months seeped for many into the struggling toil of fearing to sleep and loathing to wake. I owed Pearl then more than could be repaid; for even as I tried to stave back her nightmares, she listened when I woke in the night-morn, whispering words to soothe my fears and acknowledge my loss. She did what only she could—made me see that for the Maiden's sake I could not let her memory be one of anguish and sorrow, but one reflecting how she was in life—a beacon to be held close to the heart in stormy times, firing courage to forge a brighter future.

"It was Pearl who initiated the development of a structure that has become an integral part of our society, and which allowed the Maiden's prophecy to come true: the Fountain. It is a transportation device of sorts—it is best perhaps that I leave the description at that—yet to explain its meaning properly I must return to the effect the war had on our sea-dwelling allies. Their population was decimated by their involvement and the survivors, having as an entirely peaceful people engaged in sustained combat for the first time in their history, were severely weakened. The Sea Folk sensed instinctively that the recovery, and indeed continuation, of their race demanded now a wrenching choice: to return to open water and forsake the energy-sapping enchantments that had carved their identity as the last magic-wielders of the Realm, or to keep their unique powers and instead turn their back on the sea, their spiritual home.

"Yet magic of an equal opposing force was required to negate the sorcery of the Vetches and ensure that Snakelocks and her remained imprisoned insentient in the deepest stone of the Realm.

"The Sea Folk elected, after much soul-searching, to return to the open ocean: all, that is, apart from one Maiden. She alone chose to forsake the sea, and so became the sole guardian of the retained magic of an entire people. Turning her back on her home, the Water Nymph—as she is known, for she took thereafter the form of womanhood—retreated through the bowels of the Realm, sealing the way behind her through magic so that none other might be burdened with her duty, to the chamber of what henceforth became known as the Enchantress's Fountain, and it is her power alone that prevents the Vetches from returning. From her solitary vantage point, she views all through the bubbles designed to afford sightings of any such incidents as could precede a return of the Vetches should they ever, fates forbid, find a way to break from their restraints and mass an attack again.

"Long seasons have passed since the Nymph made her decision. She grows old, as do we all who were blessed with surviving those atrocities, and her power weakens as her time wanes. She shuns all attempts at contact; she trusts neither Fairy nor Arraheng nor any other peoples you could mention. I am uncertain whether she would help anyone any more. She cannot be judged for this, for her sacrifice has been great indeed, and the sights that have flickered, distorted and impossibly distant against the filmy surface of those orbs, could slide the most mindful into madness. Mayhap she no longer views the outside world as her Realm at all.

She refuses to venture from the chamber, and so her heroism is infused with particular tragedy, for she has not set eyes on water for many long years, save for that which crashes against the rocks beneath the Fountain—and even then she only sees it, separated by the sheer drop of the rock-face from the basin; she has not felt its touch on her skin, nor become one with it as is the wont of her peoples. To endure separation from the hallowed sea itself, to suffer the birthplace of her people fading into mere memory; her transformation must have affected her in ways we can scarce imagine. That she may one day return to complete her pilgrimage is a hope that I fear dwindles in her heart, and one that I would dearly wish to see rekindled."

The King shook his head. "My apologies; speaking of it tugs at my memory, and recalls to me those whom we must never forget. Yet my tale is not finished: before they returned to the deepest oceans to rebuild their lives, our sea cousins shared one more communion with us, helping to create a monument to our allegiance and a permanent symbol of the union between Air and Water: the Enchantress's Fountain.

"To this day, a Fairy blown off-course over the sea has never drowned; no matter how fierce a storm they have fallen into they have been borne ashore by willing hands. And on the last day of Recö we take a great feast, enough to be stored through Requë to sustain a full clan for the bleak Restë months, down to the Southern Sands. We strap the casket hampers to rush-woven rafts, and set them floating amongst the bobbing lanterns lit in memory of those who died all those years ago.

"The night of its completion saw the Sea Folk return to open waters, and thus we gathered, in the eternal quiet of the Silent Sound, and struggled to say for perhaps the last time farewells and anything else we could put into words to those who had stood by us, fought with us, and whose friends and relations had paid a price that could never be settled.

"The finality of that night churned amidst my memories, and as I walked back alone—one could easily access it then, for the Water Nymph had not yet set foot in it, nor turned it into a solitary fortress—I found myself drawn to the deserted Fountain in its new-formed splendour, its orbs glowing a soft lustre to rival the moonlight. Wandering, entranced, across the curve of the rock ledge to gaze into the fathomless vision-pools of the bubbles, I could not help but think of my dear friend who had not lived to see this structure, nor the peace it represented.

"But then—oh, joy, I saw her. I tell you true; she was in the bubble, and I saw her not with broken body and shattered hope but whole and well and at peace.

"A thousand words welled in my mind, but the suddenness of seeing her and the impossibility of having any time at all whilst knowing there must be only seconds stole all capacity from me.

"'I love you, my friend.' It was all I could manage. And yet, if I were being granted the time for but one phrase, it could not have left me wanting. After nights of futile pleading to the stars, I could ask for no more.

"She smiled—oh, that glorious smile, so beautiful through my sudden veil of thankful tears.

"'Peace, Morgan.' She stood firm in that ephemeral bubble as her words faded, and neither of us spoke, or needed to speak, in the sacred silence as she placed her hand against the film of the bubble. 'You did not need to see me now to know that it is likewise for me also.'

"And then I stretched out my hand to hers, to reach her just once more, and the bubble burst abruptly at my touch. And I was left alone, standing there in the fading twilight, tears falling from my cheeks.

"Yet I smiled, even as I tasted their salt on my lips, for to have known her was better by far than to have been spared this stabbing grief for one who now seemed lost forever but whom I would come to learn that I could never really lose. I had loved her, and she had loved me, and we had both known; and that was something worth surviving for—something precious that could never be taken away.

"I told myself that I could either let my memories of her blossom into a life-giving stream, or allow them to stagnate into the kind of pool wherein I could wallow and drown. As I resolved to honour the former I felt a light touch; I told myself it was nothing but the breeze blowing over my face, for I knew there was no one there but I, but it felt to my heart like the touch of a Sea Maiden. And so it dried my tears, even though a part of me felt they should never dry for fear that it would seem I had forgotten.

"The memory lingering, I walked home slowly beneath a sky and moon that would never more look the same. That night I feared nightmares, but instead I slipped into a clear dream wherein a Maiden swam through an everlasting green sea beneath swathes of sunset-purple sky."

Silence settled heavily as the King stared into the flames. "So that is my story." Against the glow of sinking embers his eyes glittered, bright with the vividness of memories conjured, so close he seemed almost returned there. "Now it must continue, despite and because of the shapeless terrors twisting like smoke into our minds. We will not wait for the light to come—we will grab the torch, stride out undaunted into the darkness, and send the shadows fleeing. We will accomplish this not because it is foretold as the esoteric fate of a nation in the texts the Emperor relied upon, but because it is within our grasp. We are not resigned to wait for heroes; we are compelled to become them and capable of doing so, because we know, in the deepest part of our being, that we can accomplish so much more than we might allow the doubtful masses to speculate upon. I know we will accomplish this, because instead of leaving us her name, that Maiden bequeathed us her legacy."

Roanen

In the private quarters of the castle, a curtain-edge at the entrance of the Queen's chamber flickered, and Laksha the handmaiden stepped through.

"Sorry ter disturb," the Goblin warned brusquely, eyes glittering with restless energy almost as if she were back with Gorfang, stealing him out of the Lobanian dungeons. "But there's a . . . gentleman, I s'pose, ter see yer. I told him you weren't ter be disturbed, but he relinquished his weapons an' asked usin' yer full name."

Pearl eyed her friend, an unspoken agreement conveyed within that glance. There were but two men who held such knowledge, and she was married to one. The other . . . could not be possible; the knowledge must have fallen by foul means into the possession of another. Times were evidently direr than she had judged.

"Thank you, Laksha." Steeling herself with a melancholy sigh, the Queen slipped a long-handled dagger beneath her sleeve and prepared to greet her guest.

As her guard stalked forth to bark a summons, the man stepped through in a swirl of dust-marred desert garb, his face obscured by the folds of his hood, and bowed low.

A pause hung unplanned in the air as everything the Queen had thought to say fled from her mind. She drew a careful breath, staring at the cloaked figure intently, and took care not to drop the dagger in her surprise. "Hash-hakka en hashto Rashtakka?" she chanced hesitantly, not quite believing that there could still be one to give the answer she sought. "Speak you the tongue of Dragons?"

The figure straightened, his hood falling back to reveal the creased smile, the shrewd eyes glittering warmth amidst the weathered skin and days' stubble of a travel-worn face. "Shai, ashanta wai Rashtekksho hashta-sesh," he answered softly, his voice an un-placeable combination of accents. "Yes, for I see the Realm through Dragons' eyes." He nodded courteously. "My Queen."

"And student," Pearl replied wryly, her eyes dancing with amusement as a grin of delight spread across her face and she stepped forward to embrace him. "Roanen the Wanderer—too many seasons have passed since last I looked upon the face of so dear a friend."

The Nomad's smile mingled approval with surprise. "You remember our training, all those years ago?"

Pearl smiled back, archly. "I couldn't forget." Her eyes misted as the seasons fell back . . .

"That's not fair!" she shouted, as his blows continued to rain even as she fell.

"You think fairness will save you in combat?" the Nomad retorted bluntly. "You think life is unfair, wait until you stare death in the face. You're doing well enough to have the breath to shout at me during this, so you should be proud of yourself."

"But I'm just a—" Oh, fates, she hadn't wanted to say that, but the words had already half slipped out in retaliation before she could bite them back.

Roanen's eyes flashed disappointed anger and he clipped her smartly round the head so that she had to parry once more and continue to fight. "Do not make the mistake of thinking I will allow you whatever excuse you were crafting," Roanen countered, not ceasing in his measured attacks, "for it will not be allowed to you on the battlefield or down some deserted alley in the town. It is not because you are young; it is not because you are female. It is because you are weaker and slower than you will become; you are as yet clumsy, you have no bank of techniques to draw upon, you are tired, you have never been in this situation before and you do not know how to handle it. Strength can be developed, knowledge imparted, technique honed, experience gained. Hence the practice. Now—again."

She bit her tongue, his words stinging like smarting blows even as she heard their wisdom. She dragged a dirt-stained hand across her sweat-stung eyes and prepared for the next onslaught. "Yes, Sire. Sorry, I'm ready n—"

"Your enemy—" He swung a blow before she'd finished. "—Will not wait!"

She sidestepped hastily and parried, all thoughts of speech fleeing from her mind as they clashed once more.

"Good," he barked in approval. "There will always be enemies stronger than you, Pearl, as there will always be those stronger than me—than Gorfang himself even—but your willingness to learn stands you in far better stead than some block-headed brute who is convinced he has it all already. Don't stand there listening—prove me right!"

And they strove forwards and back; tiny specks of life amidst the endless scalding desert sands skirting an outlaw town, barely visible within whatever great scheme was playing out; fighting their chances and bettering their odds, beneath the shadow of an ever-growing threat under the near-blinding sun . . .

The Queen blinked quickly against the glittering veil brimming before her eyes as she drew back to the present. "My life has followed a winding path since, but your training will ever remain the fire in which my spirit was first forged, and that flame will never be smothered. But enough of the past; you have not come merely to reminisce, Roanen. The Wanderer's path is never aimless. Why does it lead you here after so many years?"

He smiled sadly. "I wish my tidings were brighter, my lady, but I come to warn you of rumours from the desert. There has been word of an unprecedented influx of Goblins, too sudden and dangerous to ignore. Since Gorfang banished their King, they have in depleted numbers congregated to haunt the square with their accursed market, and in straggling packs marauded across the plains; but now they are massing; they remain lawless, leaderless, and yet they are gathering at the site of their last stand all those seasons ago."

Pearl stared in horror. "Their King? You cannot tell me that Thanatos—" the words stuck, unfinished, as her mouth dried.

The Nomad glanced distractedly to the doorway, as if even in this place of safety he could no longer rest. "Logically, history must have rendered that impossible," he acknowledged. "And yet the situation defies such reason."

The Queen sighed, her eyes heavy with grim realisation. "That history is slipping into legend; even you must acknowledge that. Can heroes' words still hold such enchantment as they once did? What is left to prevent the Goblins' resurgence now that magic is fading from the Realm? The entire Realm, Roanen; it is not just in Arkh Loban that cracks are beginning to show. We received word of another foe only recently, one the Arraheng people call 'Venom-spitters'."

Roanen's expression tightened. "Two monsters drawn forth," he mused in an undertone. "Mayhap there is some commonality, a single joining thread as yet unseen, which will in due course prove key to vanquishing both." He grimaced as the answer floated ephemeral beyond his reach. "The Venom-spitters I will investigate at once," he promised. "We may have just as little time to strike against the Goblins, however," he warned his protégé. "The Arkhans have heroes within their own community—there is a young woman, bestowed a volatile heritage, who is attempting to unite a broken people. She has become a figurehead to an oppressed populace, but the fate of a nation is too great a burden for one, however brave, to bear. The Arkhans need our help. How great must the numbers of Goblins swell to before we step in?"

"Our responsibility is clear," Pearl nodded. "Yet we can ill afford to fulfil it when we ourselves stand to come under siege from elsewhere. The situation presents a somewhat eldritch advantage to both invaders. Moreover, we know so little about the Venom-spitters."

Roanen spread his hands. "Both threats will reach to the furthest corners of the Realm if left unchallenged. If we must fight, far rather be it on our own terms."

"You speak the truth." The Queen's eyes closed in pain. "But, Roanen, we have borne this burden once before. To have to ask my people to do so again—" She lifted her face, steel rising in her gaze. "I will discuss this with Morgan, and send ambassadors to Loban. We cannot stand idle when lives are in danger that we have a chance of saving. I only hope our resources stretch to our requirements, however, for here meanwhile we will make the necessary preparations. Fear must not be allowed to temper our defences; we need use all the time we have to fortify our lands and protect those whom we hold dear and are responsible for. This concerns us all. We will play our part with all the fortitude we can gather."

Roanen nodded smartly. "Aye, my lady; I will send word at once." The Nomad's expression softened as he beheld the Queen's careworn face. "Times are changing, but not all for the darker. There is talk also of light . . . of Dragons," he offered carefully.

Pearl studied his face for a long moment. "The understanding has always been that they left the plains after the Sea Battle; that there was not enough magic left in the Realm to sustain them."

Roanen returned her look. "The general understanding, certainly."

Absorbing the revelation in his words, the Queen's voice faltered for the first time. "There was . . . something I wished to ask you."

Roanen watched her closely. "You have heard it, haven't you? They call to you still."

Pearl's gaze grew searching, as something akin to fear flickered across her face. "I have told this only to Morgan: three nights ago, I could not sleep. When I went to the window, from out across the meadows rang a sound that had not spoken to me for many, many seasons. One I have scarce been able to put aside since."

Roanen covered her hands with his. "Once you hear a Dragon's call, only one thing can give you peace. You search for its source the rest of your life, no matter whether fortunes good or ill visit you thereafter."

Pearl nodded wretchedly. "And yet they say that way lies madness."

"Aye," the Nomad acknowledged, unperturbed. "Some may call it madness to chase a dream; but a greater sorrow lies in letting it slip between your fingers for want of a little courage and conviction. Rather run with the madness, than drown in the sorrow."

Pearl arched a brow. "I cannot think why you are being hounded thus by the Authorities." The ghost of a smile faded from her lips as her voice grew restless. "I cannot ignore their call. They beckon me, and I know that one day I must summon them in return. Perhaps it will help us; perhaps not even they can, yet I feel bound to try."

Her voice dropped guiltily. "Still, how can I leave now, with the Kingdom and the Realm itself in straits such as these? I turned my back on the possibility of a Dragon-touched life; those years feel now like an existence I can never again claim as my own. My place now is here, with my people."

"It is your love for your people that will lend your plea strength, my lady." Roanen's lilting voice was calm, his words assured. "You remember the words you spoke to the stars on that Mid-Recö night?"

Tears quivered suddenly in the Queen's eyes at the reawakening of such a long-held dream, put to earth sorrowfully and silently as the first tendrils of magic seeped irretrievably from the Realm. She nodded, barely trusting herself to speak.

"They never came when I tried to call," she warned, her strained voice holding the fears of an apprentice instead of the confidence of a Queen. "Night after night I called them, and the skies yielded nothing. I began to believe what I had at first been told; that the language had no use, that the Dragons were dead. My training with you became a dream—a treasured memory, but one I feared could never truly be sustained through the waking world. Times have changed, Roanen, with the Realm itself. Many things have."

"Many things, like the dream, have not."

She watched him, wondering, and in her eyes he saw the curious chancer from her teenage years return, sizing up the challenge. Roanen resisted the urge to smile. She had come so far hence, but it was good to see her like this again. Contemplating her potential. Standing on the threshold of shattering her limitations.

Pearl tugged a hand through her hair distractedly as she weighed up her options. "I will never forget it," she admitted, "no matter how many seasons I am graced with."

"Then guide it to completion." The Nomad's voice wrung with passion. "Has the need ever been greater? Speak the words you learned for such an occasion as this. You alone continued learning. Your knowledge now surpasses even mine."

"My knowledge now? For all you know, Roanen, I stopped studying long ago."

"For all you know, my Queen, the fact that you didn't may prove a vital factor in the salvation of the Realm. Why continue for so many years, if not to hone your skills for such a time as this?"

Pearl was quiet. "Mayhap it wasn't just about the Dragons," she offered. "Mayhap I wanted to keep a piece of that life for myself."

Roanen nodded acceptingly. "In that case, perchance the girl you once were would not feel as though quite all the magic had faded, if you were to let yourself in this matter follow your heart. A gift is never lost," the Nomad insisted. "You were ever my best student. You alone had the tenacity to truly master that language. Call—for if they answer to anyone, it will be you."

Pearl grimaced. "You taught me the theory, but can I make it real? What if they do not come?"

"What if you never call?"

"Don't answer me with questions, Roanen, it never got you anywhere when I was younger. What if I come back empty-handed?"

The Nomad shook his head. "None return empty-handed who at least make the journey. You know how it works; it is not just the words, it is the intention behind them. You need to trust yourself, my lady, as those honoured to be close to you do. There will come a time when the need for your skill is far greater than that for our swords."

A Minor Complication

The doors cracked against the wall as Jasper strode in too hastily. The raised voices he'd heard from the hall stilled abruptly. "Sorry," he mumbled. Father and one of the horse guards, a sturdy, crag-faced individual he recognised as Magnus, were standing at opposing ends of the desk; Father tugging distractedly at his beard, the other man obstinately folding his arms across his chest. They made no mention of the Prince's indiscretion, remaining instead locked in each other's gaze.

"Your mother has received word from Arkh Loban," Morgan offered carefully by way of explanation into the silence, his voice softening in Jasper's presence even as he curtailed Magnus's obligatory interruption with a steely glance.

"The people of Loban are in trouble; the Goblins are virtually laying siege to the town. There have been uncanny sightings close to Fairymead also, both of Goblins and of a monster hitherto unknown by our people; an old enemy newly re-encountered by the Arraheng—yes, I am referring to the Venom-spitter, son. It is no great assumption that the two are linked, but we need to know why. We have already relayed a request for arms; the Queen spoke earlier with a desert Nomad who has eloquently asserted the severity of our situation by suggesting that there may soon come a time for the sake of the entire Realm—and this man does not scaremonger—when the intervention of Dragons may be necessary. And, not withstanding natural bias, there is only one person I would trust with that task."

"Impossible as it has proven for the past two-score years," Magnus broke in.

"Mother?" Jasper hazarded faintly, staring in disbelief at his father. "You mean she learnt the Dragontongue?" He could vaguely remember being told of it in lessons; but it had been described only as an archaic, long-dead language the Lobanian Emperor had, for his own disreputable motives, decreed must be learnt by all boys before adulthood. Jasper couldn't remember anyone getting a decent grasp of it. He had never got round to even attempting to read it; he hadn't seen the point.

The King guessed the extent of his son's recollection, and smiled wryly. "The ability to commune with Dragons gives one great power—the like of which the Emperor did not want falling into the hands of 'mere womenfolk.' So, of course, instead of going through the authorised channels, Pearl took herself off into the desert—as the Dragons were, or are, cold-blooded, it was ever their last refuge. There, she apprenticed herself to Roanen, a displaced Nomad who had, shall we say, a more immediate connection to the language than a textbook, and who cared nothing for the fool customs of a bigot.

"Pearl's hunger for learning, fuelled by the injustice she had experienced, fostered a single-minded dedication and tenacity sufficient to attain linguistic mastery the extent of which remains unsurpassed to this day." His smile faded into thoughtfulness. "In times after, when we were married, she tried to teach me what she knew; but in my learning I lacked the thirst for success she had needed, and so I never approached her level of skill. She alone I believe can commune with any Dragon ill-fortuned enough to have remained in the Realm without its kin."

"Sire, it has been long since any such communion," the horse guard interjected. "Any Dragon remaining would, like as not, be an abomination of the proud allies we once knew. There is no predicting the dangers we could be exposing her to."

"Magnus, what is the risk of attempting defiance, against the risk of falling prey to apathy and submission? The beings my wife still speaks of were lofty in both nature and stature, and I intend to honour both their memory and her judgement in my decision. Pearl knows the dangers better than I do, and I respect those I love enough to let them follow their own path."

Jasper stifled an unnecessary cough, but the horse guard's attention did not waver. "Sire—"

"Magnus, you may be able to soothe the wildest of Bicorns with those dulcet tones, but if you try to turn the Queen to your logic your mistake will prove sorer than any unseating they have dealt you."

His attendant's gaze remained stony. "The attempt is doomed; I cannot in good faith advise otherwise."

"So you imagine; yet it is decided."

"Should I go to Loban?" Jasper offered against the silent tension.

His father relaxed visibly at the suggestion. "Good man. We need information, and we need allies."

Jasper blinked. He'd hoped for more advice than this. "Information," he nodded. "Allies. Right."

"Loban. Of all places, Loban." Stepping out into the damp cold of the morning, Jasper slid the massive oak doors shut behind him and tried to compose his thoughts, pushing the hair out of his eyes and rolling back his shoulders. "To Loban it is."

"Great; I haven't been there in ages," a familiar chirpy voice piped up, and Jasper turned to stare with a mixture of relief and annoyance at the three assembled figures. It was irritatingly plausible that they'd been standing there listening the whole time.

"Don't give us that rubbish about needing to do this on your own," Amber warned with a glare that was half grin. "We're in this together."

"If you insist," Jasper acquiesced in a carefully neutral voice, his glance alone betraying his relief.

After briefing the others, the Prince descended morosely into silence, his impatient strides severing the company.

Glancing meaningfully to Amber, Racxen loped ahead to catch up with the Prince.

Tramping on regardless, caught in his own bleak thoughts, Jasper grudgingly became aware of a presence beside him, maintaining his pace with easy strides, keeping shoulder to shoulder with him in unspoken solidarity.

"No matter the tribe," Racxen suggested evenly, "no one expects a leader to keep them entirely away from danger. You can but guide them through it as best you can, and accept what solace lies in knowing you have attempted a role none other would risk."

"But you proved yourself, and were rightly chosen," Jasper grimaced, subdued. "I've had it easy; I was just born into it. They'll know I'm a fraud soon enough."

"You never did talk sense, Prince," the Arraheng reprimanded lightly. "You'll inspire them as a chosen leader never could—you're not here because you've dreamt of and trained for this moment your whole life; you're here for the same reasons they are: circumstance and the will to fight against it. In rising to the same challenges they face, your every action will diminish the foe before their eyes."

Jasper shrugged, but his heart lifted. "Mayhap."

"Guys?" Amber's shout cut through their thoughts as she ran up with Mugkafb. "We're getting close to the lake where I saw the Venom-spitter." Her eyes darted warily as the meadows began to drift into the flat expanse of marshland bordering Arraterr.

"Are you sure you know where we're going from here?" Mugkafb checked more pointedly, watching the Prince.

"Well . . ." Jasper fidgeted with his robe cord. "I've never been to Arkh Loban. But it should be a reasonably well-worn path from here. Can't we—okay, you—kind of scout around for it?"

"Tonak, we'll find it," Racxen promised, dark eyes gleaming as he scanned across the marsh and lake to the distant forest, already relishing the challenge of calculating a route before Mugkafb could think up a retort suitable for the audacity of the Prince's assumption.

"Doubtlessly our journey lies through the forest," the tracker surmised, "but one could wander fruitless for days beneath those eaves. Finding the right path depends on the angle of our approach. If we fan out, we can trace a broader route, and let the clues of the earth—changes in the soil; variations in the plant life—guide our footsteps. Mugkafb, you take the first quadrant; Amber the second, Jasper the third, and I'll take the last."

Mugkafb darted off eagerly, squirming with pride at having the chance to take the lead. Fearing she was going to prove useless at it, Amber followed suite, combing the ground with her gaze, determined not to miss anything that could help her friends.

Watching the others leave, Jasper stole a glance to Racxen. "I'll just refill the water-skein," the Prince mumbled awkwardly, gesturing for it. "I'll catch you up."

Racxen regarded him questioningly for a moment. Then he nodded. "Supplies. The most important part of an exhibition," he agreed, knowing full well they had plenty to last already as he loped off towards the forest.

Alone once more, Jasper trudged down to the lake's edge, fumbled for a leaf of sanitising boil-weed to drop into the skein, and thrust it into the shallows. Racxen, he supposed, would have waded out to get to the cleaner, clearer water, but then the Arraheng didn't care about getting numbed to the core in a bitingly freezing marsh.

Muttering a stream of curses under his breath as his efforts to fill the skein kept getting thwarted by the air-bubbled end wobbling up to the surface, Jasper's first assumption at the noise behind him was that the Arraheng had come back to complain about why he was taking so long. Turning to form an explanation and possibly an apology, the Prince stared instead at the reality.

Venom-spitter. Twenty yards. Stalking closer.

Fear stole his voice even as instinct warned that any sound could trigger an attack. He stood paralysed, his wings alone alive in their trembling urge to spring to flight. He'd always heard that these times flashed before you too fast to think or plan, but for now everything held still; and yet it was all for nothing, for here he stood just watching everything unfold with seconds spilling and no idea how to turn them to his advantage.

They're far enough away to not get hurt, if it takes its satisfaction now, a voice crept in. Wondering fleetingly if the fear had sent him quite mad, Jasper's resolve surged. *You've never been good at decisions. But this is your duty as their Prince. And duty's a different matter.*

Tearing his gaze from the death-bringer, he glanced over the marsh towards the far forms of the trio; the closest to friends he'd yet known. "It's not my duty," he promised them with sad solemnity. "It's my honour."

"*Creaaaaaaght!*" Possessing him of a strange fire, the ancient Fäe word sprang unbidden to his lips as he ran towards his foe.

The monster paused, uncertain at finding fight still left in its prey. Seizing on its hesitation, Jasper sustained his charge, bellowing his fury until at the last minute the shadow-stalker turned in defeat and ran to withdraw.

Jasper had no energy left to yell after it. Exhausted, he returned stumbling to the water.

Pounding earth—rasping breath: he slammed face-first into the mud, a crushing weight slamming into him as the monster's snarl exploded through his head.

Faster than he thought of the action, he squirmed onto his back, kicking out against ribs and limbs and grappling against the unassailable power of the brute as the force of its onslaught drove him into the shallows.

His head whipped back and with a sickening jolt he realised his cloak, ripped through by jagged teeth, was caught in the monster's jaws. Its folds billowed around him in the water, dragging him down as he floundered disorientated, fighting for release as the Venom-spitter shook him like a rat.

Sacrificing his cloak like a sloughed skin, Jasper wriggled free and plunged beneath the surface. Broiling river raged, closing over him. The Realm reverberated in his ears, far away now. Flailing blindly against sinking mud as he fell back, something solid—metal—found his hands, its form registering as his bloodied fingers closed around it: a sword hilt.

Sweeping it up in a fistful of detritus, he thrust all his remaining strength upwards through his only chance. Knifing through the surface, too late he saw it was only half a rusted blade, but with no choice left he plunged it through the wire-furred muscle, driving it up to the crossguard with a crazed yell.

He didn't have the strength to pull it out again. Defenceless once more, he summoned his last beleaguered reserves of strength to him for what would surely prove his last moments, and amidst the scattering water a tiny thought skittered that it wasn't going to work as the Venom-spitter collapsed onto him, thrashing mechanically as if hit with lightening-current, driving him under the icy water.

Fighting back with renewed terror, it took Jasper seconds to register that the monster was being taken by death throes.

Floundering with the cadaver, Jasper yelled as other bodies touched him.

"Engo ro fash!" Racxen shouted, hooking his claws into the suffocating corpse and dragging it away from him.

Jasper gulped and spluttered convulsively, staggering wild-eyed and unseeing towards the bank at terror-fuelled speed, each splashing plunging step sinking him further into fear until he suddenly tripped, lurching back into nightmare.

He felt a hand round his wrist, and Amber was under his shoulder, wrapping her arm round his chest before he could fall and guiding him to the bank, as Mugkafb's chirpy voice danced before them like a bouncing lantern. Staggering beneath his weight, she stayed, steadying him as he sloshed trancelike through the filthy water until the lake sank, the ground felt firmer even to his frozen limbs, and he could finally clamber onto the bank where he slumped, shivering violently as the wind whipped through his soaked clothing.

His friends watched anxiously as he caught his breath, sensation seeping back through until he pawed the fur from his mouth and spat violently, rubbing his skin sore as he scrubbed at the blood covering him, feverishly trying to remove all trace of the past moments.

Mugkafb clung to Amber's hand silently, his eyes wide with Jasper's pain.

"Prince—" Racxen tried steadily, stepping towards him.

"Bring it here," Jasper interrupted, neither looking up nor stopping.

"But—" Amber pleaded.

"I need you to." Jasper tore his gaze from his hands, and flung it instead towards the bloated, stiffening bulk now half-floating towards the shallows despite Racxen's efforts to keep it from his eye-line. His haunted stare traced the trail of blood and gore seeping in a darkening stain over the sombre grey cloud of the lake's surface.

With a resigned sigh, Racxen strode with loose-limbed ease through the water, and with more difficulty hauled the gruesome bulk back to the side.

Slipping her hand from Mugkafb's, Amber darted to the bank before her mind could catch up. Swallowing against the rising urge to vomit, she grabbed a stiff, wiry leg and pulled as hard as she could. It was slippery with mud and disgustingly cold.

When they'd manhandled it across the sodden bank and the monster had thudded at a grotesque angle at the Prince's feet, she couldn't stop an involuntary shudder, and wiped her hands compulsively on her saturated cloak.

Jasper nodded his thanks, kneeling clumsily to lean towards the corpse. "I just need to look at it closer."

Racxen laid a hand on his shoulder. "Leave it. That Venom-spitter would have killed us all; your response was necessary. Fill your eyes with better sights; the friends whose lives you've saved, and the land you've ensured we all live to see."

Deaf to his words, the Prince heaved the front leg onto his knee as if preparing to shoe some monstrous horse, studying the matted footpaw with its bloodied, yellowed talons. "Racxen, how many claws were those gashes in the cave made by?"

The Arraheng watched him closely. "What? Four."

Jasper stared, his Realm crumbling. "Only three," he muttered bitterly, letting the limb fall back with a thud. "Lords and ladies, we're dealing with two different types of monster." As they stared at him, mute with disbelief, he dragged himself up tiredly. "Sooner we get to Loban, sooner we get answers."

Still to be Found

"Look, they weren't being ironic when they named this place the 'Endless Forest'," Jasper huffed, gesturing wildly at Mugkafb to stay within view. "Loban's bad enough without courting further disaster on the way."

Pressing on, they settled into silence and, despite the Prince's mood, Amber felt her spirits lighten as the company continued deeper into the heart of the wood. The trees above them stretched broad like sheltering arms, filtering the air into a vibrant green and infusing the surrounding leaves with a warm-hued glow as here and there dazzling sunbeams pierced the canopy to illuminate sections of their path in gold-touched splendour. She didn't know along how many shadow-dappled, twisting passages they had journeyed when Racxen stilled, his eyes shining. "Listen."

She heard it too, now—the jumping notes of a panpipe spiralling towards them, joyful and intoxicating. The melody soothed their frayed nerves, the steady rhythm easing their pounding hearts until they had forgotten they had been trudging through the Endless Forest for over half a day.

The music hushed abruptly, and without warning through the trees towards them came cantering a being the like of which they had never seen before. His upper body was irrefutably that of a man; unclothed, deeply tanned and strong-faced, with long wild dark hair flowing back over his shoulders. His fierce eyes danced, and along his arms ran intricate patterns stained in plant-dyes. A reed pipe rested in one hand; in the other, two barkless short sticks. Yet below the torso his body was unavoidably equine—if as well-built in its own way—for his unkempt coat gleamed a proud bay and his long, muscular limbs adorned with striking white feathering wouldn't have looked out of place on a draught horse, each graceful move belaying a mulish strength.

He skidded to a halt in the clearing, his tail sweeping as long and dark as his hair as he watched the newcomers. Standing before them, he was a head or so taller than Racxen. He flashed a quick grin to Mug-kafb, who was staring in unabashed amazement.

"Careful," the Prince hissed to his companions. "Centaurs are rash and unpredictable."

The stranger tossed back his head in a braying laugh, kicking his hooves with a restless energy. "Indeed," he answered, his deep voice booming warmth. "We are apt to dance at a second's notice, and we will drop everything to run to the aid of one who needs it. Who ventures through Han's Forest in times such as these?"

Jasper, in the lead, stared soundlessly.

Amber glared at the Prince and stepped forwards hurriedly with introductions. "We need to get to Arkh Loban, sir," she explained.

"It concerns the Goblins, the Venom-spitters, and a foe as yet unidentified," Racxen finished. "We travel with the utmost urgency for the sake of all people."

The Centaur grinned roguishly. "Ah, do you now? The Forest has missed such talk for too many years," he divulged. "May it ring through the eaves once again. You'll need the Travellers' Pass—it's the only entrance still safe—and of course an honourable guide to show you the way. Just so you know," he warned jauntily, "it's guarded by Basilisks."

"Basilisks? Have you taken leave of your senses?" Jasper blurted, struggling to keep up with the Centaur's long strides.

Han eyeballed the Fairy. "Do you know this gentleman; this lady? Have you ever *met* Basilisks?"

Jasper glowered, but refrained from further comment.

Han snorted in merriment. "Then this will be interesting." His hooves clipped quietly against the dusty ground as he led on.

Hard-eyed, fair-minded reptilian warriors rumoured to be able to kill with a stare—

"Basilisks," Han primed the company as they neared the toll-gates, interrupting Amber's thoughts, "walked with the Dragons until the end of their age, when they settled, as much as Nomads ever can, in Arkh Loban. Remaining at the outskirts of civilization, they took it upon themselves to provide protection for the dispossessed town-dwellers from those who still seek to emulate the foul example of the Lobanian Emperor. There is a price upon the head of every Basilisk warrior; yet none will be betrayed by even the poorest Arkhan," the Centaur promised. "You may be equally sure," he added with a smirk, "that neither Goblin nor aspiring Emperor's underling would live through any attempt at claiming bounty. You've probably heard the Basilisk-related rumours that abound," he continued, "which I will not add to. You would be foolish to stand within four feet of any attacker, and the intensity of their stare can heal also, of course. A more upstanding citizen than the Basilisk would be difficult to come by, although they do not suffer fools."

Amber nodded. It was a common belief that you couldn't live in such close proximity to Dragons without some of their magic rubbing off. The rumour went that Basilisks were humans who had over time acquired certain attributes of the Dragons; their forms becoming more reptilian, their sight exceeding the limits of human capability to the extent that they could see into your soul, and their senses growing attuned to the "unmentioned element". Some believed the relationship to have been even more symbiotic, suggesting that it was through the Basilisks that the desert lizards of old became more human, learnt the art of understanding vocal speech, and evolved into Dragons in the first place.

Even disregarding such urban legends, the Basilisks were certainly not beings to trifle with. Their sand-coloured scales formed an impenetrable hide to rival the stoutest armour, and a protective film slipped across their Dragon-keen eyes during combat. Even the most foolhardy of thieves quailed before the steadfast gate-masters. As the regulators of trade between the civilised districts of the Realm and the now infamous outlaw town under siege by Goblins, they were the last remnants of justice. And as law-enforcers, they were second to none.

Han slowed, his tail flicking away flies in the stifling air. Further along the narrow dust-path that served as the highway into Arkh Loban, they saw two tall, bipedal reptilian sentries with lizard-like heads and unblinking eyes flanking the border.

"Welcome to nowhere," the Centaur breathed as Jasper stared past the sentinels to the exposed settlement beyond. Lonely snatches of wind howled between age-worn ruins and tumbledown shanties, whipping the sand into dervishes that rattled through the bundles of charms tied to the windows of spartan dwellings. Apart from a bedraggled clan of waiflike children darting between stark shadows under the blistering sky, the town seemed empty, bereft.

As the companions neared, heavy tails lashed the dust and thick black tongues tasted the air. Jasper felt his throat dry and his palms moisten.

"Sstate your purpose, travellerss." The Basilisks spoke in military unison. Their eyes drew Amber's gaze hypnotically: viperously narrow, yet with the depth of humanity—and an intensity she hadn't seen save for in pictures of Dragons. Each gripped a wooden spear with an embossed obsidian head, rough-beaten and dulled through use yet eye-wateringly fearsome. Light armour was strapped to their brawny shoulders, their chests hard-plated with scarred scales rendering any further protection unnecessary. Amber found herself staring at the metal circlet crowning the female's brow, with a jewel resting between her eyes bearing a strange insignia. *That's where Tanzan got it from,* she realised in amazement. *He saw the Basilisks.* She grinned. They must be the only people to get away with flaunting their allegiance with Gorfang so openly. Not even the oppressive Lobanian Authorities would dare risk hand-to-hand combat with one as powerful as a Basilisk over a mere trinket.

"Afternoon Rhissk; Lahssk." Han bowed a foreleg politely as he broke the fraught silence. "My friends require safe passage into Loban. What's the handover?"

"Not much concrete to tell, Ssire," Lahssk reported in a lisping, gravelled voice, not taking his eyes from the road. "Goblinss we're ussed to handling, but never in thiss number before. It'ss like they've been driven here—they're too sscared to sstay in the desertss."

"Sscared enough to plan something, too," Rhissk mused. "Word iss of a 'sskinner'. That'ss all you get if you quesstion 'em."

"Right," Han offered, uncertain for once. "Thanks. This mission is—"

"Not worth death. Now iss not the day," Rhissk warned shortly, brooking no arguments. "We have told you all we know. You musst return when the ssituation is not sso . . . volatile. Tomorrow, by thiss road, and fewer of you. For your own ssafety." The Basilisk's third lid winked across her eye as she turned back to join her companion in resuming their roadside vigil.

Thanking the Basilisks, the companions walked the long trek back mostly in silence. Amber found herself turning back to stare worriedly after their new acquaintances: their tall, armoured silhouettes solid against the purpling horizon slipping into distance and dusk. What confrontations would await them on the road tonight?

Nearing Fairymead as the sky deepened into inky night, Jasper guided everyone to the castle, Han's hooves splintering the quietness of their approach as he navigated the stone steps amidst a flurry of curses.

Waving his companions into the empty Great Hall, Jasper slung his cloak down tiredly and slumped onto the bench. "Well, that was useless, wasn't it? A 'skinner', indeed. Who makes these names up?"

Racxen kept his eyes fixed on the knot at the centre of the banquet table; he hadn't spoken since greeting the Basilisks. "The Goblins," he muttered hollowly. "It's their King, Thanatos."

The Prince stared directly at him. "And you came to know that how?"

The Arraheng didn't answer, so Jasper ignored him, pulling a few texts from a shelf in the corner and rifling irately through the tomes far too fast to read them properly. "Not a single one of these goes back far enough," he muttered fractiously. "There's no mention of either name."

He let the last book curl shut with a *thwump*. "The only place left for information is the market—it's only part of Loban," he added with exaggerated patience as Han glared at him, his tail lashing in agitation as he waited by the door, visibly uneasy at being enclosed by the stone walls. "The Goblins are articulate and charismatic," Jasper reasoned. "Maybe they'll know—"

"We will not parley with Goblins!" the Centaur snorted, hooves kicking out restlessly as he threw a savage glance towards the Prince. "They spin such a soiled web of tender words that you don't realise until too late that they've teased them softly round your throat. There is a danger far beyond enchantment in their dealings."

"The *Goblin* market?" The fear of it slammed into Amber, breaking through the shock that had clamped her tongue. "Jasper, that's madness. You can't mean it."

Jasper spread his hands resignedly. "You can buy anything there. What else would you have me do?"

Racxen wheeled to him. "But the tender there is not mere gold—it is blood, and soul, and will."

"A mere story," Jasper waved a hand placatingly. "They are pirate traders—they all take gold."

"It is not a story!" the Arraheng cried vehemently, his claws flying to his head in anguish.

Jasper watched him stonily, his frozen silence demanding an explanation for the other's outburst.

The Arraheng stared at him wretchedly, but said no more.

"'Course, they're not nasty all the time, oh no," Han pressed stubbornly in the silence that followed, unwilling to let it rest. "If they were, I wouldn't have to remind you to be on your guard. Their means are subtle, as well as savage, and the former makes them more dangerous than the latter. They'll try to force your hand, of course, but you'll be ready for that. What's harder to guard against is how you'll end up wanting to trust them. No matter what I say of them here and now, when you're out there, it will seem a completely different scenario, and you will feel you have chanced upon the one Goblin who you understand well enough to hazard viewing differently than the others. In the most beguiling means they have at their disposal, they will attempt to twist your own mind to your downfall; juxtaposing their evil ways with just enough goodness to make you question yourself until you risk losing sight of everything you once knew to be irrefutable. They can be resisted; they have to be resisted, but you need to know your own mind as well as theirs. You can't go into this thinking they won't get to you." Han's gaze settled forebodingly on Jasper, his voice heavy with discomfort, no words left.

"You're right, of course, it *is* dangerous," the Prince acknowledged in clipped tones. "Which is why I'm going and not you." He stood and retrieved his cloak. "Now—"

"Someone should check the library vaults in Loban too," Amber interrupted, in a tone that displayed scant intention of leaving him in peace. "Professor Cobalt always said they were the oldest in the Realm. Give yourself a break; you don't have to solve everything single-handedly, and if you try to cover both locations we'll just end up back in this situation tomorrow night, so I'm coming too. You got the map?"

Jasper opened his mouth to protest, then thought better and shut it again. "Good grief, Amber, you're difficult to get rid of. Just make sure you keep up. First," he yawned blearily, "everyone find yourselves spare blankets and an empty corner. I'll see you tomorrow."

Arkh Loban

Any memory of sleep fell away cruelly with the last vestiges of shade and scrubland as Amber and Jasper stumbled through the scorched sandscape heralding their return to Arkh Loban. The last reserves of their energy evaporating in the suffocating temperature, they slogged through the trek grim-faced and sweat-soaked, driven only by the entrenched spark of defiance clutched deep enough in each of them to be immune to their mind's entreaties of the impossibility of the endeavour.

"This is where we part company for now," Jasper gasped, waving at Amber to stop as a cluster of sun-blanched dwellings speckled the quivering heat of the horizon. He slapped the first of an innocuous succession of boulders protruding through the sand. "At least one of us gets to escape this accursed heat—you're taking the cavern-ways through this rock that form the secret entrance to the library vaults. It has several such entrances, from when the Emperor decided he couldn't possibly allow his subjects to think for or better themselves and outlawed such sacrilegious facilities." Jasper had the grace to look uncertain as they approached the narrow fissure. "Although I couldn't tell you when it was last used, nor by whom."

"Great."

"I did say that your assistance—"

They stalled in an unspoken truce.

"You can thank me back at the market," Amber called back easily over her shoulder with a grin, her voice shivering with echoes as she ducked into the shadows.

"It's a right then a left then a left then a right," Jasper warned anxiously, beginning to wonder if he'd made the right choice as he stared into the foreboding dark.

As Amber waved her acknowledgement, the desert wind rushed to drown her footsteps and the darkness swallowed her completely.

Hours blurred in the shimmering sand-heat until noontide saw Jasper gasping beneath his suffocating cloak, cursing the uselessness of the only map he carried and swearing an oath against the need for disguise as he staggered into view of the dilapidated historic quarters of Arkh Loban, precarious in a state of decay that echoed the ruination of this once proud town of ancient lineage.

Murmuring his relief, he stumbled on, squinting against choking, sand-gusting winds carrying snatches of conversations in tongues he could not understand and the scent of some kind of herb-encrusted unidentifiable meat being cooked at a Goblin-run stall.

Along the emerging dirt-track rode mingled traders of all descriptions: families cloaked in peasant rags shuffled beside striding merchants bejewelled in richly embroidered garments from every stretch of the Realm. The Prince had to admit, despite a festering unease at having brought his companions so far from home in such grave uncertainty, that amidst such a patchwork hub of cultures the gaps left in the limited history tomes of Fairymead could surely be filled.

His resolve shuddered as he glimpsed the wiry, omnipresent Goblins, stalking amongst the droves of buyers and dealmongers like hunting dogs methodically splitting a herd of oxen.

You're finally somewhere where no one knows you, he reminded himself pointedly as he steeled his courage. *That's got to be worth something.* Yet he tugged a hand wearily through his damp hair as the pragmatics of such a situation invaded his mind: no authority, no allies, no reputation or connections to rely upon.

"Your inadequacies follow you even to the desert," he muttered as he replaced his hood.

As the Prince wandered closer, slowing his pace to an unthreatening shuffle, it became obvious that this was the district of the city the Basilisks could not police. It was not so much the obscenely rich few that stole his attention, as the sheer mass of dispossessed. He was put in mind of a city of refugees; determined souls eking out a living however they could, street urchins running in straggling packs between the ruins, their squabbles and rare laughter anchoring the humanity of the place amongst a surreal, despondent quietness.

Maintaining his interminable pace, Jasper's heart sank lower as he saw burgundy liveries threading through the crowd in his direction; the garb of a growing minority plotting to reconstruct the oppressive regime of the Lobanian Emperor defeated by Gorfang. This road too, then, was toll-guarded—and not by Basilisks.

Jasper's mind raced for a moment with impossible ways to take a stand, but by the time the guards came properly into view he had guiltily dismissed them all—how could he help these people, and his own, if the radicals knew his identity and plans?

Sweating as if his cover were blown already, Jasper darted out of view, retreating hastily to the sheltering remains of a derelict theatre. A shadowed stone wall pressed reassuringly against his back, the Prince examined the coins in his palm, loathe to display his ignorance of the currency when his success, possibly even survival, relied on passing inconspicuously through the toll-gates.

Cursing his misfortune, he guiltily slipped into silence as he realised he wasn't alone, cursing himself instead now as he glanced to the young girl sitting amongst the rubble watching the passers-by, her bony arms wrapped protectively around a painfully thin body clothed in thread-bare rags.

He felt wretchedly intrusive just for being there. How could he hope to solve anything?

She caught him looking, scratched free a scrap of stone and threw it away. "It's eighteen to get in," she muttered dully, as if long past caring the riches of others. "It's a rotten disguise, though" she dismissed. "Yer too clean for a peasant."

The Prince sighed, cringing inwardly as he clung to his original design. "Forgive my stupidity, I'm sure you had better schooling than a, ahem, peasant like myself. Can you count me out eighteen?"

She shrugged, and pointed. "That one. And the small one."

He pocketed them and stood. Careful to keep his face hidden, he flicked the other coins back to the kid.

She snatched them from midair faster than a swamptoad snapping flies. Her eyes searched his hood with the smallest curl of a smile, and then she was darting off to who knew where.

Not for the first time, the Prince found himself wondering what it would have been like to have a brother or sister. *You're not doing such a fine job of watching out for the others,* he reminded himself dispassionately. *Mayhap it's for the best you were spared the chance of botching that up too.*

Gloomily he strode on, merging into the drift of the crowd flow-ing towards the tollgates until, too soon, he found himself before the guards. Cursing his introspection as indulgence and berating himself for not having paid more attention to his surroundings, all Jasper's plans fled from his mind and, words failing him, he mutely thrust his coins at the burgundy-liveried officials.

"Goblin bought your tongue?" the closest mocked, running his hands intrusively over Jasper's cloak, appraising it for hidden symbols of dissent; anything that could link him with the folk hero so despised by their leader.

Fear vying with anger, the Prince scraped together his story. "The market," he managed, bringing a quavering crackle of desperation to his voice, "the healers cannot cure me—I need the potions—please, good sirs, I'd give anything."

Another guard smirked nastily. "Yer got that right."

"Don't pay him no heed, you go through," the second soothed sententiously, his grip hovering on restraint. "Just the sort we like to see around here, aren't you? The kind who knows exactly where he belongs? I don't think we're going to see you come back this way, now are we?"

"No sirs, thank you sirs, I'll be on my way sirs." Jasper raised his hands in contrition, bowing and cringing and backing away until the influxing throng swept new suspects into his place and he could slip through the gateway and duck out of sight before something else could go awry.

As the crowd dispersed along the dust-road and he could breathe freely again, Jasper pulled back his hood thankfully, ran a still-shaking hand through his now sweat-plastered hair, and considered his next move. Yelping as he absentmindedly rested a bare hand on the scorching stone wall, the Prince bad-temperedly adjusted his robes and slumped down against the side of the nearest building. Pressing himself into the tiny sliver of shade, he unfolded the map from his pocket and drew out the water-skein.

His head pounding from dehydration, he loosened the cork and gulped dizzily, closing his eyes in relief as the water flooded his parched throat.

He opened them at a small, apologetic noise, and stared in a mixture of bewilderment and indignation. A rangy, tawny-coloured, wolfish-looking dog was standing in front of him, gazing at the skein hopefully, tongue lolling from its gaping mouth as it panted in the stifling heat.

The Prince begrudgingly spilled a little water into his hand. "Haven't you got a master to go and bother?"

The dog lapped gratefully, its tongue rough and warm against his palm. With a sigh of defeat, Jasper let spill the skein again until the last few drops were gone. "Look at that, you horror," he chastised quietly, spreading his now-empty hands as the dog licked its chops. He ruffled its ears, and it felt like rubbing a moth-eaten carpet. "Nothing else for you; you might as well go."

The dog, unmoving, watched him through intelligent, gold-flecked eyes.

Jasper smiled ruefully. "Do you know, out of everyone here, you're pretty much the only one who's given me a second of their time?" he confided conversationally to the wolfish creature. "Now: if you were information about three kinds of monster, where in Arkh Loban would you be?"

The dog cocked its head in a quizzical expression, and Jasper chuckled. "No answer? Be off with you, then. Can't have a beauty like you on my tail on a dangerous mission, can I?"

The dog obliged, trotting stiff-legged past the girl he had spoken to earlier.

She ran up as she saw him. "Got you through, didn't I?" she noted proudly.

"Indeed," the Prince acknowledged sagely. "It would appear I am in your debt."

The girl watched him seriously for a minute before glancing out over the sands. "Hey, if I told you—" She fell silent, her eyes upon him solemn again, and Jasper had the sudden feeling she was taking his measure. The possibility didn't fill him with confidence.

"If I told you," she blurted again, her voice edged with the smallest hint of challenge, "that my sister could fight better than ten men, and would help you if you got into trouble, would you laugh at me?"

The Prince stared across the bleak, arid landscape, between ruin after ruin of crumbled housing: a scene devoid of hope. "Once, mayhap, I would have," he confessed uncomfortably. "I'm not proud of the boy I used to be. I'm not all that sure about the man I'm becoming, either, to be honest. But no." He opened his hands in acceptance. "I am alone, in a land I know nothing of, and my task here is perilous. I would accept her help gladly, and I would ask her name of you."

The child grinned. "In that case, shout for Yenna."

"Yenna. I'll remember that," Jasper promised, puzzled. "My thanks. I'll—"

"Sash—Authorities," a scruffy-haired, scrawny-looking boy interrupted furtively, already running on to warn others.

Instantly serious, the girl grabbed Jasper's hand and cast about quickly. The boy had already vanished.

"What? They could help," the Prince argued, confused. "Couldn't—"

"'Authority' is our code for the lowlife bullies ruling the streets round here styling themselves as the dead Emperor's servants—they're as corrupt as they come," the girl warned, casting him a withering glance. "We've got to—"

The Prince's gaze flew to the tollgates as he saw the two guards joined by a larger, even more fearsome-looking man. Sweat clung suddenly as he saw them gesture to others and draw arms.

"No—you can't be seen with me," he warned urgently. "You never saw me. Keep yourself safe." Without another word to delay her, he pushed through into the mass of traders.

Darting between stall after stall, Jasper slipped gratefully into the shadow of the closest jumble of rubble, disorientated and exhausted, his nerves in shreds and his head spinning.

As he glanced to the distance to steady himself, he wondered if he was seeing things as for a second he caught sight of a poised figure, swathed in black; an illusion of stillness amidst the chaotic crush. The garment obscured most of her face, yet its edge was hemmed with brilliant golden disks, framing her glittering eyes in a juxtaposition that intrigued the Prince. Cloaked in anonymity, her identity and intentions hidden, her movements both fluid and measured spoke of a freedom paradoxically greater than those of the barefaced populace as, watching everything but remaining concealed, under the guise of submission she flaunted defiance.

Witnessing the triumph of each quiet action, Jasper was reminded of the legend in which Gorfang tricked the Emperor's gatekeepers into admitting the majestic beyond-sighted Dragon Akutan, the narrow-minded minions little guessing that the blind old lizard they saw before them would prove their downfall.

The stranger happened to turn towards Jasper for a mere second, and in the instant their gaze met he was struck by the beauty of those eyes: dark and intense, yet flecked with gold and warmth.

She looked away and yet, he sensed, not through the fear of the peasant-folk struggling to eke out an existence here on the border beneath the crushing shadow of the Old Lobanian Palace. Instead her action was performed without haste, in the manner of one accustomed to casually appraising adversity without drawing its attention, before attending to greater matters.

Fare you well, my lady. He turned to orientate himself amongst the growing crowd, and when he looked back she was gone.

Realising with embarrassment that he had tarried too long already, Jasper turned his attention to observing the Authorities. Now that Sash had pointed them out, it seemed they stood everywhere; sharp-eyed and stern or obsequious and fawning, their clothing studded or stitched with subtle symbols of their allegiance, almost as hidden as those of Gorfang's followers. Intangible and inescapable as smoke they spread through the crowd, to appear, judiciously placed, the moment dissent flickered or the denunciation of some choice rule of theirs seemed imminent, and Jasper couldn't stem the wave of despair as he beheld their work and realised they had permeated every section of the crowd through which he had to pass.

He thought then of the woman he'd beheld. *This is what she has to live with every day,* he chastised himself firmly, and pushed onwards.

Casting a careful eye over his surroundings did nothing to allay his fears as he approached: foreboding remnants of age-old buildings sprawled across the sand beyond the crowds, and behind it all shadowed ominously what he could only assume had once been some kind of arena, his view barred by the wreckage of some other building that looked as if it must have been torched. From the pillars it looked ominously like the library vaults, and Jasper's heart sank to think of Amber.

Unaware of a swift movement in the crowd as two guards pushed forwards, their eyes meeting in silent agreement, the Prince pulled his hood down so it shadowed his face again and stepped out of the shadows.

Adopting what he fervently hoped was a casual manner, Jasper wove cautiously through the crowds hurrying to ply their trades or seek succour from the merchants beneath the merciless all-seeing sun, fear prickling his scalp as Goblin eyes scanned vulture-like from both sides.

Looking down to the map to avoid their ravenous stares, he didn't see the burgundy-liveried shapes dart in from the left until the first guard was in his face, all bellows and anger, blocking his path.

"Where did you get this?" he spat, snatching the map and ripping it into pieces as Jasper made a lunge for the fragments thrown to the sands.

"That has not been *authorised,*" the second growled sanctimoniously. "Our regulation maps provide all the information necessary. The old parchments are dangerous—you want danger?" The man dealt him a smarting blow across the face, grabbing his cloak-front, twisting it against his neck and shoving him back against the building wall. "Do you?"

Grabbing the fists, Jasper managed to force the man's hands back on themselves and twist free. "Of course not," he placated, no idea how he'd got out of that and knowing he couldn't do it again, wondering fleetingly if he had the slightest chance of embroiling the men in an argument instead of a fight and knowing he had nowhere in the Realm here to run to if it didn't work. "You're probably wondering—"

Something made him stop, and for a split second he stared uncertainly at the guards. Their demeanour had changed, though he couldn't tell why. He looked down, and cursed, fear washing through him: his Gem, pulled into view when they'd gone for his throat—

"*Treason,*" murmured the first guard, as if he'd waited his whole life to charge an offence of such magnitude. "Punishable by—"

"Gentlemen, this is folly," Jasper heard himself retort, the idiocy of the situation firing him with indignation. "The only one of us with any appointed power or jurisdiction is myself. And don't tell me these lands aren't mine; neither are they yours—this land has had no democratically elected leader since Gorfa—"

A cuff to the face sent him staggering, clutching his jaw as he counted his teeth with his tongue, the swollen pulse of his lip throbbing as the salt-rust tang seeped into his mouth.

"You will not speak that heathen's name!" the first guard bellowed gleefully, like a Goblin trapping a desert traveller.

Never one for fantasy, Jasper nonetheless felt a surge of kinship with that hero, and a passionate defence for the tales that had sustained a broken people in a land from which all other possible sources of hope had been systematically eradicated. "I come to you like Gorfang!" he yelled suddenly, seeing frightened faces glance his way. "Cloaked in peasantry to hide a kingly future!" Wrestling free, he flung off his cloak. "And I swear—"

His head smacked into the sand, breath stolen by the impact as the guards slammed him to the ground and he saw in terror the flash of a knife.

"*Yennaaaa!*" he bellowed, the word ripped away by the winds and stolen in the struggle until his scalp burned and he was staring at the sky at a weird angle and cold steel pricked into his neck and he couldn't even swallow.

Jasper distractedly registered a wolf's far-off howl before claustrophobic silence crushed in around him. His neck spasmed as the guard shifted his grip on his hair to force his head further back, tracing the line of his throat with the blade-point.

Breathe, he tried to remind himself. *Breathe and think. You've got your people to live for. It's not time to die for them yet.*

"Who d'you think is going to save you?" his attacker mocked, feigning genuine surprise, jerking the Fairy's head round to stare along the dust-strewn street as the other thug stood watching impassively. "You see that? That's how powerful we are. A town full of people, and no one stops us. No one even—"

His words bled into a strangled cry as a tawny, wolfish blur leapt over Jasper and barraged into the Authority, snarling its judgement as the guard lost most of his robes trying to keep the snapping jaws at bay. His accomplice took one look at the berserk apparition and fled for his life and the guard, as soon as the monstrosity allowed him, did the same, escaping with his life and limbs intact, if not his dignity.

Having scrambled to his feet as soon as his wits allowed during the beast's intervention, Jasper stood rooted in shock until its warning growls and the shouts of more guards sent him with a last despairing glance fleeing back to the outskirts of the city.

Wrapping his torn cloak feverishly around him, Jasper passed his stinging hands across his face and chest to check for wounds, struggling to accept the situation was truly over. Taking refuge in measuring his breathing, the Prince realised he was being watched by the girl from earlier.

"What *was* that?" he gasped, embarrassed by the obstinate quiver of emotion remaining in his voice despite his staunchest efforts to quell it. He stared back, but of the creature that had saved him no sign remained.

The kid shrugged nonchalantly. "You mean *who*." She grinned as she strode away. "Told you she could fight."

Tavern Liaison

There's no knight in shining armour
Who's going to ride up upon his white horse
And brandish his sword, and smash through the door
And take me away out of here
But I can get my own white horse
I'm done with hesitating
I'm going to jump on that white horse right now, ride like the wind
I can pick the knight up later

Shoving the dog-eared book back into her apron pocket, Naya stared into the haze of punters and tugged herself reluctantly back to what had served as her reality for the past two years. The poem's urges faded beneath her harsh situation, as she demanded again for the whole price and received a raised fist and stream of obscenities for her troubles.

She watched the drunkard stumble back, to down whatever it was, her heart hammering and anger bubbling beneath her set jaw. Burgundy liveries. They allowed a multitude of evils to go unpunished.

She shivered, keeping her eyes on him. *You think I serve you by night, you think I serve you by day. You don't know what I find out, in those stables and behind here. If you knew what I did with the information—*

The next punter caught her eye, and hoping he would be more

civilised she flashed a friendly smile, drawing her mind back to the present. She would report the thief when the other girls came back, for all the good it would do; it wasn't like anyone had listened to her during the whole shift so far.

As the customer staggered back to his friends Naya drummed her fingers restlessly, wondering how much longer she was going to let herself put up with this. She fished into her apron pocket for the key to the cellar, and her fingers brushed the battered poetry book. Feeling alone for a moment amongst the commotion of the tavern, she allowed herself a quiet sigh. "Why do I bother with such stories in a town like this?" she murmured under her breath.

"To anchor you to the deepest truths through times when reality cannot provide their proof?"

Naya jumped violently at the voice, but the man's eyes were friendly and she grinned in recognition, glancing around quickly and carrying on cleaning the glasses so as not to draw attention to the Nomad. "You look like you've been travelling the desert for two weeks," she told the air pointedly in a low voice. "And you smell just as bad," she added with a disdainful sneer as the earlier punter glanced over suspiciously.

Roanen's laugh was warm and self-deprecating.

Naya coughed, poured his usual dewberry elixir, and busied herself by energetically cleaning the bar. "New law," she muttered frustratedly by way of explanation. "No one may fraternise with outsiders who are not of the Emperor's lineage."

"The Emperor? That—" the Nomad checked himself. "How about those of . . . Rashtekkn'yar lineage?" he returned softly.

"The Dragontongue is forbidden also," she hissed with amusement. "Although were it not so dangerous for you—for both of us—I would dearly love them to know who you really are. Not that it's your heritage that I admire—and they would fear—the most."

Roanen grinned, his shrewd eyes dancing. "Mayhap you should run away and join the Nomads," he teased. "Then we'd show them a thing or two about fear."

"Really—Nomads plural? You mean it's not still just you with a hero complex?" Naya shot back dryly. "And if I did let you tempt me away, where then would you get your information from? News, Roanen, and quickly; for I know you cannot stay long."

The Wanderer lowered his voice. "Fairymead has been warned. They lie directly in its path."

Naya poured a drink that wasn't needed. "Good. There are whispers here also," she added, keeping her manner conversational, but letting her voice drop so quietly that only the Nomad could hear. "I don't know if it's connected, but the markets are spreading. Goblins have been sighted not just in the square, but haunting the alleyways all over town. Even by the schools—in broad light the other day. It's like they've been driven—or lured—here by something."

"Gutless cowards," Roanen grimaced. "The Basilisks can protect travellers on the road, but they cannot be everywhere." The Nomad faded into silence until a gaggle of new customers had lumbered past.

"The news is no better from my watch," he rejoined. "Mobs have been setting up camps in the ruins, on the outskirts, anywhere they can—like they have something to prove. Goblin-chatter is that their king has arrived. They're not going to leave this time, Naya. You know as well as I that this town has been choking beneath their shadow for too long." His voice fell to an angry whisper. "They know there is no fight left in most of this city."

Naya's eyes flashed. "Then we must prove them wrong."

Roanen's expression softened. "If the fight could be won by the courage of a few alone, I would have no doubts were you to stand among them. But the city must first be united, prepared, and certain. We won't be able to delay once the storm breaks. Send word to your brother that Fairymead has need of armaments."

A chill flickered along Naya's spine, and the bustle of the room faded from her ears. Dimly, she saw someone dip her hand into the tip bowl and she didn't even care: it barely registered through the veil drawn across her roiling mind.

The Nomad saw her pale. "Do not lose heart, my lady. Such times are not fully upon us, and may yet be thwarted." Replacing his hood, he paid for his drink, his calloused hand lingering gently as he passed the coin. "Keep hope."

Naya tried to smile, storing up the look in his eyes, but she stiffened as a burgundy-liveried woman stood abruptly and began grim-faced to force herself towards the bar. Stepping out under the pretence of collecting glasses, Naya caught Roanen's wrist with a low warning. "Authority, six paces behind. Be off."

Roanen ducked towards the entrance with a wink. "You'll be such a dream-walker some day . . ."

"Yes," she admonished, shoving him hastily towards the door. "But in the meantime I'm forced to be a worker. I'll give word to Seb of Fairymead's requisition. Expect him three nights hence."

Her countenance grew more haggard beneath the flickering lamplight, amongst a room of punters who had as yet no worries worse than the price of their next drink. "You will keep me informed, won't you? I know it brings you into danger, but the Authorities tell us nothing, and we must prepare; I hate asking you—"

Roanen held up a hand. "You couldn't stop me, not for all the traitors under that name. I would understand, in my turn, if things become dangerous and you fear to share information—" He stopped at Naya's exasperated refusal, nodded courteously, and smiled to her beneath the shadow of his hood.

"My lady, despite the darkness, keep looking to the stars. I wouldn't want you of all people to miss the Dragon."

Naya stared, speechless, at the door now swinging shut.

Ambush

Running to put the market square behind him, Jasper slowed in relief as the trees of a straggling forest rose to shelter him. Amongst the sandy earth, wiry grasses sprouted to render the ground easier for travelling. Beneath the cooling dappled shadows, for the first time that day, the Prince permitted himself to relax.

Amidst the green before him, a glint of metal flashed.

The second guard. You forgot about the second guard. Jasper froze, staring helplessly, as twenty feet in front of him a bodkin-point wooden arrow far longer than the Fairies used protruded between the branches, angled from a full-drawn deeply curved exotic bow straining in the hands of a female warrior, her blazing golden eyes fixed on him, her olive-hued skin framed by a crashing wave of long black hair.

"Don't move," she commanded unnecessarily.

Adrenaline flooded so suddenly that Jasper's initial, pitiful thought was that his only response would be to vomit. Then the injustice of the past hours roared in his memory, the images of the rag-clothed girl and veiled woman firing within him a cry far bolder than himself, and he drew his sword and lunged.

The string slapped the air, the arrow gleamed.

"Which part of 'don't move' do you not understand?" the archer hissed incredulously as her arrow thrummed past, finding its target behind him.

Jasper flinched violently at the bellow of pain, spinning round to stare as the burgundy-liveried man blundered through the forest roaring obscenities and clutching his pierced-through hand, his knife fallen impotent to the ground.

"The Wolf Sister of Arkh Loban has shown you mercy today!" she yelled after him. "It is more than you deserve and will not be bestowed again!"

Jasper retched. "Sorry," he murmured, stunned, his sword heavy in his limp hand. It took him two attempts to sheathe it, so violently was his arm shaking with adrenalin.

"Moon and Realm, stranger, I could have shot you," the woman muttered. Pushing angrily through the trees, she wistfully recounted her remaining arrows before turning her attention back to the Prince.

"I saw him follow you, after that magnificent specimen of a wolf rescued you," she offered by way of explanation, her voice tinged with humour. "He is one of those known as the Authorities in these parts," she advised in a gentler tone, stepping into his line of sight to stem the fear lingering on the young man's face. "The term is necessary to retain some level of covertness in these times."

Jasper met her gaze gratefully. "I need to thank you for your rescue, my lady," he managed awkwardly. "But for you, I could have lost more than dignity and injured worse than pride."

"That was assistance, not rescue," she assured him honestly, her golden eyes sparkling. "You fought adequately, as evidenced by your being here to bemoan your fate."

Jasper grimaced, not convinced. Then his mind caught up, and he shot her a direct look. "How in the Realm did you know I was attacked? You weren't in the audience, I would've—"

The woman merely smiled slightly.

Taken aback, the Prince watched her closely for a moment. "What are you doing here?"

"I could ask you the same question," she replied irreverently. "And your obligation to answer me would be greater, seeing as these parts are closer to my home than yours. Fine," she growled in an undertone when no answers were forthcoming from the Fairy. "As a gesture of good faith I will tell you why I am here, as it couldn't be more obvious who you are and where you have come from whether you choose to answer me or not, for the Basilisks have informed me of strangers journeying to these parts, seeking answers to the questions few dare to voice aloud."

Jasper snorted uncertainly. "Your words could mean anything and nothing."

She shot him a measured look that warned him to waste neither his breath nor her time voicing such trivialities. "We are in bandit country, Prince, and you should know none can speak plainly for fear of the information falling into enemy hands."

"I guess," Jasper offered, cowed, and then cursed himself inwardly for not saying something less inane. "But why are you trying to help me?" he tried again. "Who are you?"

"My allegiance is known by deeds, not words," the woman replied, with more fervour than he'd expected. Before he could interject, she added in a drier tone: "If you are here for the Goblin market, I suggest you proceed with greater caution than you have so far shown. All evil I know stems from and gathers there."

"Come on, you can't just—" Jasper broke off, the fierceness of his companion's expression quashing his certitude.

"The markets have been at the square for longer than my lifetime," she continued, refusing to back down. "They have always been a haunt for the desperate and despairing, and those seeking to take advantage. The Goblins running them used to be a tolerated minority; they could not lawfully be punished for petty misdemeanours and whispers of crimes never proven, so they were allowed to stay unchallenged, eking out a tainted existence at the edge of society. Yet now their numbers are swelling to the point where they will soon be able through sheer force to overthrow the remaining vestiges of justice and democracy in this town, and in doing so smother the last hopes of free will and a future still smouldering in the hearts of the people.

"To fall under Goblin-thrall is to slide into a cursed sleep with scant chance of waking. It is not a fate I intend to leave this town to. The Authorities, of course, submit to the Goblins' demands for their own ends, and such an undercurrent is drawing this land to its ruin. The grey ones may be awaiting their leader, but never before have they felt so dangerous; it's as if they've been caught through with a fire I cannot sense the origin of. These things you must know, before you choose to involve yourself."

"It is no longer a choice I can turn away from," Jasper mused, his brow creasing as he regarded her. "I feel like I've met you before."

The woman smiled slightly at something he was sure he wasn't aware of. "You have. And you will again." She hooked her bow over one shoulder to leave.

"That was you in black, wasn't it?" he realised, wondering. "You appear to be something of a master of disguise."

Her smile broadened, its cause still veiled. "You've no idea."

For a moment Jasper was tempted to offer to accompany her on her way, but seeing the almost worryingly familiar way she handled that hunting-bow and noting that the quiver slung at her hip retained several brightly-fletched arrows, he gave up and settled for performing a slightly awkward bow and wishing her all success in her quest.

Her eyes glowed in response, and she darted away beneath the trees, leaving him with but a memory.

Alone in the forest, staring after her, Jasper realised he'd neither offered his name nor received hers. Dismay rose, but he allowed himself a smile. She wouldn't be hard to recognise, even if she were in some new disguise, not with those eyes. They didn't just seem to see past the façade of royalty forced upon him, they didn't just flash with strength. They were gold-flecked, like the wolf's.

Something flicked in his mind. Arkh *Loban*. City of *Wolves*. So when she'd called herself "Wolf Sister" . . .

Awash with confusion, Jasper hurried on, and circled the same clump of trees twice before realizing it and hastening back towards the library vaults.

Rraarl

Amber's feet slapped against the cold rock as she padded through the fissure-like opening of the tunnel. Shivering at the sudden chill after the heat of the desert, a sudden warmth bloomed within her as she beheld, almost invisible amidst their shroud of cobwebs, the rudimentary torches more ancient even than the ceremonial ones at the castle, propped against the blackest nooks in the wall.

Amber's breath caught with emotion as she contemplated how long they had been left there in bold defiance by those who'd opposed the Emperor at the height of his power, to help those they trusted would follow after. Somehow she felt better just to know that someone all those years ago had believed enough to help the someone who was now her.

Grimacing at the greasy tickle of the cobwebs dusting her hair, Amber disentangled a torch carefully, thought better of lighting it right away in case the ventilation proved bad, and pushed more confidently into the darkness.

Left, then right . . . that's what he'd said. Wasn't it? As she journeyed further, growing more acutely aware of the depth of the blackness and the closeness of the walls, alone with her shallow breathing quickening as she groped along the rough rock, she felt her heart slam as her shaking hands parted to yet another fork in the passage. What in five seasons was she supposed to do now?

You haven't taken many turnings yet, she insisted, struggling to talk herself out of panicking even as she felt the sweat prickle the back of her neck. *You'll be able to trace your way back if you need to. Stay calm and make a choice.*

With clammy fingers, she extricated the flint firestone in her pocket from its leather pouch, half loath to use it in case she drew attention to herself.

Left?

Her footsteps faded into muteness, her flustered breathing the only audible presence now as her fears clamoured in time to her racing pulse. *Give it time—no, it's too far. Is it supposed to be narrowing like this?* Her heart thudding so heavily she felt sick, she clung to the slim promise of light as the swimming blackness grew the slightest dimensional tinge. Amber scrambled towards it, her vision blotching weirdly as the darkness lifted into a heavy twilight. *Please let this be it.*

She tried to tell herself it was just her beleaguered senses struggling to adapt to the eerie lich-light after so long in pitch darkness, but through the ambiguous shadow-night she felt the sudden prickling sensation of being watched.

Spinning round, she nearly screamed as she saw amongst the ghost-grey of the chamber a dark figure crouched silhouetted as if rising from the mists.

Her fingers flying to her pocket, clumsily in her terror she struck the flint against the torch. As she thrust it forward and welcome light spilled into the shadows, giddy relief brought laughter tumbling from her lips. *A statue. Just a statue.*

Emboldened and intrigued, lifting the torch high she tiptoed towards it. Illuminated in the flickering light, studded into the savage face of the life-size Gargoyle the jet-black eyes glistened hypnotically, staring fixedly into the darkness beyond the Fairy.

But what a statue . . . The torchlight accentuating each aspect into a play of warmth and shadow, she studied the carving, unable to help marvelling at the detail that had gone into it. Seemingly hewn out of the roughest cavern-rock in stark contrast to the marble reliefs displayed in the castle halls, it was a figure unlike any other.

Half crouching, half kneeling, the Gargoyle took the likeness of a man—his build as powerful as she had seen, the musculature intricately carved, and with pointed ears and sharpened teeth and features contorted into a soundless snarl—but a man nonetheless. A rusted chain hung immobile from his clenched fists, and his fathomless eyes gleamed with an intensity that frightened her. But as she stepped round quickly to get out of that fixed gaze in the eerie, inconsistent light, her glance fell upon strange cuts tracing across the stone back and shoulders. They had to have been just accidental strikes from the unwieldy carving tools used long ago, but to Amber they looked almost like the lashings of a whip. Instinctively her heart, and her hand, went out to the figure, and she touched the stone shoulder gently.

Torchlight flared in the piercing obsidian eyes, and although it had to have been just a trick of the light she flinched back nervously, snatching her hand away as if stung. Spooked, she fled the alcove, racing back until she rejoined the tunnel, cursing her curiosity and nerves in equal measure.

The gritty dampness of the underground air withered into dry heat as Amber stumbled from the tunnel, squinting as her eyes adjusted to the dust mote-strewn near-daylight to stare in a mixture of triumph and despair at the row upon row of cobweb-encased tomes piled precariously onto fragile-looking shelves stretching from floor to shattered ceiling. In this state of disrepair the library looked even older and more ravaged than Jasper had described, and Amber trod carefully over the uneven, sand-blown tiling. So this was the place the Authorities feared so much they outlawed. Even now, it held its own defiant beauty.

Running a hand along the shelves, she turned her attention to the books themselves: true histories, not the Authorised versions . . . a battered *Rashtakkan*, holding words of the Dragontongue, slim enough to slide into any dust jacket . . . entire volumes of songs . . . but where were the maps?

Painfully aware of the hours, judging by the now-streaming sunlight glancing through the glassless window arches, that she had already wasted getting lost, Amber forced herself to dismiss the half-heard wisps of sound behind her, focusing instead on her search. What use would she be to the others if she jumped at every noise? It was probably just a feral dog anyway, wasn't the city renowned for them?

She tugged at a faded cover in excitement, coughing as the dislodged dust billowed up. *Maps of the Dragon Ages*—this looked more like it. But as she lifted it, the spine tore from the age-weakened cover, sending the slab of pages crashing to the floor and forcing her to spin round to avoid it landing on her foot. *That was close*—

Her eyes flew to a movement behind the shelves and she barely stifled a shriek at the sight of the blood-matted, black-furred spectre.

Dropping to the floor, she crept in the opposite direction, silently begging that the tiles beneath her feet would not this time crack; would not this time shift.

Surrounded by more shelves, she clenched her teeth round a curse, no idea where the exit could be.

She shrank back as turning a corner she glimpsed another Venom-spitter; its massive head low to the ground, viscous ropes of venom shaken free with each searching sweep of its muzzle.

Sickening weakness flooded through her. *They're close enough to scent you.*

Despairingly she cast left and right, trying to grapple her mind, alien and unwieldy in the clutch of terror, into thinking straight. *It's not over till you submit to the fear. Think. There has to be another way. They didn't build these things so they could get trapped. Jasper said they always built a way out; one that they knew, but the enemy wouldn't see.*

Dragging her protesting mind through the options, Amber forced her petrified limbs into action and, begging her terror-stolen senses to serve her once more, crept to the end of the shelf. Staring wildly in every direction for fear of confronting the monsters, she backed against the wall and began sweeping her hands over the stones, feeling along the joins, scanning desperately across the room for anything out of the ordinary; anything different. She almost cried aloud as the rising flood of panic threatened to engulf her. There had to be a weapon, an exit, a hideout, anything.

Entire shelves crashed amidst dust clouds, the ground shuddering into the crumbling scuffle of talons over rubble as suddenly the monsters converged and caught sight of her, charging through the ruins, sending rock and debris smashing as they gave chase amidst baying, manic howls.

Terror stripping her of all reason, tearing herself from the deadly paralysis of fear she turned towards the only other wall and ran.

And there was nowhere. She reached the wall in seconds, and there was nowhere else to go. Injustice overtook fear. There wasn't going to be a secret exit. There wasn't going to be any way out at all. And they were coming.

She turned, and with nothing else to do, bellowed at them until her eyes streamed and her throat seized, her voice's echo the only returning cry.

Gasping down air, everything seemed now unnaturally quiet, and a small part of her wondered whether something had happened to her already as she stared into the hypnotic eyes as they encircled, watching her with something akin to curiosity. She couldn't tear her stricken gaze away as the monsters stalked stiff-legged and inescapable towards her.

The fraught air splintered as the ruins erupted again in a rumbling crash, the ground shuddering with a violent impact that sent Amber sprawling to the floor, the Realm distorting into the screaming protest of stone on stone.

Growling and whining uncertainly, the Venom-spitters turned.

Coughing against the sand-cloud billowed up from the impact as the air filled thick and choking white, Amber squinted up through streaming eyes to see a dark figure, indistinct against the swirling particle-fog, rise slowly from the haze.

As the dust settled, she stared at the apparition in disbelief.

The scarred, awesome stone physique.

The piercing jet-black eyes.

The rusted chain, hanging motionless in his grasp.

The—he was the—

The air throbbed, electric, as in a fluid movement the chain snaked out, whipping taut around the central pillar with an echoing *crack*.

The Gargoyle's snarling visage shifted into a vicious smile, and in the potent silence, Amber felt reality slipping away. *You've got backup,* her mind murmured faintly. *You're going to question it?*

For a heartbeat, all held still. Then dissension shivered through the Venom-spitters, and one rushed.

The Gargoyle hauled at the chain and pandemonium fell around them as with a thunderous crash the pillar gave way, the ancient ceiling plummeting in an ear-splitting scraping protest as, section by section, the ruins crumbled in a deafening cascade that sent Amber curling in terror as tightly and small as she could, arms wrapped pitifully over her head, pleading that the shards and spears of stone would miss her, hearing them explode around her so close that she knew it could only be seconds before—

A scream tore from her throat as something slammed into the ground around her and her eyes flew open in panic.

Jet-black eyes locked blazing into hers, teeth inches from her face, as shuddering with the impact of every boulder that hit him the Gargoyle braced over her.

All thought fleeing in that single moment, shielded from harm and held safe in that unwavering stare with the yowls of the monsters trying to escape piercing through the chaos resounding in her ears, Amber flinched at every assault the Gargoyle took as the debris thundered down.

The tattoo fading with the last fleeing whimpers of the Venom-spitters, she risked drawing breath properly again and was wracked with coughing against the whipped up sand. Weakly she rolled over, gasping and spluttering, and wiping clear her smarting eyes, she realised she was alone.

You're safe, she reminded her pounding heart. *The monsters have gone.* She pushed herself off the ground. *The monsters and the, well . . . Gargoyle?*

Her rescuer . . . She spun round, trying to make sense of it. Where was he? Who was he? And how was he . . . how he was?

Wandering dazedly through the wreckage, Amber had to consciously remind herself that now that she was outside she was arguably close to the market square, and that the Prince would probably be waiting there for her with a huge amount of information and a distinct lack of understanding as to what in the Realm had happened to her in the meantime.

But even as she meant to hasten from the ruins, her mind lingered: questions and feelings churning as she turned back. In the tunnel she had seen him so alone, so hurt. To have gone through that, and who knew what else, and still be able to save someone . . .

Tears welled in her eyes, as the thought that she could never thank him, and even more the fact he had felt it necessary to leave before she could, seemed suddenly unbearable.

She bowed her head in gratitude, and as she did her eyes settled on shapes—no, letters—scraped into the sand:

RRAARL

Crouching to touch the fragile inscription, a wondering smile drifted slowly across her face. He'd gifted her his name.

Thank you, she traced, adding her own name next to his.

With a final glance back to the ruins, she coaxed her aching joints into standing and pushed on towards the market square, preparing herself for what Jasper was doubtless going to say when he realised she hadn't found anything out. *It'll be fine,* she told herself firmly. She was empty handed, but she was alive and safe. Saved. He'd understand. Probably not completely, but still . . .

And whatever Jasper had to say about the matter, she admitted to herself, unable to check a self-conscious grin as memories flooded, it was going to take a while to get that encounter out of her head.

The Goblin Market

I shouldn't be here. The mantra repeated through her fear-trapped mind as Amber threaded through the swarms of traders drawing towards the infamous markets.

Swept along by the crowd, the desperation of so many lost and searching souls seeping into her, Amber began to feel chillingly alone. What if the situation at Arraterr had grown so dire that Racxen couldn't leave? What if Jasper got lost? What if Han had been delayed by the Basilisks?

No, she promised herself. *Somewhere amongst the tricksters and traders are your friends, as worried about you as you are about them. You'll find each other, and the map, or information, or whatever, and you'll leave this accursed place together.*

As she watched the multitudes disperse, drifting as if bewitched towards the stalls as they entered the market square, Amber forced the alternatives from her mind, knowing instinctively that she would need every scrap of her focus to avoid succumbing to the insidious enchantments of the Pedlars within.

As soon as she stepped over the threshold onto the age-cracked filigreed tiles of the square Amber felt a subtle alteration of reality: a gravitas, an uncertainty. The cloying air hung pungent with sticky aromas she couldn't name, and the whistling quiet of the open city had been replaced by furtive mutterings punctuated with Goblin cackles as the vendors bartered with deaths and futures. Waves of nausea swept over her as the heady scent of spices assailed her senses and she clutched at her brow, dizzy already, knowing she still had to search the stalls and find the map.

Drawing her breathing back under control, she risked moving closer to examine the stalls flanking the sand-strewn cobbles. *No one's being forced to stay,* she tried to reason, nerves on edge. *We could all walk away if we chose.* But the atmosphere hung as heavy and fraught as a sea biding its time before a storm, and she felt her fists clenching as she approached the closest stall. Bone-charms clacked from the overhanging gnarled branches of a withered tree behind it, and in a jar the frozen form of a Pixie floated suspended, its tiny fingers groping through a bluish liquid and its skin paled by death. Amber turned away, sickened, unable to quell the bile rising in her throat.

"Fairy wings," a cracked voice cackled behind her. "Crisp and dry. For all your potions. You know what they say about—"

She dragged her cloak tighter around her in the heat as she pushed away through the crowds, feeling naked beneath their rapacious stares.

Everything started blurring. Rattles sounded, like the shaking of snake-tails. Goblins clothed in tattered cloaks of strange fabrics descended from crumbling stone walls or stepped out from behind ruined remnants of fallen towers. Their gait grew shuffling and innocuous when she turned to them directly, but she shivered to glimpse the steel-like gleam in the scouring eyes lowered in feigned respect as united groups of citizens strode past only to fix hungrily on subdued peasants and over-confident gentry alike, sending them hurrying to the relative safety of the Travellers' Pass.

All this time, the marauders' numbers were growing: she could see the death-grey figures slipping through the unknowing crowd, subtle and unstoppable as rivers flowing to a drowning pool.

The warnings she'd had drummed into her ever since she was a winglet rose like jittering moths in her mind: *Never sample Goblin-wares, no matter how beguiling the lies that the Pedlars weave. From the moment they touch your lips, they will have a hold on you. You may not think so at first; you may not feel it until later, but you will never be free again. You will find no peace; the hold will tighten until your life is not your own and everything you wagered for will come to ash. Eventually, it will catch up with you. You go there to buy; you end up sold.*

And here they are coming, her mind interjected, strangely detached in the inevitability of it, even as her deeper soul quailed at the sight:

Goblins—stalkers of innocents and abusers of fears.

Goblins—breakers of dreams and stealers of souls.

Goblins—advancing in droves, the atmosphere shifting with their presence into a tangible aura of malice and rage. Each darting movement from the horde betrayed a restlessness, an impulse barely controlled, and all the while the rheumy yellow eyes emanated a watchful, considered callousness that scared her in a way not even the Venom-spitters could.

Before her instincts could paralyse her, Amber pushed forwards amongst the crowds to scan stall after stall, careful not to get too close and rushing past when they held no parchments. But then—

There it was. Had to be. Cold sweat clung to her. This was where it started. This was why they always won. They always had what you needed. And she had to get the map, or she'd be letting everyone down.

Steeling herself, she strode up to the stall, her hands jammed into the pockets of her cloak so the Goblin couldn't see how much they were shaking. She made her eyes flit neutrally over each of the items, although she was panicking so much she could barely take any of them in.

So absorbed was she in racing through what she could possibly say that, when the Goblin slipped out from behind the table to spring lightly to her side, she started violently.

"I think this is yours," a strange voice advised, handing her back her coin pouch.

Amber's heart slammed. How had—

"Pick-pockets," the Goblin shrugged, with a roguish grin. "Round here we get used to it, but I'm guessing such a beauty doesn't as a rule frequent these parts."

Amber managed an embarrassed smile, shaken that someone had managed to grab her pouch, and he of all people had—

"So," the Goblin spread a hand theatrically across the stall, interrupting her confusion. "This is the only place in the Realm where 'anything' means 'anything'. Faint heart or fair maiden—which will it be, I wonder?"

Her heart hammering in her ears, Amber barely dared let her eyes linger over the map for fear of betraying any emotion for the Goblin to pounce on. "Where's that of? Looks too old to be any use to anyone."

The Goblin smiled to himself, and considered. "My, we are feeling brave today, aren't we?" With a flourish, he spread out the map. "The oldest corners of the Realm, my girl. Not the sort of thing you'd want falling into the wrong hands, am I right?"

Amber kept her mouth clamped shut even as her tongue itched to be drawn into a response. Jasper had made it clear this would be vital to the quest; the sooner she had it, the sooner they could leave.

"Out of curiosity, how much?" she risked.

The Goblin's grin widened imperceptibly. "Well now, seeing how this is just out of curiosity, and as we don't want anyone else getting their filthy hands on your money, how about the word of a lady?"

Amber stalled. There had to be a catch. "My word?"

"Yeah. Means nothing, no offence, 'cept to you an' me."

Amber thought frantically. She didn't know much about magic, let alone sorcery. Could you do anything terrible with someone's word of honour? And she'd convinced Jasper she could handle this. If she came back empty handed, he'd lose what tenuous faith he still had in her. "What kind of map is it?" she stalled, cursing herself for not knowing what to do.

"Normal one. For round here, anyhow. Don't look too closely at the ink. Or the paper, actually."

She couldn't help noticing how the edges curled, yellowish and almost transparent, crisscrossing into infinitesimal squares amongst larger grooves. She couldn't place how, yet there was something so wrong about it. "But what kind did you say—"

"No more questions, wench," the Goblin snapped, all trace of favour evaporating from his harsh voice. "I've done you a favour; I could have kept that purse, but you don't trust me. I've spent my good time dealing with a complete stranger as a respected equal, and I'm beginning to think better of it. If you can't take what I say on trust, you don't deserve my custom. I thought you were different from them peasant girls; I thought you had more backbone, thought we understood each other. Give your answer—and make it sharp!"

Amber felt suddenly terrified of his reaction. "I can't just—"

"What?" the Goblin barked venomously. "Should've known. 'S people like you who give women a weak name. Take no risks. What're you going to do; wait for some Prince to rescue you and take responsibility for what you should have done yourself? Pah—I thought you were better than that. Never been more wrong. You want your friends to see you as an important part of this quest instead of some stupid hanger-on, you better get used to making sacrifices, or why should they do the same for you?"

Too miserable to stay for the rest of his judgement, Amber pushed away from the stall as the tears squeezed from her eyes at the reawakening of her fears. What would Jasper think of her? And worse she'd let Racxen down, and the others: the Goblin was right.

Running blindly from the square, she found the nearest derelict wall and crouched in its shadow, bunching the corners of her cloak into her eyes to hide the tears that however angrily she tried to prevent just wouldn't stop.

Fuming at having been left behind by the Prince, Mugkafb wandered the market alone, wide-eyed at the strange items lain out on dusty, old-patterned cloths. It would serve Jasper right if he were the one who found the map; then the Prince'd have to admit that Mugkafb was just as important as some stupid royal who couldn't even follow an hour-old trail.

The Arraheng jumped at a voice by his ear. "Would there be something I can help you with, young master?"

Not as scared as he'd thought he would be, looking up at the Goblin Mugkafb hesitated. The Pedlar's voice was quiet, but there was something in his manner that smacked of danger, and the boy found himself uncomfortably wishing that Jasper were here, even if it did mean getting shouted at. But the Goblin was smiling at him, and Jasper, having done nothing but snipe at him for slowing him down or for going on about Gorfang, hadn't smiled at him all day.

"I don't suppose," Mugkafb tried in what he hoped was a fearless voice, suddenly hoping the Goblin would say no, "that you sell maps?"

"Well, I'd *like* to say no," the trader confided, looking Mugkafb up and down as if appraising his worth for possessing such a treasure. "But you, my friend, you've shown such . . . bravery . . . in coming all this way, and quite alone. You look like someone who'd put the artefact to ethical use; I can tell it would be in good hands. I can also tell that you're no fool, so I'm not going to ask you for your money up front; instead I'm going to let you view the map yourself first—make sure it's the genuine article, like. Come on through."

Before Mugkafb knew it, the Goblin's wizened hand had clamped vice-like round his wrist. His skin felt like it was burning. He didn't like the Goblin's smile now, and he didn't like the way those filthy claw-nails were digging into his arm.

"How much for that—I need to reach my money," he managed quickly, gesturing at the first thing his fevered gaze fell on, and the Goblin's grasp loosed like a spring at the possibility of completing a transaction. Mugkafb snatched his hand away quickly, stepping back under the pretence of looking into his coin-pouch and, shoving aside the embarrassment of everyone turning to stare he ran, faster than he could ever remember having run, until he was in the middle of the square and when he spun round the only people clustering around him were the fraught-eyed buyers.

His heart tattooing out of control, trembling overtook Mugkafb as in the suffocating heat he felt gripped with a creeping chill, knowing instinctively that he'd escaped something more terrifying even than the lake predator he'd fled with Amber.

"Mugkafb!" The Prince's strident voice cut through the dusty air like the breaking of an enchantment, and the boy ran to him, burying his face in his robes.

As he hugged him, wishing he could protect him from the vicious hurts of the Realm, Jasper realised his eyes were watering too. "You can hate me, okay?" he whispered fiercely. "You can curse me, you can tell me you wish me to die. You just can't ever be scared of me, Mugkafb. You never need to run away, and that is a vow as solemn as any I've made at the Royal Council. While I'm even half-standing I will not let anything bad happen to you, but I can't do that if I don't know where you are. If you're under my care, you're to stay in my line of sight. I know Racxen always seems to magically know where you are and what you're doing and steps in at just the right time, but I'm not your brother so my methods are somewhat more mundane."

Mugkafb scrubbed at his eyes with the palms of his hands and swallowed a gulp. "Sen."

Jasper released him gently. "Right, then," he considered. "I need to get this map and find Racxen and Amber, but there's another equally important mission, if you're up for it?"

Mugkafb nodded eagerly, back to his usual self.

The Prince scanned towards the Endless Forest, keeping his voice low. "We have an unexpected ally, it would seem," he advised the young Arraheng. "Her name is Yenna, and I saw her last in the Forest. She saved me from the Authorities; she has wolf-gold eyes, the longest black hair and olive-bronzed skin and she carries a rather intriguing hunting bow. We're going to need her help with this, although if you don't tell her I said that it might make my life easier."

Mugkafb straightened with pride. "I'll find her," he promised, darting away at once.

Jasper watched in relief as the youngster fled the Square. With a whispered "fly free" out of habit, he pulled up his hood and strode back into the crowds.

As he neared the stalls, having told himself for years that the rumours about the market were nothing but the fool superstitions of uneducated peasants, Jasper found himself in the proud but despairing position of no longer being able to believe nor glean comfort from his previous assumptions. *You wouldn't last one turning of the hour here,* he told himself bitterly, *whilst everyone else proves enterprising enough to carve out not merely an existence but a life. What good is being a royal, or a scholar, here—and what else are you to anyone?*

Trying to shake off his self-doubt, Jasper sighed, set his jaw, and strode towards a stall displaying parchments in various states of disrepair. "I'm looking for the oldest map of the Realm possible," he started, continuing before the Goblin could break in: "and I will give you thirty high coins for it, not one copper more. It's all I have in my wallet—look."

The Goblin regarded him for a long moment, and Jasper felt fear creep in. But the trader merely nodded. "You'd be a fool to carry more in bandit-country, and I can see that you, sir, are no fool."

Jasper nodded curtly. "I have no time to loiter, my good man. Your speed and discretion are appreciated."

The Goblin shrugged. "Very noble way you have about you sir, if I may venture to express an opinion. Almost Princely, I'd wager? I'll get it for you directly."

Jasper kept his breathing measured. This was evidently the way to deal with Goblins: concise, direct, no nonsense. He stared uncertainly as the Goblin spread the map with a flourish. His eyes watered; the map looked like it had been inked in blood.

"Worst kind o' criminal," the Goblin assured him. "Deserved it. Dead now anyway, so it doesn't even matter."

"I don't think I can," the Prince managed, his throat drying.

The Goblin's eyes hardened. "Sorry? A moment ago you were talking like royalty, but now you're going back on your word like some common serf?"

Jasper took a step back. "I just—"

The Goblin pushed closer, his voice rising in judgement. "But you told me—word of a Prince an' all—that it was important. An' if it's important to you, it must be vital for your people. But you're saying no. You're putting yourself above your own people."

Jasper opened his mouth, cold sweat clinging to his brow. *Good grief,* he thought to himself in panic; *all I said was—*He checked his thoughts; the people next to him were staring. "It's not that—"

"Take it then, go on—"

"No wonder no one respects yer authority," another Goblin materialising behind him broke in, loudly enough to gather more traders. "No wonder yer just yer father's son. You change yer mind every time it gets a bit tough for yer. What does that say about the King you'd be?"

Their taunts echoing irrevocably, dragging together as much dignity as he could muster Jasper fled the Goblins' persecution before they could savage the last remnants of his conviction.

Pulling his cloak protectively around him as he stared into the mass of glassy-eyed strangers, he hoped Amber had fared better and suddenly wished she were there with him. Even when she didn't agree with him—and it was frequently, he remembered as a ghost-smile twitched across his lips—she knew he'd changed; believed in what he could become.

"Jasper!" Her voice shrilled high with relief as she pushed through the crowd.

The cares of this accursed place lifting, the Prince ran to meet her, but against his pale, drawn face his smile couldn't have been convincing, for he saw concern fill her eyes as she gripped his hand tightly as if fearing the strange sorcery at work here would conspire once more to tear them apart.

"I don't suppose 'engo ro fash' would sound the same, coming from me," Jasper grinned, giving her hand a reassuring squeeze. "But we'll be out of here soon. I haven't acquired the map," he added guilty, hating himself for having put her through all this to no avail. "I believe it's for the best."

"I said no too; it wasn't worth it," Amber added awkwardly, wishing she'd trusted earlier that he wouldn't have a go at her. "I'm proud I refused, but I know you were convinced it was the only thing that could help us, and I'm sorry we've ended up finding nothing."

"Not quite nothing," insisted the Prince, grimfaced about the Goblins but clinging to a bud of pride. "We've each found the line we will not cross despite temptation, provocation, and pressure. Following which," he added more lightly, "it should be a mere trifle to ascertain how to achieve our goal without needing that accursed scrap of paper they want us to barter our souls for. I've sent Mugkafb off to the Forest to keep him safer, so let's find Racxen and get out of here."

Determinedly, he stomped off, and grinning, she followed.

Slipping through the horde of buyers and hawkers, Amber glimpsed Racxen's form and darted on ahead, breaking away from the Prince.

"Racxen!" Her shout melded into a warning cry of horror as she saw a Goblin reach him first. Shoved and jostled by the multitudes as she tried in vain to struggle through, she could only watch as Racxen turned to confront his foe.

"Hello, son," the Goblin growled, her perversely soft voice loud enough to shiver across the crowded distance and into Amber's soul as she thrust her long, leering face closer to his, her point-filed teeth showing in a wicked, leisurely smile. "Remember me?"

Suddenly a buyer laden with a sack of apples backed into her, and Amber stumbled, automatically blurting an apology and fumbling the things hastily back into the bag, but when she stood again she couldn't see the Arraheng.

Cursing, she pushed forward, searching frantically, her mind replaying the scene as fear trickled in: *the Goblin knew him—really knew him.*

So close, yet to Amber unreachable, Racxen's world shrank into the immediate as the Goblin's voice lowered. "What's the matter—Goblin got yer tongue?" she taunted. "Don't worry yerself, won't be long now."

"Keep your distance," Racxen growled. "You will never take my soul."

"Wouldn't dream o' denying His Majesty the pleasure," the Goblin retorted with mock civility. "I'd sleep with one eye open, son. Them that're friendlier with the darkness than you will come knocking one o' these nights. The words you speak alone to a starless night are always those you would be wisest to remember. And I wouldn't get any foolish ideas about changing the future," she rasped sneeringly before he could recover his senses. "You ain't had much luck amending the past."

Racxen staggered back as if he'd been struck, but the Goblin's wizened hand whipped out and pulled him close. "Hear this, earthcrawler," she hissed. "Our armies are massing. Days from now this city will fall, as the Realm starts to crumble. His Lordship—or should I say *your* Lordship now—nears these plains as we speak. He will claim the debt you owe: your body will fall and what's left of your soul will be taken."

The Goblin's eyes gleamed dangerously. "Make no mistake, he will find you. Just as I have, after all these seasons. The boy lived, son. And we don't leave a debt unpaid."

Shoving him back roughly before he could retaliate, the Goblin sprang away without another word, already lost amongst the crowd.

Unable to move, washed through with shame and fear, Racxen stared after her, oblivious to all else; to Amber now standing shocked beside him having shouldered through the crowd, to the trembling that overtook his body; everything. Nothing registered save for the terrifying words of the Goblin, and the death knell they sounded.

Finally catching up, having missed the whole exchange Jasper unwittingly broke the silence by admonishing them all to leave. Racxen led on, stalking off ahead without another word, and with an exasperated sigh the Prince let him be, throwing a plaintive look to Amber.

Running to catch him up, Amber matched the Arraheng's pace wordlessly until they were out of the market and far from the eyes and ears of the Goblins, her heart feeling squashed in her chest and everything she thought she knew spiralling into uncertainty.

Locked into his fears, Racxen barely noticed the distance, but for Amber the minutes beside him, not knowing what to think, were more excruciating than all her time in the Market. *This is Racxen,* she forced her mind to repeat. *There'll be a decent explanation.* Clinging to that thought, though, was getting harder.

Realising despairingly that he wasn't going to say anything, Amber stopped, feeling awkward and sick. "What was she talking about?" she asked in a small voice, dreading the answer with all her soul.

The Arraheng didn't look at her, kept his eyes to the ground.

Before her throat could seize up and her mind fall blank, Amber blurted everything out in one breath: "Racxen, I'd hoped you knew that you could trust me by now. Don't insult me by saying 'nothing'. I trust you, but this is starting to scare me. Tell me what's going on, or I've got no choice but to rely on my own awful conclusions, and I refuse to do you that disservice. If you're in some kind of danger, I want to help, and I can't do that if you won't let me in."

He glanced at her then, more trapped and hopeless than she'd ever seen him before.

"Sen," he chanced wretchedly. "I'll tell you."

Racxen's Tale

"You're going to need to know how this started, if we are to have any hope of deciding the ending for ourselves," Racxen admitted miserably. "It was many seasons ago. Mugkafb was too young to now remember it, or so I still fervently hope."

His voice shook, the words dragging years of buried pain to the surface, raw and overwhelming. "It was my fault," he blurted desolately, fixing Amber in a pleading stare. "He was always begging to come with me on my treks, and one day I relented. I needed to scout towards Loban, but these were volatile times, and as we were crossing the border we were caught in the crossfire of some rebel faction who had hijacked a convoy of goods. Mugkafb was hit by a stray poisoned arrow—" his face contorted at the memory. "It went so badly for him; nothing I did could stem the bleeding and we were nowhere near civilisation. I knew he couldn't make it back to our lands; it was a day's trek, and we were too far for the Zyfang to hear a summons. Our only chance, so I thought, was to carry on through the desert and hope to reach an Arkhan healer in time.

"Caution now was worthless, so I cradled my brother in my arms and strode through the desert in as straight a path as possible. It would have been a perilous trek at the best of times, but we had little water, the winds were high, the sun harsh, and within the hour I was no longer sure Mugkafb was still with me. The nonsense words and frightened murmurs he had at first uttered had drifted away entirely, and none of my pleas could rouse him. I had no reason to believe him to still be alive, save for a vague feeling and the burning hope that this young soul in my arms who'd filled my life with purpose and pride hadn't quite left."

A grimace twisted Racxen's face and his head jerked involuntarily as if attempting to dislodge the memory he had never been able to free himself from. "I can remember thinking: I would give anything—anything at all—to save him. And it was then the Goblin caught up," he spat bitterly.

"A lone Pedlar. She must have trailed us for the last hour, I neither knew nor cared; a hundred would not have made me change my course. But this Goblin—" he couldn't look at Amber now, instead dropping his eyes to the dirt ground as he forced himself to continue. "She offered me something for myself, and I refused. But then she presented something else. A phial of potion, for my brother."

Racxen stared into the distance through haunted eyes. "I will never forget what she told me then: 'He will certainly live until nightfall—and just as surely die before dawn.'"

His eyes swam with unfallen tears. "I thought it would buy him time," he managed wretchedly, gulping air as he strove to keep his voice steady. "I accepted the Goblin's terms. In those few hours, I knew I could get him to Loban; to a healer . . . I thought he'd be okay . . ." Racxen flexed his hands, rubbed his claws to steady himself.

"I took the potion. The Pedlar merged into the heat-mists of the desert, and I was left with a cursed chance." His eyes took refuge in the horizon again.

"I held my brother close. I told him that I loved him and that I was sorry. I urged him to hold on, to fear neither pain nor darkness. I promised I would get him to the healers and stay with him. And then I dripped the liquid into his cheek, and waited. For seconds I dared not count there was no sign, and I began to fear it would not work; that my brother truly was dead. Then—how will I ever be able to forget that sound—he screamed. The most terrible sound I have ever heard, and he would not stop.

"All the way to Loban, I carried him—and all the way he screamed; the heartrending wail of a tortured soul. I grew terrified that my choice had been wrong; that it would have been kinder to have let him slip away back there; to have allowed that small, quiet step from unconsciousness into nothingness.

"Instead, my choice was destroying him; ravaging him with unthinkable pain. Never before had I encountered the treachery of Goblinwares, and I despised myself more than any monster I'd tracked for having in my naivety subjected my brother to such torture.

"Cursing myself to the earth itself, I stumbled into the first healer's hall I found in Loban, clutching my brother as if I could sustain him through will alone.

"They did what they could; cleaned the wound, staunched the bleeding, administered transfusions, bound the wound. It appeared everything that could be done had been done—yet still he would not stop screaming.

"I think at that point I just wanted to follow my brother and die. It drew me the closest to madness I have ever been, but with nothing else left to cling to, I convinced myself that hope might lie undiscovered just around the next corner if only I could will myself that far on his behalf. Thus somehow I made the journey back to the grasslands, and screamed a cry to the Zyfang.

"Faint from hard flying, she threw down her answering call to me, and if I'd had breath I would have praised her to the moon she flew by.

"I clambered onto her back, and in my feverish state the pulsed waves of sonar she rained upon the landscape resounded like whip cracks in my head, until I glimpsed to the south a silver thread ripple through the darkness below, and my heart sang as I guided her in a slurred gasp to the stream, for I knew that the only hope now lay with the near-lost healing skills of the Sea Folk.

"My steed-friend called as she alighted, and as I half-fell from her and ran stumbling to the water there swam already three Maidens and two Knights to greet me. They gave me no reproach as I tried to blurt what had happened, half incoherent I was so distraught, and they looked on me as welcomingly as if I were one of their own kin as they took my brother from me and swam with him into the centre of the pool.

"Watching them, I knew that if there remained any hope for Mug-kafb outside the reversal of my actions, it lay here. Yet I knew something now of the twisted way in which the Goblin-arts worked and, although I feared that it was just my delirium urging me towards such things when the most I could really hope to offer might be to be here when he awoke, I could not sit by and watch others drained in their efforts and not do everything in my power to try and help my brother, no matter the risk to myself. And so it grew, in the adrenalin-depleted logic of my mind at least, clear as to what I must attempt.

"That night, I went to the ruined palace, and proffered myself before the Goblin King, pledging my life to him in exchange for my brother's, asking him to transfer the blood-debt to me.

"Mayhap it appealed to his idea of sport to have a willing victim for an arrangement of such depravity, for he eventually agreed. To seal the bond he cut my hand with his own blade; not deeply, but it hurt savagely, for it was laced with a weak poison so that as a reminder of our bargain the wound formed a scar that has never fully healed."

He opened his hand to reveal the mark, and Amber wondered why she hadn't really noticed it before. She'd just assumed it was from tracking; that he'd cut himself on something sharp in the undergrowth. She thought with sadness of how little she truly knew him, and of how alone he must feel even when they were together.

"I slipped back to the lake," he mumbled self-consciously, "to be greeted again by those who passed no judgment. All night they stayed with Mugkafb, and at midnight they bade me sleep, beneath the trees whispering their lullaby beside the lake. One of the Maidens told me she would come to me should any ill befall my brother, and those people do not lie.

"Despite vowing I would stay awake in case I was needed, exhaustion must have taken me, for I was woken by the cooling fingers of a Knight upon my shoulder, his scale-patched skin iridescent in the predawn gloaming and his eyes shining with such a light that I knew all had gone well even before I could ask. Bidding me follow, he hauled himself gracefully towards the bank to reunite with the water's embrace, and as I padded light-headedly after him I heard the brook-like laughter of a Maiden in the Glade Pool itself, and it was as if a veil had been lifted from the Realm as I stared at my brother, curled in the most comfortable-looking slumber as she held him safe in her arms in the shallows.

"The Knight slipped beneath the surface with barely a ripple, beckoning me to join them—Mugkafb was beginning to wake as I ran down the bank into the welcoming water. And heal him the Sea Folk had, for he opened his eyes and seemed content, if slightly confused and not knowing what the fuss was over, nor why his big brother had tears streaming down his face, nor why he was with the Maidens and Knights as he could not recall having needed healing in the first place.

"Over time, he recollected fragments from the ambush, which we talked about in front of the fire wrapped in a blanket. He remembered being pierced by an arrow, and feeling very sick, and me carrying him through somewhere hot and windy, and me stumbling when I walked, which hurt him.

"Yet of the Goblin and what happened after—nothing. His memory is awash instead with the warm calm of the water, the strong hands of the Knights as they cleansed the wound and bound it—and I know he remembers the Maiden's healing song; sometimes I hear him singing it to himself at night if he's upset.

"Such were the skills of the Maidens and Knights that the Goblin-potion has tainted neither his mind nor his body, and the shadow of that time does not rest on his brow." Racxen paused. "I am sure of it," he murmured in an undertone, brow creasing as he mentally re-trod the path as if searching for a missing piece that would hold more comfort, and Amber nodded quietly, wishing achingly that she could help him believe it.

"I should have known that Goblin-trysts are never what they seem," he whispered feverishly into the silence. "I should have known that he would suffer."

"How can you say 'should have' when you could not?" Amber countered. "You saved him," she reminded him carefully. "No one can say that was the wrong decision; you did what was necessary, and he is safe and well as a result."

Racxen's eyes lingered on her face as if trying to ascertain whether she truly thought so, and he smiled weakly. "I am grateful for your words, but I can take no solace from them. The healing I owe to the Knights and Maidens alone. I cannot regret my decision—to save him I would pledge my life a hundredfold. Yet the remembrance of what I did twists splinters into my heart, for what if there had been another way I could have found? I still hear his screams in my head some nights; I just—whether it's from guilt or the potion—I feel so poisoned." He flinched away wretchedly, his claws hovering over the earth in anguish.

Amber quietly covered his hands with hers, holding them gently. "You told me the earth sustains your people through all things. She didn't desert you or Mugkafb—she nurtured the medicines that helped heal him; she filtered the waters of the Glade Pool; her breath was the high wind that carried the Zyfang swiftly to you."

In his silence, Racxen's eyes spoke gratitude. "The full story of what happened, my brother does not know," he admitted more steadily, his voice full of tiredness as a look of absolute certainty crossed his care-worn face. "Lonely burden as it is, I can never tell him."

Amber kept a respectful silence, trying to take in the enormity of her friend's disclosure. "You're braver than me," she offered. "To have carried that memory alone every day . . ."

Racxen shook his head. "Like I've told you before, it has nothing to do with bravery," he mumbled. "You've just never been in that situation."

Amber grimaced. "Racxen, I'm so sorry; it must have brought every-thing flooding back. The Goblin you just saw, did she hurt—"

"I'm fine," Racxen promised unevenly, attempting a smile that didn't reach his dulled eyes. "She brought a warning. Well, from that night hence according to Goblin-law, that which it is, my life belonged to their King. I railed against it the only way I could: I became a tracking scout, monitoring the Goblin colonies in these parts, hoping to protect my tribe against that from which I had failed to save my brother. On my trails I strove to confront my nemeses; to acquaint myself with their fighting styles and behavioural traits—anything that could lend me the advan-tage, lessen the paralysis of fear they instilled in me and help me to acquit myself honourably in my brother's eyes in the hope that he will come to know that I will never again let him down. I have done everything I can to try to atone for what I did and stave back what must happen.

"I had never returned to the markets until now. I thought it would no longer haunt me," he muttered brokenly. "I thought I could escape it, but all the miles I have trekked have not been far enough. I have just been waiting out the inevitable; it is finally catching up with me, just as he told me it would."

He let out a staggered sigh, his eyes bereft of hope. "It has been slowly eating me away, and I can gain neither peace nor closure. This guilt, this weight, has poisoned me and tied me to the accursed Goblins as surely as if their concoction had itself destroyed me, and it will stay with me the rest of my life."

Amber shook her head. "The influence of the Goblins falls away before the magnitude of your own actions. You burdened yourself, sacrificed yourself, so that your brother might be spared. That is love, Racxen—and that is what saved him." Her smile strengthened. "If there is one person the Goblins can never submerge with their darkness or bend to their will, it's you. They wanted you to become so guilt-ridden and afraid and angry that you would become a prisoner to the idea behind the blood-debt. But instead of giving in, you've become the bravest, most compassionate person I've ever known. Every day you endure gifts you further strength—I know you will outlast this, and be rewarded by seeing better times."

His spirit flickered with her words for a moment as his eyes met hers. Yet he glanced away as if in shame, and a great sadness grew with realisation in her eyes. "That was why you led the monsters away," Amber whispered, almost unable to speak it aloud. "Why it had to be you. You wanted to die."

Racxen stared at the ground, retreating within himself. "When you rescued me, I wished so much that you had not . . ." He faltered, choking on emotion.

His words squeezed hurtfully around her throat, and she felt the hot pinpricks of tears stabbing in her eyes as she turned away quickly, churning all her strength into not letting them fall, a hollow sickness twisting her stomach.

Racxen shifted, gently guiding her face with a shaking hand so that his eyes could meet hers again, warm and intense. ". . . At first." His voice shook as he tried to explain. "I know you well enough now to recognise that you would do that without thinking for a friend—and that is extraordinary enough. But the fact you did the same for me when I meant nothing to you—as long as you're here, there's enough magic left in the Realm for me."

His eyes lingered wonderingly, and she realised how safe she felt beneath his gaze; thinking suddenly of how much it would hurt to have to watch him walk away when this was all over. "You're going to defeat this," she insisted fiercely.

Racxen's smile was sad as he squeezed her fingers tightly. "Not this time, I fear," he warned, trying to keep his voice light. "I can neither run nor fight forever." Releasing her hand, he stood abruptly to leave.

Amber sat feeling helpless, thoughts rising chaotic as a sandstorm in her head. "Okay, look," she blurted, as he was about to walk away. "You're right; I don't know if this is conquerable or not, Racxen, any more than you do. But I know that, either way, you're not carrying it alone any more. It's never going to be just you against it ever again."

Racxen's eyes rested guiltily upon her. "Even though it can neither be changed nor escaped?"

Amber nodded steadily. "Maybe what victory there is to be claimed lies in bearing it out with courage. Along that road, we will find answers as yet hidden, and they will equip us to defeat this."

Racxen stared at her in amazement. "Where did that certainty come from?"

Amber shrugged honestly. "Maybe, in my turn, I know you well enough now to recognise that."

Racxen smiled shakily, sitting back down next to her.

"Mugkafb showed me one of his books the other day," Amber offered, buoyed that Racxen seemed to be lifting from the despair he had so bravely admitted. "There was a picture of a woman; kind of an Arraheng but with wings like a Zyfang—she had the calm bearing and kind eyes of one who inspires hope, and she was standing in a tunnel bearing a torch of moonlight."

"The Guide," Racxen explained reverently, his eyes growing distant. "Legend tells that she led the ancient tribes to the caves, and so to safety, when all seemed lost in the clutches of an infamous battle seasons ago that rent the peoples of the Realm apart and began the persecution of our kind." He looked thoughtfully to the horizon. "She would say that a way could be found through the deepest recesses of darkness."

"Sounds like she was right before."

Racxen smiled self-consciously. "She also said that although she was but one, after her there would always be others walking the path in different guises to be found in times of peril, who would lead travellers safely through the dark when all hope failed." His smile broadened as his gaze rested on Amber. "And I know she's right about that."

Amber grinned, her heart swelling as she returned his gaze. "Me too," she said softly, wishing she could think of something more memorable.

Tentatively, Racxen reached for her hand. "No more shutting you out in a misguided attempt to protect you."

Hesitantly, Amber curled her fingers round his. "No more jumping to conclusions in a needless attempt to protect myself."

Racxen shifted nearer, and Amber found herself acutely aware of the narrowed distance between them; the reassurance his closeness brought.

"I thought I was being brave," he admitted, "when I told you to stay away that night; when I meant to leave just now. But it's braver to let you in when I don't have the answers and I can't fight the battles."

It felt the most natural thing in the Realm to rest her head acceptingly against his shoulder in response, and she felt all her worries about their awful predicament lift for a moment as his arm encircled her comfortingly in return. "Racxen, you've seen my frightened side more than anyone else in the Realm," Amber murmured. "Yours is safe with me. I admire you for all that you are, and the stories that make you so, not just the parts you let everyone else see."

As his gaze met hers again, no words were between them necessary as he held her, and gradually Amber found in the warmth of his touch and the steadiness of his heartbeat the courage to recount her own fraught memories of the market and its journey.

"The links between the three monsters are becoming indisputable, if ever more tangled," Racxen interjected finally when a carrion bird wheeling high above broke the sacred silence that had settled. "I was trying to glean the courage to explain," he promised. "Not long before I met you, this quest started for me when I was found by a Goblin, on the outskirts of Arraterr, on his way back from the desert. He warned of a great evil that would sweep across the land—the usual Goblin-chatter.

"Yet something about his words compelled me to retrace my steps to the place where I had long before bargained with the Goblin King. Upon the aged walls of those same tunnels I had traversed that starless night, I found claw-like gashes. I assumed they had been gouged by the Venom-spitters, which were known to frequent caves and had recently begun haunting our swamp-lands—I confess part of me concluded that mayhap the Goblins, returning to their hallowed ground, were seeking to use the Venom-spitters for their own ends.

"However, after Jasper noted the discrepancies in the prints from that carcass, I realised they were instead Vetch markings: the Venom-spitters had been driven out of their caves by the reformation of an earlier evil—hence their new hunting grounds. The Goblin King is the only one who can bend monsters like the Venom-spitters to his will; and it seems my imaginings were correct: now they have encroached on Goblin territory he cannot resist the temptation, for whispers are growing that he is returning to gather his hordes, now that—so they say—Gorfang no longer lives to stop him."

Racxen sighed heavily, returning to the present with a conscious effort. "Against such things, we pledge our unconquerable souls," he promised, the old fire and conviction kindling in his eyes as he turned to Amber, and she grinned to hear him talking as if the Goblin-thrall no longer held sway in his mind.

His face tightened as his gaze lowered. "Yet amidst the threats erupting around us nowhere will remain out of reach, nothing will be left unscathed. The only possible outcome is war, and I fear such a conflict can no longer be prevented." The silence stretched as he grappled uncomfortably with words Amber couldn't guess. "Rraarl sounds a good man," he offered finally, his voice carefully neutral. "I know he can protect you better than I."

"Where did that come from?" Amber couldn't keep the hurt from her voice as she pulled back from his embrace in confusion, studying his face even as she wanted to bite her words back. A thousand things to say in repair fluttered on her tongue and skittered out of reach.

"Racxen, I think Rraarl is a good man," she started hesitantly. "I think it's amazing that he's come back from whatever he's been through. And yes, I valued his protection. But do you think I'm proud that I needed it, or that I'm comfortable with everything that comes with it; the darkness locked inside him simmering so close to the surface, how easily he killed? Do you think I take *that* as the measure of a man? I wished he could see himself as human—and yet at that moment, to survive, I needed the monster. I hate that I put him in that situation; that because of me he slipped a little further along a path he deserves to leave. I'd never want to put anyone in that position. And how could I expect anyone to rescue me when I can't know, however much I want it to be true, that I could save them in return if needed? I couldn't demand that from a—a guard dog, let alone anyone . . . you know . . ."

He didn't. *How could he?* she reminded herself miserably. "I'm looking for someone who sees me as an equal, not some fragile thing always needing protection," she tried again. "Someone who fights foes with me, not for me. I'm looking for—"

"Goblins," Racxen hushed suddenly, staring beyond her. "Split up—find the others."

Amber watched him dart towards them. "Goblins," she murmured awkwardly, cursing her leaden tongue and ridiculous nerves. "Yeah, that's simpler. Maybe we should just stick with that." Squashing the alternative firmly into the very back of her mind so it couldn't make a fool of her again, she strode morosely through the crowds.

A Risk and a Wish

Lashing his tail in frustration as his appearance caught the attention of two Authorities, Han darted abruptly into the nearest alleyway. His priority was to find the four companions, and although as a rule he would have dearly loved to cause a scene, no burgundy livery was going to delay him on this occasion.

He was snapped back to the present by a scuffle from the shadows: shadows that shifted into forms everyone in these parts knew too well.

The nearest Goblin caressed his dagger hilt lazily. "Say, boys. We haven't had *horsemeat* for a while."

From either side, floating laughter answered as more of the horde pushed into view.

Han snorted derisively, heart tattooing in his chest. "If I'd thought you worthy adversaries I'd have floored you before our eyes had met," he boasted to buy himself time, quickly assessing the numbers as the mob tightened around him. But more slunk towards him, blocking the whole alley.

"Well, Centaur," the leader growled, drawing a blackened dagger as the horde closed in. "Believe in evil now, do yer?"

"Evil?" Han snorted, rearing up to flail his hooves in a warning. "I'm merely forced to acknowledge its presence. But *good*—"

He gave a piercing whistle and a familiar golden-eyed Wolf-form sprang from the rooftop, snarling her allegiance.

Han grinned roguishly. "Now *that's* something worth believing in." Before the mob's attention could snap back onto him, the Centaur leapt clear over the closest Goblins, the Wolf Sister's growls and the cries of the thugs forced to dive to safety ringing in his ears amongst the crack of his hooves against the cobbles as he galloped away with Yenna speeding before him, guiding him on.

Slipping through the endless swathes of traders, with Mugkafb even less likely to shut up now that he'd proudly completed his mission of finding the Wolf Sister, Jasper wasn't sure whether he was more relieved or irritated to find Han, embroiled as the Centaur was in some heated argument or other with two Authorities, his strident voice drawing incredulous stares before the townsfolk's courage failed them and they hurried on with downcast eyes.

"You must be terrified of these stories," Han was taunting them, and Jasper's eyes flew skyward in disbelief to hear it. "They're the only ones you can't twist to your depraved ends—I'm not surprised you have such strict censors."

"It is grossly irresponsible to encourage false hope," the first official insisted piously. "How can you plant such dreams in their heads when these children live daily with the far-reaching clutch of evil that chokes us all, and require our surveillance and sanctions to ensure their safety?"

"Because every fulfilled ambition begins with a dream someone said could never come true," Han retorted, irritatingly cheerful. "A seed of an idea—it's all any of us have ever had to carry us through; it's all the heroes whose memories you tried to stamp out started with. As insubstantial and eternal as the wind, and even harder to catch. I'm sorry," he goaded, turning hastily to leave as the second Authority signalled for reinforcements. "I didn't realise I was making you feel so threatened."

An apoplectic stream of curses spewed in response, and Jasper hastily pulled Mugkafb out of earshot.

Emboldened by his company, the Arraheng snuck past the Prince with a sudden idea. His eyes darted curiously over the wares on the closest stall: crinkled, brownish parchments scrawled with writing in a language he couldn't understand; probably curses in the Goblintongue, like in that story where Gorfang—

There's no time for that, Mugkafb checked himself, refocusing diligently. *Find it, quickly, for all of them.* Garish charm adornments with scribbled price tags hung from the display behind the table, and amongst bowls of anyone's-guess herbs that made his head ache, a tarnished old lamp nestled against strange-patterned fabrics.

Mugkafb glanced back to check where Jasper and Han were, and the next thing he knew, the Goblin stall-holder was bellowing in pain and clutching his scorched hand as he cursed virulently at the lamp, its spout now plugged with foul-smelling cloth.

Horror rising, Mugkafb almost collided with Jasper in his haste as he ran back to him, tugging urgently at his robe. "There's a Genie in the lamp—he's trying to kill it."

"How much?" Jasper interrupted hurriedly, seeing Han's eyes harden.

"Two hundred high on the label," Mugkafb blurted, bunching his hands in scared impatience.

"What?" the Prince countered weakly. "This is Goblin territory—I can't carry that much around, you know that."

"But we've got to save it," Mugkafb beseeched. "It's—"

"Out of the question," Jasper hissed, terrified of Goblin retribution any minute. "By the time I went back for funds, it would already have died. I'm sorry, Mugkafb, but we can't possibly just steal it; such action has consequences."

"So does inaction," the Centaur retorted mulishly.

Jasper ignored him. "It's sold by Goblins; think of the repercussions," he tried lamely.

But the young Arraheng was grinning, no longer paying him any attention at all.

"Curse you, Centaur, in all the tongues of this Realm," Jasper growled helplessly in realisation as he turned. But Han had already gone, and with Mugkafb now following, there was no other option left.

Light-headed with elation at having managed to avoid the Goblins, Amber was greeted by the sight of Racxen, Mugkafb, Han, and Jasper looking in turn relieved, triumphant, smug, and embarrassed. Jasper had bundled something up in his travel cloak in a vague attempt at making it appear unobtrusive, and had thereby rendered it tantalizingly conspicuous.

"See for yourself," the Prince pre-empted in despair at her questioning gaze, unwrapping the lamp furtively and holding it out with the air of one thinking it might burst into flames.

Gingerly, Amber watched the antique. It sat motionless in the Prince's hands, shining quietly in the sun and doing its best to look innocuous.

"So what are we going to do with it?" she asked, for wont of a better question.

"Leave it somewhere safe out of sight," Racxen cautioned. "We've saved its occupant."

"Rub it," Mugkafb urged her, before she could ask what his brother meant by "occupant".

"Pawn it in the town for supplies," Jasper reasoned. "We could use food and weapons. More water wouldn't go amiss either." The Prince lifted the lamp closer to peer inside. "There's not really going to be anything in there."

At that precise moment, what looked very much like an insubstantial but bulging eye peeked from the spout, blinking hard in the dazzling light before disappearing. "Some *thing*? I like *that*," an expansive, remarkably human voice protested amongst tinny echoes. There was an apologetic cough of smoke, and a greyish-purple spectral entity floated from the spout amidst a weak puff of hazy blue cloud, startling Jasper so much he almost dropped the lamp on his foot.

"A Genie!" Mugkafb whooped happily into the stunned silence.

"*The* Genie, if it pleases you," the apparition managed grandly, attempting to bow before being overcome by a coughing fit. "Don't worry," he managed, catching Amber's concerned gaze as he wheezed sorrowfully and sneezed some soot. "It's my smoke, not theirs. Stage stuff, completely harmless, purely for the theatrical effect, you understand. I just—" he broke into coughing again "—need some air."

He drew a great breath, and his whole form seemed to swell, until he appeared to the friends' astonished gazes now so light as to be in danger of floating away.

"Ah, that's better." He wafted up to eye-level, his spectral hands weaving a figure-eight pattern, looking for all the Realm like a fish trying to stay immobile against a current.

"Is there anything we can do for you?" Amber asked, not sure if she was being helpful or just ridiculous. "You must have been through quite an ordeal."

"Nah, don't worry," the Genie reassured her chirpily. "It's difficult to hurt someone who's not much more than a wisp of thought on a trick of the light. Although," he added mournfully, "the fact that I'm the colour of a bruise isn't entirely coincidental. But on the much brighter side, I'm free now—my unending gratitude to you all."

"Our pleasure," Jasper returned guardedly, determined to be courteous if only to hide his confusion.

"Please do we get a wish?" Mugkafb broke in, unable to contain himself any longer.

"A wish?" The Genie tasted the word carefully. "Haven't done this for a while. Don't see why not. Be careful, and all that." He twirled showily, and his voice grew deep and dramatic. "Tell me your wish, o worthy travellers."

Jasper shrugged. "We wish for our quest to succeed."

"Excellent!" the Genie enthused. "Now tell me how you're going to go about it."

Jasper blinked. "I thought that was your department."

"*My* department?" the Genie echoed innocently. "Your faith in me is touching, but observe: I'm made of smoke. Do you honestly expect me to whisk four great heavy—no offence—bodies across miles of unknown territory dodging unspeakable dangers ending up who knows where? What a notion. And anyway, it's *your* quest. You don't even know where you're going—course you don't; if you did it would merely be a journey."

"But if we knew where we were going," Jasper interrupted, struggling to keep his patience, "you could in theory do it then, yes?"

"Course I could, and not just in theory." The Genie swelled his incorporeal chest. "I *could* take you anywhere. But I'm not going to."

Jasper gave up with a sigh. "Then we wish for five hundred high golds," he corrected smoothly.

"Oh really?" the Genie countered, fixing his spectral eyes on the Fairy. "In Goblin country? You sure?"

"All *right*," the Prince acquiesced grudgingly. "But you are a wish-granter, are you not?"

"A common misconception," the Genie mumbled uncomfortably. "I'm more of a—well, a wish *facilitator*. Since Gorfang, wish *granting* has somewhat gone out of style. It's all about empowering the wisher nowadays, you see?"

Bathed in a stony glare that established that the Prince, in fact, did not, the Genie spun a theatrical gesture. "You dream of sword-fighting prowess? Go speak with Roanen. Taming a Bicorn? You know where you can find them, and that for every two thousand four hundred and seventy-nine people who do not succeed, there are two who do. The hand of miss—"

"Enough," Jasper interrupted testily. "What are we supposed to do, then?"

"Ah," reassured the Genie brightly. "You're in luck. I have a feeling you're about to work it out. *Cough*—something-closer-to-home—*cough*."

Amber stared. "The castle."

"*Library?*" the Prince challenged, eyeing their latest acquaintance dubiously. "I could have thought of that."

"You just did. You should have more faith in your own resources," the Genie advised mildly. "Go on, prove me surplus to requirements, it'll be cathartic. Cheerio for now." With that, he slid like water down a plug back into the lamp, leaving the four companions staring mutely at the spout.

With a disgruntled snort, the Prince thrust the lamp towards Amber. "You take it, for pity's sake. Mugkafb?" Jasper clapped a hand on the young Arraheng's shoulder. "You probably know more about the old stories, and their lands, than the rest of us put together. Mind helping me with the research tonight?"

Mugkafb glowed with pride. "No problem. After wyshep though, I'm starving; c'mon, Racxen."

Waving his goodbyes to the others, Racxen laughingly took off after Mugkafb as the boy raced away down the hill.

"I'm going to, um—if it's okay?" the Prince asked awkwardly, now that it was just the two of them. "I haven't for a while, you see, and—"

"Fly," Amber shrugged with a too-brief smile, trying not to mind. "It's okay. There's no point neither of us being able to." She tried to laugh, but it didn't work.

Jasper nodded quietly and leaped to the sky, heading quickly for the clouds as if he didn't want to mock her by remaining in view.

"I really have to make this be okay, don't I?" Amber mumbled sadly to the silence. "If I'm not going to end up one of those bitter—"

"Couldn't have said it better myself," approved the lamp from her hands, making Amber jump violently having forgotten all about it.

"I'm going back to Fairymead," she explained to change the subject. "Is that your way?"

"*Everywhere* is my way," pronounced the Genie languorously. "You'll have to excuse me," he added quickly in embarrassment. "I've been stuck in that lamp with no one to talk to; I've somewhat lost the art of conversation. Let's be off."

They walked in silence for a while, the lamp weight sloshing gently from side to side with every step as if it were filled with water instead of, well—

"Genie?" Amber asked.

The incorporeal form materialised again, wispy hands grasping the spout to steady himself as he swayed slightly with the Fairy's gait, eyes swivelling to watch her attentively.

"You know . . . Gargoyles?"

"Ah," agreed the Genie sagely. "So you've met Rraarl."

"Just Rraarl?" Amber stared at her companion. The smoke floating across his face made his expression enigmatic at the best of times. "You mean there aren't, I don't know, a whole bunch of statues that come alive or something?"

"Statues that come alive?" echoed the Genie, bewildered. "Amber, how do you think these things up? No," he divulged with a sad smile. "It really is just him. You see, Rraarl was a man. Well, he still is, obviously—but now he's also something else entirely."

"Okay," Amber encouraged quietly, half fearing what kind of tale was about to be told. "Since when?"

"Your King and Queen have no doubt told you stories of the Sea Battle," the Genie noted. "Well, I say stories—of course they are no more tales than the blood of those fallen is red ink, but they are part of our history, and in order for their dearly-bought lessons not to die we must continue to tell them how we can rather than let their memory crumble. Attend: the Sea Battle marked the end of an age, for in those days before there lived not only Centaurs and Fairies and Arraheng, but also all manner of wondrous beings. There were Satyrs and Pixies, Shadow Folk as well as Sea Folk, and Unicorns before the Bicorns, and of course Dragons, who, it seems, have never been able to drag themselves away from the Realm entirely. Anyway, you will have been told most of this, so I shall keep my account brief. I need only speak of the Vetches—you've heard of them, no doubt?"

Amber nodded, her mouth dry.

"Rraarl stood against them, and they captured him," the Genie surmised grimly. "They turned him to stone in an attempt to kill him, but he kept his mind somehow and lived, despite his altered state. There are certain things that if they are to be told, must come from him alone. But the Vetches I must warn you about.

"You know, do you not, that Snakelocks, the Vetch Queen, began to form an army: half-rotten remnants of the dead of her horde reanimated through the darkest of arts? Evil begot greater evil, until Snakelocks's power grew such as to render her able to manipulate the forms of her minions' flesh to her own ends; an abhorrent technique proving the Vetches near invulnerable, for their Queen grafted into their construction the ability to turn into stone.

"Her gaze achieved this petrification as effectively when turned upon her luckless prisoners as upon her subjects, for Snakelocks also used this torturous practice to devastating effect upon imprisoned rebel forces. Rraarl is, to my knowledge, alone in having survived.

"Yet the Vetch Queen's original use for her repulsive proficiency was far more self-serving, for the technique meant that her army could join with the very rock enclosing the tainted waters it patrolled. Henceforth if attacked the Vetches could meld with the rock, biding their time in the dark places—at the bottom of murk-filled pools, in the flow of the deepest cavern waters—for the opportune moment to spring forth as if mechanized, when their prey approached, with wraith-like, paralysing cries.

"Being cold blooded, and through the link with Snakelocks and everything; you know how vipers locate their prey through being able to sense body heat? Well, it's a devastatingly effective method."

Amber felt herself go cold. "*That's* why Rraarl awoke when I touched him?"

The Genie gave her a direct, if not unkind, look. "You of all people should know you are perfectly capable of becoming far more than you were born to be. Good things and bad may happen in this life, but our destinies remain our own."

Amber nodded, chastened, in turmoil over what she had heard. "So, how he is now, he can't physically feel things at all?"

The Genie spread his hands expansively. "In a—rather negative— manner of speaking. He can feel, as you've already experienced, the warmth of living touch. And he has proprioception, but not tactile differentiation. He has a sense of where his body is," the Genie continued hastily in response to the Fairy's confused expression, "so he can walk through darkness. But you could run a feather along his arm or a knife, and he wouldn't feel the difference."

Amber fell silent. "What a curse to live with," she murmured, churning it over in her mind.

"Mm," the Genie acknowledged. "But mayhap it can be lifted."

"By . . . ?"

"Something stronger than sorcery," the Genie predicted, fading with a self-assured grin. "Wake me when we're there."

Amber nodded guiltily, realising how much time she'd unwittingly let herself lose getting caught up in the Genie's story—Rraarl's story. She'd be miles behind the others now. With her hands sweat-slippery in the heat, her pockets pointlessly small, and miles ahead left to trek, she nestled the lamp carefully into the deep hood of her cloak, and concentrated on the long walk home.

Twilight was gathering in lengthening shadows before Amber neared the familiar sights of Fairymead. As she reached the castle, staring up to marvel at its iconic silhouette, with a jolt she recognised the Gargoyle: a silent sentinel crouched in watch on the ramparts, framed against the darkening purple-streaked sky.

She hesitated. *You'd probably just annoy him, going up there,* she reasoned. *He's a Gargoyle; it's not as if he can't take care of himself. And think of what he's been through—precisely, you can't.* She stalled uncertainly. *But none of that is a reason,* she admonished herself sternly. *It's just an excuse to hide your embarrassment at not knowing what to say—and your discomfort isn't exactly the main priority here, is it?*

So, as the evening breeze rippled through the meadow-grasses, she climbed the stairwell. The Gargoyle was crouched on the parapet, staring out immobile with his back to her. The moonlight lifted the scars from long ago so that they traced his body like a map of the past.

"Rraarl?" She walked over quietly. Those black eyes unnerved her, but she found herself wishing that he'd look at her again. "It's cold up here. Are you okay?" *You fool,* she immediately thought, feeling stupid. "I don't suppose you actually feel the cold, do you?" she mumbled. "Sorry."

At first she felt painfully awkward in his silence. Ruby always filled pauses with chatter; about anything, it didn't matter what, and she'd got used to it, found it comforting. But now perhaps the opposite was liberating and necessary. *Every word counts,* she told herself. *You've got time to say it.* "Rraarl, I'm sorry I ran. You could never scare me; I know that now, even if you don't. I won't look away again."

He traced something over the moon-blanched bricks, but it was too quick for her to read.

Amber stared at the patch of tiles, trying to conjure again the words he had formed. "I'm no good at this," she mumbled, feeling stupid again. "I didn't catch that."

The Gargoyle traced again, slowly. *SLEEP*. The ghost of a smile flickered through his carved snarl. *YOU WILL BE WELL GUARDED. FROM HERE I CAN SEE FAR ENOUGH INTO THE KINGDOM, WHILST SENSING YOUR WARMTH AND KNOWING OF YOUR PRESENCE.*

Emotions roiling, Amber stared out into the deepening night until its landmarks merged into a further darkness beyond sight, fleetingly envying Jasper's elegant turn of phrase as her tongue thickened in confusion around words that remained unsaid. "You saved me." She fidgeted with her sash.

LIKEWISE, he traced onto her arm, the coldness of his touch shivering onto her skin as darkening clouds gathered overhead, and then he did look at her.

As small footsteps skittered through the deluge, beneath his sodden cloak Jasper strode out from the haze of the Fairy Ring into the further darkness, a soft ring of light still emanating from his lantern despite the flame within skipping precariously in the howling wind as if threatening to abandon him altogether.

Beneath the shadow of his hood, the Prince glared at Mugkafb. "Do you know how long I've been out here in this confounded weather?" he hissed, the candlelight dancing wildly across his features as he glanced warily into the surrounding shadows. "This is not a night for decent folk." He gathered his saturated robes around him more tightly and squinted through the driving rain. "Follow me."

They ran across the squelching grass until the Prince drew up before a towering stone structure, unfamiliar in its state of dereliction.

"Tradesman's entrance, as it were," Jasper explained with embarrassment. "We don't have money for maintaining the whole structure;

Father says that funds must go on other things. Here, hold this."

Thrusting the lamp towards Mugkafb, the Prince fumbled in his pockets and drew out a rusted key, jamming it in the lock and wrestling vocally with it to no avail. "Curse this place." He kicked the door savagely. It remained obstinately shut. "Okay, I apologise," he muttered, and it creaked open smugly.

"Welcome back to the Fairy castle." The Prince ushered Mugkafb out of the rain. "In circumstances such as these living in a dry, warm cave does hold a certain appeal," he admitted, coercing the ancient fireplace into life as the Arraheng's footsteps echoed along the stone corridor to the accompanying *drip, drip* of the roof surreptitiously leaking from a great height.

As the fire crackled welcomingly into animation, amidst a noise like a gust of leaves stirred high in a Requë wind hundreds of tiny, thin-winged creatures of all colours flitted around the corner and en-masse made a beeline for the night, sending Jasper slamming the door shut with a startled yelp.

"Typical," the Prince complained, dragging a rusted grate to the hearth as Mugkafb stared around in delight at the scattering rainbow. "Out there it's raining a torrent, and in here it's infested with Dartwings. No, you can't go out, it's not safe," he argued tiredly in the general direction of the creatures, ducking as several fluttered erratically past overhead. "Shoo." He waved his hands aimlessly in their direction as, unperturbed, they lazily changed course and fluttered straight back towards him. Jasper gave up with a sigh. "This place is a disgrace."

"I like it," Mugkafb grinned, dragging—priceless, no doubt, Jasper worried—volumes haphazardly off the shelves and dumping them on the banquet table. He held out a hand and one of the flying creatures settled on it. "So who are these little guys?"

"The Dartwings?" Jasper coughed genteelly amongst the dust Mugkafb's efforts were billowing up. "They're our messengers; there's one for every Fairy in the whole Realm. When you come of age, you get an invitation to receive your Gem from the King and Queen, and you meet your very own Dartwing for the first time when it brings you that invitation."

He reached out his hand and a dark red Dartwing with flecks of blue and gold fluttered down to settle on his open palm. "This one is mine," he said, speaking quietly so as not to disturb the creature. "Well, she is kind enough to humour me in this folly. I call her 'Petal'. Because, well, obviously." He had the grace to look embarrassed, and turned his studious attention to the books.

As the Prince threw down a threadbare tome, the pages bounced open at a weapons section. His eyes drawn feverishly to the description of one particular blade, Jasper felt a chill grip his core despite the now roaring fire. Slamming the text shut guiltily so that Mugkafb wouldn't see, with racing heart Jasper promised himself that he'd research that particular possibility tomorrow, if a possibility it were to prove.

"Anyway," he interrupted his dismal thoughts with forced jocularity, turning back to his young companion with an effort. "Where were we?"

"Closer," Mugkafb divulged with a smirk, spreading a map out triumphantly.

Whispers in the Night

Shivering against the sudden cold after the coal-fired warmth of the tavern, as Naya let the oaken door swing shut on the end of her shift the chatter and jeers from the Golden Griffin faded, leaving her with only the sub-zero chill of the desert night for company. Normally, she'd wait for one of the other girls to finish, and Yenna had developed a reassuring habit of hanging around particularly late into the night in Wolf-form under the guise of wanting kitchen scraps, but with news so urgent she could afford to waste neither time nor caution in getting to Seb's.

That was what she told herself; yet the darkness seemed to surge closer around her with every step, her boots clipping loudly on the sand-strewn cobbles as she hurried along the deserted street, the muted halo of streetlamps spaced too far apart only serving to deepen the shadows between them.

The wind sent dried leaves scudding along the path with the sound of scuttling footsteps, and Naya quickened her pace anxiously, hugging her cloak protectively around her. *You used to walk this route all the time,* she tried to tell herself. Yet tonight, when it was completely deserted, her senses were tightened and her thinking narrow. She couldn't shake the feeling that something was wrong. It pervaded every fibre of her being.

It must be along here, her memory insisted at the next turning. It had been far too long since last she'd visited. *Just a little further.* Invasive images of bandits and horse-thieves and worse squirmed into her mind as the path seemed to lengthen, and she struggled to tell herself she was merely being foolish. Eyeing the winding path ahead, she found herself questioning the kind of purchase the slippery, uneven cobbles could afford should she have cause to run.

Even as she was dismissing such thoughts, upon a wailing gust of wind harsh voices lifted. Instinctively Naya darted onto the sand to dull her footfalls, back-stepping into the night.

Bristling desert scrub scratched into her face as she crouched, rattling and shivering so loudly in the wind that she bit her lip in exasperation, scared she'd miss vital words carried on the air. *Who could they be?* her mind insisted on asking, although she dreaded any response she could think of. The stables were shut, the voices too low to be those of benign drunks.

She froze as they neared. Nabb? The head stable hand? The Realm seemed to chill. She knew several of the hands were Authorities—one even flaunted it—but *Nabb*—

"I came as quickly as I could," she heard his gruff voice mutter, uncharacteristically obsequious and out of breath as he followed the stranger striding on ahead. "It was only born earlier today; no one else has seen."

The shock hit Naya with staggering weight. What in five seasons would they want with a newborn foal, unless . . .

She could barely force herself to remain concealed as the men passed. *You can't follow them,* she tried to reason with herself. *Get Roanen's message to Seb—then head to the stables. It's your only chance of thwarting their plan undisturbed.*

She crouched there, her hands stinging from the cold and her breath clouding in the air as she let the seconds stretch into minutes, choking on her frustration as she waited. She couldn't risk her presence being known. How many left in this town would heed a cry for help if she let herself get careless now?

She felt the familiar bubble of anger well up as she peered along the path, listening to the fading footsteps. Within her memory, Loban had been a proud and thriving trading town. Now, in the creeping thrall of Goblin-rule, all that was good about it was crumbling away. The ethical healers, the unbiased teachers, the free-minded craftspeople, the honest tradesfolk: most had now fled, and amongst the intricately carven marble structures from the height of expressive freedom now slunk Goblins, their lamp eyes reflecting in the gloom.

The recollection chilled her more deeply than the wind. Picking up her skirts she ran the rest of the way, her eyes streaming in the cold, until glowing windows winked through the night and a ramp dulled her footsteps as she knocked the door, breathing on her hands for warmth.

"Come on in, sis!" a yell floated, and Naya prised the sliding doors carefully apart.

Seb wheeled to meet her, his smile easy as the welcoming light from the fire glinted in his eyes and off the spokes of his chair to flood out into the darkness and render the fears of the night, if just for now, neutralised.

Seeing that her brother's messy blond hair was as soot-flecked as ever, and that he was wearing that ridiculous slashed shirt to show off the brawny arms he was so accursed proud of, Naya impulsively leaned and hugged him, even though the stench of the smithy still clung to him, realising suddenly how much she'd missed him. She saw he'd made himself another spoke-cover, with "my other ride's a Dragon" emblazoned, and she had to grin.

"Nice to see you've been busy," she noted archly.

"I'll have you know, it's been a slow week," Seb admonished, squeezing her tight in response. "But obviously, I had no time at all to tidy up," he added, waving at the tools strewn across the table.

"It's partly Tann's fault, too, you know," a sleepy-haired girl added yawningly, wandering into the hall and blinking in the light. "Can we stay up because Auntie Naya's here?"

"You know what, Sama?" Naya broke in apologetically to rescue her brother. "I've got to check on something up at the stables in a minute, so I'm going to have to properly visit you another time. I'll bring Taiko—you'll be big enough to ride him soon," she added conspiratorially as Sama's face began to fall, and the girl grinned concedingly before darting away.

"Auntie Naya?" a boy's voice called next, as amongst a thudding scramble a mischievous face stuck round the door. "Check out what I made for Taiko." He proffered the scrap proudly. "D'you think he'll like it?"

Naya examined the leather flower closely, trying to stifle the sense of urgency shying in her gut like a fretful horse. *It would be safer to stay awhile,* she acknowledged uncomfortably. The thought felt like a betrayal, but if she arrived too early it would ruin everything. "That's really good work, Tann," she answered honestly. "Keep it safe so that I can put it on his bridle the next time I ride him over."

"Tell him I made it 'specially for him," Tann insisted, disappearing after his sister as Seb eyeballed the clock meaningfully.

"*'Auntie',*" Naya groaned theatrically. "Like I don't feel old enough already." She snorted with laughter and wriggled out of her boots, tucking her feet up beneath her on the sofa, as her brother wheeled into the kitchen to make drinks. "They're lovely kids, Seb."

Only so many heartbeats remained before her brother's return, and face-to-face without the children she could no longer hide her ill tidings. "You got much work on tomorrow?" she called anxiously, clinging to normality for a few precious moments longer. She let her eyes rove across the jumbled shelves climbing the walls, and admired amongst the half-finished metalwork pieces adorning them the twisted steel model of a running unicorn he'd finished since last she saw him.

Seb had hankered after being a blacksmith for as long as Naya could remember, as a way of repaying the majestic creatures to whom he felt he owed his life, carriage-driving having returned to him a level of freedom he'd never trusted he'd feel again. Naya had never seen anyone so attuned to the needs of a horse, nor so adept at translating their nature into the fluidity of metal as he was now.

Seb pushed a mug of cocoa into her frozen hands. "Nah," he admitted, taking a swig from his own as he watched her astutely. "So, how big is the order and what's the deadline? And," he added lightly, "how's your hero?"

"Shut *up*," Naya squawked indignantly, feeling like she was seventeen again for the briefest moment. "The order," she rejoined, instantly subdued and feeling in that moment as if she were bringing war to their lands just for speaking of it, "may prove the most grimly significant contract since the Sea Battle. Roanen delivered it, for King Morgan of Fairymead. To put it briefly, Roanen tonight confirmed the extent of the Goblin stronghold in the further reaches of the desert—I know your team have equipped the Arkhans already; but there's more. He's been to Fairymead, to find that its people lie in the path of attack from Venom-spitters, monsters driven from the deepest caves by the recent Vetch movement and steered by the Goblins to their own ends. The Fairies need—" She passed the parchment over helplessly.

"Ah," Seb murmured hollowly as he scanned the list, serious for once. "This is what I hate about my job. Creating tools that can betray as well as save."

"They'll only be used if there's no other choice," Naya offered quietly, knowing the words were obscenely inconsequential. "If my life depended on the blade I held, I'd want it to be one forged by you."

Seb smiled sadly. "We all knew, didn't we, that it could only come to this? It just doesn't feel real yet. And I wonder if it'll ever feel right."

"If the accounts I've heard are correct—and I'd trust Roanen with my life and the Basilisks being Dragon descendents cannot lie—I'm sure we'll all get to the stage where we can justify it to ourselves, wherever the truth may lie," Naya returned bleakly. Her gaze strayed to the window as she sought the significance of Nabb's threat amongst the falling leaves scrambling over each other like pieces of a puzzle.

"Naya?" Seb pressed, following her glance.

She chewed at her lip. "There's something I've got to check at the stables."

Seb watched the restlessness in her eyes for a second before, as always, he nodded his assent. "Be careful, yeah?"

She smiled her gratitude for his unspoken understanding. "Good luck with the shipment."

Seb forced his voice to stay light. "No rest, huh?"

"Well if you will be the best blacksmith in the whole Realm," she retorted airily, but she couldn't quite conceal her pride as she hugged him quickly before turning towards the night again. At least focusing on the means could block out the end—for now.

But as the doors slid shut behind her, closing off the light and warmth, and the cold air stung into her eyes again, there was nothing left to stop the tears from falling.

Rebirth

Heart slamming as her hands fumbled with the latches, Naya slipped into the deserted yard, willing the most tenuous of silences to eke out just a few minutes longer as she scanned the stalls in turn. Hurrying past dappled-grey Allantaro, flighty bay Leena and retired, bow-legged Hodge, she breathlessly eased open the single remaining door.

By the cloud-veiled moonlight Naya beheld the newborn, and against her gaping, night-ridden uncertainty her heart softened in amazement as she watched the foal totter towards her, his spindly legs splaying out and his quivering muzzle misting hot breath into the dark.

Relief flooded through her with the realisation that it hadn't been harmed. The foal nuzzled at her hand, and she reached automatically to stroke the white star of its brow.

Her heartbeat scudded as her fingers touched a strange, unyielding bump. Parting the wispy forelock, she stared mutely at the gnarled protuberance extending like a rough-layered shell.

She couldn't catch her breath. The foal was a—She couldn't let herself think it. A regressive deviant, a threat to progress, that's all the Authorities would view a Unicorn as: a throwback to the old days and a reminder of the old stories. She shuddered, bile rising to her mouth. *That's why they want to kill you,* she realised, as the newborn stared innocently back at her.

Footsteps punctured the womb-like darkness of the stables, more menacing in their subtlety than the march of an army. Wretchedly Naya froze, fear coursing through her.

Spooked by the intruders' approach Allantaro whinnied, and the noise galvanised Naya into action. She darted out, loosed the grey, and with clicks of her tongue and whispered entreaties led him into the foal's stall, ripping open the straw bale outside and flinging it around, covering the foal in most of it and coaxing Allantaro into such a position as to hope that his shadow would fall judiciously. He must have sensed her fear, as for once he stood immobile; a flecked marble statue more suited to times long passed. *Times of nobility and courage,* the thought flitted as she waited impotently. *Times long passed indeed.*

She flinched violently as the door of the stall next to them creaked open amidst the tramp of heavy boots.

"You sure this time?" a man's voice—Nabb's again, she realised with a sinking heart—spat venomously.

A second man yawned blearily. "Jakar must've killed it this morn'; none of the others are empty. C'mon, we can check with him tomorrow." This voice was younger, uncertain. Naya's thoughts raced through the darkness.

"Wait. Check the next." Nabb's voice impaled her through the door. "For a young lad, your memory ain't that sharp."

Naya pressed herself weakly into the corner, wondering too late if she had time still to reach across for the pitchfork. The men would—

"Naya?"

She almost fainted in the echo of his voice as Nabb's harsh features glowered at her beneath a sputtering lantern held high. Its flickering light imparted upon him an almost ghoulish air, and she couldn't have looked more suspicious if she'd been standing there with the foal in her arms.

Her mind draining, Naya managed to gesture towards Allantaro, who was still mercifully shadowed. "He hurt his foreleg hunting," she entreated shakily. "My lord requested deeper litter for a week. I'm just attending to it, I'll be done soon, I promise."

Nabb grunted impatiently. "By the Emperor, woman, you work even worse hours than us. Make sure you get him back to condition; that horse is worth more than your year's wages. Don't forget to lock up—and don't think you're getting paid extra for this."

As he stamped off again, Naya leaned back into the darkness, allowing herself to breathe once more. *Hurt his foreleg hunting?* she ridiculed herself silently. *For how long could he possibly believe that?*

Yet now that it was quiet enough to think again, the germ of a plan shivered tentatively into her mind as she sank into the straw beside the foal. *What was it the legends spoke of?* she found herself questioning. *Did they not say that a free-running Unicorn could never be caught, save for by those good of heart?*

She sat back on her heels, her eyes gleaming with something other than fear now in the darkness. Had she not read also that Gorfang had been challenged to catch one, and catch her he did—only to release her with whispered words for the creature to run across the length and breadth of the Realm, bearing a message of hope to those oppressed that their long-awaited freedom lay now close at hand.

"That story will be retold once more," she breathed to the foal. Her eyes danced as it raced through her mind: the Authorities had never actually read the legends they so despised, for they feared their power too much. Thus had the stories continued to circulate unde-tected amongst the townspeople; the passages within closely guarded, shared between those needing succour and sustenance through a secret language of shared meanings woven as subtly as Gorfang's insignia stitched understated and overlooked in the folds of garments or carved intricately into jewellery.

"It starts here and tonight," she murmured, willing the words she hardly dared speak towards the foal. "I'll free you. I'll tie a message amongst your mane, on the smallest scrap of parchment, and you will gallop unfettered past both the Authorities and their tyranny and the Goblins and their savagery—carrying word of the uprising to the free and oppressed in all corners of the Realm."

Allantaro snorted, and she almost shrieked at the noise in the silence. But now that she had hope, she collapsed into furtive giggles and hugged his broad neck.

"The Authorities promised us justice, and gave us corruption," she warned him, a fierce grin flourishing across her face. "But no longer. Now, wherever there are the Authorities, there *will* be justice."

Heart fluttering, she fished into her apron and tore out a page from the poetry book she'd been reading in her break—okay, not *just* in her break—and closed her fingers around the stub of pencil she used for taking orders. Agonising over the words until they finally spilled joyously across the page, she coiled the note up and tied it with several coarse strands in amongst the foal's mane, then rubbed his neck soothingly.

As if hearing her thoughts, the foal wobbled gawkily into standing, tottering towards the great chasm of darkness beyond with ever steadier hoofsteps, his whiskery muzzle quivering as the breeze reached out, lifting the scent of freedom towards him.

Touching his warm neck in farewell, Naya watched the foal skitter into the yard and trot away, until he shone no bigger than the smallest star amongst the devouring blackness of the night.

Survivor's Dream

Black eyes vacant and rolling in sleep, Rraarl flinched and snarled weakly as lurid broken images rained like blows through the only dream he'd ever had.

Their claws gouging into his bubbling throat. The pitiful gurgle as he fought to breathe through his own blood. The man he used to be shackled to the pillar, welts weeping over his skin where the whiptail had lashed.

"When the Realm witnesses our retribution . . ." their deathknell hiss seeped like poison, severing all hope, "none will dare stand against the Vetches again."

His world turned to bellowing fire as the seconds wracked into a reprieveless eternity, their acid promises echoing as he slipped from consciousness into what death must feel like.

Later that night, clouds gathered and in time rain, its incessant rush the only murmur to wash his mind clean of the malevolent voices before, the storm's impartial tears the only witness to what the Vetch monsters left behind, their liquid caress his only comfort.

Thunder rolled and amidst the relentless deluge the straggling clouds parted, rock glistening wetly as moonlight passed over the immobile figure.

The black eye gleamed, moved. Stone muscles bunched and heaved as laboriously he forced air into leaden lungs and lifted his face to the sky.

His scream tore from his dream into waking and sent him lurching to his feet, the rusted chain taut in his shaking fists. He tried to focus on his only possession, real in his hands. The chain that once bound him as a victim, which he now carried broken as a survivor. The chain he'd let rust with the years as a reminder of how long ago that . . . incident had now been. The chain he could count the links of to quieten his mind when the ghosts of memory clamoured too loudly.

His feral stare relaxing, he allowed his gaze to lift to Fairymead Castle, its silhouette as reassuring as the caves that had previously shielded him, its bulk shrouded in predawn mist until the sun cautiously admitted her first glimmering rays and a pink-tinged dawn eased over the land.

The nightmare would never leave. He knew that; had learned it cruelly afresh each night over so many fragmented years. And yet a fierce smile stole to his snarling lips with the realisation that last night had been the first time since that he had slept through until dawn.

Transformations

As she stepped out across the Meadows in the crisp, hesitant light of the new morning, the still-dewed grass wet beneath her feet, Amber saw a crouched darkness against the pale light, and with a start realised that Rraarl must have, true to his word, been there all night.

I HAVE BEEN ROBBED OF THE CHANCE TO FACE MY DEMONS, the Gargoyle traced by way of explanation as she approached. *PERHAPS THERE IS SOME RELIEF TO BE FOUND IN FIGHTING YOURS.* His hand hovered for a moment over the rock. *AND IF NOT, SO BE IT. MY CHOICE IS MADE.*

Words failed Amber. "I can't ask that of you," she managed inadequately.

That strange ghost-smile flickered amidst his snarl. *THEN NEITHER CAN YOU REFUSE IT OF ME.*

Amber stared at him, overwhelmed. "If you're certain, I need to check out the caves; Racxen found claw-gashes, and we now know that the monsters we originally feared didn't make them. We think they're Vetch markings." She stood there wretchedly in the silence, feeling awful for even asking him. "The only place we know for certain they have haunted is—"

YOU DON'T HAVE TO ASK, he traced quickly. *I WILL BE THERE. IT IS NECESSARY.*

"Rraarl, I don't deserve this," she mumbled, half-disbelieving. "Anything I ask of you is too much; you saved my life, and then what do I do? Ask the impossible of you."

The Gargoyle grinned fiercely. *YOU GAVE ME MY LIFE BACK, YET YOU TALK OF "IMPOSSIBLE"?*

She smiled back, embarrassed, and shrugged. "'Beautiful and impossible things'," she corrected comfortably, remembering a quote from Professor Cobalt's lessons. "Till tomorrow?"

The Gargoyle nodded, watching her through blackest hawk eyes as she ran off across the meadow, and slowly he touched his shoulder where the warmth still lingered.

As the diminishing sun sank beneath the horizon Rraarl stood in the bleak shadows of the shore cliffs, buffeted by the roaring wind, staring out impassively to the foaming waves dashing the rocks beyond. The only way a Gargoyle could die was by drowning. For years he had felt no pain, and now there was an agony inside him that could not be stilled.

Maybe this was the only way.

Maybe this was best.

Slowly, as the lonely wind whipped across the sand-flats, he began to walk towards the raging waters.

Striding ahead of Amber, anxious to reach Loban before nightfall as the sky shifted ominously into twilight, Jasper froze as tremulously against the rising winds the desolate howl of a wolf's cry lifted, shivering familiarly into his soul.

"Yenna!" Jasper broke into a run, Amber pelting after him.

The howls distorting now amongst the cliff-top winds, gulping down waves of nausea Jasper reached the peak, with Amber close behind, in time to see silhouetted against the darkening sky a running wolf fall and rise stumbling into woman-form.

"Man drowning," Yenna blurted, grappling her unfurled bandana into a semblance of decency knotted at her hip, her breath tugging raggedly as she thrust a hand to the seething ocean below. "He went under."

Instantly, the Prince leapt to the air, swooping low over the churning waters even as Yenna scoured the slopes, her sharp golden eyes searching for a route down.

Skidding frighteningly as she started her ill-planned descent, spitting a furious curse at herself for not being able to fly down to help whoever it was, Amber in relief felt strong soft fingers close around hers, and Yenna led her unhesitatingly down the cliff-path. Her dark hair whipped out in the perilous winds, but her grip never shifted from the Fairy's hand, and she guided her as sure-footedly as if she had been in Wolf-form.

Stealing a glance at her new companion, Amber felt an odd pang of despairing admiration knowing that kind of confidence and poise would never be hers. It felt strange, coming face to face with the kind of woman she realised she privately wanted to be: grace and fierceness all in one, compromising neither half of herself. It was embarrassing to look at her own self in comparison—and yet, she realised, Yenna knew none of these worries, and had just taken her by the hand and run. *Mayhap you should try the Wolfren way of thinking once in a while,* Amber challenged herself with a shivering internal grin.

"Thanks," she gasped, remembering herself as she fought to keep her balance on the skittering stones whilst clinging tightly to the Wolf Sister.

"Don't mention it. You're part of the pack now, sister," Yenna promised, her eyes shining steadily amidst the chaos. "I know this is getting kind of intense. The night's long, the way's hard—doesn't even begin to cover it; but you're forgetting something. Not only are you stronger than you know, but you're not alone. So you remember that. Forget your fears, forget your doubts, forget your worries—and remember that, when times get hard." Yenna rolled her eyes embarrassedly. "This human tongue, it runs away with me. It's easier as a wolf. One glance, one shift of expression: no ambiguity. Get ready," she warned, steeling herself to jump as the night-silvered sands spread beneath them. Amber leaped with her, sprawling as the grains clung to her hands and hair, and then she was running like a wolf herself after Yenna to the roaring sea.

Buffeted mercilessly by the battering winds, the Prince flew as low as he dared over the roiling swell, searching the glittering mass of darkness for any signs of life.

The gale screaming in his ears, the rain lashing at his wings, he had no way of knowing for how long he'd been flying save for the aching protest of muscles seizing along his back. Disorientating spray flung up from the waves and stung salt into his streaming eyes, and his gulped breath caught in panic as he glanced back to the shore—no man could be this far out and live.

Terrified of what he'd find, he banked sharply to turn inland, flying still lower, sensing the air thin warningly until he feared nothing was keeping him airborne save for obstinacy of will. He knew he couldn't sustain this; yet he forced himself onwards, the elemental roar of the sea throwing its deafening challenge against him as he darted between the heaving waves with the last dregs of his strength.

Impossibly, he glimpsed a solid form amidst the fickle swell and instinctively he swooped, but in his haste he misjudged the manoeuvre, plummeting uncontrollably into the crest of a wave. Fighting to stay afloat as he groped through the surge, his wings spattering pitifully against the surface and spilling out to drag him under like some ineffectual cloak he couldn't remove fast enough, Jasper snatched air in panicked splutters as the depths fought to claim him. The memory of the sunken man viscerally near, in a final explosion of desperate effort he dove.

As she breathlessly reached the shore, the Wolf Sister's sharp eyes glimpsed the white of Jasper's shirt flickering into vision on the rise and fall of the swell, and she threw herself into the surf with Amber.

Immobile beneath a crushing weight and the sucking hiss of dragging waves, Jasper lay silent, voiceless and breathless, time slipping irreversibly.

The tomb-silence splintering into shouts and yowls, in a surge of moonlight and streaming water Jasper felt an impossible weight lifting as he gasped burning air above the surf, salt-crunched sand scuffing beneath his heaving chest as he felt himself hauled slowly to firmer ground, a lupine shadow over him as Yenna gripped the neck of his robe between her jaws, her four limbs light across the sands that would have claimed two.

"Show-off," he managed hoarsely, slumping prone as they both collapsed on the beach and pulling her weakly towards him to kiss her wet fur before he could think better of it.

"Where—?" Spitting sand as he shakily pushed himself off the ground, the sight of a corpse-still fallen figure, unmistakeable from Amber's description, silenced him momentarily. "Fool!" he railed at the motionless form as he slumped down beside Amber, his salt-clung throat clutched by an icy hand now that the Gargoyle hadn't moved. "Don't you *dare* try that again. How are we supposed—"

At a glance as sharp as a nip from Yenna, he fell silent.

"Rraarl," Amber whispered, disconsolate, his stone body as cold as death in her arms. "Rraarl, come back to us." She didn't know what to do, what else to say. You couldn't shock a stone heart back into a rhythm, could you? Couldn't do anything Sarin would teach.

Silently, Yenna padded over to the still form and nestled against his side, for all the Realm like a treasured pet consoling her master.

Following her lead, awkwardly Jasper took the stone hands in his.

Her eyes clouding with tears, Amber cradled the blank-eyed head in her lap, her fingers tracing the snarling lips, the savage teeth, the cutting scars from so long ago. Softly, she leaned to press her lips against his and exhaled, wishing she could gift him the warmth from her own heart if only it would let him stir again.

Creepingly slowly, the heat began to seep through into his soul, and the obsidian stare flickered, latching onto each of the vigil keepers. Was it Amber's imagination that he held her gaze longest?

"Rraarl," Jasper warned as gently as he could as the blackest of eyes now fixed on him; understanding the Gargoyle in those few moments more than perhaps he acknowledged himself. "Times have changed, since you were—I'm so sorry, after the Sea Battle, the Sea Folk forsook their powers. They can't give you a flesh form. That knowledge was lost to them so many years ago. The Water Nymph," he added hastily, as anguish shuddered through the tortured form, "is the only one who can now. She is aging with every passing season, but—" the realization caught in his throat, "tonight is Mid-Recö Eve. Her power will be at its strongest. It's probably," he faltered at the enormity of the words, "now or never."

"Rraarl, you don't have to." The words squeezed, painful in their urgency, from Amber's throat. "If you're not a man, it's because you're more. Curse it, why didn't I stop him?" she cried wretchedly as the Gargoyle knuckled away without a second glance at any of them.

"Because you know the choice is not yours to prevent," the Prince insisted. "I should have realized he'd do it this night," he admitted miserably. "I ignored his pain; I didn't want to intrude."

"Come," urged Yenna evenly. "Our duty is not to make choices for him, but to help him bear the consequences of his own."

Amber nodded gratefully. "You guys go back," she offered, seeing the look Jasper gave the Wolf Sister and wanting to give him a break after his trials. "I'm going to stay, in case."

Yenna returned her glance, her fierce eyes now tender. "Understood."

For once, Jasper didn't protest, and Amber settled herself to wait, a knot she didn't entirely understand curling itself in her stomach.

"The pain that lies before her cannot be borne by another." A voice as crisp as ice cut through the cavern, her face turned away despite the heavy footfalls. "You cannot save her from it, despite all your strength. It would help, would it not, if I were to ease your choice and say that she could not possibly do this alone? But I will not. The Realm is changing, and she managed without you before."

The Gargoyle stalked round to face the Water Nymph, throwing the words to the rock so she could not avoid them: *YOU SPEAK THE TRUTH. SHE COULD. BUT SHE WILL NEVER HAVE TO AGAIN. CHANGE ME,* he finished, blazing eyes brooking no argument. *MAKE ME A MAN.*

Her gaze as heavy and fate-laden as his words, the Nymph turned to him, her eyes betraying that she had always known it would come to this.

As she stepped forward, visions in the bubble behind shimmered into a far ambush.

Staring uneasily into the deepening haze of distance as twilight sank into night, Amber finally tore her gaze from the horizon to trudge tiredly home. Locked in worries, she registered the rustle of grasses too late.

She was thrown to the floor, the impact punching the breath from her as she half glimpsed the black-furred bulk of the monster leap and heard a slamming crunch bleeding into a whimper as if the Venom-spitter had thrown itself at a stone wall behind her. Disbelievingly her eyes flew to Rraarl as the fight erupted around her, flooding paralysis into every part of her until she had to remember to scramble to her feet; force her body to obey her once more.

As soon as she did the monster was coming at her, faster than thought, and moments later she was bleeding but free and unable to remember how, left with shaking limbs and stinging hands and cuts she only felt as itches, and blank patches in her mind where she could place little but panic and reaction and somehow a solid presence with her through it all. The fear caught up with her swiftly, and she retched at the closeness of it all.

Rraarl's shadow fell across her then, and lifting her head shakily she stared at him. "But you said this was the only day she could have changed you," she managed hoarsely, her voice raw through with emotion and adrenalin. She had to swallow against the bile before she could speak again. "That this was your only chance to become a man again."

Memories of the struggle reared, wrenching everything away, and it wasn't until she forced herself to match Rraarl's measured breathing and replace the unthinkable alternatives, so nearly played out and now rampaging through her mind unchecked, with the picture of reality: of the Venom-spitter running yowling into the distance, defeated and away, that she could allow her gaze to fall upon the Gargoyle's response, gouged into the churned earth:

I WAS WRONG. WHAT KIND OF MAN WOULD I HAVE BEEN IF I HAD LEFT YOU NOW?

A Perilous Equilibrium

Having checked the manuscript under the cloak of midnight as soon as he had reached the castle, Jasper set off again before dawn. Yet it was nearly midday by the time he reached Loban, and another hour of wandering in increasing infuriation through the throat-scorching heat before he actually found the elusive Yenna. It hadn't helped, he tried to console himself, that he'd had no idea whether he'd end up finding a woman or a wolf.

"You know they say the blade is cursed, I presume," Yenna interrupted bluntly, as he stumbled over his plan. She was wearing her hunter's garb, in broad daylight in the middle of the square, and the Prince's nerves were thoroughly shredded now that the Authorities had approached twice with the intent to reprimand her and been warded off with barely-human vocalisations and the choice appearance of certain feral companions.

Jasper faltered, wishing he could demonstrate her kind of bravery. "I read something like that a while back," he conceded, remembering his original track with difficulty beneath her golden eyes. "I was trying to shed some light on a riddle Amber heard that still has not helped us, and it barely registered at the time. As I understand, the 'First Blade' is the only weapon that can be used against Thanatos. I allowed myself the indulgence of believing you to be the one person who might take me seriously enough to answer were I to ask you of its history and location."

The Wolf Sister regarded him for a long moment. "About its history I can tell you," she acquiesced. "And I will do so truthfully, to the best of my power. But of its whereabouts I know as little as the rest of my kin. None but the Goblin King himself knows where he hid it." She stared out to the shimmering horizon before shifting her gaze back to the Prince. "What exactly do you know of the artefact?"

Jasper dug the toe of his boot into the sand. "I didn't read much of the passage; I'd scanned through hundreds of scrolls by then and thought I was beyond caring, but the First Blade kept coming up. Something about," he paused uncertainly, "Thanatos being scared of it?"

Yenna's voice was quieter now. "And did it tell you why?"

"The inscription carved into the blade? A curse upon Goblins, I suppose it must have been."

A growl slipped from Yenna's tongue. "Not a curse upon just Goblins. A curse upon *anyone* who wields the sword."

Jasper's façade of confidence slid miserably to the ground. "So what am I to do?"

"What you *could* do is not in question," the Wolf Sister cautioned. "What it would *cost* you is the issue here."

Her eyes flashed with anger. "Goblin traders believe that with suitable recompense anyone can be incited to surrender anything: their freedom for protection, a soul for a life, morals for riches. Your debt would be equal and opposing to any potential reward you stood to gain."

Jasper smiled tightly. "Well, they didn't think that through. This could save the whole town; help the entire Realm—but they could still only kill me once. On reflection, not a poor balance."

Her look quelled him.

"I think I had better tell you the whole story," she advised carefully in his silence. "It happened at the time of Gorfang—the time your young Arraheng friend is so eager to hear about. You would be wise to listen to him more, Prince. He probably knows this better than I do." She shivered uncharacteristically. "Legend tells that Thanatos, the Goblin King, ordered his slaves to forge him a certain weapon—and you know by now how the Goblin-arts work.

"In his lust for dominion, he decreed that the sword must be bound by the worst of all curses. And so it was. So full of his own grandiose sense of invincibility that he had overlooked the possibility, he found himself in possession of a weapon to strike terror into even his dread heart—a weapon that turns against the one it should protect, a weapon that the slaves in defiance had imbued with the only sense of balance the Goblins would understand: whatever destruction intended for others would be meted to the one who wielded it.

"Even after tasting its justice, Thanatos could not resist the pull of wielding such destruction even unto his own doom. Thus he tasked several of his followers with hiding the blade deep and far and dangerous enough that none could ever find again either the chest containing the sword nor the key to release it. On their return, Thanatos murdered the slaves, so that knowledge of the locations died with them, thereby keeping his secret safe."

Staring blankly into the ground long after Yenna had finished, Jasper roused himself with difficulty, not looking at the Wolf Sister. "Thank you for your honesty. I didn't want to mention the possibility to the others before I knew exactly what it would entail."

Yenna tried to smile, but the attempt twisted with guilt. "This is why you're meeting them at the Griffin? To explain that you're going to try it?"

"No." He shook his head tiredly, as if his whole being had suddenly drained of all energy. "That I'm going to do it."

Yenna looked at him levelly. "I shouldn't have questioned."

"No, you shouldn't have." He tried to sound severe, but had to grin. "Anyway," he continued briskly before he could let himself wallow in despondency, "it has to be me. The Goblins have hurt Racxen too deeply as it is; I don't know the details but something horrendous happened with them in his past and I don't want him to be put through it. And," he shrugged, "Amber winds me up something rotten, but she's a good kid and she wouldn't deserve it."

Yenna's eyes narrowed. "No, but do you feel that you would?"

He gestured aimlessly, wishing she couldn't see right through him. "Anyway," he mumbled again awkwardly, but Yenna did not rush him. He realised suddenly how much he admired her stillness, her poise, her acceptance of silence. Emboldened, he risked continuing, spilling out in one breath: "I appreciate your help more than I have ineptly conveyed, but I can ask of you nothing more; I must find the key and sword alone."

She regarded him calmly, one leader to another. "I know."

Relief flooded through him, strange in the circumstances, he mocked himself. A smile touched his lips. "You're the only one who understands."

Her tone was mischievous but her eyes held a solemn sadness. "What we do for our people."

Within her gaze Jasper touched for the briefest instant the extent of her loss; the aching burden she shouldered, every time she changed to Wolf-form, for the sake of those who would persecute her if only they knew. His heart wrung for the insidious toll it must take on her, and he found himself realising why she kept herself so keenly guarded. *And I thought I had it bad,* he worried uncomfortably.

He must have let more than he'd meant to show in his gaze, for Yenna's voice softened. "Take heart, Prince; the Fates say we shall meet yet in better times."

He regarded the pragmatic Wolf Sister in surprise. "You believe in fate?"

When her eyes danced, she looked younger. "We must believe in everything we create for ourselves, surely?"

And before Jasper could think of an answer, she was gone, but her memory guarded him as he pushed on towards the Griffin.

Mirrors and Demons

At the mouth of the tunnel, Rraarl hesitated, staring into the waiting darkness with blazing eyes.

Amber, catching up, followed his gaze to something that glinted dangerous and innocuous within the blackness. "Mirrors?" she blurted, confused. "But who—"

VETCHES.

Amber shivered at his certainty. "But everyone says the Nymph's magic still binds them." Her voice sounded tiny, as pitiful as the argument. Her stomach twisted in fear. "Rraarl, if not, we can't—"

MIRROR, MIRROR, ON THE WALL, Rraarl traced with finality, his eyes holding an odd gleam. *I HAVE NO NEED FOR YOU ANY MORE.*

He flinched, glancing to the Fairy as if remembering when and where he was. *IF I WERE TO FIND THEM,* the Gargoyle warned falteringly. *IF I WERE TO LOSE MYSELF DOWN THERE*—He stopped himself, his stillness potent against a rage Amber saw edge closer to the surface of those burning eyes, the nearest thing to fear she'd seen etched deep into his face now.

I KNOW WHAT LIES DOWN THERE, he threw the words to the stone, so fast Amber barely had chance to read them. *THE MEMORIES ARE THE ONLY THINGS I CANNOT PROMISE I WILL BE ABLE TO OVERPOWER. AND SO I CANNOT ALLOW YOU TO*

GO ANY FURTHER. IT IS A RISK I WILL NOT TAKE.

Amber scuffed her toe against the rough ground, her jaw clenching. "*You* can allow *me* to go no further?" she demanded. "Do you think so little of me that you believe I'd countenance you going through this alone? Or, now that we know they're in there, going through with this at all? Rraarl, I just assumed their old haunts would be a good place to glean information about their habits, anything that could help us fight them. I thought the Nymph would have bound them somewhere, I don't know—somewhere other than their original stronghold. We're both going back: this was a terrible idea from the beginning and now it's a thousand times worse. I'm so sorry, I should never have involved you."

Rraarl shook his head slowly, his gaze remaining fixed on the shadows. *IT WAS DESIGN ON MY PART, NOT OVERSIGHT ON YOURS, WHICH LEADS TO THIS DECISION.*

A chill seized Amber as she realised his intention. "Precisely," she argued, scared for him now. "You don't get to just decide my choice doesn't matter, oversight or none."

The Gargoyle looked at her then. *YOU KNOW I DO NOT SAY THIS TO HURT YOU,* he traced carefully onto her arm. *I COULD NEVER DO THAT.*

Her skin tingled at his cold touch. Curse him, why did he have to leave? Didn't he know she couldn't do this without him?

AMBER, THIS IS ALL I KNOW HOW TO GIVE. LET ME PRO-TECT YOU. I LOST MY OWN LIFE YEARS AGO, BUT YOURS—

Abruptly he turned, and knuckled into the tunnel without a backwards glance.

At a loss, Amber stared after him until the darkness merged against the shadow of his form and he was lost to her eyes. In wretched indecision she stood, glaring into the chasm. What could she hope to achieve by following him? She couldn't fight, couldn't fly, couldn't even find her way.

Amber twisted her sash in her hands. And she couldn't leave him.

As the skeletal trees shivered their displeasure through the greying sky behind her, she turned and strode into the darkness.

Squinting through the pressing shadows, no time to let her eyes adjust to the darkness as she skittered through the tunnel, Amber struggled to ignore the growing monologue of doubt clamouring inside her mind. She hadn't so much as glimpsed Rraarl when the tunnel widened into an echoing chamber, its keen chill seeping towards her.

Amber's misted breath caught in her chest as glimmering ice formations loomed forth like ghosts released after centuries of darkness, piercing the false twilight with an otherworldly glow. Daggered icicles draped over the rocks like clinging bone-white fingers as she crept past, realising in trepidation that there were two exits further on and she had not the slightest clue which to take as she tiptoed past endless swathes of ice. Dripping like stalactites and hanging in curtains like flowstone, they glittered their ethereal brightness fit to turn the chamber to crystal.

The cold crept numbingly into her, making it harder to breathe, and she might as well not even still be wearing her cloak for the pitiful extra warmth it gave her, although she clutched the edges to protect her hands should she need to break her fall as she slid across a floor as slippery as a Goblin's tongue.

Just as she was berating herself for not being able to judge which exit to take, a groaning, splintering crash resounded, sending Amber racing through into the next chamber to see Rraarl, crouched at the edge of a frozen pool, impassively raising and then smashing his fist through the ice. The noise frightened her, but not as much as the dead blankness of his eyes.

Oblivious to her presence, he continued the ritual until she walked right up and sat in front of him; smashed grey-veined slush lodging in the narrow, cut-glass channel of coldest blue between them. Without looking up, the Gargoyle shifted his position slightly so the shards would not hit her, and raised his fist above the ice again.

"Stop." Her voice escaped in a strangled squeak, and he flinched violently in shock, his hand dropping instantly. Amber realised there was water in her eyes, and she smeared it away quickly. "Rraarl don't, you'll—"

HURT MYSELF? the Gargoyle traced, although his touch over the rock was steadier now.

Miserably, Amber realised she had no answer to give him.

I HEARD THEM. THAT'S WHAT I THOUGHT. IT FELT SO REAL. The Gargoyle watched her with a confused expression. *I PUT YOU THROUGH ALL THIS, WHICH IS INEXCUSABLE. AND YET YOU ARE NOT AFRAID.*

Amber felt like screaming at him. "Of course I am," she snapped. "Every time I'm with you. What you refuse to realise is that I'm scared *for* you, not *of* you."

Further words coiled up dry and tight within her as she stared at the man in front of her, so close yet locked away inside himself, drowning in a world of horror from so long ago that even if she could imagine it, how could she hope to guide him safely home? What could she possibly say to him that could help him back from a place she had never been?

"You think it would help?" she tried hollowly, not knowing what else to do. "If you felt the pain?"

The Gargoyle's glance shifted. *PERHAPS,* he traced lightly, as if not wanting to involve her in this. *THE FACT I CANNOT PROVES I AM A MONSTER.*

"You really think that?" Amber glanced to the ice, her voice curling into a tight knot. She couldn't believe the dent his fist had left. Unseen by him, she let her fingers stray to the ground, gauging the sensation. The searing cold bit into her, the shards of ice sticking in her smarting unprotected skin as if barbed. The pain seeped inwards with the cold, flooding into a scalding sting. She distractedly realised it might've been a better idea to have spat on her hand first, as she withdrew it carefully.

"And you really think you can't feel pain?"

YES, he traced quickly.

Amber gritted her teeth, anticipation stinging behind her eyes. "Fine," she challenged. When she raised her own fist the Gargoyle's lip lifted in a warning snarl, and as she punched down the cavern exploded with his roar and Rraarl caught her hand, face contorting instinctively as if the pain would have been his own.

"You have your answer," she insisted stubbornly, her gaze as fierce as his despite the frantic tattoo her heart beat against her chest. "You feel pain—the kind that separates men from monsters: the pain of others."

His eyes lifted, the weight of his gaze tangible, and tentatively Amber relaxed her fist within the iron of his grasp, and let herself take hold of those cold hands. "Rraarl, I know that when you try to hurt yourself, it's because of them. But they've already made you suffer more than anyone should have to endure in a hundred lifetimes. Don't let them hurt you any more. Let go of what they made you have to do to survive. The fault is theirs, and the triumph yours. You broke the chains that bound your body; I know you can let fall those that haunt your mind. It's not just you alone in the dark now. Talk to me; we've got enough time in these accursed tunnels. Tell me," she clutched for ideas, and realised he had only one thing of his own left from before the Sea Battle, "about your name. What's the story behind it?"

Silence gaped between them, and Amber was about to apologise, worried that she must have inadvertently breached something, when Rraarl's hand shifted awkwardly.

THEY TOLD ME I WOULD SURVIVE, IF ONLY I COULD SPEAK MY NAME AFTER. The Gargoyle unclenched his fist with practised care, and Amber saw the crest of muscles jut along his jaw at the memory. *I REMEMBERED THEIR WORDS. I SCREAMED*

MY NAME TO THE STARS, AND WITH MY BODY RE-FORGED IN STONE, AN INHUMAN ROAR TORE FROM MY THROAT. I CHANGED MY NAME. I LIVED.

A fierce smile etched his scarred face. *SO IT IS AS RRAARL THAT I STAND BEFORE YOU.*

His hand moved steadily now. *IT WILL BE NIGHTFALL OUTSIDE.*

Amber nodded light-headedly. Yesterday's trials still raced in her mind, and she'd had so much adrenalin coursing through her last night that she'd barely been able to lie still, let alone sleep. The inevitability of another night passing without shutting her eyes suddenly seemed unbearable.

I WILL KEEP WATCH, Rraarl promised. *FEAR NOTHING. SLEEP.*

A grin seeped across her face in relief, and spreading her cloak out over the ice, as Amber turned over to say goodnight she caught sight of the Gargoyle in a frame that would forever be etched into her memory. Crouched at the mouth of the tunnel, silhouetted against near-impenetrable darkness, the weird gloom-light heightening the gleam of the tarnished chain-links and the whitening scars that traced his form, he waited: a motionless guardian, a silent watcher through the night.

At first it had unnerved her, the gaze from those flint-sharp eyes and the undeniable power that lay behind, but now such unwavering strength anchored her in a night of uncertainty, and she slept.

Letting out a deep sigh as he beheld her, Rraarl's breathing eased. Turning back to his post, eyes burning, he stared into the unknown, daring it to yield its worst.

When she woke, perhaps it was just her imagination hinting that grey pre-dawn had filtered into the strange twilight of the cave, but the words scratched into the ice-bound floor seemed to glow with a muted light as in a flood of panic she realised Rraarl had gone.

I HEARD SOMETHING. WHATEVER HAPPENS, DEATH CAN CALL BUT ONCE—AND BECAUSE OF YOU, I GOT TO LIVE TWICE.

A hot grip tightened round Amber's throat as she tried to focus on his words, willing herself to find some other meaning in the spartan message. "Oh, Rraarl," she hissed despairingly. Her vision swam now, and not just with the obscuring haze of the cavern. Furious with herself for having let him go alone while she'd slept on regardless, she dug a knuckle into the corner of her eye until she had her tears under control.

"You said you'd never hurt me, and then you go and leave," she challenged, desperately wishing he'd appear to refute her accusation with that unwavering gaze. "Curse you, Rraarl. When are you going to realise that we care about you, even if you don't? You feel my pain so acutely; why can't you understand that I feel yours? And curse me for caring, but there's some pain worth feeling."

Snatching up her sodden cloak, she plunged further into the unknown.

The echoes of her gasps crowding behind her like a breathless assailant, the claustrophobic distance fell away as the tunnel shattered amidst a thunderous, agonized roar.

All thought draining, Amber pushed rashly through the darkness, following the echoes blindly.

She skidded to a halt as she reached the next cavern, her breath catching in her throat as her appalled stare flew to the Vetches' poisonous scrawl, stretching indelible and inescapable as far as she could see over walls no longer ice-entombed but covered in a crueller savagery:

BODY OF A MONSTER.

Her gaze fell to Rraarl, surrounded by the shards of broken mirrors, curled hunched in the furthest corner as if that last reserve of strength had finally been drained from his body. His once-fierce eyes rolled fitfully and unseeing, his hands mechanically gouging into the clayish floor as Amber stood in frozen anguish, wishing mutely that there was something she could do to take the pain away; some way to reach him through the dark.

The memory of her failures flared painfully and yet, decisively, her fingers closed around a tiny talisman in her pocket: a piece of chalk that in another time and Realm Mugkafb had found, proudly telling her would bring her luck, and which she had carried faithfully as promised for all this way.

Clutching the fragile gift, she picked her way across the jagged rocks and shattered echoes of distorted images, to where the Gargoyle, heedless, flinched and snarled at things she could neither see nor hear. Silently, in bold white letters as large as she could, she wrote, right across his field of vision and over the Vetch's obscene taunts, four new words to drown out theirs:

SOUL OF A MAN.

No further words were necessary as his eyes locked onto hers, blazing once more, and together they approached the remaining mirror, beyond which lay the next chamber. Rraarl stared deep into his reflection, his snarl of anguish shifting into a fierce smile.

MIRROR, MIRROR, ON THE WALL, he traced, the strokes unhurried and deliberate. *YOU HOLD NO FEAR FOR ME ANY MORE.*

They stepped together into the waiting dark.

Continue the quest
with *Earth-Bound* in 2014

Acknowledgments

This story has been over eleven years in the making, and I am thoroughly indebted to those who have believed in me through it all. You know who you are, and I thank you from the deepest place in my heart. Inexpressible gratitude will always be owed, in addition, to those who took that chance, made that decision, and brought my world into this world.

Finally, of course, a book would be a dead thing without a reader. Thank you so much for giving it life; it will always mean more than I can say. I really hope you have enjoyed it, and that you will join Amber, Racxen, and allies old and new on their continuing adventures in the next instalment of the series, *Earth-Bound*.

Fly free!

About the Author

As a qualified Occupational Therapist with a Master of Arts in Psychoanalysis and experience working in a variety of psychiatric settings, Laura is especially passionate about using writing and other creative pursuits therapeutically to help children, teens, and adults cope with and recover from mental illness and trauma. A steadfast believer in the value of fantasy as a nurturing space and safe escape, she draws inspiration from everywhere wild and magical and seeks to both celebrate and inspire the indomitable nature of the human spirit through her writing.

Printed in Poland
by Amazon Fulfillment
Poland Sp. z o.o., Wrocław

49463505R00190